Moon's Lament

Iris Retzlaff

Moon's Lament (Moon's Lament #1)
Copyright © 2024 Iris Retzlaff
Cover Design © Iris Retzlaff
All rights reserved.
No part of this book may be reproduced in any form or by any electronic or mechanical means, without written permission from the author, except for the use of brief quotations in a book review.

Ebook ISBN: 978-3-9826675-0-8
Paperback ISBN: 978-3-9826675-1-5
Hardcover ISBN: 978-3-9826675-2-2

Author's Note

The Empire of Tsukiyama is not a representation of real life Japan at any given time, nor was it ever meant to be. It's a world all of its own that was strongly influenced by Edo Japan, with 19th century Europe in the mix.

That being said, I do apologise for taking some licence with the Japanese language. I promise I will continue to study hard. 申し訳ございまます。もっともっと勉強しなければなりません。頑張ります！

Content Warnings

Violence, death, loss, (false) accusations of abuse, prejudice

Dedication

Because stories can only live through the reader – this one is for you.

Part 1

Encounter

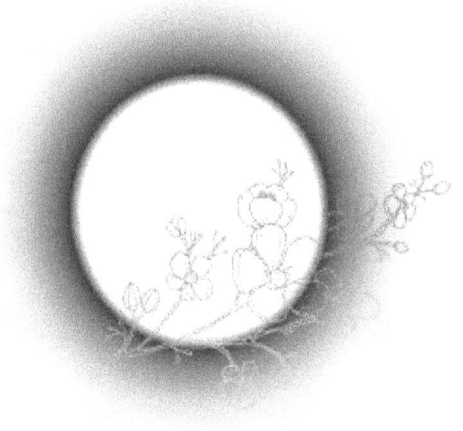

Chapter 1

The past had always had the bad habit of creeping up on him in his dreams.
Suzu opened his eyes. Morning sunlight streamed in through the window. He was twisted up in his robe, the soft fabric now half strangling him; the thin blanket long gone. He blinked at the ceiling's wooden beams and took a deep breath. Other people's nightmares left them sad, desolate, or frightened, his left him with rage burning inside him.

A timid knock came from the door, and a small voice inquired, "Suzu, are you awake?"

"Yes, come in." Suzu sat up and tried to pull his twisted *nemaki* straight, but only succeeded in almost undressing himself. The door slid open, revealing a kneeling boy with a tray of food beside him. The boy bowed low.

"G-good morning."

"Rani," Suzu sighed, "stop that. How often do I have to tell you not so be so damned formal when we're not working."

"But I am working."

"You know exactly what I mean. We're in our private rooms, no need to stick to that stuffy routine here. Well?" He raised an eyebrow at Rani, sitting and staring at him. "Do I get my breakfast or not?"

Rani practically jumped to his feet, picked up the tray and hastily carried it over. He was a painfully shy boy of about twelve or thirteen – the boy, himself, wasn't sure about his age. Working in a pleasure house couldn't be easy for one as meek as him. Naked skin, lewd jokes, and flirtatious behaviour early in the morning was enough to leave him stammering and blushing throughout the day. He would, of course, never be anything else than a servant boy – unless he chose to become a cook or gardener or whatever else the house needed. But he was as much a part of this cobbled together family as every other inhabitant of the Singing Dragon.

While Suzu picked at his breakfast, Rani put away the futon and laid out fresh clothes.

"You were having nightmares again, weren't you?" the boy asked quietly.

"How do you know?"

"You're all sweaty."

"It was very hot this night," Suzu pointed out, lifting a bowl of miso soup to his lips. It was even true. Though still a month from midsummer, it was already as hot and humid as at the peak of summer. People were constantly complaining about the heat, but Suzu liked it. He could have done without the thunderstorms, though.

He could tell Rani wasn't convinced, so Suzu put his bowl down and looked the boy straight in the eyes. "Don't you worry about it, all right? They are just dreams. Look, I'm the one having them and I don't give a damn. They are annoying, that's all. So, really, don't worry. All right?" And to emphasise his words Suzu put on a broad, dazzling grin. It finally gained him a small smile from the boy in return.

"Shall I prepare the bath for you?" Rani asked.

Suzu took a sip of tea. The thought of a bath was tempting, but he quickly reconsidered. "No, not yet. I go to the dojo first."

The dojo was at the back of the estate, far away from the rooms in which they entertained customers. Gekka no Kazue – or Mother, as her boys called her fondly – put a lot of stress on the health and fitness of her Furyusha. Which was why she not only enforced strict rules against drugs, she also made sure everyone, who lived and worked at the Singing Dragon, was well trained and could defend themself. Haldor, the dojo's master – a master of both the northern and southern sword style, as well as in unarmed fighting – taught them his skills, but also acted as their bodyguard. Where Kazue had found him, no-one knew. When she returned to Yūgao more than a decade ago, she had brought him with her.

Haldor was a northern Hun: huge, broad shouldered, scary looking.

"I'd really, really like to know where in the world you learned this," Suzu commented, panting hard. He stood across from Haldor, a wooden training sword held up in front of him, sweat running down his face. "One of these days I will make you tell me your entire life story."

Haldor snorted, and rushed Suzu. The message was clear: less talk, more fighting. Although Haldor was more than a head taller than Suzu and packed with muscle, they were an almost even match. Their sparring was vicious and intense. Haldor had always had a kind of intuitive sense for Suzu's moods, and so they fought and fought until they were both drenched in sweat and exhausted.

Suzu lay on the hardwood floor, spread-eagled, breathing heavily, and grinning. Oh, he had needed this. It had been a lie when he had told Rani the nightmares didn't bother him. The rage they kindled inside him demanded an outlet, lest it burnt him to ashes. Now, despite the sore muscles and the exhaustion, he felt relaxed and happy once more.

Haldor nudged him and handed him a cup of water. Suzu gratefully accepted it. That was one of the things he so appreciated about Haldor – there was no need to talk. People often mistook Haldor for being mute, because he tried to avoid speaking at all cost. But the big man had never needed words to convey what he had to say, or to understand others. It was his gift, even more so than his fighting skills.

Haldor had never pestered Suzu about his past, about his bouts of anger, or the nightmares. He had simply taken him to the dojo one day, put a wooden sword in his hands, and let him sweat out his rage.

"All right," Suzu said, getting to his feet. "Guess it's time to take a nice long bath and get presentable." Haldor nodded, gave Suzu a pat on the back, and went to stow away the training swords.

Suzu slowly walked through the garden towards the bathhouse. Every pleasure house in Yūgao had its own private bathhouse. A luxury, but also a necessity.

He took a deep breath. The air was fragrant, rich with the perfume of flowers and the aroma of herbs. Birds sang from the rooftops, bushes, or trees, or were splashing around in one of the many ornamental bird baths. Sunlight glittered on the surface of the small koi pond. It was a peaceful place of tranquillity, sheltered from the hustle and bustle of Yūgao by its high walls. To Suzu it was a piece of heaven.

The bathhouse was quiet this time of day, but the pile of clothes in one of the baskets told him he was not alone. Suzu pulled his own sticky clothes off and threw them in another basket. A cloud of steam greeted him the moment he opened the door.

"Phew, isn't that a bit too hot for the season?" he complained.

Pleasant, deep laughter answered him from somewhere within the mist. Suzu squinted and found a young man sitting on one of the little stools along the wall, meticulously scrubbing his fingers. Rivulets of water ran down his muscular back and dripped from the long strands of his dark wet hair. He looked over his shoulder at Suzu, a smile on his handsome face.

"And here I thought it couldn't get hot enough for you," he chuckled.

Suzu sat down next to him, pulled the string from his hair, allowing it to fall like a black silken curtain down his back, and reached for a bucket of water.

"I just don't like being cold. I never said there was no such thing as too hot. All this steam is suffocating." He lifted the bucket and poured the – comparatively – cold water over his head. "Ryū, have you been digging in the dirt again?" he remarked with a grin, squinting sideways at his friend.

Ryū mirrored his grin. "No. I've been planting flowers – you know, that pretty stuff growing in the garden *someone* likes so much."

"And that's why I love you so."

Ryū, laughing, pushed a dish of soap towards Suzu and stood up. "Here. Mistress Ayame's latest creation: lemon and thyme. Oh, and Rani threw a whole bucket of orange blossoms into the water."

"Did he now? What's the occasion?"

Ryū shrugged. "Said you had nightmares again and he wanted to cheer you up."

"They're not nightmares," Suzu protested.

"So you keep saying," Ryū retorted and slowly let himself sink down into the hot, orange blossom filled water of the pool. "But they're obviously not very pleasant either."

Suzu ignored this, busying himself instead with working the soap into a nice lather. The fresh scent of lemon and thyme enveloped him. From behind him he heard Ryū's exasperated sigh, but he knew his friend wouldn't nag him about it. He was one of three people in the world who knew what his dreams were about. There was nothing to say. All that Suzu needed was a way to let out his aggressions and to know his family was there for him no matter what.

He squeezed the water from his hair, bound it in a knot on the top of his head, and joined Ryū in the pool. The water was almost scalding. Droopy, exhausted blossoms drifted lazily across its surface, their scent yet lingering in the air. He slid down closer to his friend than was necessary, their shoulders almost touching. For a while they sat in silence. It made Suzu drowsy. Deciding it was too early in the day for that, a mischievous grin tugged at the corners of his mouth. He rolled sideways and straddled Ryū, throwing his arms around the other's neck.

Ryū opened his eyes slowly. "And what exactly are you planning to do now?" he asked with a stern expression.

"Hm, what would you like me to do?" Suzu purred.

"Suzu," Ryū sighed, exasperated. Suzu laughed and tightened his arms around his friend, pressing cheek against cheek. "You're strangling me," Ryū gasped.

"But I just had a really fun idea. You know, we could –" A loud clatter, an exclamation of pain, and the sound of a wooden bucket rolling across the floor cut Suzu off. Ryū twisted in his grip to look over his shoulder, forcing Suzu to let go. They found Rani kneeling on the floor, rubbing his right ankle, face flushed a furious red.

"S-sorry," he stammered. "I b-brought fresh clothes and… um… and … Suzu, Mother wants to see you."

Suzu sighed dramatically. "Another time, my love," he breathed into Ryū's ear, climbing out of the pool. His friend retaliated with a playful slap on Suzu's naked rump.

Suzu threw a wink over his shoulder, sauntered across the room and accepted a towel from Rani, who held it out as far as his arms were long and tried to look everywhere but at Suzu. Shaking his head, Suzu ruffled the boy's hair.

"Run along, Rani. Tell Mother I'll be right with her." Rani practically flew from the bathhouse.

In the anteroom Suzu found two sets of fresh clothes: a maroon coloured yukata, and a black jinbei set – Suzu's preferred type of clothing when he wasn't working. He grabbed the jinbei, pulled on the loose trousers and the top, combed his wet hair out with his fingers and headed for Mother's room.

It was already past noon now and the private quarters of the Singing Dragon resembled a bustling beehive. Boys and young men were running to and fro, laughing, arguing, practising their instruments or dancing, carrying piles of clothes or trays of food. The Singing Dragon – one of the most expensive and exclusive pleasure houses of Yūgao, the entertainment district of Tsukiyama's capital Getsuro – housed ten Furyusha, twelve younger boys, a cook, Haldor, a stylist, and, of course, its proprietor: Gekka no Kazue. Yet in moments like this it seemed there were hundreds of people living under the same roof.

On his way, Suzu was waylaid by some of the other Furyusha. It was a common occurrence that they asked Suzu for advice, despite them being in the business longer than him. With months away from his twentieth birthday Suzu was one of the youngest Furyusha in Yūgao – but also the most expensive one. And it had taken him less than a year to gain his status. Even the most spiteful, jealous competition had to grudgingly admit that he was achingly beautiful, smart, witty, and gifted with many talents. He had captured the eye of quite a few rich and powerful men, but his greatest conquest was the Earl of Tsukikage, Mori no Toshiaki. The most eligible bachelor, but also one of the most feared man in Getsuro, for the Earl was known to be unsocial, cold, even rude. With the exception of a select few, the young earl didn't seem to care for the company of other people. He had – as far as the public knew – no interest in marriage and had never taken a lover, and visits to any of the pleasure houses were for business only.

That was, until he had met Suzu. It was no secret that he was head over heels for the young Furyusha.

Mother was already waiting for him in her parlour, two trays of steaming food set in front of her. A boy was putting the finishing touches on a beautiful, artistic flower arrangement.

"Excellent, Miharu, you've become quite accomplished. The arrangement is magnificent. Well done," Mother praised him. Miharu beamed, picking up his tools and a few stray flower stems, and brushed past Suzu with a nod, glowing with happiness. Suzu smiled.

"Miharu has a real talent for arranging flowers."

Mother looked up at him, her warm brown eyes sparkling. "That he does. Come, Suzu, it's been a while since the two of us had lunch together."

Suzu slid the door closed behind him and took a seat. "He still doesn't talk, though," he commented quietly, casting a glance at the flower arrangement. Delicate blush pink and white bell flowers complemented a single majestic white peony.

"No," Mother sighed. "He doesn't. But, I've found a good place for him. You know Aiyana, don't you? The flower artist? She saw his work when she delivered flowers the other day – well, she liked what she saw, so she offered to take him on as her apprentice. I think it's for the best, so…"

Relief rushed through Suzu. He had been worried about Miharu for quite some time. With seventeen the boy was supposed to decide where to go from here: begin training as a Furyusha, or stay on in a serving position. But Miharu had been badly traumatised when he had arrived at the Singing Dragon three years ago. He hadn't spoken a single word in all this time. Suzu understood, he had been there. But he had found his voice again quickly. Perhaps because the rage inside him wouldn't be silenced. Miharu was different. According to the woman who had brought him to the house, Miharu had always been a quiet and sensitive child. Even before... Before what exactly, no-one but Miharu knew. The woman – a neighbour – had found him, bloody, dirty, nearly starved, sitting immovably by his dead mother's side.

To apprentice him, although he would have normally still had years to work at the Singing Dragon, was Mother's way of ensuring the boy would have a good and happy life no matter what happened. She was prepared to lose a great deal of money over it; it showed how much she cared about her boys.

"You know, some say your heart is too soft for this work," Suzu commented.

Mother snorted. "As if. And he'd be wasted as a serving boy. What's the use throwing away such talent?"

"True. But another house would not have taken him in the first place. You have a soft spot for the broken ones," Suzu added quietly, a small smile on his lips. Apart from Miharu, he had probably been the most broken of them all.

"I don't know what you're talking about," Mother retorted. "There, your food is getting cold, and Sabia has prepared it especially for you. So eat."

Suzu looked down on his tray and found the dishes to be some of his favourites: ginger spiced chicken with noodles, the scent of herbs and spices delicate and well balanced. He took a bite and hummed in bliss. Sabia – in his opinion – was the best cook in the entire empire. They ate in companionable silence.

At last Suzu put his chopsticks down and sighed. "That was delicious. May I ask the occasion, though? No, let me guess: Rani told you about the dreams, didn't he?"

"I don't need Rani to tell me you're having nightmares again. I know you, Suzu, I can see it in your eyes. And let's not mention the hours you are spending at the dojo right after breakfast."

"They're not nightmares, they're only dreams. And I am fine."

"So you keep saying. But Suzu, those dreams – they had stopped, hadn't they? You didn't have them in over a year. So why are they back now?"

Suzu shrugged indifferently. It was probably to ensure he didn't grow too complacent. They had stopped once, they would stop again.

"Want to know what I think?" Mother asked and didn't wait for Suzu to answer. "I think it's because of the Earl."

"What? What's he got to do with it?"

Mother didn't answer at once. She reached for a pot and poured herself a cup of tea, then regarded Suzu with a mixture of exasperation and pity for a moment. He didn't like it. Mother took a deep swallow, sighed, and said, "The whole world knows how the Earl feels about you. You know he wants you to be with him. And it scares you. It scares you to accept him, it scares you even more to accept your own feelings."

"I… I'm not… it doesn't…" Suzu stammered. He stared at Mother defiantly, not knowing what to say, how to deny it. How did this woman know him so well, how could she see right through him?

Suzu had mastered the art of putting on masks from an early age on. It was part of his nature, one of his gifts as an Ethereal – descendents of the Gods' Blessed. Whatever people wanted him to be, whatever it was they wanted to see, he would give it to them. It was what made him so good at this work. But when he was younger, he had almost lost himself in the persona he had created, and when it broke, he had been lost. Mother had found him then. It had been she, who had told him to be himself, and she, who had accepted his true self. And after her there had been Haldor, and Ryū, and the rest of the Singing Dragon family. Here, surrounded by his family, he could be only Suzu. Not Yūzuki no Suzu, not the Furyusha, not the many different versions of himself that he donned like a gown, only to rip them off again the next moment. He loved his family for it, for loving him for himself and despite himself, unconditionally.

"All right," Mother relented. "I just want you to know – not that I ought to remind you – that you can always talk to me. Whatever it is." She fixed him with her sternest glare, and waited expectantly. Suzu swallowed the lump forming in his throat and nodded. "Good. That's not why I wanted to talk to you anyway. But because of this." She pulled an envelope out of her sleeve and held it out to Suzu. The card inside was expensive, heavy paper, written in an elegant, and obviously professional, hand, and embossed with a familiar seal.

"His Lord General Jarick ax Varg has invited you to his birthday party the day after tomorrow. It's probably the most anticipated event this year, after Tsuki no Matsuri, and you can bet that the entire high society will be there, except the emperor, of course. So you know what that means."

"That I have to practice playing the koto for the rest of the day?" Suzu asked confused, staring at the card in his hands.

"No, you idiot, leave the entertainment to the professionals. You are a guest."

"Isn't it rather uncommon to invite a Furyusha to a ball such as this?"

"It is. But we're talking about the General here," Mother laughed. "That man gives a damn about societal conventions."

Suzu laughed. It was true. He remembered an episode in which the General had been running around Yūgao all evening, dressed in the – far too small – furisode his wife had been wearing to her coming-of-age ceremony some thirty years ago, heavy make-up on his face, because he had lost a bet – to his wife, nonetheless.

"So, you understand now, Suzu, what that means?" Mother asked again.

"I am Yūgao's number one, and I have to look the part, so… shopping?"

"Shopping."

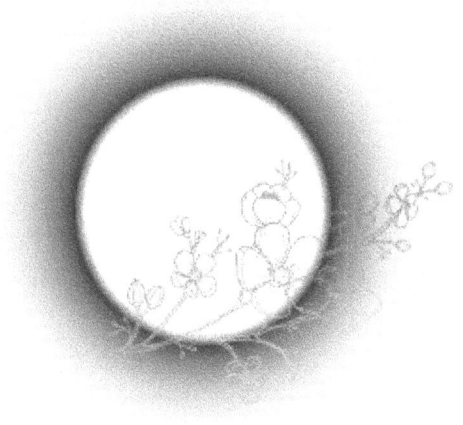

Chapter 2

"… Nonsense!" The voice of the old lady drifted down to where Jin sat in the shadow of the house. Cantankerous, as always. Amongst the susurration of voices that had been competing with the birdsongs and the stridulation of insects for more than an hour, this word alone stood out. Succinct. Unmistakable. Jin turned his head, met his friend's eyes, and rolled his eyes.

"The old crow is at it again," he remarked.

Niall chuckled. "Oh, you know how much she loves arguing," she said.

"How much longer will this take, do you think?"

"Who knows. If the geezers got their teeth in a good bone it might easily take all afternoon."

Jin groaned and leaned his head back against the cool stone of the wall.

"Long night?" Niall asked, wiggling her eyebrows suggestively. Jin shrugged a shoulder. "You know, one of these days you'll end up in real trouble."

"Why? My partners are consenting and willing adults. More than willing, I might add – and they leave quite satisfied," Jin retorted with a cocky grin.

"Right. Until you break their heart, or you seem forget about the jealous husband, wife, father, brother, uncle, boyfriend, girlfriend, cousin, pet--"

Jin put a hand over his friend's mouth to stop her tirade. She glared at him with eyes that had the blue of a raging sea. How often had they had this very conversation? She pushed his hand away. Her auburn hair and slightly vulpine features gave her a naturally mischievous and sly expression. At this very moment, however, she was every bit the scolding big sister she had been to Jin for the better part of four years.

"Do I really have to remind you of that incident with the umbrella maker's daughter last month?"

Jin winced. How could he forget. He wasn't proud of what had happened, but how was he to know that the girl had a fiancé? It had been most unfortunate then that the young man had stumbled upon them. Worse still that he had dragged the poor girl, wailing and pleading, only half dressed and with tousled hair, to her father's shop and broke off the engagement. The scene the erstwhile fiancé had made had not gone unnoticed by the neighbours either.

"How... how's she now?" Jin asked quietly, avoiding his friend's eyes.

"Wow, you don't even remember the girl's name, do you?" Niall accused. Filled with shame Jin hung his head. "*Hinami*," Niall enunciated the girl's name, "has been sent to live with her relatives – somewhere up in the north, far away from the town and gossip."

"Why can't you just go to Yūgao, like everyone else?" Jin's head snapped up, startled. A tall woman was leaning against the gate, one hand resting casually on the hilt of the sword at her hip, in the other she held a long-stemmed pipe. In appearance she could have almost been Jin's sister. The same black hair, dark eyes. The same lean, muscular physique, tall and broad-shouldered. But whereas Jin's face was smooth and unblemished, his hair unkempt by nature, the woman's long glossy hair was pulled back into a messy bun, a nasty scar cut across her full lips, the remains of a vicious bruise coloured her left cheek.

"Risa," Niall exclaimed. "What are you doing here?"

"Boss said to meet him here," Risa explained, sauntering towards them. "Don't ask why, I haven't the slightest."

"Well, get comfortable, this might take a while," Jin said.

Risa took a drag from her pipe, blew out a cloud of smoke, and grinned evilly. "All the more time for Niall and me to roast you over your love life." Jin's groan made the two women laugh. He was aware, though, that it was his own damn fault. If only Issei had been here, but his other best friend had left town indefinitely.

"To answer your question, Risa," he snapped. "I won't pay some poor bastard to have sex with me."

"There he is, the little temple boy." Risa grimaced. "Do I really need to explain about Yūgao again? *Again*? 'Cause I will, though you never seem to listen. Fine." She pulled the sword out of her belt and plopped down on the ground, sitting crossed-legged in front of Jin.

"I know what Yūgao is, damn it. The pleasure district. A town within the town, with its own rules and laws, blah blah.

It was basically the first thing I learned when I came to town. But if I want to sleep with someone I want them to want it too – and not because it's their job and they have no choice."

"Very commendable. And who says that no Furyusha wants to have a little fun with you. You're a handsome – apparently -, kind, gentle – they'd eat you for breakfast." Risa laughed. Niall, chuckling along with her, nodded her head in agreement, much to Jin's annoyance. "Might be their job, doesn't mean they can't have fun doing it. They'll say no if they don't want to, you know. You can't force them – it's against the rules. Trust me, they are protected by more laws and rules than the average person. Whereas you, my hypocritical friend, cause all kinds of trouble with your little flings."

Jin looked away from his friends. Risa was right, of course. Yūgao had the strictest rules and laws, often harshly enforced. Most Furyusha also had a better life in one of the houses than they ever had before. Mistreatment of a Furyusha resulted in an instant and permanent ban from the house and a painfully high fee. Repeat the offence and the ban was effective for Yūgao as a whole – which also included the bars, gambling houses, and other establishments.

Harsher yet was the punishment for a house proprietor who mistreated their boys or girls: they lost everything – name, reputation, the house, everything. They were run out of Yūgao, and often out of the capital altogether. Yūgao's council, consisting of the most influential members of Yūgao's society, ruled with an iron hand. But it was this what made the small town within the town what it was: a safe place for those who were in need of one. Children of poor families were often sold to the houses. Here they received an education, were fed, clothed, and had a roof over their heads. no-one was allowed to touch them. It was their own decision whether they worked as a servant or a Furyusha once they were of age. Whatever they decided, at the end of their term each and every one of them walked out of Yūgao with their heads held high and enough money in their pockets to start a new, good life.

Yes, Jin knew all this. His friends had explained it to him over and over again, and yet... Perhaps Risa was right, perhaps he was a hypocrite. Or perhaps it was his temple upbringing, after all he had spent most of his twenty years of life in a Hôjô temple, where his parents had dumped him with the monks when he was only four years old.

"How long's it been now?" Risa asked suddenly. Jin looked at her, confused. "Since you lost him. How long has it been?"

"Four... no, almost five years," Jin answered quietly.

"It's time you got over him."

"Risa's right, you know," Niall agreed. "All these meaningless affairs... Don't think I haven't noticed that you have a very specific type. None of them will ever be able to replace your Kari. You need to let go. For your own sake, Jin."

"And ours. It's annoying as hell, just so you know," Risa added, earning herself a vicious jab in the ribs and Niall's dreaded scowl.

Five years – it felt like a lifetime and it felt like only yesterday. Jin regretted the choices he had made then every single moment. Leaving Kari in the temple until he, Jin, had ensured a life for them here in the capital – it had seemed the right thing to do. But life in the capital was not as easy as Jin had thought it would be. A few months after his arrival he had ended up in some backside alley, starving, delirious with fever. No money, no food, no roof over his head – nothing. Dying slowly, abandoned by an uncaring world – until Niall had stumbled over him. She had saved his life, and given him a new one.

"I should have never left him behind," Jin mumbled.

"Yeah well, what's done is done. Besides, might I remind you, you weren't even able to take care of yourself then."

He knew that. He had told himself so a hundred times over, but it didn't stop that nagging feeling that he should have done things differently. That something had been wrong from the start. What it was, though, he couldn't say.

"Cut yourself some slack," Risa interjected. "How were you to know the boy would suddenly vanish."

"Yes. But that's what's been bothering me ever since. That's just not like him. He wouldn't just disappear like that. Something must have happened, and--"

"And I'm stopping you right there. Don't. Just don't. We've been over this so many times. Durin went to the temple. Durin, not you. And why was that again?"

"Because I'm not allowed to show my face at the temple," Jin grumbled. He didn't like being reminded of that particular fact. And even less did he like to admit that he cared.

"Yes, 'cause you ran away. And then Durin asked for Kari, and they basically slammed the door in his face, yelling at him that there was no such person and never has been. I'd say it's pretty clear that Kari had enough of sitting around and waiting for you, and took off."

"Fine. Then tell me why the villagers acted pretty much the same when Durin asked them. That's not normal. And where is Kari now?"

"How should I know. And how do you know the villagers don't do exactly what the monks tell them to do. Anyone ever run away while you were at the temple?" Jin grudgingly shook his head. Risa had a point, he didn't know.

"See," Risa said smugly. "Which brings us back to Yūgao. Come on, I know the absolutely perfect Furyusha to cheer you up. He's exactly your type."

"Woah, wait a minute, do you have any idea how expensive he is?" Niall exclaimed before Jin even had a chance to protest. "I mean, yeah, you're right, he's totally Jin's type – like he's everyone's type. I mean... hello! He's gorgeous – even you have to admit that."

"I know, right? I'd make an exception for him." Risa grinned, wiggling her eyebrows. Frankly, this did spark Jin's curiosity for a minute. Risa took as much notice of male beings as a stone of an ant. That Furyusha had to be quite something – not that Jin would ever know, not if he could help it.

"If we all throw in together, I'm sure we'd get enough for an hour or so," Risa continued. "Jin's birthday is in a few days, so..."

"No, no, no!" Jin waved his hands around as if he could disperse Risa's half-formed plans. "Don't I have a say in this? You know I don't want to go to Yūgao," he added weakly. From the looks the women gave him he could protest as much as he wanted, they would do as they pleased anyway. With a sigh he leaned his head back against the wall, closed his eyes, and tried to ignore their laughter and excited plotting.

When their boss finally came strutting out of the council hall, followed by the rest of the Crescent, Jin was so glad he could have kissed Naloc. Niall, psychic that she was, seemed to read his mind and gave him a sharp jab in the ribs.

Murasaki no Naloc was a tall, slender man in his late fifties. He was handsome and charismatic, and radiated authority. But Jin also knew him to be warm-hearted, caring, and fatherly. His eyes were the same grey as steel, but never cold, and his smile was easy, seeing his people waiting for him.

"There you are," he called as if they hadn't just spent hours waiting for him in the exact same spot he had left them in. "I need tea. And something sweet. Let's find the nearest tea house, shall we?" Without waiting for an answer he passed

---

them right by. He knew they would be following.

They found a lovely tea house with a terrace over the banks of the Opal River. Naloc ordered tea and sweet dumplings for them all. For a while they enjoyed the view, the tea, the gentle breeze.

"So, what's wrong? Don't tell me the ladies were teasing you all afternoon," Naloc asked Jin eventually.

While Jin mumbled incoherently around his mouthful of *mochi*, Risa and Niall protested the accusation.

"Hey, we were only discussing Jin's birthday present."

"Yes, thought it was time he got a taste of the delights Yūgao has to offer – if he wants it or not," Risa added. "Any chance you could get Kazue to give us a discount?"

"You want to take him to the Singing Dragon? Quite the pricey present for someone who doesn't even want it," Naloc said with a glance at Jin's annoyed expression.

"Well," Niall drawled, "yes, we were thinking Yūzuki no Suzu..."

Naloc huffed a laugh. "Oh dear, not a chance. You do know Kazue's golden boy is the Earl of Tsukikage's favourite, don't you? He hasn't been serving anyone but his regular patrons in months. They say it's only a matter of time before he quits for good and accepts the Earl's proposal."

The women deflated. Jin, on the other hand, found his spirits lifted. At least now they had to discard that stupid plan. He hoped.

"Ah, but Niall, you might get a chance to show Jin the boy, so he knows what he's missing," Naloc continued with a mischievous glint in his eyes. And as quickly as Jin had cheered up, his mood plummeted. But Niall and Risa perked up, leaning forward, eyes shining. "At the General's birthday party!" Naloc's announcement was met with a collective groan, eye rolling, a shake of the head, and Risa even buried her face in her hands.

"What?" Naloc asked innocently.

"Boss," Risa moaned. "Let the man celebrate his birthday in peace. His gods damned birthday!"

"I don't know what you mean." Naloc sniffed, looking deeply offended.

"Seriously," Niall scolded, "isn't it enough you stole the man's beloved pet peacock? Do you really need to crash his birthday party?"

Naloc stiffened, picking imaginary lint from his sleeve. "Just so you know, I did not steal the bird" – his denial was met with more eye rolling – "it followed me home." Naloc ignored the doubtful snorts. "And who said anything about crashing the party? On the contrary. You, Niall, and you, Jin, will go there to gather information."

"What?" Jin and Niall cried in unison. But before they could argue further, Naloc held up a hand to stop them. His friendly and fun demeanour changed abruptly, his mien became stern. He changed from Naloc, their fatherly friend, into their boss: ambitious, ruthless, and inscrutable.

"It's all been arranged already. The General has hired personnel from outside for the evening. You will serve drinks and food – and while you do so, you will keep your ears pricked for any kind of gossip, rumour, or scandal, and your eyes peeled for what is happening in dark corners. Got it?"

"Yes, boss."

The first time Jin had been sent to gather information, he had asked why. The answer he had gotten was that the right information could be more valuable than gold. An event like this, with the crème de la crème of Tsukiyama's high society present, was simply too good to let pass.

With their spirits a little dampened at the prospect of a job they both didn't want to do, Jin and Niall went home. Their two small houses stood face to face enclosed by a high wooden fence and divided by a little brook running through their grounds. Stepping through the gate, it felt as if they entered their own world. Looking straight ahead, one could see the well at the opposite side of the grounds. To the left of the gate stood a magnificent big ancient ginkgo tree. A table with chairs had been arranged in the shade beneath its canopy. A gravel path led from the gate to Jin's house, a small bridge across the brook to Niall's. Random patches of colour caught the eye: a rose bush here, a hydrangea there, cornflowers, daisies, and other wild flowers growing wherever they wanted. Capriciously, free, with its own rules – this was their very own sphere inside this hectic town, their private haven.

"Would you really have dragged me to Yūgao?" Jin asked. To his amazement – and shock – Niall nodded her head. He had expected as much from Risa, but Niall?

"This time, yes. Look, Jin." She stopped and turned to look her friend in the eyes. "I know you miss him. And I know this time of the year it's always the worst. But you can't go on like this. This stubborn refusal to go to Yūgao – I don't get it. You're not stupid, you know that it's not bad. I can't let you keep ruining your life or the life of others. And don't shake your head at me, young man, because that's what's going to happen one of these days. All those casual flings with people who are unavailable and damn the consequences. There will be consequences eventually, serious consequences. And not even Naloc will be able to help you then. So whatever this is, it stops now!"

Jin sighed. His friend was right, of course. He *was* being stupid. Incredibly stupid. He couldn't even say why he was so averse to Yūgao, except that he wanted something real, not make-believe and pretence. He shook his head at himself. Even that was a lie. His affairs – they were nothing but pretence. He pretended to like his bed partners, that it was them he wanted. When all he ever really wanted was to be with Kari. He assured himself that his partners were like him, that there were no feelings involved. He refused to even consider the alternative.

"Well." Niall squeezed his arm. "Tomorrow you will feast your eyes on the infamous Yūzuki no Suzu – and if that sight doesn't make you forget even your own name, then, my friend, you are truly beyond help." She grinned at him cheekily, and despite himself, Jin laughed.

"He's really that beautiful?"

"Oh, you have no idea. But for now," she hopped over the brook, ignoring the bridge, "I'll cook us something nice, and you run over to Take's and buy us some cold cider."

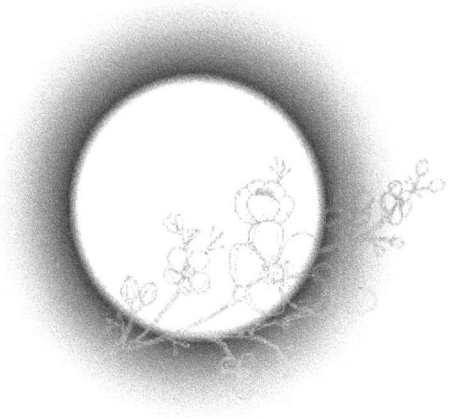

Chapter 3

Suzu stood in front of the full-length mirror, his thoughts drifting. *Yūzuki no Suzu* – they had named him after one of the Seven Bells, the Moon Goddess's regalia. The Evening Moon – it stood for charisma; the bell was said to produce the most beautiful sound in the world. Kazue and Ryū had chosen the name, claiming it befitted his otherworldly beauty and allure.

Suzu stared at his reflection, trying to see what the rest of the world saw. Glossy black hair, as black as a moonless night, fell over his shoulders and down to the small of his back. It was a stark contrast to the lightness of his flawless skin. Suzu seemed less like a real human being and rather like a piece of art. Sculpted out of jade by a master's hand. Every muscle well defined, his face symmetrical fine lines, elegant brows, sensual lips, brilliant big eyes, slanted, emerald green. Suzu blinked. That wasn't right. Only his left eye was green, as vivid green as his father's eyes had been, as his mother's – it was all he remembered of them. But his right eye was almost colourless with the barest blue-green shimmer. A thin silver scar ran from the middle of his forehead across his brow and down to his cheekbone. His only blemish – the crack in all that perfection, the fissure that revealed his humanity. A permanent mark. A reminder. A symbol of pain.

He held his hand in front of his left eye. Darkness – almost. The merest hint of movement, shadows, the idea of light. Suzu sighed. If he had been treated earlier he might not have lost sight in his eye, or so the doctor had said. But then, he wouldn't even be here now if he had been found any later – or never. He had no clear memories of that time, of how long he had wandered about, how long he had been lying in the street, more dead than alive. He remembered nothing but pain – emotional and physical.

But that was the past, and he had sworn to forget the past, even if his nightmares seemed bent on reminding him. He had a new life now. A good life. The past didn't matter.

He tilted his head and leaned closer towards the mirror. He couldn't recall his parents' faces. Nothing but the eyes. So vibrantly green, just like his. Suzu had never met anyone else with eyes this colour, although he had met other Ethereals. They all had uncommon eye colours, but many were less vibrant, paler, less noticeable. There weren't many full-blooded Ethereals around anymore – and even less with green eyes, it seemed. Suzu didn't know which god had blessed his ancestors. His parents might have known, but his father had died before Suzu could walk, and his mother had lost her voice then. no-one else could tell him either. He was a rarity even amongst rarities.

A knock at the door made him jump. He quickly turned his back to the mirror, just as Rani came in, carrying a bundle of fine cloth. The boy closed the door behind him, looked up – and flushed furiously.

"W-w-why are you n-naked?" Rami stammered, trying and failing to look anywhere but at Suzu.

Suzu was proud of himself for not bursting out laughing. "Rani, you see all of us naked every single day. We take baths together for fuck's sake. You do work in a pleasure house, you know. You've seen – and heard – worse."

"Yes... yes but it's... it's y-you."

Suzu sighed. He'd forgotten that Rani had a crush on him. For the longest time he had meant to talk to the boy about this, but he just didn't know how. He didn't want to hurt him. Perhaps Ryū could have this particular talk with Rani, the boy did look up to him more than to anyone else after all.

Noticing Rani fidgeting nervously, Suzu took pity on the boy and reached for the *nagajuban* hung on the back of the mirror. The thin underrobe seemed to do the trick.

"I've brought your kimono for this evening. Do you want to put it on now, or do you want Tomiko to do your hair first?"

"Tomiko first. It's too hot to wear this kimono any longer than I have to. And Rani, be a dear and fetch me something cold to drink, would you?"

Tomiko styled his hair in a simple but elegant fashion and adorned it with a hairpin in gold and green jade, shaped like a flying dragon. Neither she nor Rani would stop lavishing compliments on Suzu. It was highly irritating, but Suzu tried not to snap at them.

"Like a masterful piece of art." Suzu turned to glower at Ryū, leaning against the doorframe. His friend grinned wickedly as he sauntered into the room and took a seat on the windowsill.

"Don't you have work?" Suzu snapped.

"No, I've taken a bit of time off so I can admire you in all your glory."

"You mean to annoy the living daylight out of me."

"Aww, you say so now, but we both know how much you like me admiring you," Ryū drawled, and winked.

"Why don't you –" The sound of someone loudly clearing their throat cut Suzu off. Mother stood in the door, Haldor looming behind her. She had her business expression on, which was usually a sign she was dissatisfied with something. Probably the fact that Suzu was going to spend the evening out of house. Mother hated her boys being outside the protection provided by the house. The laws of Yūgao were far-reaching and iron-bound, but people had a tendency to forget them outside the walls of the district. It was why they had bodyguards, and why Kazue insisted on her boys being able to defend themselves.

"Are you ready? The carriage is here," she said, eyeing Suzu critically. The emerald green kimono Mother had picked out for him, and his flawless porcelain skin gave Suzu the impression Mother had been aiming to make him look as if he were a jade sculpture.

"Yes, perfect," she said. "All right, Suzu, listen up. You are an invited guest at this party. And as such you don't have to take any shit from anyone. So if anyone tries anything funny..."

"I'm allowed to punch them?" Suzu suggested with a wicked grin.

"Please do try not to break any bones, will you?" Mother sighed, but Suzu noted she hadn't forbidden him. "Remember, your are a guest, you are to be treated as such. Any whispering, snide remarks, jealous glowers – don't let them get to you."

"Great," Suzu groused. "You know, actually I'd rather spend a quiet evening at home."

Mother chuckled and shook her head. "Nonsense, if anyone can handle them, it's you. Oh, and the Earl will be there, so..."

"So what? I'm the General's guest."

"Yes, but I bet he also invited you for the Earl. You know how unsociable that man is, and how much the General dotes on him. You're probably the bribe to get him to come... or the reward. So go, have fun, break a few hearts if you must."

They smiled at each other, then Mother grabbed him and hugged him tightly enough Suzu thought she might actually break a rib or two. It seemed Kazue could never stop herself from worrying about her boys. And perhaps she worried about Suzu the most. The anger that seemed to forever simmer deep within the boy, she fretted, might one day be his undoing. But not tonight. Tonight Suzu would dazzle the high society of Tsukiyama, show them the rare gems Yūgao hid. He would have a few hours of well-deserved fun, and then come back to her and tell her all about it.

Kazue held him just a moment longer than necessary, then planted a kiss on his cheek, and let go of him. Her precious boy. Who had known what a rare treasure was hidden beneath the blood and grime when she had found him lying half dead in a ditch by the road. Her brilliant, sharp-minded, fierce, beautiful boy. He had no idea how precious he was to her, how much he had helped her heal her own wounds. One day she would tell him. One day, but not today.

A hansom waited outside the gate. Suzu stepped into his shoes and off the porch. Behind him, Rani struck the flint three times for good luck. Mother was particular about keeping the customs.

Taking his seat in the hansom, Suzu shook his head. There they stood, Mother, Ryū, and Rani, as if he was about to set out into the world, never to return. He was certain, if the others hadn't been busy getting ready for the evening, they, too, would have stood there on that porch. They were ridiculous and overdramatic, and he loved them so much. His weird family.

The hansom dipped sideways as Haldor joined him. Suzu fondly watched the giant man squeeze himself into the small carriage. Father, uncle, and teacher – those were Haldor's roles in this strange, motley family.

Day after day after day Suzu was amazed by how lucky he was. It filled him with a bright sunny warmth – pushing the ever-present, lurking darkness aside. *It won't last*, a voice in the back of his head whispered to him. A shiver ran down his spine. It was a thought he could never really get rid of, but in this moment it felt like a premonition. *It isn't yours to have.*

The town of Getsuro consisted of five districts: Yūgao was snug in the middle between the oldest district, Eigetsu, and Kigetsu, which had become the bustling, crowded centre of the town. East of the River Opal, which cut the town in half, was the home of the nobility, the rich and famous, and the academy – Mangetsu. The imperial estates with the Moonlight Palace, its private gardens and stables, Moonlight Square, the public gardens, and, of course, the Temple of the Moon Goddess, highest deity in a pantheon of thousands of gods and patron goddess of the empire, slowly gave way to mansions, town houses, expensive shops and tea houses. If it wasn't for Yūgao and the Moon Fair the rich of Getsuro had no reason to cross the river. The southernmost corner of Mangetsu was reserved for the Academic Quarter.

Crossing one of the many bridges was like crossing into another world. The noise and closeness of the town fell away to be replaced by tranquillity and splendour.

The General's mansion was situated close to the river, with a private little quay, and stood in the centre of a park-like estate. Just like his neighbours' the General's property was enclosed by high stone walls. However, the enormous wrought iron gate was wide open this evening. Blooming rose bushes in various shades of red lined the long driveway, the courtyard in front of the house was already filled with carriages.

"I stay outside with the drivers," Haldor announced as they drew slowly to a halt. Suzu smiled. He couldn't hold it against the man, he would prefer to stay outside, too. All those rich snobs... it wasn't his world.

"I know. Don't worry, I'll try not to murder anyone or cause too much of a scandal," Suzu said and accepted the helping hand of a servant in the General's livery. He could hear Haldor snort as the hansom rolled away to make room for the next one. Suzu envied him a bit. Everyone knew the General, generous and kind soul he was, provided the servants of his guests with not only a cosy waiting area, but plenty of good food and drink. Very often that turned into the livelier gathering than the one inside the mansion – even the General himself had escaped his own party on more than one occasion to join the drivers and footmen.

Suzu took a deep breath and entered the magnificent entrance hall, wearing the mask of the sophisticated, aloof, and slightly haughty Furyusha he was supposed to be. He felt a multitude of eyes following his progress the moment he stepped into the ballroom. Admiration, envy, hostility, desire – he could feel all of it directed at him, and let it all glance off him. He could see ladies whispering behind their fans as he passed. One or two of those fans were snapped closed in irritation, before giving the presumed spouse, gaping openly at Suzu, a hearty smack with it. He tried not to laugh.

A woman blocked Suzu's way. She wore a kimono of vermilion silk, embroidered with golden leaves. Her dark eyes found his. He braced himself, expecting some kind of unpleasant confrontation, but the woman smiled. A warm, disarming smile.

"Yūzuki no Suzu," she said, her voice gentle, quiet, and yet ringing with authority. "Thank you for accepting my husband's invitation. I'm Mori no Akari, General Jarick ax Varg's wife."

Suzu gracefully bowed low. He had heard stories about Mori no Akari from her husband, but he had never met her personally. If he was being honest, he had always assumed the General – smitten as he was with his wife – was largely exaggerating her beauty. He saw now that he had been wrong. She had lustrous black hair, warm brown eyes, fine, delicate features, and truly one of the most beautiful smiles Suzu had ever seen. Despite the fine lines around her eyes and at the corners of her mouth, Akari looked far younger than her sixty years.

"Thank you, my lady," he replied. "It was most kind of you to invite me."

"You are most welcome. I know my husband enjoys your company. I do admit," she leaned towards Suzu and lowered her voice, "I have been very curious about you."

"Hm, I see. I do hope you are not too disappointed."

Akari laughed. "Not at all, not at all. On the contrary, words do not do you justice."

Suzu humbly bowed his head. "Come," she linked her arm with his, "my husband is on the terrace with Toshiaki. I'll take you to them."

They found the two men as promised on the terrace, looking out on the garden. Servants were already busy lightening torches, candles, and lanterns scattered all over the place. The sun was a red glow in the western sky.

"Ah, my lovely wife," the General exclaimed. He bent down to place a kiss on his wife's cheek. Jarick ax Varg was a tall and powerfully built man, even with more than sixty years on him. He couldn't have denied his northern heritage even if he had tried. His hair and goatee were snow white, and rumour had it, it had already turned white when he was still a young man. His watchful yellow eyes held a perpetually playful twinkle. And although Suzu had a hard time imagining Jarick as the tough, authoritative commander the rest of the world knew him to be, Suzu had to admit the man's biography was impressive. Having been born into the unimportant side branch of the clan, Jarick had risen through the ranks of the Silver Guard through hard work and a wit sharper than a fine blade; eventually he had been appointed a member of the Moon Council, advising the emperor in all matters.

But it was the man next to Jarick most people, commoners and nobles alike, were intimidated if not downright scared of.

There was no playfulness about him, no easy manner. His light grey eyes were like chips of ice. He stood tall and proud, power radiating like heat waves from him. Cold, aloof, and unsocial: Mori no Toshiaki, Earl of Tsukikage. He was a distant cousin of the General's wife, and perhaps that had been the reason Jarick had taken him under his wing, or perhaps he had recognised a similar mind.

"And you have found Suzu for us, my dear." The General beamed as Suzu bowed respectfully, first to the General then to the Earl.

"Happy Birthday, my lord. And thank you for the invitation."

"Of course. Suzu, you do know you are one of the handful of people I do actually like, don't you? Let's be honest, most of these people here?" The General shuddered. "Dreadful bores. You, at least, bring some glamour and fun – I need a few decent people around me."

"Oh hush," Akari chided him, but she wasn't serious.

"Fine, well I also did have to give Toshiaki an incentive to come."

"You know I would have come," the Earl grumbled.

"Right, right. And you would have stood in a dark corner, gloomy and miserable, glaring and growling at everyone who dared come too close. And as soon as possible you would have fled." Even the Earl laughed at this, albeit a bit ruefully.

They each accepted a glass of champagne from a servant and toasted the General. And then the General regaled them with funny anecdotes. One such featured the Earl. Suzu glanced at the man, blushing slightly from embarrassment. It was a rare thing, to see him like this in public; Suzu, of course, knew a very different man than the public. Laughter transformed him, it evened out the worry lines, and emphasised the man's handsomeness. Suzu drank him in. The hard lines, the grey eyes, glittering with sudden happiness. The expression on his face as he looked back at Suzu that made Suzu's heart skip a few beats. Suzu had the sudden urge to run his fingers through the Earl's hair, the thick white streak above his temple that cut across the deep black in stark contrast, despite his young age. Some people claimed it was a sign he was cursed.

After a while Akari dragged her husband away, admonishing him not to neglect the rest of his guests, and left Suzu and the Earl alone. They sat on a bench and watched the fireflies, flitting between the bushes, filling the dark patches left by the torches and lanterns with sparks. A myriad of twinkling little lights, almost mirroring the sea of stars above them.

"Are you really related to the General's wife?" Suzu asked eventually.

"Thrice removed, or so. She's from a side branch of the family." He turned to look at Suzu. "Apparently her father wasn't happy about Akari choosing some irrelevant minor noble from the north as her husband. He ordered Jarick to prove his worth before he agreed to give him his daughter's hand. Which, of course, he did. You know what he's like when challenged. They were married within the year."

Suzu chuckled. "That sounds just like the General."

Toshi's laugh – it was one of the most beautiful sounds in the world, in Suzu's opinion. It was so rare, so precious. The man must have caught the fondness in Suzu's gaze, for he cast a quick glance around, making sure they weren't watched, before he leaned towards him. A warm tingle went through Suzu as Toshi pressed his lips against his. Tenderly. Careful. As if he was afraid he might break him. Oh, he had no idea the things he did to Suzu.

Grabbing the lapels of Toshi's jacket, Suzu pulled him closer, lips parting slightly. He couldn't care less if anyone watched them. There was only Toshi – his closeness, the heat from his body, his taste. And when Toshi broke the kiss, Suzu couldn't help the protesting sound that escaped him.

"Sorry, but we ought to stop," Toshi said quietly, not without regret. "You know, I have to uphold a reputation as cold, unapproachable, and stoic."

Despite his disappointment, Suzu laughed. "Fine."

"Tomorrow. I'll come to you tomorrow."

"Promise?"

"I promise."

Suzu smiled and tilted his head back, looking at the stars. He liked Toshi wanting him, touching him, kissing him – loving him. He liked the warm fuzzy feeling he got, thinking about Mori no Toshiaki. It had a name, that feeling. Suzu knew it. He had felt it once before. And he hated it with every fibre of his being.

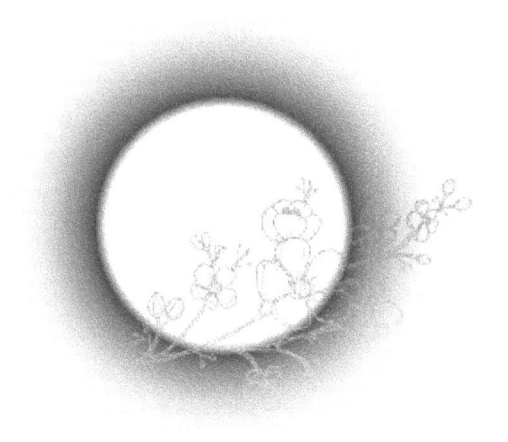

Chapter 4

"I can't believe we're really doing this," Jin grumbled, struggling with the unreasonable amount of buttons on the jacket of his borrowed livery. He felt ridiculous. And far too hot. Seriously, what were these people thinking? Wearing that many layers of thick cloth in this heat.

Niall stepped out from behind the partition she had been changing behind, and Jin's struggle turned into an altogether different one. The frilly skirts, the laze... the bonnet!

"Yes, thank you very much, I know I look ridiculous," Niall grumbled and aimed a hearty kick at Jin's shin. Jumping aside at the very last minute saved his leg from getting bruised.

"No... really... you... you look... beautiful?" Jin tried rather pathetically.

"Hmph. I'm letting this slide. Anyway, you, my friend, look by no means any better. Do something about your hair before that battle-axe of a housekeeper gets on your case."

Jin smoothed his hands over his unruly hair. They both knew it was a lost battle, his hair had the bad habit of doing the exact opposite of what he wanted it to do. Especially in this humidity. Perhaps he should just let it grow out, but he didn't have the patience for it.

"But to answer your question: Yes, we are really doing this. A hard day's work will do you good, you lazy sod," Niall joked, and although Jin laughed as well, he felt the words like a stab in his stomach. Wasn't it true after all? Most of his days were spent sitting around and waiting for either Niall needing his help with a patient, or Naloc having some errand for him to run. But Naloc had people for the real jobs: the spying, the meaner ones, the subtler ones, the ones that were never mentioned. Those were people who knew what they were doing and were good at it. Naloc had tried to find work for Jin in his own business – the legitimate one – but Jin had neither a knack for fine cloth nor for numbers. At the end of the day, Jin was a simple farm boy, who had difficulties reading, despite a temple education, and was a slow learner. Naloc had said they would eventually find the right profession for Jin – years later no-one even mentioned it anymore. And Jin lent a helping hand wherever one was needed. Usually his were the banal, small tasks no-one else wanted to do.

Niall, on the other hand, was a trained doctor. How she wasn't already fed up with him was a miracle to Jin.

"It's simple," Niall said, clasping Jin's shoulder. "You've helped out serving drinks before, so you'll be fine. You carry a tray around, and while you're at it, you prick your ears and catch what they are talking about. The tray gives you the perfect excuse to get close to them, and to rich folk the servants are basically invisible. Piece of cake, right?"

"I'm just surprised Naloc sent me, that's all."

"Why shouldn't he?"

Jin mumbled something unintelligible and averted his eyes. Niall was accomplished, smart, skilled – everything he wasn't. A foot collided with his shin, he hadn't seen it coming this time.

"Ouch... what was that for?" he cried, rubbing his smarting leg.

"For being an idiot. There's nothing for you to be ashamed of. Nothing. You hear? You haven't found what you're good at yet – so what? Some people need a little longer than others. Doesn't matter. You go at your own pace and that's good enough. You'll find what you are looking for eventually, stop comparing yourself to others, their life is not yours. And believe me, Jin, you are so much better than you think you are." She looked up at him. Her dark blue eyes full of fondness. Earnest and direct. "I will fight anyone who dares belittle you – and that includes you!" She squinted her eyes at him, daring him to argue. He didn't. One simply didn't argue with Niall about something important to her. Instead he smiled and nodded.

"All right."

"Good. Then let's do this."

Niall had been right, the older grey-haired lady, who seemed more like a military instructor than a housekeeper, was not happy with Jin's hair. But after consulting another older woman who seemed to be responsible for the wardrobe of the General's wife, she dropped the issue with stoic resignation.

Most of the afternoon was spent decorating the garden and the ballroom, polishing glassware and cutlery, and every surface they could find.

The day was sunny and hot – too hot to wear layers of stifling cloth while working, and Jin found himself not only sweaty and uncomfortable, but mentally cursing the livery every other minute, even though he had at least been allowed to take the frock-coat off. He would never understand the rich folks' taste in northern fashion.

When finally the last flower pot had found the perfect place and the ballroom glittered and glowed in the evening sun, they were allowed to rest before the guests arrived.

"There will be supper for everyone in the servants' mess, but you are free to take it out into the garden behind the kitchen," the housekeeper announced, walking up and down the row of servants very much like the military woman Jin suspected her to be. "The guests arrive at sunset. You will be on your stations fifteen minutes earlier. Until then, you can rest. Don't dare to be late or in anything less than an immaculate state. Dismissed!"

Jin and Niall followed the others to a large dining room in the back of the house, next to the kitchen. It was a nice, friendly room with a set of large glass doors that opened to a small garden. Tables and chairs were scattered across the green. Niall grabbed Jin's arm and pulled him quickly to a table set in the shade of a chestnut tree. It was already laden with bowls of food and jugs of cold water. One of the chairs was already occupied but Niall did not seem to care or ask for permission as she shoved Jin into a chair and claimed the last one for herself. The girl at the table didn't seem to mind.

You could say what you wanted, but the General did take care of his employees. The food was plenty and various. Next to freshly baked bread there were small bowls of cold soba, plates of cold meats, an assortment of seasonal fruits – something for every taste.

After the initial hunger had been stilled, a general chatter filled the air.

"Hey, have you heard about Genta?" a red-haired woman at the table next to them asked.

"Genta? The Earl's gardener? What about him?"

"Apparently he eloped with the maid."

"Nonsense!" the girl sitting next to Jin at their table snapped, turning in her seat to look at the woman behind her. "Numie would never just run away. Never. She has a sick mother and a little sister to take care of."

"Well, yes, but perhaps she got tired of it, and perhaps Genta was tired of waiting for her."

The girl shook her blonde head. "No. She wouldn't. Never."

"Mari, I know she's your best friend, but…" another girl spoke up, her voice carrying a hint of pity. "But perhaps she didn't tell you everything. I mean – when did you last see her? I haven't seen her around for at least two weeks, not even at the market. And don't you think the Earl would have allowed her to help out here today, after all she does need the money. So where is she?"

The girl called Mari hung her head, fiddling with the frills of her skirts. "That…"

Niall gently poked Jin in the ribs. She raised an eyebrow at him, leaned in and whispered, "There, you feel this? This tingly feeling that tells you something interesting's afoot.

Might be more than just a morsel of juicy gossip." She winked at him then leaned across him to address Mari directly. "Hey, you know, I've been worried about her, too. I was afraid she might be sick, or that something happened with her mother. I would really like to check on her, but I don't know where she lives."

Jin tried not to choke at the obvious lie. It always took him by surprise how quickly his friend could pull the lies out of her sleeves like it was nothing at all. Usually she was a very honest person, but she had told Jin once that she was so honest because she found honesty of more use, if necessary, however, she was able to lie without batting an eye. In order to not sabotage his friend's act, Jin tried to look politely concerned. Mari regarded them with big blue innocent eyes, probably wondering how these strangers knew her best friend.

But then she said, "Well, see, that's the weirdest thing." Niall gripped Jin's arm excitedly, she obviously liked the sound of that. Her face didn't tell, though. "I went to her house – repeatedly – but she's never there. Her mother and her sister seem to be doing fine... but they're acting strange. Like they hardly know me. And every single time they claim I've just missed her."

"Hmm, you say they act strange. Strange how?" Niall prodded.

"Like I said, like they hardly know me. But we've known each other all our life, Numie and I. Her mother took care of me when my parents had to work. They'd always tell me if something was wrong with Numie, but now they try to get rid of me as quickly as possible and don't want to speak to me instead. Weird, isn't it?"

"But they seem to be fine, you say? They don't seem to be in need of money or anything?"

"No. Apart from Numie never being around, and her mother and sister not wanting to speak to me... Look, I know, everyone tells me it's nothing and that I'm overreacting, but I know Numie. I know her. She's my best friend. She's basically like a sister, her family is also my family, so..." she trailed off as if the energy to argue further had left her.

Niall's eyes met Jin's. He could see the matter had caught his friend's interest. She had a good instinct, she could tell if there was something wrong about a story. And right now, Niall looked like a hound who had caught the scent of prey. Jin gave her an almost imperceptible nod to let her know he understood.

"I can tell you this, though," an older man sitting at the table opposite them suddenly spoke up, "Genta's definitely run off. My son's a friend of his. And when he couldn't find him anywhere, he went to the Earl's and asked about him. Do you know what they told him?"

"What?" came the impatient, curious inquire out of several mouths all around them.

"Said that two weeks ago, the Earl's valet – out of the blue – announced that there'd be some changes in personnel but that none of them had to be afraid to loose their jobs. That's all. Just like that. No more explanation, nothing. But neither Genta nor Numie were seen since that day." Everyone was staring at the man now. Jin couldn't help but think that Niall was right, there was something fishy about that story.

"Couldn't he... I mean... why didn't he... ask the Earl?" Mari asked in a small voice, but even before she had finished several people were already shaking their heads.

"Girl, you don't go asking the Earl. You do what he tells you to do and keep your mouth shut," one of them said and got a collective affirmation of those around.

After that, people slowly began to drift away from the tables, probably to catch a moment of rest, or freshen up. Eventually the only ones left beneath the chestnut tree were Jin, Niall, and the young maid, Mari. She looked terribly young, sitting there looking lost and sad. She didn't seem able to stop fidgeting with the lace on her apron. Jin and Niall exchanged worried looks. They wanted to help her, but what do you say to someone, being anxious about their best friend; what words could ease their mind?

Niall, always the one who knew what to do – or at least to appear as if she did – reached a hand out to put on the girl's shoulder. But before her hand had even crossed half the distance between them, Mari suddenly sat up straight and slapped her own cheeks with a resounding clap, making both Niall and Jin jump. She then took a deep breath, and hopped lightly to her feet.

"I'm going for a little walk. The General's wife apparently has the most beautiful roses in town – I want to catch a glimpse of them while I can. See you later." She beamed at them, her cheeks red, and not waiting for an answer, turned away and left. Her golden locks bounced happily at the spring in her step.

"Um... that's a professional maid for you, eh?" Jin joked half-heartedly, taken aback by the girl's sudden change.

"That... or truly worrying mood swings," Niall replied.

Jin stared at the tablet in his hands. Pastel coloured, enticing little morsels of some kind of sweets he had never seen before stared back at him, trying to lure him into trying them. He stomped down hard on the temptation.

"Don't be nervous," Niall whispered at his side.

"I'm not."

"Good. Keep your eyes and ears open. Oh, and hey, if you get a chance to get close to the Earl... he might let something slip about his missing servants."

"I doubt it." Jin hesitated. Niall – responsible, rational, level-headed as she usually was, sometimes had the tendency to let her imagination run wild. "Niall, you are not spinning stories in your head again, are you? I'm sure the Earl is not a blood-thirsty serial killer who bathes in the blood of young innocent women to retain his youth."

"And how do you know?" Niall hissed, squinting suspiciously at Jin. Jin glared back. After a moment she sighed, shrugged, and said, "All right, all right, he's probably not. But there is something strange going on in the Earl's house and I will find out what." She straightened and made for the entrance to the ballroom. Resigned, Jin followed.

The sun had begun its slow descent, and with the encroaching night the guests arrived. First one polished carriage, then a second, a third... rolled up the driveway, unloading men in bespoke suits and women is evening gowns or expensive kimono.

The General had set up a waiting area for the drivers, beautifully decorated, and supplied with more than enough food and drink. His own grooms – supported by a handful of young cadets – took care of the horses in the meantime.

So far, everything Jin had seen or heard strongly contradicted the tales Naloc kept telling about the General.

The man, himself, and his wife had at first welcomed every guest in front of the house, but soon too many people were vying for the General's attention. The musicians began to play, the glittering ballroom filled with people, the party spilled out onto the terrace, into the garden.

Jin drifted among all the finely dressed people, offering drinks and food, keeping his ears pricked to the hubbub of voices, the meaningless chatter, and baseless rumours. Here and there he caught an interesting titbit and stored it away as if he were collecting pebbles.

He was so focused on his work that when he finally had a minute to catch his breath, he was surprised to find night's reign had already begun. The goddess showed herself as a gibbous moon in a sea of stars, fireflies flitted between the trees and bushes, ephemeral in contrast to the steady glow of the lanterns.

Jin sagged against the wall next to the open doors and inhaled the fragrant night air. The calming scent of herbs filled the breeze, lavender and rosemary. Now that he had stopped moving, Jin noticed the ache in his back, the soreness of his feet. How much longer would this night last?

"Hey there, champ," Niall greeted, sidling up to him. "I see you've been working hard."

"How can you tell?"

"You look knackered. But if you think your feet are sore – try wearing these shoes all day. I don't know what these people are thinking, those things are torture devices." She stretched a leg out and wriggled her foot. The glossy, polished shoes with their small heels did indeed look terribly uncomfortable. Although he hated them, Jin was suddenly thankful for the loafers he had been forced to wear.

"Anything good?" Niall asked.

"Define good. A few bits and pieces that might come in handy, but nothing much."

"Same. ... Oh, but you know what?" Niall's eyes sparkled as she suddenly grinned up at him.

"What?"

"Get this: The General is still whining about the loss of his peacock to anyone and everyone."

"He isn't."

"He is. Heard him bemoaning the bird and cursing Naloc's name in the same sentence at least five times already this evening."

Jin chuckled. It seemed ridiculous that the theft of a pet bird could re-ignite an old rivalry like this.

"Honestly, I feel bad for the man. Anyway, did you get a look at the infamous beauty, Yūzuki no Suzu?"

"I don't think I have, but then again I don't know what he looks like, so..."

"Trust me, you'd know if you'd seen him. Come on, I think he's still outside on the terrace with the Earl – and before you ask: No, the Earl has not mentioned his missing servants, nor has anyone else."

Niall grabbed his arm and dragged him out onto the terrace. They nonchalantly sidled up to the bench on which Niall had last seen the Earl and the Furyusha. They weren't there anymore, the bench was empty. Only a few people were left on the terrace, the ballroom, too, had begun to empty.

Jin felt only a fleeting disappointment. Admittedly, he had been curious to see the Furyusha everyone was talking about. Though he had a feeling that the boy's beauty was grossly exaggerated. People were like that.

Niall suddenly tapped her hand repeatedly against Jin's chest, drawing his attention. She pointed in the direction of the ballroom's folding doors. "There, look, that's him." Jin, still wondering what Niall and his other friend's were trying to achieve by showing him someone, who apparently was far out of reach of any common man anyway, sighed in resignation and let his gaze follow Niall's pointing finger. There, talking to the General and his lovely wife, stood a young man so impossibly beautiful Jin wondered if he was even human or perhaps rather a spirit sprung from legends. Enticed, Jin took a few steps into the room to get a better look. The General's wife – against protocol – gave the young man a quick hug, then pulled her husband away, laughing. And in that moment Jin got an unobstructed view of the young Furyusha.

It felt as if he had suddenly been thrown into freezing water. His breath caught, his heart missed a few beats. He stumbled backwards, caught himself against the doorframe. It wasn't possible. His vision blurred. He gasped for breath.

"That's not possible," he whispered.

"Jin?" Niall frowned at him, worry plain on her face. She tried to make him look at her, but he couldn't take his eyes off of Yūzuki no Suzu. Through a sheen of tears that marred his vision he saw the young man turn and leave. Niall was shaking him now, calling his name again and again.

Jin's body reacted before his brain could. He tore himself away from Niall and ran after the youth.

At the foot of the marble stairs he caught up to him. Torches lit the driveway, a single carriage, simple and unadorned, stood waiting.

"Kari!" Jin cried – and the young Furyusha stopped, frozen, tense. Slowly, oh so slowly, he turned around and looked at Jin – with murder in his eyes.

Chapter 5

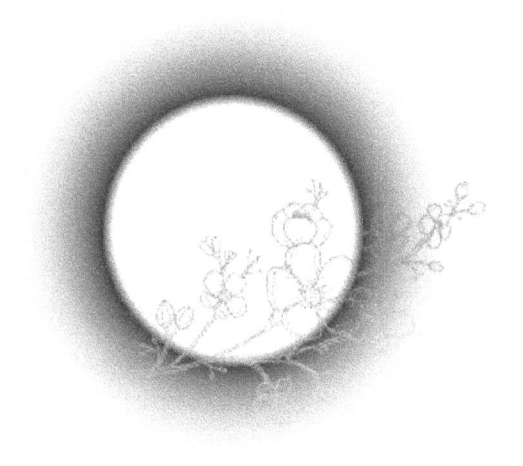

The evening flew by in a swirl of glittering lights, too much champagne, laughter, and familiar and unfamiliar faces. The only ones that lingered, however, were the Earl's family – his sister, brother-in-law, and nephew. Suzu had considered a hasty retreat when he saw them making their way through the crowd out onto the terrace. To his surprise they had greeted him as if he were family, or rather soon-to-be family. Suzu was overwhelmed. He didn't know how to deal with it and with the emotions bubbling up inside of him. In consequence he acted far shyer than he normally would. Although not as shy as Takara, the Earl's nephew and heir. The poor boy blushed furiously every time Suzu's looked at him, stammering his way through the evening. The relief when his parents finally decided it was time for them to greet a few more people before leaving for home was palpable.

Soon after, the party began to slowly break up. Toshi, after promising again to come visit him the following evening, bid Suzu goodnight. And after the obligatory quick conversations with a handful of the Singing Dragon's prosperous patrons, Suzu decided it was time for him to return to Yūgao as well. Finding the General and his wife wasn't difficult, but to take his leave of a more than tipsy General was a different story. In the end Akari pushed her husband forcibly aside, gave Suzu a quick kiss on each cheek – one more surprise he had no idea how to react to – and finally dragged the General away. For a moment Suzu stared after them, dumbstruck. Then he turned and left the brightly lit ballroom behind.

Haldor and their driver were already waiting for him. Suzu had wondered if the servant girl he had sent to tell them he was ready to leave had found them in the short time, but he guessed his description of Haldor as the tallest, broadest man around had been most helpful.

His feet had hardly touched the gravel when there came a voice from behind him, loud and crystal clear. "Kari!" Suzu froze, his body tensed. That name – like a dagger to the heart, struck true. And that voice – that voice, as familiar to his ears as his own...

If Suzu had to be honest, he was always angry. He didn't know exactly when it had started, but there was just too much anger inside him. Now, through the cracks of his once broken and mended heart a rage seeped through unlike anything he had felt in a very long time. He clenched his teeth. His hands curled into fists, fingernails digging deep into his palms. Slowly, with monumental control on the building storm inside him, Suzu turned around.

The young man's face was deep in shadow, he was taller, shoulders broader than in his memories, but Suzu would have recognised him anywhere, under any circumstances.

"Kari?" the young man asked. Uncertainty tainted his voice now. "It's me. Jin."

"I'm sorry, you must have mistaken me." Suzu was surprised how cool and calm, how polite he sounded, despite the voice in his head screaming for blood.

"No, I don't think... Kari. I know it's you. I –"

"I said, you have the wrong person," Suzu cut him off, a vicious edge creeping into his voice. "And I don't know anyone by that name either."

He could hear Haldor climbing out of the carriage behind him, could feel the giant's presence, saw the young man involuntarily take a step back.

"But..."

"If you'd excuse me now, I'm expected," Suzu threw the words out, then whirled around and almost dived into the carriage. Haldor glared at the young man once more, for good measure, then climbed in after Suzu.

As the carriage began to move, gravel crunching beneath the horses' hooves, the wheels, Suzu heard him call that hateful name a last time – a spectre that haunted his nightmares.

They were silent on their way home. Haldor didn't ask, and Suzu was glad about it. The old northerner never pried, never prodded, he simply knew what his children needed, by some instinct, always ready to catch them should they fall. So when they arrived at the Singing Dragon, and Suzu jumped out of the carriage and ran for his room, Haldor let him. When the boys, curious about the party, tried to follow Suzu to his room, he chased them away, telling them to leave Suzu alone. When Suzu nearly ripped his expensive kimono, struggling out if it, and even threw the jade kanzashi carelessly on the floor, he stood silently by and waited until Suzu fled his room again. And Haldor followed, like a shadow, like a guardian spirit. Followed Suzu to the dojo, lit the lamps for him, stood guard at the door. When Kazue and Ryū came to investigate, worry written all over their faces, he held them back. He did what his child needed him to do: to let him rage. And rage he did.

Suzu attacked the dummy with his wooden sword viciously enough the sack cloth ripped and the stuffing spilled out. But he cared little about it. It wasn't pretty, it wasn't graceful, there was no skill in what he did. Suzu hacked and slammed and beat until one tiny cracking sound was followed by another, and the sword splintered and broke. With a ferocious, rage filled cry he hauled the rest of it across the training hall, then stood, heaving one breath after the other, shaking and drenched in sweat, in the gloom of the lamps.

At last he fell to his knees, spent, exhausted, the rage inside him not gone, but tempestuous no more.

After a little while he felt someone come up behind him, felt a hand on his shoulder. A gently squeeze. A reassurance. *It's all right, you are not alone, your family is with you.*

"Ryū, help Suzu get cleaned and then take him to his room. I'll join you later." Kazue's voice was quiet, soft, and tinged with deep dark sadness. Suzu didn't look at her, he couldn't. He didn't want to see the sorrow she felt for him, the pity. He let Ryū pull him to his feet and lead him from the hall. As they passed Haldor, Suzu brushed the big man's arm. A quiet rumble in return, an acknowledgement. It was all Suzu had wanted and needed. Haldor didn't need words or grand gestures, he knew Suzu was sorry about the sword and the dummy, grateful for Haldor's silent guardianship.

Ryū, too, asked nothing, said nothing as they made their way to the bathhouse, nor while he waited for Suzu to finish cleaning himself. Nor on their way to Suzu's room. Silently he sat beside Suzu on the futon, close enough Suzu felt his warmth, the tiny electric tingle that passed between two bodies.

At last Kazue arrived with a steaming cup in her hand. "Here," she said, thrusting the cup at Suzu. "Drink, it'll calm you. It's lavender tea," she added as an afterthought. Kazue sat down in front of her boys and watched Suzu sip the fragrant infusion before she finally asked the question Suzu had dreaded. "What happened?"

Suzu took a deep breath. "He was there. When I was leaving, he was suddenly there." His hand tightened around the tea cup, he put it quickly down before he could break the fragile porcelain.

"Who?" Ryū asked.

But Suzu couldn't, wouldn't say his name. It was poison, acid, burning his throat, his tongue – his heart. He clenched his teeth, and all he spat out was "He." A single syllable, tiny and irrelevant. Yet Suzu filled it with so much hate, so much rage, such despise, raw pain, it fell heavy like a smith's hammer on the anvil.

Kazue was the first to understand. "I feared this day would come," she sighed heavily. "If he had come to town, as you said he had intended to, then sooner or later you were bound to run into each other. We all knew this, and dreaded the day it would happen."

Suzu scowled at the tatami floor. What if he had left the party earlier? Could he have avoided this encounter, or was it meant to happen eventually as Kazue believed? Oh how he had hoped and wished to forget, to erase his past, pretend it had never happened, then he wouldn't always feel this anger inside him, could forget the pain... could allow his broken heart to love. No such luck, it seemed.

"What if he comes here?" Ryū voiced what Suzu refused to ask. "It's not like it's hard to find Suzu."

Kazue stood up and smoothed down her kimono. "We'll deal with it then, but now – sleep. You need your rest, both of you. Ryū, you better stay here tonight."

Suzu smiled at her, a tiny but grateful smile. She must have known Suzu would plead Ryū to stay, he didn't want to be alone with his thoughts. How was it that everyone in this motley, thrown-together family of his always seemed to know exactly what he needed. Kazue smiled back at him and left.

Sleep, however, was elusive. Whenever Suzu closed his eyes, he saw him again, standing there in the soft light of the lanterns, flushed, excited, expectant. Gods, how he wanted to punch that damned familiar face. Destroy that easy smile he had once adored.

Suzu kept tossing and turning, softly growling, until Ryū pinned him down. "All right," Ryū huffed. "It seems you still have too much energy left. So tell me what you want me to do."

Suzu stared into his friend's eyes for a long moment, then reached up and framed his handsome face. "Then make me stop thinking," he said roughly, and pulled Ryū towards him, claiming the young man's lips, hard and needy.

Jin sat in the dark, staring at the flickering flame of an oil lamp. He didn't remember quite how he had gotten home. It was a blur, a white static spot, a void. Nothing but the sound of his pounding heart, the dizziness of a whirlwind of emotions: elation, confusion, doubt, hope, disappointment, heartbreak. Dimly he remembered Niall at his side, calling his name, asking questions, and eventually dragging him away from the General's estate. The rest was as nebulous as the mist that so often hovered on the surface of the Opal River.

He heard the door open and close; a moment later Niall sat down across from him. She carefully pulled the oil lamp out of the way and replaced it with a steaming cup.

"Drink this," she said gently. When Jin didn't respond she added more sternly, "Doctor's orders." That did the trick. It usually did.

Jin inhaled the warm scent of lavender and chamomile. Gentle, calm, a mother's touch, a friend's embrace. He obediently drank the tea, then set the cup down and looked up at his friend. Between her brows a frown puckered her smooth skin, worry was written in every line of her fox-ish face.

"It was Kari," Jin said at last, and wasn't surprised by his friend's reaction. The young woman sighed and shook her head.

"No, Jin. He's not Kari. Perhaps they look alike, but --"

"No, it's him," Jin cut her off. "I know you don't believe me, I don't blame you. But, Niall, I'd know him anywhere no matter how much time has passed. Even blind I would know him." Niall was quiet for such a long time, Jin wondered if she had fallen asleep with her eyes open, until she shook her head again.

"If that were true, why didn't he know you? Why did he claim not to know who Kari is?" Ah, so Niall had been there the whole time, had witnessed what had transpired between the two young men. The realisation should have stung or made him angry, but Jin knew her well enough to know she hadn't spied on him out of curiosity, but out of concern.

"I don't know," Jin admitted. The boy's reaction had been strange, to say the least. But it hadn't been the reaction of someone being mistaken for another. There had been a moment of recognition. Eyes widening, breath catching. Jin hadn't imagined those. Yet he also hadn't imagined the sudden rage, the hate that had flared across the boy's face, made his body tense. The intensity of it had shocked Jin to the core. Before it could burn him to ashes, however, it was gone, so suddenly the world seemed askew, hidden away behind a mask of pleasant neutrality. If Jin hadn't felt its heat, he would have been sure it had been nothing but a trick of light and shadow.

"The way he reacted," Jin tried to explain, "that's not how you react if someone mistakes you. You didn't see it. I don't even know why it was there, that... that... anger." Jin could not bring himself to speak of the hate he had felt, if only for a second, rejected the thought that it been directed at him. It couldn't be, could it?

"Jin," Niall sighed, "let it go. It's been a long day and we're both exhausted. Sleep, and tomorrow you'll see clearer."

"All right, I guess you are right."

"You know, I usually am."

Jin smiled. He knew he was right about Kari, but he understood why Niall found it difficult to believe him. Too often had he been crushed by disappointment whenever a quick glimpse had turned out to be nothing but a fleeting similarity. And Niall? She had been there every single time to pick up the pieces and glue them back together. She also definitely was right about both of them needing sleep, so...

"Good. Oh!" Niall suddenly exclaimed. "And it's your birthday tomorrow! Well, today I guess, but seeing as I haven't been to bed yet, it is still today as in yesterday-today, not today-today, and not yet your birthday, which is tomorrow."

Jin blinked at Niall, who looked back at him with the defiant smugness of someone who had just explained the universe itself and was daring him to disagree. Yes, they needed sleep. Overcome with fondness and gratitude, Jin pulled her into a crushing hug. He would never stop thanking the gods for sending Niall to find him on that rainy winter's day. What would he ever do without her?

"All right, all right," Niall chuckled. "You can let go now before you squeeze me to death." When he did, she planted a kiss on his cheek. "Sleep tight, little brother of my heart."

"You too. And thank you for always being there... for... for having found me, sister of my heart."

Niall smiled at him. A smile full of warmth and love, and he knew, no matter what, he would have her on his side, always.

And then she was gone and Jin lay in the dark waiting for sleep to come. But when he closed his eyes, Kari was there, green eyes sparkling with joy, and love, and laughter. And suddenly his expression changed, grew cold and hard, his jade eyes burning, not with love and laughter, but with barely contained rage, with hate. Where had this hate come from, who was it directed at, he couldn't say. Out of a dark corner of his mind came a tiny voice, whispering, jeering, scolding: *You, he hates you.* No. It couldn't be, why would it? But doubt was nagging at him, making him toss and turn. Sleep didn't come easy that night.

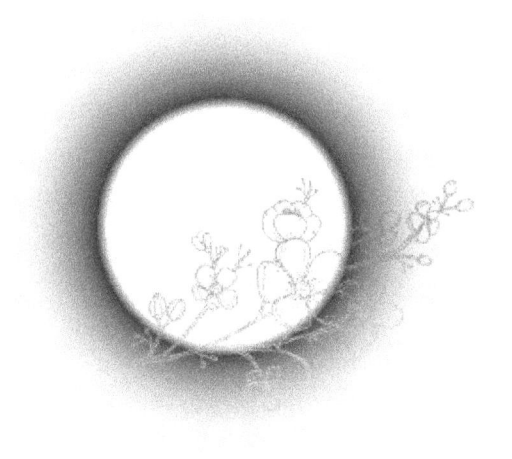

Chapter 6

"You seem distracted today."

Suzu lifted his head from Toshi's chest to meet the man's eyes. "I'm sorry," he muttered.

"You don't have to apologise. I'm just curious. Should I be worried that you are growing tired of me?"

Suzu cocked an eyebrow at that. "Did anything we did in the last hour seem to you like I was growing tired of you?"

Toshi laughed, slung his arm around Suzu's waist and rolled on top of him. "Well," he said in this low, resonant voice of his that always sent shivers down Suzu's spine. "No, as a matter of fact that was... I don't know how to put it. Very... creative."

Suzu smiled coyly. "Did you enjoy it?"

"Did I...?" Toshi sputtered. "You little minx. You very well know I did." Suzu laughed. The mischievous side of him enjoyed making Toshi blush. It wasn't easily achieved either.

He lifted his head and kissed Toshi. But this, this was something Suzu couldn't get used to. The heady feeling kissing that man in his arms elicited, the electric sparks the whisper of Toshi's skin against his sent through his entire body, the way he wished time would stand still whenever they were together. It was addicting, it was dangerous. And he didn't want to think about it too much. So instead he slung one slender leg over Toshi's hip, grinding their bodies together, still slick with sweat from their earlier exertion, stoking the fire of lust that still kindled between them.

But Toshi suddenly pulled away, flinging open the veil of desire. A rush of coldness dowsed the fire as Suzu looked up into eyes like chips of ice. Desire turned into anxiety.

"You are also unexpectedly demanding today. Is something the matter?"

Yes, I want to be fucked stupid until last night's encounter has been erased from my memory. But of course, he couldn't say that. It would lead to questions he didn't want to answer, to revelations he wasn't ready for. Suzu cursed inwardly. He had been so intent on making himself forget, he only now realised he was out of character. What if Toshi saw through him? He couldn't risk it. So far the man seemed to be pleasantly surprised, but Suzu had to be careful, Toshi knew him only as well-mannered, graceful, and kind. Gods, this wasn't like him. He never slipped up like this.

All Furyusha learned to play different roles. It was part of their profession. But Suzu had made it a special kind of art. It was one of his Ethereal gifts to instinctively know what another person wanted, what they needed, and to give them exactly that. Never, not once, no matter how drunk or exhausted he was, did his mask slip. The only ones who knew the real Suzu were the people he had made his family. But

Mori no Toshiaki, Earl of Tsukikage, had been a challenge from the start. Suzu hadn't been able to read him the way he read all of his customers, couldn't tell what the man wanted, what he needed. In the end, Suzu had opted for a persona very much unlike his true self: docile, submissive, soft-spoken, and kind, a little timid sometimes but flirty enough. Powerful men like the Earl liked this kind of person, did they not? Someone to protect. It worked – or at least Suzu liked to think it did. But there were moments in which Toshi looked at him with those inscrutable grey eyes and it felt as if he was able to see straight into the deepest, darkest abyss of Suzu's soul. In those moments Suzu felt an inexplicable fear – not of being exposed but of losing this man. Toshi would never love the real Suzu, would he?

And yet, each time they met it became more and more difficult to retain this persona, to not tear off the mask. A part of Suzu wanted Toshi to know him, to see him – another part of him, however, wanted to run and hide from him forever. These feelings the other man awoke in him, Suzu didn't want them. Feelings he had discarded, abandoned, vowed to never let into his broken heart ever again. Feelings that scared him the most.

Unbidden the image of a handsome boy with messy hair and a smile brighter than the sun emerged in his mind. There had been a time in which Suzu had been willing to discard his own self forever, to become someone else – for that boy. He had given him everything – and he had thrown Suzu away like so much garbage.

"Suzu?" Toshi's voice jerked him out of his thoughts. Suzu willed his clenched jaw to relax.

"I'm sorry, I..." he trailed off, uncertain how to finish the sentence.

"You know you can tell me whatever it is that is bothering you, don't you?"

Suzu forced a smile. How he wished that was true, but he had his doubts. He closed his eyes and took a deep breath. When he opened them again, a worried frown creased the skin between Toshi's brows.

"I'm fine, Toshi, really," Suzu assured him. He could see Toshi didn't believe him, but was relieved when the man didn't press the issue.

"All right. Well, I think you could do with a little change of scenery."

"Change of scenery?"

"Why don't you come stay with me for a couple of days?"

"You mean at your place?" Suzu mumbled. It was tempting, no question, but also daunting. Could he really maintain his mask, spending so much time alone with Toshi?

They both knew Toshi was trying to show Suzu the life he could have, the life they could have together. But how could he ever accept, when the one Toshi wanted wasn't really Suzu?

"Only a day and a night. What do you say? It might do you good." Or it might destroy him.

"I need to ask Mother first," Suzu hedged.

"Of course. Although I'm pretty certain I already know what she'll say." Toshi cleared his throat and declared in a haughty, high-pitched voice, "That's entirely up to Suzu."

Suzu snorted. "That was the worst imitation of Mother ever," he laughed. And just like that, his mood brightened, his worries dissipated like mist being burned away by sunlight. Toshi's grey eyes warmed. A smile brightened the man's face, full of happiness and fondness, and Suzu relented. "All right. One day and one night."

Toshi brought their lips together. Suzu could feel the smile on Toshi's lips, as that heady feeling spread through him once again. If he could live only in moments like these, he'd knew himself to be blessed beyond measure. But all too soon Toshi pulled away and sat up.

"Sorry, my love. Business calls."

"And what am I to do with myself this evening?" Suzu pouted. "I absolutely can't accept any other customers today."

"Oh? Have I worn you out?"

Suzu playfully slapped the man's naked rump. Toshi laughed and got to his feet. "It's rather that I don't want to spoil our time together," Suzu admitted in a small voice. It was worth it, for seeing Toshi blush.

"Well," Toshi said with a little cough, "it's a full moon. When was the last time you went to the Moon Fair?"

A piece of art made of strawberries and cream, topped with lime peels, dominated the centre of the low table like a prima donna on stage. It was enormous, almost too tall for the delicate wooden piece of furniture. Jin had an inkling of how the table must have been feeling. For when he looked at the grinning, expectant faces around him, he felt nearly crushed by their expectations.

That cake was too beautiful to eat. He knew where it had come from, there was only one baker in town who was capable of creating something like this, and her baked goods were as expensive as they were exclusive. It must have cost them a fortune. Jin couldn't let his dark mood ruin his friends' efforts. They seemed determined to make his birthday the best he ever had, so he could at least make the effort to show them how much he appreciated it by putting on a smile and enjoying his day.

"W-wow... thank you," he mumbled – and was promptly punished for it when Risa punched his arm.

"Oi, show a bit more enthusiasm, please," she demanded.

And of course she was right. Jin shook his head at himself, his smile becoming a bit more naturally, and tried again. "Sorry, but really, thank you. This is amazing, I'm speechless."

"Can we please get to the cake-eating part now?" Niall whined, and Jin couldn't help but laugh. He wasn't the only one. Niall's love for cake was notorious. She could have easily eaten the entire thing herself and died a happy sugary death. The fact that she hadn't even tried to steal one of the flower-shaped strawberries was proof of her iron will and her love for Jin. So Jin offered her the first piece, the ache in his heart soothing at the sight of happiness on his friend's face. It was one of the things he loved best about Niall – the joy and wonder she felt about even the smallest things.

The cake was almost gone when Naloc joined them, waving away their half-hearted attempts at respectful bows. He accepted a piece of cake and a cup of tea, joked and laughed with them, congratulated Jin to his birthday like an uncle would his favoured nephew. This Naloc wasn't their boss or the leader of the Crescent, but the man who had taken them in off the streets, gave them a home, work, people they didn't only call friends but family, and they loved him for it.

Despite his broken heart, Jin found himself enjoying his birthday party and the company of the people most important to him.

Eventually, however, the cake was eaten, the tea drunk, and Naloc had business on his mind. He leaned back, looked at

Jin, then at Niall and said, "So?" The laughter and chatter around them died down at once.

Niall swallowed the last bite of her third piece of cake. "Well, there was a lot of the usual nonsense. You know, stuff like 'By the gods, have you seen what Lady Blah is wearing – and at her age.' But," Niall paused and looked at Jin, prompting him to continue.

"Something odd seems to be going on at the Earl of Tsukikage's. Or at least it struck us at odd," he complied, then explained about the missing gardener and maid, about the strange way in which their disappearance was treated. Naloc listened closely, pulling at his goatee all the while.

"It might be nothing at all. Perhaps they really just eloped?" Jin finished. He felt foolish. Yesterday, listening to the other servants, to the girl Mari, he had felt as if there was some big conspiracy behind it. But now, recounting it, it seemed silly to think so. The gardener and the maid were known to be lovers, they vanished at the same time – every child could put two and two together. And Mari? The missing girl was her best friend, of course she wouldn't want to believe her friend abandoned her family and ran away.

Jin sighed. He wondered if he could ever do anything right, ever be of any use at all.

"Durin, get your boys ready, find out what the Earl's been up to lately," Naloc ordered, much to Jin's surprise. Durin, a small, mousy man in his forties, nodded his head once and sprang to his feet. As he passed Jin he gave him a quick smile and a wink. Jin was too taken aback to react.

"Aika," Naloc continued, "see what you can find out about that gardener." Aika, as quick-footed and silent as Durin and as graceful as a dancer, stood up without a word. Before she could leave, however, Risa interjected, "Wait, what about me?"

"You remain here as my ever loyal bodyguard."

"Aw, but--"

"Risa, darling," Aika stopped her protest. "Sweetheart, this is no work for you. You are as subtle and inconspicuous as a giant golden dick covered in glitter, standing in the middle of a temple court."

While Risa blinked like an owl and flushed a furious read, the others roared with laughter at the colourful picture Risa's lover had created. Niall was laughing so hard, she was bent double, holding her belly. Even Naloc, shaking his head, chuckled.

"Rude," Risa said at last. Then a crooked grin tugged at the corner of her mouth. "Also true."

When they were alone, Naloc finally turned back to Jin and Niall. "Do you think you can find that Mari girl? I want to know more about her friend. And if possible check in on her family."

"Sure," Jin agreed, happy to be called into action like his friends. For a moment he had feared that his usefulness had already been exhausted. But Niall didn't move, nor did Naloc stop mustering Jin in a rather disconcerting way. "Um..."

"Jin, Niall told me about what happened last night."

"What do you mean?"

"Jin!" Niall snapped. "Cut it out. We're family, aren't we? I know that you won't let it go, but I also know that you won't ask for help. So here we are, trying to help. You still think Yūzuki no Suzu is your Kari, don't you?" Jin's silence was enough of an answer. Niall sighed and shook her head, but before she had a chance to continue, Naloc took over.

"Lad, I don't see how that could be. From what you told us about the boy, and what I know about Yūzuki no Suzu, it doesn't add up. Suzu came to Kazue – or rather, she found him

– months before you met Niall. Actually, if I remember correctly, it was right around this time of year, almost the exact same time you first came to town. She called on us back then, you know. Needed a doctor, a good one. I saw the boy then, it wasn't a pretty sight. When she'd found him, he was more dead than alive, but stubborn, so very, very stubbornly holding on. Covered in dirt and dried blood, half starved and dehydrated, cuts and bruises everywhere, some worse than others. A cut that split his right brow all the way to his cheekbone. It was too difficult for Niall to handle at the time, so I called in a favour with someone at the academy. And she did a remarkable job, though the boy lost the sight in the eye. You probably didn't see the scar last night."

With a sinking feeling Jin sat down heavily. Was it possible? Were Kari and Suzu two different people? True, it shouldn't be possible, at the time Suzu came to town, Kari should have still been at the temple. But what if he hadn't been? What if he had followed Jin despite Nobu's promise to keep him there, to explain to him why Jin had to leave, to keep him safe. Kari had always been a sweet and timid soul, but he could be stubborn as a mule. So what if Kari had followed Jin? What had happened to him? Why had the boy been injured? And why was he working as a Furyusha? To pay his debts? Out of gratitude towards his saviour? That kind of work – it disagreed with Kari's personality.

"I don't know what happened, but I do know one thing: That young man I met last night was Kari. My Kari. I know this with all my heart. I know him."

Niall drew a breath and opened her mouth, probably to tell Jin he was a thickheaded idiot. But Naloc stopped her with a small gesture of his hand.

"All right," he said soothingly. "We don't have to discuss this now. Let's focus on the work at hand. Find this Mari, get her to take you to the maid's family."

Agreeing – and relieved, in Jin's case, while Niall seemed rather put out – they got to their feet and made for the door.

"Oh, and don't forget: sundown at Take's oden stall. I've had him prepare an exclusive table for us," Naloc called after them.

"What? Why?" Jin whirled around, staring at his boss. A table at any stall during the Moon Fair was an extravagance not even Tsukiyama's nobility indulged in, except for very, very special occasions.

"What do you mean, why? Because it's your birthday, that is why!"

He followed Niall through the narrow streets of Kigetsu with no idea where they were going – not to mention how to find the girl. At last Niall stopped in front of a small shop close to the river.

"How in the world are we supposed to find her? It's a big town, you know!"

"Which is why we ask for her address," Niall stated as if Jin should have known this all along.

"Ask... ask who?"

Niall gestured at the store front, at the sign above the door. Jin looked up at it, and felt like a fool at once. The shop wasn't a shop, it was the office of the town's biggest job agency, placing servants into Getsuro's most illustrious houses and employees in the town's biggest enterprises. And they provided people for special occasions such as the General's birthday party.

"I see," Jin said. "But they won't just give us the girl's address."

"Leave that to me. You just look awkward and uncomfortable." Niall looked up into Jin's face. "Yes, that's good. A little less confused perhaps."

Easier said than done, but Jin knew better than to argue with Niall about how to get information. She was by far better at this than he would ever be. Therefore he followed his friend and tried to do as she had told him.

A heavyset man with a rather out of control moustache sat behind a desk, scribbling into a big ledger. He spared them the quickest of glances before bending over his work again.

"Niall ax Corbin," the man said, "if you are here to collect last night's wage you are at the wrong place. That fury of a housekeeper dispenses the payment."

"Oh, I see, our bad," Niall replied sheepishly. "But man, that lady's scary."

The man snickered, put his pen down, and finally focused his attention on them. "True. You know," he lowered his voice conspiratorially and leaned over his desk, "rumour has it, she used to be the General's right hand back in the guard. They rose through the ranks side by side. Allegedly she could have become general herself, but instead she decided to stay by his side, even when he quit the active service." He raised a thick, bushy eyebrow suggestively.

"Sven ax Helge, is even a single word of that true?" Niall demanded.

Sven barked a laugh. "Who knows. As I said: rumours. Anyway, if you want money, you have to go to that old harridan. But I guess you didn't want that job for the money anyway, did you?" He grinned knowingly. Niall ignored the comment.

"Look, Sven, the reason why we are here is that you have to help us find someone." Sven's beady eyes glittered with curiosity. "A serving girl. She was also working at the party last night. Her name is Mari. Golden locks, big blue eyes...?" Sven frowned, his focus suddenly latching onto Jin, who dropped his gaze to the hardwood floor and shuffled his feet, looking as awkward as possible. It wasn't difficult. "Ah... um... she lost something and we would like to return it," Niall mumbled.

"Right," Sven drawled. "Well, you know I can't just hand out the addresses of our clients. We are a discreet agency and value our clients' privacy." Despite his words, his tone suggested otherwise.

Niall cast Jin a quick glance, twisting the hem of her shirt between her hands. When she spoke next, there was a kind of heartbreaking desperation in her voice.
"I... I know, and I would never ask... but... you see, my friend here..." Again her gaze flicked to Jin. "Y-you know... he's... and... it's his birthday today," she finished in a small, wavering voice. Sven's expression softened. They watched him for a moment struggle with himself, before Niall turned to Jin, rubbing his arm consolingly. "Sorry, love, it was worth a try. But if the two of you are destined for each other, I am sure--"

"All right," Sven cried suddenly, throwing his hands up in defeat. "But you have to promise not to tell a single soul you got that address from me. Not. One. Single. Soul. Got it?" Niall and Jin nodded their heads emphatically. Jin took his cue from Niall and let a hopeful smile spread across his face. Sven grabbed another ledger on his desk and flipped through the pages. Having found what he was looking for, he ripped a piece of paper out of the back of the ledger and scribbled down the girl's address. He looked at them sternly as he handed the piece of paper over. "This is an exception."

Outside, Niall waved the paper at Jin and grinned broadly. "Let's get a bite to eat first."

"I can't believe this worked. And without bribing him."

"That's because Sven ax Helge is a hopeless romantic. He'd never miss a chance to play love's advocate."

The address Sven had given them led them to a neat little neighbourhood in the north of Kigetsu, inhabited mostly by well-to-do working class families. Mari's home was a friendly northern style brick house with a small front garden. A rose arch granted visitors entrance, sweet smelling and welcoming. A tall, slender woman with hair as golden as Mari's locks and eyes the colour of periwinkles opened the door. Curiosity twinkled in her blue eyes.

"Hello, sorry to disturb you," Niall said. "But we are looking for Mari. Is she here?"

The woman frowned at the familiarity. "Are you friends of my daughter's?" she asked with a hint of suspicion. No doubt she knew all of Mari's friends and was wondering why she had never seen nor heard about them before.

"Well, kind of. We worked together at the General's yesterday." Honesty – at least a measure of it – seemed the correct choice, for the woman's expression relaxed.

"Well, come in then," Mari's mother said, pushing the door wide, allowing them entrance, and called for her daughter.

They heard a door creak open on the upper floor. A moment later Mari's heart-shaped face appeared at the top of the staircase. "Oh!" she exclaimed, nearly stumbling down the stairs. Her mother shook her head at her daughter's clumsiness and disappeared deeper into the house. "Um... sorry, I think... I've forgotten your names," she added sheepishly.

Having grown unbearably tired of letting Niall run the show by herself, Jin put on his most charming smile, feeling ridiculously satisfied when Mari blushed. He ignored Niall's snort. "Don't worry about that," Jin said. "My name's Jin, this is my friend Niall."

"R-right," Mari stammered, as taken aback by the familiarity as her mother had been. But Jin, who had never had a family of his own, had been granted Naloc's name when the man took him in – and leading with that wasn't always the best course of action. It tended to make people nervous.

They followed Mari into a small but cosy sitting room with tall windows overlooking a lovely little garden in full bloom. A pitcher of cold water infused with lemon slices was already waiting for them on the table, three glasses, each containing a sprig of rosemary, next to it. Jin hadn't noticed just how parched he was until he accepted a glass and let the cool, subtly flavoured water wash over his tongue.

"So," Mari said at last, "this is a nice surprise, but I don't think this is a social call, is it?"

"Well, not really, no," Jin admitted. "Actually, it is about what you told us yesterday about your missing friend. We would like to know more about this."

"Oh. Um... why?"

"Because... that is... well, we--"

"Do you know who Murasaki no Naloc is?" Niall interjected, causing Jin to bite his tongue in his surprise. So much for trying to keep Naloc's name out of this for now.

Mari's sky blue eyes widened. She nodded her head slowly, her gaze flitting from Niall to Jin and back. "He is... the Crescent's First Seat?"

"Correct."

"My papa says, he's a scoundrel." Jin snorted, earning himself a jab in the ribs."But that he takes care of his people," Mari continued. "So, do you think he'd help find Numie?"

"I don't think, I know it. Look, Mari, we work for Murasaki-tan. He sent us to you because he wants to help you find your friend. But we need your help to do so. You have to tell us everything you know. Can you do that?"

Mari worried her bottom lip for a moment before coming to a decision. She took a look over her shoulder, making sure her mother wouldn't overhear."What do you want to know?"

"Everything you can tell us might help. Why don't you start by telling us about your friend's employment at the Earl's? Did she like it there? Did the Earl treat her well?"

What the girl told them came as a surprise to Jin, who had always thought of the Earl of Tsukikage as a cold, ruthless man. Mari, however, painted a different picture of him.

When Mari and her friend Numie were little girls, Numie's mother, a widow with two children and a frail health, had found employment with the Earl when no-one else had wanted her. The young earl had treated her well, paid her extra to send her girls to school.

Until two years ago, at the birthday party of the Earl's nephew, when Numie's mother had suddenly collapsed. The Earl had taken her to the academy, paid a lot of money for the best doctors to treat her, but in the end, there wasn't much anyone could do.

The small family had thought they were ruined. Numie had yet had to finish her apprenticeship, her little sister Nami not yet old enough to work. Again it was the Earl who had saved them: he had offered Numie a position as his maid. Her wages included not only fair compensation for her work, but also the payment for both, her mother's medication and her little sister's tuition fee.

Jin slowly slurped another glass of water, speechless. If any of this was true, the Earl wasn't just a far better man than he was generally perceived as, he was almost too good to be true. There had to be a fly in the ointment.

"What about that gardener? Numie's fiancé? Any problems with the Earl?" Jin asked abruptly. Niall shot him a scowl at the almost desperate undertone in his voice. Luckily Mari didn't seem to have noticed. She took her time considering Jin's question, then shook her head.

"No, not Genta. He knows the Earl since he was a little boy. His father was already their gardener when the old earl and lady were still alive. He told me once, that they were all like family there."

"Really?" Jin grumbled. Gods, he couldn't stand the man. Oh, until a mere few minutes ago he had always thought of him as a cruel bastard, the worst kind of aristocrat: elitist, arrogant, entitled. Now he sounded like some blasted saint. And to top it all off, Yūzuki no Suzu was the man's favourite Furyusha. *The* Yūzuki no Suzu, who – as Jin had only just found out – was his Kari. Oh how he'd love to punch the Earl's aloof handsome face.

A hard pinch in his thigh almost made him yelp. Niall was glaring at him. Mari looked confused, but continued her tale.

Numie and Genta had met at the Earl's and fallen in love almost at once. One and a half years later, Genta had proposed, with the blessings of his father, Numie's mother – and the Earl's. Which was the very reason why Mari doubted her friends had run away. And in all fairness, she had a point. Nothing suggested the two young lovers had had any reason to run. On the contrary. But that made the Earl's apparent disinterest in the disappearance of two of his people all the more suspicious.

"This doesn't make any sense at all," Jin exclaimed, exasperated.

"I know, which is exactly why I want to find Numie. And Genta. It's not right. But everyone pretends like nothing out of the ordinary happened, like them disappearing was an every day occurrence."

"Hold on, what do you mean, 'everyone'? What about Genta's and Numie's families?"

"They... um..." Mari's gaze dropped to her lap where she had begun twisting her skirts anxiously. "They, too. They don't want me to make a fuss – as they call it," Mari pouted.

Jin turned to Niall, raised an eyebrow questioningly. His friend nodded. It seemed she, too, had the feeling they had stumbled upon something rather strange. What exactly it was, Jin couldn't say. There was a glint in Niall's mossy green eyes, the glint of a hunter having caught scent of its prey. She got like that sometimes when she found something that intrigued her.

"Mari, could you give us the address of Numie's family?" Niall asked. "Perhaps it's best if we spoke to them."

"Oh." For a moment Mari seemed utterly taken aback by the request. "W-well, I guess. But perhaps it would be better if

I accompanied you there. I don't want them to get scared by strangers suddenly showing up and asking about Numie."

"Fair enough. Could we go right now?"

Half an hour later they were standing in front of a tiny house which couldn't have been more of a contrast to Mari's if it tried. It was more of a glorified garden shed than a house, situated right smack on the border between Mari's neat neighbourhood and one of the oldest and poorest part of the town – Eigetsu. From here on it would only get worse, the houses more and more dilapidated, the people sadder and more desperate. Until even the houses, once grand and majestic, stood empty, abandoned, decrepit. Jin knew this desolate place, had breathed its hopelessness, drank its resignation, absorbed its forlornness. It was a place of broken dreams, of failed existence. And it was the place that had nearly cost Jin his life. He shuddered at the memory of it and was grateful they didn't have to go deeper inside.

They had to wait for an answer to their knocking on the crooked door of the tiny house for so long, Jin didn't think anyone was at home at all. Until the door creaked open a tiny sliver through which they could make out a dark brown eye, rimmed in black shadows, in a ghostly pale face.

"Who is it?" a harsh croaky voice asked anxiously.

"Auntie, it's me, Mari."

"Oh, Mari. Numie isn't home right now."

"I know. Can we talk? Please."

"Um... I'm not feeling well today," she croaked hastily, already withdrawing into the shadows of her house. "Come another day." The door began to close, but Niall was quicker. She grabbed the edge of the door and yanked.

"Ma'am, I am a doctor, I'm here to help," Niall declared in her bossiest voice. It was the voice she used with her most obstinate patients, and even they knew better than to argue with her then. The frail, painfully thin, tiny woman, staring with big round eyes at them, shocked and trembling like a leaf in the wind, however, did not.

"I... I don't need your help. I have all the help I need. I have my medication, and--" Niall stepped over the threshold and kept going, forcing the woman to back into her house. "Oi, I didn't allow you to enter my home. Go away!"

"We are only here to help."

"I don't need your help."

"Auntie, please," Mari pleaded, closing the door after her. The inside of the house was dim, almost dark. Mari stepped up to her best friend's mother and gently took her hands in hers. "Please, auntie, we're only worried about Numie. *I* am worried about Numie. These people, they want to help, I promise, just..."

Seeing how much her daughter's disappearance affected her friend, Numie's mother at last relented. Her shoulders sagged, she heaved a sigh. "You don't have to worry, lass. She's fine. Genta, too."

"How can you be so sure?" Jin asked.

"Because the Earl told me so. He... he sent her and Genta to his estate in Tsukikage for a while, that's all."

"And you believe him?"

"Of course I believe him," she snapped and Jin was taken aback by her vehemence. A moment later, though, she deflated. "The Earl knows what he's doing. When he says it's going to be all right then it will be all right. Mari, you just have to wait, Numie will soon be back, you'll see. All right?"

"All right," Mari agreed in a small voice.

Neither Jin nor Niall had the heart to keep pestering the woman. She was like a baby bird: tiny and oh so very fragile. So instead Niall insisted on examining her and make sure she took her medication correctly. Jin and Mari went to wait outside.

They had only just closed the door, when Jin noticed a small figure peeking around the corner of the house, beckoning them. "That's Nami," Mari whispered and went to the girl. Jin followed.

Nami, although looking a lot healthier, was her mother's daughter. The same brown eyes and dark hair. But her face still retained a bit of the roundness of a baby's, her cheeks were rosy. She looked from Mari to Jin, frowning, before she seemed to come to a decision and waved Jin closer. He squatted down so they were eye to eye, and Nami said very quietly, "She was acting strange before she left. My sister."

"Strange? Strange how?"

"Fidgety. I asked her, and she... hmm... I'm not supposed to tell anyone, not even mama, but now she is gone and everyone is being weird and I don't know if she ever comes back."

Jin's felt a rush of excitement and dread. Had Numie stumbled upon the Earl's dark secret and been afraid he'd find out. If so, was the Earl trying to cover up his crime by reassuring and caring for the girl's family, or had she and her fiancé fled and he was trying to track them down? Jin swallowed hard. "So... what was it she didn't want you to tell anyone?" Nami cast Mari a quick apologetic glance before she leaned towards Jin and whispered into his ear.

They delivered Mari at her home with assurances that she didn't have to worry about her friend and promises to tell her should they find out Numie's whereabouts. Jin waited until they were far from Mari's house before he told Niall about his little encounter with Numie's little sister, Nami.

"As it turns out, despite her mother's insistence that the Earl can be trusted, the man seems to be directly or at least indirectly responsible for Numie and Genta's disappearance. In the days before she vanished, Numie was apparently very worried about some 'shady and scary men' who had come calling on the Earl on numerous occasions lately."

Niall's eyes widened slightly and she slowly nodded her head. "I see. I wonder with what kind of people the Earl has been doing business with lately… and about the nature of that business."

Jin grinned. They might have actually stumbled over something exciting after all. And if he could knock the man from his pedestal, even better. He wisely didn't tell Niall so, however. She would only chide him for harbouring unjustified animosities towards a man he didn't even know – and of course she'd be right to scold him, but he couldn't help it. Not since he had found out that the Earl was paying his Kari for sex, demanding who knew what-- No, no, no. Jin shook his head furiously. He didn't even want to think about it.

Niall gave him a sidelong glance. No doubt she knew exactly what was on his mind – parts of it, at least. But she didn't comment. Instead, Niall linked her arm with his and grinned broadly.

"All right, enough work for today, we'll think about it again tomorrow. Tonight, we party!"

Chapter 7

"I feel I'm keeping you from work – again," Suzu remarked, strolling down the street with Ryū and Rani.

"Please," Ryū waved a hand dismissively. "You know that I don't have to serve customers anymore. Unless Mother needs my help with something, I am free to do whatever I want."

"So you say. But you are Mother's heir, shouldn't you be... I don't know... learning the business from her?"

"I do. And she told me to accompany you. So there. Why are you complaining?"

"I'm not complaining," Suzu laughed and hooked his arm around his friend's.

The sun had already ceded the sky to a glorious full moon, bathing the town in silver light. It was a perfect night for the Moon Fair, Getsuro's monthly night market along the banks of the River Opal. Between stalls, selling everything from fresh fruit to the finest of jewellery, soap and perfumes, musicians and artists showed off their skills. The food stalls were swarmed by customers, who came to the fair as much to spend money as they came to meet friends and have a good time. Which was why, when Mother had sent them off with a smile, wishing them a lovely evening, she had also given them a long list of items to procure: necessities and various things the Singing Dragon's inhabitants wanted.

"Actually," Ryū drawled, grinning lewdly at Suzu, "I'm surprised you're able to walk at all. You – ouch!" Ryū laughed, skipping out of Suzu's reach before Suzu had a chance to punch him again. He ruefully rubbed his shoulder. "I mean... come on, you two were at it all afternoon... Wait, wait, wait. Don't hit me!" he cried, fleeing Suzu's fists. It was his misfortune, however, that Suzu had always been the faster runner. He jumped onto his friend's back and held on tight. Ryū swatted a hand at Suzu's arms, locked around his neck. "I give up, I give up!" he gasped, out of breath, partially from running and partially from laughing.

Suzu let go of Ryū, but not before he delivered another punch to the other boy's arm. By now Rani had caught up to them. He was panting, his face, even the tips of his ears, flushed a furious red. Suzu threw an arm around the younger boy's shoulders.

"Damn it, Ryū, watch what you're saying in front of our little brother," he said in mock sincerity.

Ryū just waved his hand dismissively. "Oh, he's heard worse – just this afternoon, for example." Suzu aimed a kick at Ryū's shin, but this time Ryū was quicker.

"We were at the far end of the house, so unless you were standing right outside in the hallway the whole time, pervert..."

"What?" Ryū exclaimed with fake indignation. "We had to move everyone else to the front and make sure no-one ventured down that hall, for all the racket you were making. All that moaning and screaming –" Suzu pounced on him again. Amidst reboant laughter they even dragged little Rani into their horsing around, until they were all three of them dishevelled and out of breath.

"Jerk," Suzu said fondly as they straightened their clothes and rebound their hair. He couldn't help the big stupid grin on his face. He loved times like these the most: no fancy clothing, no pretence... no masks. His hair bound back with a leather ribbon, wearing a simple black yukata, and two of his most favourite people by his side. As long as he had them, he needed nothing else. Nothing was stronger or worth more than the bond they had: they were best friends, they were a family. Ephemeral love might sparkle and shine like precious jewels, burn like a sun, but the sturdy roots of this purest of affections would stand the test of time, even if their paths should diverge.

He felt Ryū watching him, and when he met his friend's gaze, a warmth spread through Suzu, as soothing as the first warm rays of sunshine after the winter cold, for the depth of love he beheld in those amber eyes. Ryū – his best friend, his brother, his mentor. They enjoyed each other's company in many ways, yet it was the bond between them, this invisible connection they had felt from the moment they had met, which Suzu cherished the most.

"Suzu?" Rani asked quietly.

"Hm?"

"Do you love the Earl?"

"What?" Suzu turned to the boy, surprised and slightly shocked.

"Do you love him?" Rani asked again, staring up at Suzu with big round eyes full of curiosity and apprehension. Suzu could also feel Ryū's eyes bore into him.

"That's... that's complicated," he replied uncomfortably.

"Why? It's not supposed to be complicated, is it?"

"That... I... Let's not talk about that now, all right?"

He had hoped he could just snuff that particular conversation before it really started, and normally Rani was quick to humour him, but it seemed Rani was plagued by a specific worry, for he reached for Suzu's hand, grasped it tightly, and without looking at Suzu murmured, "I think the Earl is scary."

Suzu was so taken aback he couldn't help but laugh. "Oh Rani, he's not scary at all."

"He is. He wants to take you away from us."

Suzu sighed. He took Rani's chin and gently forced the boy to look at him. Unshed tears glistened in the dark pools of Rani's eyes. Suzu smiled. "no-one can take me away from you, promise. Not even the Earl."

"So... so you won't go living with him then?"

"No, I won't. So don't worry, all right?" Relieve washed over the boy's small face. Rani nodded and smiled broadly. Ryū hadn't said a word, and Suzu knew he wouldn't. Not here, not in front of Rani, not unless Suzu wanted to talk about it. Again Suzu was profoundly grateful for his friend's understanding. It was more than he deserved.

The closer they got to the riverbank the more crowded the streets became. Already they could hear music, laughter, and vendors hawking their goods. All around them people were cheerful, excited. The atmosphere was infectious and the three of them found themselves hurrying along, eager to reach the market.

The riverbank was lined with stalls. A myriad of lights illuminated the scene, even the multitude of bridges was brightly lit. In contrast, Mangetsu, on the opposite side of the river, was shrouded in velvety darkness. High above, the moon, big and round, a warm orange blush on her silver face, laughed down on them, glittering on the night black waters of the River Opal.

Suzu's face lit with delight. It had been too long since he had last visited Getsuro's famous night market. He still remembered the first time he had come to the fair, clutching Ryū's arm like a little child; the crowd had scared him. He had never seen so many people in one place. And the sight of it, the lights, the noises, the smell. It had been terrifying and exhilarating at the same time, overwhelming to the senses. Now, Suzu took a deep breath. He still felt overwhelmed by the crush of people, the sights, the cacophony of music and voices. Navigating crowds with his limited field of vision was always a challenge, one that had taken him a lot of time and courage to face, but he'd be damned if he'd let that hinder him. Bracing himself, Suzu turned to his companions to signal he was ready to go, only to find them with their heads together, conspiring in hushed voices. Suzu frowned, put his hands on his hips, and cleared his throat loudly.

"Excuse me, young men, but what is it that you are plotting, may I ask?" It was almost comical, the way they sprang guiltily apart. Despite the wan light he could see Rani blushing furiously. Unlike Ryū, who looked as innocent as a baby bird. Well, no surprise, the man had no shame.

"Plotting? What a nasty word, we don't plot," Ryū claimed rather unconvincingly. "But glad that you ask. Seeing that we have quite the list to work through, I suggest we split up. It's a good thing they all have pretty much fixed spots. Each of us takes one part of the market. All right?"

Suzu nodded, took out the list and held it up so the moonlight allowed them to read it. It seemed Mother had had the same thought for she had neatly grouped the items according to where they usually could be found. Carefully Suzu tore the list in three pieces and handed Rani and Ryū each one piece.

"Good. We'll meet on Twilight Bridge in... let's see... two hours? Two and a half?" Ryū said.

Suzu stared at his piece of the list and mentally traced the route he had to take from stall to stall and finally to Twilight Bridge, the biggest and most central of the bridges across the Opal. "We'd better hurry then," he remarked.

And so, each with their own errands to run, the three split up and threw themselves into the hustle and bustle of the Moon Fair.

His first stop took Suzu to Mistress Ayame's stall. It wasn't hard to find. Not only did she prefer a spot close to Yūgao, Ayame's many scented oils, soaps, and candles lent a herbal, flowery aroma to the night air. As always Suzu marvelled at the old woman's ingenuity at blending different scents into one harmonious, well-balanced fragrance. Some of which brought to mind a cosy winter night in front of a gently crackling fire. Others filled the air with petrichor – warm, gentle, rain-kissed earth. There were candles that soothed strained nerves, ointments that refreshed tired limbs, incense that helped clear the mind. Suzu would have had a hard time picking a favourite one. Luckily, the Singing Dragon needed a lot of soap, incense, and scented oils in a variety of fragrances, depending on the occasion and the customer's preference.

Mistress Ayame pulled a crate out from behind the back curtain of her stall. Big bold letters on the sides of it read "The Singing Dragon". It was the custom to deliver purchases made at the Moon Fair, even smaller amounts, for few people bought so little they didn't mind carrying it around for half the night.

Suzu stooped to give the old woman a peck on the cheek before happily sorting through the soaps and oils, packing the crate to the brim. A flagon of perfumed oil caught his eyes. He carefully pulled the stopper out and sniffed at it. A heady scent of roses filled his nose. It was chased by a smoky undertone, a herbal freshness.

"Ah, I see you still have a knack for finding my hidden treasures," Ayame chuckled, coming up beside him.

"What is it?"

"It's a little composition I dreamt up a long time ago. Haven't made it in ages, though. A rose overtone, blended with passion flower and guaiacum wood. Nice, eh?"

"Very." Suzu took another sniff of the flagon's contents and closed his eyes. It made him think of Toshi. He had promised to spend a day and a night at the Earl's the coming week. Suzu held the flagon out to Ayame. "I'd like to purchase this – for me, personally."

Ayame smiled. "With pleasure. It suits you, you know." She put the flagon in a small padded box and handed it to Suzu in exchange for his money. "Always a pleasure doing business with you. You should come by more often, Suzu, I've missed you."

"I've missed you, too, you old scoundrel." Suzu smiled and winked, making the old woman giggle.

It took Suzu the better part of two hours to make his way through the market, hunting for teas, cups, *tabi* socks, and hair ornaments. Yet when he finally reached the Twilight Bridge, a cup of cider in one hand, a skewer of dango in the other, he was still the first to arrive. He leaned against the railing, pulled one of the sticky little dumplings from the wooden skewer with his teeth, and looked out over the market bustle, the myriad of twinkling lights – an imperfect imitation of the starry path across the glittering velvet ocean of the night sky. Laughter drew his attention to a group of people sitting around a huge table on the grassy riverbank. Suzu had never seen tables set anywhere during a market night. Usually people just sat on the grass or brought blankets, in winter they stood around warming fire baskets. He watched the group a while and realised that they seemed to be celebrating. A cheer went up from the group when a tall man stood up and lifted his glass. Although Suzu couldn't see him clearly, he thought the man looked familiar, but he couldn't place him.

Suzu was still wondering about where he had seen the man, pensively munching on his last dango, when another figure caught his eyes. His hand clenched around the wooden skewer, breaking it in two. That one he would recognise anywhere. No need to stand right in front of him, to see him clearly by the light, he knew him – by instinct, his entire body, every part of him knew him. The cracks in his heart, the anger in his soul. Jin – the name a steel barb in his heart. He had tried to tear it out, forget all about it, yet its claws dug deep.

The rage simmering deep inside him sprang to life. After all these years, when at last the hurt, the memories had begun to fade and blur, Jin just had to appear in front of him. Why? Why couldn't he simply forget the past?

Suzu couldn't tear his eyes away from the scene. The familiarity with which the group treated each other, long-time friends, perhaps more than that. It sparked a sudden realisation in Suzu and he wondered why he had never thought of it before. Of course, Jin, too, was living in this town. It had always been Jin's plan to come here, he had constantly spoken about the life they would have here – together. Suzu clenched his teeth. They both had a new life here now, but not together. Nothing had been as Jin had promised. Only lies and betrayal. But how come Suzu had never seen Jin in Yūgao? He recognised some of the people Jin was celebrating with, but he had never seen him with them. What were they celebrating? A memory, unbidden, but clear. Jin's birthday. They were celebrating Jin's birthday. Years ago it had always only been the two of them celebrating their birthdays. The last time –

A sudden rush of hate and anger left Suzu dizzy. He gripped the railing, gasping for breath. As if he could feel the intensity of Suzu's emotions directed at him, Jin suddenly turned towards the bridge and looked up. Suzu froze. Could Jin see him?

Suzu whirled around, shaking his head at himself. So what? Who cared if Jin knew he was here, that he knew now they were living in the same town. It didn't matter. This town was big enough, they each had their own life. Suzu took a deep steadying breath. He was not the boy he had once been, Jin had nothing to do with him. The young man was nothing but a remnant of another life, a bad memory.

"Suzu!" He looked up and saw Rani running towards him, Ryū following closely behind. Relief and the affection he felt for his adopted brothers chased the anger and hurt away, like sunshine burning away the mist. "Sorry, did you have to wait long?" Rani panted.

"No. So," Suzu turned to Ryū, "what have you been up to? And don't pretend you don't know what I'm talking about. I know you two have been up to something."

"Yeah, well, all right, you caught us," Ryū said, grinning broadly. "Go ahead," he told Rani.

Rani, shy as always, shuffled his feet, not meeting Suzu's eyes. "We... we got you something."

"Got me... it's not my birthday."

"Doesn't have to be your birthday for us to give you a present, now, does it?" Ryū remarked and gave Rani a little push. The small boy held his hand out to Suzu, slowly opening his clenched fist. On his palm, glittering in the moonlight, lay a delicate silver necklace. Tiny flecks of moonstone were set in intervals between the links of the chain. A pendant hung from it, an oval disc of black onyx with a stylised dragon of jade on its smooth surface.

"It's... it's beautiful," Suzu stammered.

"And look, we had it engraved." Rani turned the pendant over and angled it towards the light so Suzu could see the fine inscription. "Ah, it's difficult to read in this light, it says... it... it..."

Ryū took the necklace from the flustered boy, took a step towards Suzu, and fastened it around Suzu's neck. "It says," Ryū said quietly, fumbling with the catch of the delicate necklace. "'Wherever, whenever, for ever.' It's from all of us, Mother, Akito, Haldor, us, the boys – in short, the Singing Dragon. It's to remind you that no matter where you are, or how long we may be apart, we are your family and we love you. A lot, actually."

An emotion Suzu had no name for, fiercer, more intense than anything he had ever known, stole his breath away. He swallowed the tightness in his throat, grabbed his friends, and pulled both into a hug.

"You are such... whatever." His voice was huskier than usual. "Thank you," he whispered. "Thank you for loving me."

His friends – brothers – didn't reply. Instead they hugged him back as tightly as they could. It said more than a thousand words. It spoke of their love, their understanding, of how they accepted him without pretence, without any mask.

Down below, on the grassy riverbank, Jin stood staring at an empty spot on the bridge. Like a moth enthralled by the moon he had felt compelled to look up at it. And there he had been: Kari. Jin hadn't exaggerated when he had told Niall he'd always recognise Kari. Even embraced by shadows Jin knew him. And for a moment time had stood still. Jin hadn't been able to make out the boy's expression, to know if he was even looking at Jin, if there was that depthless searing rage in his eyes Jin had caught a glimpse of the night before. The urge to call out to the boy, to run to him, had rushed through Jin, so sudden and strong it nearly swept him away like a spring tide.

But then Kari had abruptly turned and was gone, leaving Jin with a nearly unbearable longing.

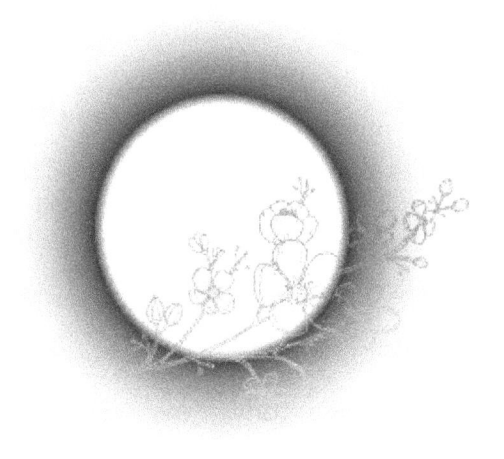

Chapter 8

The following days Suzu felt as if he was sleepwalking. He grew more and more irate. Sleep kept eluding him, and when he did sleep, he dreamt of a past he had thought forgotten. But ever since he had run into Jin, the young man stole unbidden into his thoughts. Distractingly. Irritatingly. And so Suzu spent every free minute in the dojo, better to be physically exhausted than having too much time to think.

Except for Ryū, Mother, and Haldor, the rest of the Singing Dragon family took pains not to bother him, avoiding him altogether if possible. Rani, on the other hand, followed him around, silent as a ghost, loyal as a puppy, yet always keeping his distance.

Knowing they did all this not out of fear of his temper but out of consideration, just irritated Suzu further. To a point where it became difficult for him to entertain customers.

"Perhaps you ought to take a break," Kazue said; it wasn't a suggestion. She had found Suzu, lying stretched out on the verandah outside his room, in a drunken stupor after playing a drinking game with the General and one of his friends. It had been a lot of fun actually.

"Going on holiday anyway," Suzu pointed out, hiccupping. "Next next day."

"It's called the day after tomorrow. And you're not going on a holiday, you are going to the Earl's," she corrected, then sat down at the edge of the verandah. The garden was dark, the lamps had already burnt out and fireflies were now the only light, painting strange ephemeral patterns in the air. "Is that why you are acting like this? Are you nervous?"

"No." Suzu rolled over onto his side, resting his head on his arm. "He just won't leave me alone."

"Who? The Earl?"

"No! *He!*" Suzu put what he considered a very meaningful emphasis on the word 'he', but it seemed lost on Kazue. He glared at her until he finally saw comprehension dawning on her face.

"Oh. He." Kazue sighed. "But Suzu, how is he not leaving you alone? Has he come here? Sent you letters? Is there anything I should know?"

"Yes, he shows up, unbidden. Here." Suzu tapped his temple. "I can't get rid of him."

"Suzu, have you ever considered that perhaps you have been dealing with this the wrong way. Trying to ignore the past, shove it aside, and pretend it never happened – it doesn't work that way. You are not over what happened, and you are not over that boy."

Suzu sat up abruptly, swaying. He pointed an accusing finger at Kazue. "Not true!" he cried. "I'm so over him." He gestured wildly in an attempt to clarify just how much he was over Jin. Kazue seemed unimpressed. "Honestly. But he... he just h-had to show up and ruin it all! I just have to forget it all again, that's all... that's all I need. That's--"

"That's not how it works." Kazue reached out and framed Suzu's face between her hands, forcing him to look at her. "Look at you. Darling, this mess is driving you nuts. Some of the boys are even scared of you, all of them are worried sick. And what about the Earl, hm?"

"What about him?"

"Don't think I'm blind or stupid. I have been playing this game far longer than you. I can see it clear as morning: you are in love with the man. Don't!" she snapped, forestalling Suzu's protest. "I know, you'd rather continue to deny it, to lie to yourself. But have you ever wondered why? Why it is you are fighting so hard against the possibility of being in love with someone?"

"I love a lot of people," Suzu grumbled.

"You know we are talking about different kinds of love here, don't play stupid."

Suzu pushed her hands away and struggled to his feet. He couldn't deal with this now. He had been in such a good mood after playing with the General, it was ruined now. This was all Jin's fault. If only he had never shown up again. If only Suzu had never met him in the first place. If those final months at the temple had never happened, how would his life be now? Could he allow himself to embrace Toshi's love, allow himself to love Toshi the way the man deserved? Gods be damned, but he had to hit something. Hard. He was too drunk to hit anything, though. Damnation, but Mother was right, this was driving him mad. His rage was slowly becoming an untameable wild beast, utterly out of control. How long until he ended up hurting someone he loved?

He flinched violently when Kazue suddenly put a hand on his shoulder. The sudden movement almost made him lose his balance.

"Suzu," Mother began, but Suzu's vehement, snarled "No!" cut her off. She took a deep breath. "All right. Come on, you are drunk and tired. Let's get you to bed." Suzu nodded and let her steer him inside.

Once again Jin found himself in Naloc's sitting room, listening to the reports of the others, with Niall providing their own findings. To Jin's surprise, it seemed they had been the most successful ones so far. Even Durin grudgingly admitted that he had been unable to break through the wall of unshakable loyalty of the Earl's servants. Not a single one had had one bad word to say about the man, not a single complaint about their working conditions.

"His neighbours, though," Durin proclaimed with a hint of desperate triumph. "They may not have a lot to say about the man himself. But they have noticed some rather suspicious folk hanging around the place lately."

Naloc perked up. "Suspicious how?"

"Well... to be frank, the descriptions leave much to be desired. What it comes down to is that apart from his family and the General the Earl has no regular visitors. Especially not ones who only visit after dark. Until now."

"Hmm, that's not much to go with." Naloc tugged at his goatee, humming, pondering. "Though sudden changes in behaviour and missing servants – sounds to me like those two lovebirds might have witnessed something they shouldn't have."

"Really? That's the conclusion you make?" Niall snorted. "Don't you think you might be making a roaring fire out of a candle?"

Jin gaped at Niall. Everyone knew Niall was like a daughter to Naloc, and as such she was always more outspoken towards him than the rest of them. But talking like this to Naloc in front of his people...

Naloc, however, still tugging on his goatee, merely furrowed his brows, and grunted in acknowledgement. "There's only one way to find out: we need to get some inside information."

"Inside information? None of his servants – excuse me, employees – their words not mine – are talking. They are too loyal to him," Durin pointed out again.

Jin clicked his tongue in irritation. He didn't get it. What about the Earl inspired such loyalty in these people? Granted, he had only seen the man once – well, twice now – and only in passing. But that aloofness, that coldness had sent a shiver through him. This was a man who, Jin was certain, would tear apart his enemies, who would damn the consequences to get what he wanted, and who would go through everyone who stood in his way.

He had voiced his opinion earlier – and got scolded by Niall. She had accused him of feeling antagonistic towards the Earl because the man was close to Kari. Another thing Jin couldn't wrap his head around. Unless, of course, Kari was forced to keep the Earl company, to entertain him, be friendly with him... sleep with him. In all honesty, Jin would enjoy punching the Earl's handsome face, break his perfect nose. Anything. Just the thought of the man putting his hands on...

"You do know that no-one, not even the Earl of bloody Tsukikage can force a Furyusha to do anything they don't want to do." Niall rolled her eyes at him, easily reading his thoughts. By now she had probably explained a thousand times to him how Yūgao worked. How the laws of Yūgao protected its people. "If your boy – assuming he is your Kari – didn't want to serve the Earl, he could just reject him and the Earl would have to accept it."

"Yeah yeah," Jin grumbled. When it came to Yūgao Jin had a hard time believing anything he was being told. "And what do you mean 'assuming he is your Kari'? I told you I know it's him."

Niall just sighed and shrugged and shook her head at him, but decided to drop that particular line of conversation.

"We might still have another option," Naloc said slowly, his storm-grey eyes focusing on Jin, who frowned in confusion. "We might even kill two birds with one stone."

Jin was still wondering what could have possibly gone wrong. He had had a plan, he had had assurances that Kari would be safe. And that they would explain Jin's decision to the boy. It wasn't that Jin didn't think Kari would be angry, but he was smart, he'd understand. Right? So why, when Durin went to the temple for Jin to fetch the boy, was he gone? There could be only one reason the temple had denied any knowledge of a boy called Kari, and that was that Kari had run away.

For long months afterwards Jin had hoped Kari would eventually show up in town. Even Naloc's merchant colleagues had been on the look-out for him on the roads leading to Getsuro. Nothing. Had Kari really been here almost exactly as long as Jin – how was that even possible? What was he doing in Yūgao of all places? Why had he never come looking for Jin? Were the others right and this young man wasn't Kari?

The questions had been crowding Jin's mind since the General's birthday party. They were sure to drive him mad eventually, he needed answers. Yet when Naloc ushered him into his small carriage and drove the two of them and Niall to Yūgao, Jin felt panic rising in his chest. He wasn't ready for this. He couldn't face whatever revelations there might be. Neither Naloc nor Niall relented to his pleas to let him go home.

And so they passed through the massive ornate gates that separated Yūgao from the rest of Getsuro, through quiet streets that were almost deserted this time of the day, past beautiful tea houses, gambling dens, ateliers, and pleasure houses. Everything was clean and well-kept, aesthetically pleasing.

Eventually they left the broad main road. Large estates lay hidden behind high walls, sprawling mansions nestled within beautifully tended grounds. Scattered in between were expensive restaurants and even more expensive tea houses.

"This particularly nice little corner of Yūgao houses the most exclusive and oldest of the pleasure houses," Niall explained. "See? They have no signs proclaiming the name of the house, you need to know how to read the carvings on the gates." A moment later they drew up beside a heavy wooden gate at the end of a cul-de-sac. There was a magnificent dragon carved into its polished surface, head thrown back, maw gaping wide open.

The mixture of excitement and sheer panic made Jin light-headed. He stumbled out of the carriage, wiping his sweaty hands on his trousers. "Why exactly are we here?" he asked. Jin winced at the whine in his voice.

"I told you, we're going to kill two birds with one stone. We need information that we probably can only get here. And at the same time we can confirm whether you've really found your Kari or not." Naloc banged his fist against the heavy gate. Nothing happened. Jin prayed to any god who might listen that no-one would answer and they had to return home. Frowning, Naloc knocked again, more persistently. And Jin's hope dissipated when the gate creaked open a sliver and a boy of perhaps twelve years of age peered out. He had huge chocolate brown eyes, almost too large for his small face. He appeared intimidated, almost frightened, until he snapped, "We're not open yet."

"Hey there, Rani," Naloc chuckled, taking a step to the side, into the boy's line of sight. Rani jumped and stood straighter at once.

"Oh, it's you... sir." Rani struggled to pull the gate wider, then stood back and bowed deep. "Good day, Murasaki-tan. I... um..." he faltered.

"It's all right," Naloc appeased. "I know you are not open to customers yet. But we are not here as customers. I need an urgent word with Kazue. Mind if we come in?"

The boy obviously did mind. He shifted from one foot to the other, looking between the three of them uncertainly, his fingers worrying the hem of his shirt. "Um... I don't know... it's--"

"Rani!" came a call from behind the boy. Relief washed over the boy's face. He looked over his shoulder at a young man coming their way. "What's going on?"

"Ryū, they want to talk to Mother."

The gate fully opened, revealing an extraordinarily handsome young man. He was tall and well-built. His raven black hair was pulled back from his elegant face in a messy knot at the back of his head. He wore a midnight blue yukata, which was hanging too wide open, revealing too much of his smooth skin, his muscled chest. Most striking, however, were the young man's eyes: a brown so light they seemed golden, with specks of green like agate. Jin wondered if he was part Ethereal. The man radiated charm. For a moment Jin had the unreasonable urge to start a fight with him.

"Murasaki-tan," Ryū said respectfully enough, yet his bow was a mere nod of his head. "What can we do for you and your... associates?"

"Hello, Ryū. We'd like a word with Kazue – if she's available."

"Of course. Rani," Ryū turned to the younger boy, "please go and inform Mother that she has visitors. And then go and fetch tea." Rani gave a curt nod of acknowledgement and hurried away. "If you'd follow me, please."

They stepped from the dusty road into lush greenness, following a gravel path winding its way from the ornate gate to the main house, lined by stone lanterns. A magnificent cherry tree dominated the centre of the green, to the left of the path ran an artificial brook, the rhythmic clacking sound of a bamboo fountain harmonised with the singing of the birds. A place of tranquillity and beauty. A group of adolescent boys, tending to the flowers, cast curious glances at them, but didn't stop in their work.

The doors of the main house stood wide open, revealing an empty entrance hall. But instead of entering it, Ryū veered sharply right and led them around the corner of the house. Behind the main building, arranged in a square around a bigger and even more beautiful garden, were three smaller buildings. Jin couldn't help the impressed gasp that escaped him. He had not expected this. The entire estate of the Singing Dragon was almost as tall and sprawling as that of the temple he had grown up in. A brilliant red bridge spanned a koi pond, stone lanterns and bird baths were scattered all over, enormous old hydrangea bushes burst with colour, from a soft pink to dark red, deep purple to a bright sky blue and clouds of white. The air was sweet with the scent of flowers, the heady aroma of herbs.

"This is your first time here, isn't it?" Jin turned to Ryū, who smiled knowingly. "This," Ryū pointed at the tallest building, "is the main house – as you've probably already guessed. It's where we entertain our customers. That one," he indicated the small building on the opposite side of the garden, "is the bathhouse. The one at the back end of the estate is the dojo, and this is our real home," he said with warm affection and pride, leading them to the building on to their left, which was only slightly smaller than the main house. They walked down the verandah until they came to a set of sliding doors standing wide open. A woman sat within, awaiting them. When she saw them coming, she got gracefully to her feet and held her hands out towards Naloc. He went to her, took her hands, and gently placed a kiss upon her brow. Neither of them spoke a single word. For a long breathless moment they stood like this, close, yet so far apart. Jin felt an uncomfortable twinge in his chest, a sudden, short bout of vertigo. There was so much in what they didn't say, so much Jin couldn't even guess at, a story no-one had ever told him, another of the many things he didn't know. He felt left out, but he also knew that what his mentor and this beautiful, graceful woman shared, was not for anyone else to intrude.

At last she stepped away from Naloc and looked at the rest of them. "Niall, my dear, it's been too long," she said in a voice as warm and smooth as honey.

Niall bowed to her. "That's true, although I am, of course, glad that my services were not needed in quite a while. May I introduce," Niall grabbed Jin's arm and pulled him forward. "This is Jin." Jin bowed hastily. When he looked up again he found Kazue studying him. Jin had heard of Gekka no Kazue. How could he not, not only did she lead one of the most exclusive pleasure house in all of Yūgao, she, herself, had once been a very successful Furyusha and people still talked about her. But more importantly, for a while she hadn't been Gekka no Kazue, but Murasaki no Kazue. Jin didn't know what had happened, why their marriage had fallen apart, but he knew that Naloc still loved her. This stern, formidable woman. She must have been breathtaking in her youth, but the gravitas, the confidence, grace and wisdom that age had given her were staggering, overwhelming.

"Are you new to Naloc's little gang?" she asked.

Fumbling for words, Jin shook his head, while Niall chuckled. "Oh no, he's been with us for years. But can you believe it, he has never set a foot inside Yūgao until today." Kazue raised one perfect eyebrow. "Grew up in a Hôjô temple. It shows."

Jin noticed both Kazue and Ryū react to the mention of the temple, but neither said a word. They exchanged an unreadable look, then Kazue bid them all to take a seat. Jin had the sense that Ryū's attitude towards them had suddenly grown cold.

As if he had just waited behind the door for the moment they all were seated, the boy Rani appeared with the tea. Tense silence filled the room while he poured the cups. Only after he had made a hasty retreat, did Kazue break the silence.

"So." Her dark brown eyes fixed on Naloc, calculating, intense. "As much as I enjoy your company, I doubt you've come for the tea."

"Darling, that hurts. You know I love--"

"Enough with this nonsense." Kazue cut him off with a harsh gesture. "Don't insult me. What is it you want? Out with it."

Naloc rubbed his chin sheepishly. "Fine. You know me too well. But it's less what I want and rather what my young friend here wants." He indicated Jin with a jerk of his head. When all eyes suddenly turned his way, Jin blushed and stared hard into his tea cup.

"Then you should have come during business hours," Kazue snapped.

"No, no, that's not what were are here for. Look, Kazue, Jin has been searching for his friend he grew up with, a boy he dearly loves, for years now. And it seems – or so he believes – that he has finally found him."

Kazue turned her piercing stare on Jin. There was suspicion in her dark eyes. Next to her, Jin noticed, Ryū clenched his hands into fists, his golden eyes cold and hard. And yet, their expressions betrayed nothing, perfect neutral masks, stoic, void of any emotions. It caused a prickling sensation down Jin's spine.

"One of your boys," Naloc added slowly, not ignorant to the reaction his words had drawn from Kazue and her heir, miniscule as it may have been.

"Is that so? And who, if I might ask?" Kazue inquired haughtily. But Jin didn't miss the way she seemed to brace herself, or Ryū's intake of breath.

"Yūzuki no Suzu."

The name fell between them like a declaration of war. After a breathless, motionless, silent moment Ryū sprang to his feet, eyes blazing, nostrils flaring. Even anticipating a reaction not in his favour, Jin was utterly taken aback by the raw hostility directed at him.

Kazue, her expression dark, reached a hand up and grabbed the young man by the wrist. "Calm down," she hissed.

"Calm down?" Ryū snarled. "You know what he did." He pointed an accusing finger at Jin, who felt more confused than ever. What he had done? What had he done? Why was this young man he had met for the first time only minutes ago so furious at him? Jin remembered the way Kari had looked at him at the General's party. The intensity of the anger he had felt from him. Jin didn't understand. He didn't understand where all this came from, what Ryū was accusing him of. So instead he simply sat there and stared at the tea cup sat before him.

Unlike Niall. "What's that supposed to mean?" his friend snapped. "He didn't do anything. He's been looking for his friend for years. He's been worried sick when he found out the boy wasn't at the temple any more."

"And you believe him?"

"Of course I believe him. Jin is like a brother to me. And unless you come out with what he has apparently done, you better watch it."

Jin glanced at his friend, grateful and surprised. He knew she had had a crush on Ryū for years, Risa liked to tease her about choosing the most unavailable man possible to fall in love with. But Niall kept denying being in love with the young Furyusha, even though she admitted she found him attractive. Either she had been telling the truth all along, or her loyalty and affection towards Jin outweighed her attraction. Whichever it was, Jin was glad to have Niall on his side.

"It's not my place to tell you. But Suzu is like a brother *to me*, and I will not see him getting hurt again."

While Niall and Ryū glared at each other, and Jin wished the ground would open up and swallow him whole, neither Kazue nor Naloc spoke a word. Eventually, however, Kazue sighed deeply, dejectedly.

"Ryū, fetch Suzu," she ordered in a tone more defeated than determined.

Ryū whipped his head around to look at her. "But Mother--"

"No," she cut his protest short. "I think it is time Suzu confronted his past. He will never get over it otherwise."

"But..." Ryū didn't finish whatever he had meant to say. Perhaps he realised it was futile to argue, perhaps he agreed with her reasoning. His shoulders slumped, but he gave a curt nod and without another word left the room. Jin stared after him, his mind and heart in turmoil.

He could hear his heart pounding, his blood rushing loudly in his ears. He was hardly aware of the minutes ticking by, of the tense silence in the room, the way they avoided each other's eyes. Jin could not recall ever having been so nervous in his entire life. What if Kari refused to see him? But why would he? Jin didn't understand all the hostility and accusations, he didn't understand why Kari had refused to acknowledge him before. The boy had clearly recognised him. Nor did he understand why Kari had run away, vanished without a trace, by the time Jin had sent for him. All Jin did know was that he wouldn't be able to deal with losing Kari again now that he had finally found him, or with leaving all those questions unanswered.

Jin took a deep breath. No, there was some kind of misunderstanding here, so much was clear. A misunderstanding. Easily solved. And then he would finally be reunited with Kari. After all those years yearning, grieving. Missing half of his heart. The longing for his love was at times a physical pain. But finally it would have an end. Finally, life would be as it was supposed to be.

Yet the door slammed open, revealing not a lovely boy, long missed, eager to reunite with the other half of his heart, but a raging god.

Jin felt trapped, pinned to the spot by the intensity with which the young man glared at him. His eyes – and only now in the light did Jin notice the right one was the colour of a leaf hidden in the fog, a mere suggestion of its former jade colour remaining. A thin silver line cut across his brow to his cheekbone. A glimmer of doubt, a voice, unbidden: Was this really his Kari? His gentle, sweet Kari, who could be stubborn as a mule, but never lost his temper.

Jin stared back at the furious young Furyusha. His beauty was overwhelming, unearthly. His rage palpable, almost visible like an aura, all consuming, hungry for destruction.

A tug at his sleeve brought Jin out of his stupor and allowed him to finally tear his eyes away from Kari – no, Suzu. He glanced at Niall who was beckoning him to get to his feet. And so he did, yet the moment he was standing, Suzu sprang at him with a roar. Jin stumbled backwards, but Suzu never reached him. Ryū had his arms tightly around the thrashing boy, hands clawing at the air, trying to reach Jin and... and what?

"Suzu, stop it!" Kazue cried, but Suzu didn't listen. Ryū held on to him with difficulty.

"Let go of me!" Suzu growled. "I want to scratch out his eyes."

"What is the meaning of this?" Naloc demanded in a mixture of outrage and shock, while Niall held on to Jin's arm as if afraid he would bolt. Jin, for his part, stood frozen to the spot, stupefied, his heart pounding, the floor beneath his feet swaying. Confusion warred with agitation. Who was this wild creature that wore his beloved's face? Where did all this rage and hatred come from. And why?

"I'll tear that fucking liar's tongue out! Let go, damn it!" Suzu continued undeterred, neither listening to Kazue nor to Ryū, both trying to calm him down. Neither cared to give an explanation, no matter how often Naloc demanded one. Suzu's threats, Kazue, Ryū, Naloc – their voices vanished beneath an onslaught of white noise. Jin felt dizzy. It was too hot, he had trouble breathing. And then, all of a sudden, Kazue stomped her foot and cried, "Not on my tatami floor, you won't! I had those mats changed only a month ago!"

The absurdity of it wrenched them all to a standstill. Even Suzu stopped, blinking at the woman. At last he huffed, shrugged Ryū off, and folded his arms in front of his chest.

"Fine, I'm not going to murder him. But you could at least let me punch him in the eye – that wouldn't soil your mats."

"Suzu," Kazue sighed, and shook her head, but Jin could have sworn there was a smile tugging at the corners of her lips, just like there was a smirk on Ryū's.

"I don't understand," Jin said quietly. He was aware of all of them turning their attention to him, but he only saw Suzu, brows drawn together in a frown, eyes blazing. "I don't understand," he repeated. "Why are you so angry?"

"Why?" Suzu's voice was dangerously calm. "You don't understand? What did you expect? Did you think the moment I saw you I would throw myself into your arms and just forget how you betrayed me? How you destroyed everything?"

"Betrayed? Kari--"

"That is not my name!" Suzu roared, making Jin flinch.

"Sorry. But... I still don't... betrayed? I... yes, I left you behind, but only because I needed to make sure I could take care of you," Jin spoke, quickly so no-one would interrupt him. "I know it wasn't right. I didn't want to do it, but I also didn't want you to live on the street, be hungry, cold. Nobu gave me some money, but it was never going to last long, so I thought it would be best if I went ahead, got a job and a little place for us to stay. I knew you'd never agree if I told you, you can be so bloody stubborn sometimes. And I'm sorry that it took me so long, it kind of didn't work out as planned. But betrayal? I'd never betray you! Never. You were gone. Why were you gone? Why did you run away? Why are you so angry, why do you hate me so? I don't understand."

Jin stopped talking then. He stood in the middle of the room, panting and trembling, swallowing the thickness in his throat, blinking away the tears that stung his eyes. Suzu stared at him with wide eyes, bewilderment having chased away the heat of rage. Jin could feel the others gaping at him, no less taken aback by his sudden outburst. Perhaps now they felt as confused as he did.

"Nobu?" Suzu asked at last into the silence.

"Huh?"

"You said Nobu gave you money."

"Y-yes. He said... he said it was better I left before I got thrown out of the temple. H-he agreed I should not take you with me until... until... you know... and he gave me money... he promised... Wait. Why did you leave? I... Nobu – he promised he'd explain to you, that he..." he trailed off. With each word Suzu's face darkened. He closed his eyes and took several deep breaths.

"All right. Come with me," Suzu beckoned. He didn't wait for Jin, but brushed past him and Niall, flung the sliding door to the verandah open and left. Jin hesitated for a second only, then followed, ignoring Niall, calling his name.

Suzu quickly crossed the garden to the main house. Doors and windows were wide open, wherever Jin looked someone was there, cleaning, arranging, making the house ready to welcome customers in the evening. He followed Suzu inside and down a broad hallway to the far side of the building. They entered a room awash in red. Red silk hangings hid a futon laid out on a raised platform. The wallpaper was a deep burgundy with golden flowers. A folding screen with a depiction of red camellias divided the room in two: on one side the hidden futon, on the other a low-legged table and sitting cushions.

"Go and tell the others to concentrate on the other side of the house for the time being," Suzu told the young man dusting the room. "And I don't want to be disturbed."

The young man nodded, gathered his utensils and with a curious glance at Jin left, sliding the door closed behind him. Suzu took a seat at the table, gestured for Jin to do alike.

"You really intend to keep this up?"

"Keep what up?" Jin wondered.

"Pretending not to know what I'm talking about. Pretending to be innocent."

"Ka-- Suzu, I swear, I don't understand. I shouldn't have left you behind, I know that now. There's not a day I don't regret that. But... This! This anger. It makes no sense. None of it makes any sense."

"Well, then let me help you make sense of it all. Let me tell you a little story: the story of how you made a fool out of me for half my life, how you destroyed everything. How you betrayed me. Shall I?"

Part 2
Betrayal

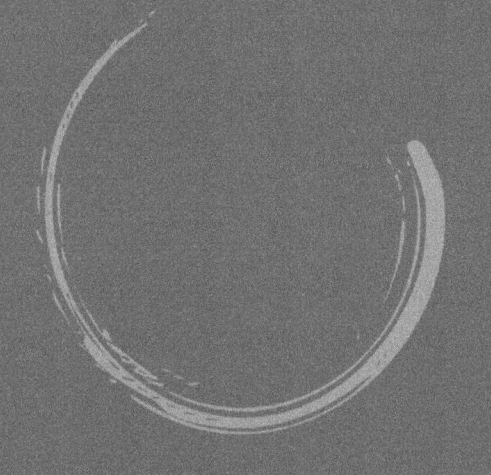

Chapter 9

Temple of Hôjô, Aoioka village, 13 years ago

Tiny hands were clutching at wet cloth. Rain was pelting down, drops fat and icy cold, painful like little stones. It was hard to see through the deluge. Strong winds whipped the rain this way and that, tore leaves off of trees, reached icy fingers beneath their wet clothes. Lightning flashed, thunder roared.

He pressed his little face into the monk's shoulder, his hands fisted tightly into the fabric of the man's robes, tight enough that his knuckles showed white. Nothing good ever happened during a thunderstorm. Though he hardly remembered, it had been a night like this when papa hadn't come home again. When mama had stopped laughing, when she had stopped speaking. When the warmth and safety had been ripped from their lives. A night like this. Thunder and lightning. And now mama had stopped altogether. Stopped smiling at him. Stopped brushing her fingers gently through his hair. Stopped plastering little kisses all over his face. Stopped hugging him. Stopped seeing, stopped breathing... Stopped being mama. Nothing good ever happened during a storm like this.

His throat hurt, his eyes stung. He had been screaming and wailing almost the entire way from the place where mama was, up the hill and its many many steps. And suddenly the storm had broken loose and the boy had been too scared even to cry. He had ceased struggling and instead clung to the big monk who had come to take him away from the empty husk that had been his mama.

Tentatively he peeked out from under his arm. They were crossing a big open courtyard. The storm seemed closer here than beneath the canopy of trees. Another clap of thunder. Another flash of lightning. With a yelp he buried his face in the monk's wet robe again.

"It's all right now, we're almost there," the man called over the wind, his voice a deep rumble in his chest.

At last they stepped out of the rain. The monk pounded his meaty fist against the heavy door. With a creaking sound the door opened almost at once. Warmth brushed against the boy's back, the welcome yellow glow of lanterns greeted them.

"Dear gods, Brother Askr!" a voice exclaimed from within. "We thought you would stay the night in the village. What in the Goddess's name possessed you to go out in that storm."

"The mother died. I had to get the boy away from her as soon as possible. And the storm was still miles away when we left." Brother Askr didn't mention they would have arrived at the temple long before the rain began, if the boy hadn't fought him like a feral cat to get back to his deceased mother.

"The poor little thing. Come inside quickly, Brother. I'll fetch warm water, tea and food for the both of you. It'd be better if the boy stayed with you for the night."

"Of course. Thank you, Brother Momotaru."

Brother Askr carried the boy down the hall, leaving a trail of water drops on the polished wooden floor. Outside the storm was still raging, but beyond the thick walls it was less frightening, and so the boy lifted his head from the monk's shoulder and curiously looked about. On either side of the hall were doors, all of them shut. Lanterns, hanging from big wrought-iron hooks in the space between those doors, cast a warm but dim light. At the very end of the hallway, Brother Askr turned to the door on his right and opened it. It was pitch black inside.

"Drat," the monk huffed. He gently pried the little boy off him and stood him on his feet. "Just wait here a moment while I light us a lamp, all right?" The boy nodded and watched the big man vanish into the darkness beyond the door. He could hear some clanking, a muffled curse, and then the monk reappeared, a lamp and a taper in his big hands. He lit the taper on the lamp beside the door, then lit his own with it. "Good, now... come on in."

The room was much bigger than what the boy was used to. If mama and he hadn't camped beneath the open sky they had slept in crammed little rooms, tiny sheds, or in barns amidst the animals. He thought it had been different once, when papa had still been with them. Before. Before the bad thunderstorm.

There was a big bed in the room, a table with two chairs, and a chest at the foot end of the bed. No decoration, nothing personal. But there were books. So many books. An entire shelf of it – more than the little boy had thought possible for a single person to have. He was curious what they were about, but he stood dripping and shivering and swaying with exhaustion, and all he really wanted was to go back to where mama was. Fatigue rooted him to the spot, however. He watched the monk rummaging through the wooden chest. He was a big man, the monk, much taller than any man the boy had ever seen, broad shouldered, bald, a ruddy complexion. But his big round blue eyes had a merry sparkle, his face was gentle and soft, as if he knew no anger.

A knock on the door, and the monk, who had let them into the temple, entered without waiting to be invited in. He carried a tray with food and a pot of tea. Behind him followed a small horde of younger monks. Two carried a tub between them, three more carried buckets of steaming hot water. They cast curious glances at the little boy while they prepared the bath.

"Here, I've found the boy some clothes," Brother Momotaru said, handing Brother Askr a bundle of clothes. "They may be a bit too tall, but better than those wet rags."

"Thank you, Brother Momotaru. And you, Brothers," Brother Askr addressed the younger monks, who, done with their task, bowed and left. Bother Momotaru followed them, but before he closed the door he said, "Ah, right. The Head Priest will stop by before night rest." And with that he was gone as well.

Brother Askr sighed. He eyed the boy, exhaustion drawing his little face tight, eyes drifting shut only to be stubbornly forced open.

"Come, little one, that bath is for you. It'll warm you right up. Can't have you catching a cold now, can we?" The boy fidgeted. He was so cold, and the bath looked very enticing, but... he was in a strange place with a strange man, and he didn't understand why. All he wanted was his mama – but mama wasn't here anymore. Mama had stopped. Fresh tears blurred his vision, ran down his cheeks in fat drops. Half suppressed sobs racked his narrow chest.

"Oh, little one," the monk said, kneeling down in front of the boy. "I'm so sorry. I truly am. Believe me, I wish there had been a way to save your mama, but alas... Look, you're going to be fine here. It's what we do, we give little boys like you, who are all alone in this world, a home and a family." He helped the little boy out of his wet clothes and into the hot water.

While he was soaking in the warm water, Brother Askr gave him tea to drink – a herbal infusion that made him even drowsier – and fed him small pieces of buttered bread. He didn't taste the bread, nor did he feel particularly hungry although he couldn't remember the last time he had eaten. After a while the big monk helped him out of the tub and into dry clothes that were only slightly too big for him. Suddenly, the boy felt so very tired, his eyelids so heavy, his body sluggish. Before he could clamber into Brother Askr's bed, however, there was another knock on the door. A second later, it swung open and a tiny old man entered. He wore similar robes as Brother Askr's, but where the larger man's were the yellow of sunflowers, his were a deep dark red. His snowy white hair was piled on top of his head in a rather messy knot, his white beard long and wispy. A myriad of fine wrinkles mapped his face, but his eyes, the dark brown of ebony wood, were sharp and clear.

"Brother Askr," he said in a raspy voice, "I see you've brought us a new member to the family."

"I have, Head Priest." The boy, though swaying on his feet, fighting to keep his eyes open, looked curiously between the two monks. It registered dimly in his tired mind that the older man was someone important. "I was called down to the village this afternoon," Brother Askr continued. "The old couple at the southern edge had found him and his mother in an old lean-to just outside the village boundary. The mother... no-one knows how long he sat there all alone with only his dead mother for company. He refused to part with her."

The Head Priest shook his head, his expression sad. "It's always a tragedy when one is torn out of life before one's time. Do we know who she was, where she came from?"

"No. The old couple said they had met both, mother and son, a few days ago, when they came to their house looking for food to buy. Apparently the mother couldn't speak. They said she looked ill and fragile but refused to go further into the village or even stay at the couple's house. They assumed they were only passing through and had all but forgotten about them when they found them today."

The older monk pulled at his beard, contemplating the little boy, who met his gaze stubbornly despite his exhaustion. "I see," the man said slowly. "Well, I guess it is safe to assume there is no-one else to take care of the child," He nodded at his own words, then his expression softened. "So, little one, let's have a look at you." It was only then, when he really looked at the boy for the first time, that he noticed the fine features – the child looked like a delicate porcelain doll – and even more so the startlingly green eyes. "Oh my," the old man huffed, surprised. "Ethereal? And full-blooded, it may seem."

Brother Askr coughed awkwardly. He was well aware of the reservations some of the monks had towards Ethereals, but the little boy was all alone in the world now. They couldn't just abandon him. "He is but a small child, who is all alone, it is our duty to give him a home and educate him as we would any other child," he countered.

The Head Priest didn't look convinced, but he dropped the matter, much to Brother Askr's relief. "Well, do you have a name?"

My name, the boy thought, startled by the question. A name. He had a name, he was sure he had. In his dreams he could hear his mother laugh and sing, call him by his name. Another, faceless deep voice beckoning him. A sound so warm and full of love and joy, as bright as the sun. Never did those two voices speak with more affection, with a deeper love than when they said his name. A name – which he could not remember. Which not even his dreams recalled. Tears welled up in his eyes, his lips quivered.

"He can speak, can he not?" the priest whispered with a frown between his bushy white brows.

"I..." the boy said, his voice so quiet the two men almost missed it. "I d-don't... remem... remember," he sobbed at last.

A warm, big hand landed on his small shoulder. The boy looked up at Brother Askr's sad face. Sadness, in the monk's eyes, in the lines at the corners of his mouth – sadness, not pity. He knew pity, Shigeru had explained it to him when he and his mama were travelling with the theatre troupe. Pity was what made him feel so small and helpless, what made his mama seem so fragile and weak despite her strength, her tenaciousness. Pity was what caused this strange urge to scream and rage, to hit those who pitied them, inside him. Shigeru had provided a name for the unwanted sentiment, an explanation. He had taught the boy many things. If only he could be with Shigeru now, but the theatre troupe had left them behind a long time ago. The little boy was alone in this world now.

"Well, all in good time," the Head Priest assured. "Don't worry, I am sure Brother Askr will think of a wonderful name for you. For now, get some rest, the both of you."

Brother Askr bowed his head low when the old priest left the room. Then he picked up the little boy and planted him on the bed, pulling the blanket over him. "My bed will have to do tonight. Tomorrow I'll introduce you to the other boys. You will stay with them in the dormitory. Sleep now, little one. Sleep."

And sleep he did. Exhaustion pulled him under the moment his head hit the thin pillow. The darkness of oblivion was welcome, a respite from the ache in his little heart.

The next morning the world looked brighter – or at least the weather did. The storm had washed the air clean, a fresh crispness that hadn't been there before replaced the sultry heat of the past weeks.

"Looks like autumn has finally arrived," Brother Askr remarked, turning from the open window to the little boy sitting at the table and sipping tea. Every now and then a sob escaped his tiny chest, unbidden and unexpected. Brother Askr sighed. There wasn't much that could be done to lessen the pain of loss the boy felt. Moving forward was all that was left.

"So, first things first: a name. Without a name I can't introduce you to the others, now, can I?" The boy mumbled incoherently into his cup. "What is it? Did you remember your name?" Shaking his head the boy put the cup on the table. In the night, in his dreams, he had almost remembered it. But no matter how hard he tried, he couldn't. And then he had woken up and the dreams were gone like fog burnt away by the sun.

A single tear fell on his lap. He pawed his eyes viciously. The sound of the other chair scraping over the wooden floor made him look up. Brother Askr sat down, grabbed the tea pot, and poured himself another cup.

"Well, we have to call you something, don't we? Let's do this: Until you remember your name, we pick another one to call you by. All right? Only until you remember." The boy considered it for a moment. The big monk was right. Most people they had met and travelled with for a while had always called him "little one". Shigeru had called him Tsukiko – his little moon. But that was Shigeru's name for him, he didn't want anyone else to use it. So he gave a curt nod.

"Good. How about... Fiete?" The boy pulled a face. "No? Too northern perhaps? All right. Kjell? ... What?" Brother Askr demanded of the boy, shaking his head vehemently. "It's the emperor's name, you know. Fine," he sighed. The monk rubbed a hand over his bald head, considering a moment, before he fired off one name after the other, all of which met the boy's rejection. "... Kotetsu?... Takumi?... how about... Isoldr? I guess not... Ren?... I give up. I'm not good at naming people, and I have no more ideas." Brother Askr stared at the boy in front of him, the shaggy black hair, the big jade green eyes. He was a pretty little thing – and admittedly perhaps a little otherworldly. Was it the boy's Ethereal blood that made the monk feel an instant fondness of him? Did it even matter? "Kari," he said softly, and sat up straight, suddenly, surprised at himself. The little boy cocked his head questioningly. "Oh, that... K-Kari. It was my son's name... a long time ago, in another life." Brother Askr cleared his throat and blinked his eyes rapidly as if blinking away tears. The little boy was confused, he didn't understand what the monk was saying, but he felt a sudden connection to the man. Perhaps they shared the same kind of sadness. "So... well... how about it? Would you like to be Kari – for a while at least?"

'Kari' – he was a stranger, borrowing the name of another stranger, 'Kari' wasn't the little boy. But perhaps he could be – for a while. Perhaps being Kari was better than being who he was now, a little boy all alone in the entire world with nothing but a handful of bittersweet memories and too much pain and sorrow for his little heart. *Would you like to be Kari?* Yes, he would be Kari now, and Kari could be whoever he wanted him to be.

Kari looked up into the dark eyes of Brother Askr and forced the ghost of a smile on his lips, nodding his assent. Brother Askr's face lit up, the smile, although it crinkled his eyes, made him look younger.

"Well, that wasn't too difficult, was it?" the monk laughed.

After breakfast Brother Askr took Kari by the hand and together they explored the temple and its huge grounds. The monks' private quarters were separated from the temple itself with its altar, headed by a statue of polished wood, twice as tall as a man. Its face was as stern as it was gentle: Hôjô – patron god of orphans and unwanted children, god of prosperity, guardian of farmers and family. Kari had heard the name of the god occasionally on his travels, mostly in small farming villages. Once, they had passed a temple and nunnery dedicated to Hôjô. There, too, had been many children, all of them girls.

Smaller rooms for individual meditation and prayer bracketed the altar room. On the other side of the temple was the dormitory, where the novices stayed, together with the flock of orphaned boys the temple raised. Enclosed by both dormitories, flanking the main building, was a beautiful small pleasure garden. The earth still smelled from the heavy rain of the last night. Two ginkgo trees dominated the centre, already their leaves were changing from a lush green to a golden yellow. Dahlias and chrysanthemums added bright splashes of colour.

They left the temple through the same heavy doors they had entered the night before. Now, in daylight, Kari could see just how big the courtyard was. To one side was a stone garden, two elderly monks were busy raking intricate patterns into the white marble pebbles. A path lined by stone lanterns led straight across the yard to an archway, guarded by two stone lions. Beyond the arch a myriad of steps, overhung by the canopies of the trees that covered the hillside, went all the way down to the village.

They crossed the vastness of the courtyard left of the path. Only the statue of another guardian lion, taller than the other other two, disturbed the empty sea of cobblestones. A garden, much bigger than the other one, sprawled between the novice's dormitory and what Brother Askr explained was the school, a squat building much smaller than the others, where the orphans received an education together with children from the village. Kari, too, would soon join them, but first he needed to learn how to read and write. At the back of the garden loomed the last building of the complex: the library.

Kari followed the monk into the garden. Unlike the pleasure garden this one wasn't meant to just look pretty. Beds of herbs and vegetables alternated with rows of flowers and flowering bushes. Here and there fruit and nut tress provided as much shade as nourishment.

On a stone bench beneath a gnarly walnut tree sat a boy, about Kari's age, swinging his feet and glaring sullenly at the gravel.

"This," Brother Askr gestured towards the boy, "is Jin. He's my other ward. And like you, he needs to learn his letters first before he can join the others in class. Jin!" he called. The boy looked up listlessly, but upon seeing Kari next to the monk he sprang to his feet and ran towards them at a sprint. Kari edged closer to the Brother Askr, almost but not quite hiding behind the big man. He wasn't sure what to expect from the other boy, he had no experience with other children, and the abundance of energy that radiated from him put Kari on guard.

Jin skittered to a halt in front of them, staring wide-eyed and full of curiosity at Kari, not even acknowledging Brother Askr. There was something in his dark brown eyes, a glitter Kari had no name for. Kari stared back defiantly. The other boy was taller than Kari, his mop of black hair stuck out to all sides, his skin was a dark, sun-kissed bronze as opposed to Kari's porcelain.

Jin cocked his head to one side, and suddenly Kari knew what it was, the energy, the glitter in the boy's eyes: he was like a puppy, lost and found. A hopeful, strong need. Kari had found a puppy last spring, begged his mother to keep it. The dog had looked at him with much the same eyes as the boy in front of him now: sad, hopeful. The same feeling as then overcame Kari now; an urge, an instinct. He took a step towards the other boy.

Brother Askr squatted down so he was at eye-level with the children, and said, "Kari, this is Jin. Jin, Kari is new here, so I hope you can look after him for me."

"Kari." Jin said the name more to himself, like testing the sound of it. "But he doesn't look northern."

"Who says you can only have a northern name when you are from the north? Brother Momotaru has blond hair and blue eyes, yet his name is southern."

"Hmm." Jin contemplated this revelation for a moment, then shrugged, and with a big smile turned his attention back to Kari. "I'm also new... well not really... not now anyway... Did your parents leave you here, too?"

"Ah, Jin, don't--" But it was already too late. At the mention of his parents, Kari's eyes filled with tears, his heart constricted painfully. He sniffled, lips trembling in an effort not to start crying.

"I... s-sorry... sorry..." Jin stammered, distressed. Small hands reached out towards Kari, only to hang helplessly in the air.

"It's all right, Jin, you couldn't know. But, you know, everyone's situation is different, so it's not good to ask so bluntly." Leaning forward he whispered into the boy's ear. Kari didn't need to hear what the monk said, he knew it already. His parents were gone. Jin clapped his hands over his mouth. Kari swallowed his tears, a spark of anger chasing his sorrow away. Surely now Jin would pity him, just like so many others had before when they looked at Kari and his mother. He hated pity, it made him angry. And sure enough, just like that the expression in those warm dark eyes changed – but it was no pity, it was something... fierce but no less comforting.

"All right, you two. I just have a tiny errand to run, and then I will see which room is available to us. Jin, why don't you explain to Kari how we do things here?" Brother Askr stood up, ruffled both boys' hair, and left them standing awkwardly in the middle of the path.

"Um... so... the temple is..." Jin mumbled, shuffling his feet. "It's a... temple of Hôjô. Do you know Hôjô?" Kari hesitated before shaking his head, after all, what did he really know about the god and his worshipper? "Oh... um... well H-Hôjô is... um... that big fellow in the altar room." Jin flashed Kari a grin. Yet when he didn't get the hoped for reaction out of the other boy, he coughed and continued. "So, actually I don't really know either, but he's a god, and they – the monks – they take care of children who don't have parents, or whose pa- parents d-don't want... don't want them," Jin forced out with a sob. Kari wondered how Jin had come to be here, and what he meant when he said parents, who didn't want their children. Didn't all parents want their children? "Th-they do so because Hôjô told them to. And they have this school where they teach us and the children from the village. And... and when you are sixteen... I think... you can also become a monk, or you stay a bit longer and then leave... um... yes." He shifted uncomfortably, not looking at Kari, a flush creeping up his neck.

Was he supposed to say something, Kari wondered. But what? Until now he had been travelling alone with his mama, only occasionally joined by other travellers. Even Shigeru and his troupe had eventually parted ways with them, although their time together had been the longest they ever had been with other people. And now Kari was stuck in this place, surrounded by strangers, with a name that wasn't his. What else was he supposed to do, though? Run away? Where would he go, he didn't even know where he was in the first place. All he did know was that he was all alone in this world with no place to go.

Kari suddenly felt dizzy. His head spun with questions, his heart was racing, his blood pounding in his ears, his chest constricted, he couldn't breath. His mama was gone. Gone, just like papa. How long until he wouldn't be able to remember her face, the way he couldn't remember papa's. The pain that came with that thought was too much for his little body. He crouched down, hugged his legs and pressed his forehead against his knees. A strange keening sound escaped his throat, more small animal than boy. He wanted to scream, and had no air to do so.

"K-Kari?" Jin exclaimed in shock. He dropped to his knees beside the other boy, hand hovering uncertainly over Kari's shoulder, not daring to touch the smaller boy. "Hey... um... what's wrong? Do you hurt somewhere? Are you sick? Sh-shall I go fetch someone?" Jin fretted, looking anxiously about the garden, but there was no-one else.

Kari gasped for air. He could feel the other boy's presence beside him, warm, comforting, and despite himself he reached out his hand and grabbed a fistful of Jin's shirt, holding on to the other boy. Jin's fretting stilled, allowing his hand to gently touch Kari's thin shoulder. A strange feeling spread through Kari, a warmth he had thought he'd never feel again after his mother's death, a grounding, a sense of belonging. He looked up into the dark brown and worried eyes of the other boy. There it was again, that something in the depth of those eyes, lurking beneath the concern. Fierce and gentle all at once. It mixed and overlapped with the forlornness and need that had already been there.

He couldn't say why he did it, but Kari took Jin's hand in his. Surprise flitted across Jin's face ere his fingers tightened around Kari's and a little smile tugged up the corners of his lips. That fierce gentleness in his eyes grew ever stronger, the forlornness receded. Strange, Kari thought, but his breath came easier, the pain dulled.

Brother Askr returned to find the boys huddled together like life long confidants.

"Why are there no girls here?" Kari asked.

"Girls... um... they are..." Jin faltered, looking up as if an answer might just present itself, and instead found Brother Askr looking down at them, smiling.

"Girls are with our Sisters at our sister temple in Akagawa," the monk replied.

"Why?"

"That is something you will understand when you are older. It's enough to know for now that the Path of Hôjô doesn't allow men and women to live together under the same roof unless they are married. Of course that doesn't mean that we exclude the village girls from our school. Denying them an education would be a violation of our laws as well."

Kari didn't understand why boys and girls could not share a roof. He had always lived with mama, and mama had been a girl. Many of the people they had sometimes travelled and shared a camp with had been girls. But he chose not to say so out loud, it didn't matter much to him anyway.

"Well, come along then, time to do some work." Obediently the boys followed Brother Askr to a small corner room of the school, past doors from behind which they could hear voices. The room Brother Askr had found them was too small for a larger group, with just four of the low desks, but adequate enough for them. Suzu and Jin each sat down behind one of the desks, paper, brush and ink were already set out for them.

Brother Askr sat down, facing them, his knees making popping noises as he crossed his legs.

"Ah, I'm getting old," the monk sighed. "All right. Before we start with our writing lesson – Kari, what do you know about our empire?" Kari shook his head. He didn't know what an empire was, but didn't dare say so, lest Brother Askr and Jin thought him stupid. "Do you know what it is called?" But how was he supposed to know that, when he didn't even know what it was? Brother Askr smiled benevolently and ruffled Kari's hair. "That's all right. I didn't know either when I was your age. That is why we have schools. So that we can learn things like writing and reading, numbers, and also about the world we live in. Jin, why don't you show Kari what you've learned so far?"

For a moment Jin froze like a hare in front of a snake. Then he noticed Kari's wide-eyed expectant look. Blushing, he sat up straighter, cleared his throat, and recited, "The country we live in is called... it's called Tsukiyama. Well, actually it's two countries, but they are one now, that's why it's not a country but an... empire? Th-the Moon Goddess is our patron god, She is the highest of the thousand gods. I think. … um... the emperor – that's the one who rules the empire – is... um... is called Kjell? The Moon Goddess chose him, because that is what She does." Jin grinned proudly at his new friend, and was rewarded with admiration sparkling in those jade green eyes.

"Very good, Jin," Brother Askr praised, letting Jin's breast swell with more pride. "I admit, I am surprised, I just never know if you are actually listening to me or not." Jin deflated. "Today," Brother Askr continued, ignoring Jin's sullen grumbling, "I will tell you how our empire came to be, so listen closely."

And so, sitting in a small room with his new friend, Kari listened to the old monk, wide-eyed, soaking up every word like a sponge, stoking a hunger inside him, a hunger for knowledge. He sat and listened to how many became one.

A thousand years ago there were two countries, separated by water and by rock from the rest of the world: the peninsula Tsukishima, and the rough mountainous Calthean. It was said that this land, from the mighty sea to the impenetrable sky-high mountain range in the north, was created when the Moon Goddess, for one single swift moment, set foot on earth. So despite all their differences, the people of both countries shared their love for the goddess.

But neither country was peaceful. In Tsukishima the four major clans were in constant war for supremacy. While Calthean's myriad of clans fought each other, when they didn't fight the harsh nature of their land.

Eventually the goddess grew tired of the never-ending strife. And so She appeared in front of a young priest and told him to go and find the one She had deemed worthy to rule all of Her lands. The priest spread Her message amongst his fellow priests and together they searched the land for many years, until, at last, they found the goddess's chosen one: a young noble named Asayake no Takao. Under his rule the clans united the country and declared Takao Emperor of Tsukishima.

Peaceful at last, the country prospered.

Soon, however, the Calthean clans took notice of their neighbours' new-found wealth. They felt betrayed and abandoned by the goddess. Why did they have to live in hardship, suffer hunger and sorrow, whilst Tsukishima alone was blessed? Enraged, the clans settled their pity disputes and united against the empire.

Yet the Moon Goddess had chosen wisely. Takao was a man of greatness, of mercy and benevolence, a clever strategist, but also a man who always chose peace over war. And so he met the Caltheans – not on the battlefield but with an offer: unite their countries into one empire under his rule, and he would do everything to end their suffering. The Caltheans – though many argued against it – saw Takao's sincerity and the wisdom in accepting the offer. Perhaps the goddess had not abandoned them after all. In the end they accepted, and the Empire of Tsukiyama was born.

"Yes, but how did they know Takao was the chosen one?" Jin demanded to know.

"By a sign from the goddess herself."

"What sign?"

"A sign only the Heavenly Council knows."

"Why?"

"How do you become emperor?" Kari interjected before Brother Askr had a chance to answer Jin.

"The Moon Goddess chooses her or him."

"How?"

Brother Askr sighed. "The Heavenly Council meets in seclusion and meditation. Until the goddess sends them a sign. A sign that has been passed down from one generation of Head Priests to the next. Only they know what it is and how to read it, and thus know our new emperor or empress."

"But wouldn't it be easier if we all just knew what it was so that we knew if we happened to meet the chosen one? That would save the Head Priests a lot of work, wouldn't it?" Jin remarked smugly.

"I doubt that would make it any easier."

"No, think about it, perhaps I'm the next emperor, and you just don't know it because you don't know the sign." Jin's eyes took on a far away look as if he was already imagining himself in some glamorous palace.

"Jin," Brother Askr said flatly. "The Moon Goddess is known for Her wisdom. It would mean the end of time is near, if She ever chose you."

The rest of the morning Brother Askr had them practise their letters. When the bell told them it was lunchtime, and they joined the monks, novices, and other children in the refectory, Jin took Kari by the hand and led the boy to a long table at the far end of the room – the children's table. At once they were surrounded by boys of all ages, curious about their new companion. Questions rained down on Kari, questions he had no answers to. Overwhelmed by the press of bodies, the cacophony of voices he couldn't even put faces to, Kari felt panic rise. Frightened, he clung to Jin, skinny arms slung tightly around the other boy's arm.

As suddenly as the onslaught had begun, as suddenly it stopped, however. The children took their seats obediently, murmuring very quietly. Kari looked up. A tall, lanky boy, much older than him stood behind Jin, his arms crossed, his face stern. When all but Jin and Kari were sitting quietly around the long table, the youth turned to Kari, his stern mien melting away into a gentle smile.

"I'm sorry, they get excited when they see a new face. You don't need to be afraid, they are all harmless, I promise. I'm Nobu, I'm currently the oldest among the children, but I'll join the novices come spring," the older boy introduced himself, leading Kari and Jin to open seats. Nobu had a gentle face, a winsome smile, and a seemingly pleasant disposition. And yet something in Kari flinched away from him, some instinct that told him to stay away from the older boy. He couldn't explain it, didn't understand it, he just knew it to be true. His grip tightened involuntarily on Jin's arm. Jin looked at him, surprised and a little bit confused, but the moment their eyes met the most beautiful smile lit Jin's face.

"Don't worry," Jin whispered, "I'm with you, I'll protect you."

Warmth seeped into the cold places of Kari's broken little heart, mending some of the cracks, like gold glueing pieces of a broken vase together. Perhaps Kari wasn't alone after all.

Chapter 10

    Jin, it turned out, was very serious about his promise, leaving Kari's side only when he had to. And soon the two boys had become inseparable. Even after they joined the others in school and found friends about their age among the village children, they stuck together like glue. To his surprise Kari found that the pain over the loss of his mother lessened in time, that he could smile and laugh again without having to pretend. That he could be happy. And what made him happy the most was Jin.

    In all honesty, Kari didn't need Jin's protection, but of course he didn't tell the other boy. Years had gone by since Kari had been on the road with his mother, many memories had become blurred, faded. Faces, places felt unreal, as if they had only been a dream. But he hadn't forgotten the time they had travelled with the theatre troupe. He hadn't forgotten

Shigeru. Oh, true, Kari couldn't recall the man's face, or what his voice had sounded like, but he remembered what he had taught Kari as clearly as the lessons he now received from the monks.

"Tsukiko," Shigeru had said one day, looking very serious, "listen closely, this is important. Your mama is very ill. Her mind is strong, but her body isn't. As long as you are with me and the troupe, you and your mama are safe. But out there are many people who do not look kindly upon Ethereals."

"Why?"

"Well, some are envious, some think it is wrong that we exist. Do you know what an Ethereal is, Tsukiko?"

"It's what mama is, and I, and Shigeru..."

Shigeru had laughed and ruffled his hair. "Yes, sweetling. But what does it mean to be Ethereal? I guess you are too small to know yet. Ethereals are god-blessed. But when the gods blessed our ancestors, what they really did was give them a spark of their divinity. Our beauty and our special gifts come from that spark. And that is why not all people like Ethereals, and some would like to own them."

"Own? What for?"

"That is something you will understand when you are older, but they don't have good intentions. But don't be scared, my little moon, not many people know this, but the gods also gave us a little bit of extra talent, so we'd be able to defend ourselves. I'll show you a few tricks, but remember to keep learning, whenever and however you can. Become strong, learn how to defend yourself and your mama."

And so, Shigeru had shown him those tricks, little things even a small boy like him could do. He had practised them every day, even after mama and he had parted ways with the theatre troupe. Mama had also known a few tricks of her own and had added those to Kari's repertoire.

At the temple Kari didn't have a chance to practise his tricks at first. There were too many people, and Jin was always by his side. He didn't want the others to find out, not even Jin. For only now did he understand what Shigeru had meant, when he said that some people did not look kindly upon Ethereals. He could hear the whispers, felt their eyes on him wherever he went. The Head Priest had looked at him the same way – suspicious, almost hostile. Ethereals, he heard them say, were creatures that went against nature. Hôjô had never granted such unnatural gifts to any mortal being. For them to accept him, there was only one way: Suzu had to make them believe he was a good little boy, harmless, acquiescent. Make them forget he was an Ethereal.

Time past. Kari learned to read and write, he discovered the joy of books, the knowledge and wisdom they granted, and while Jin was often stuck for hours in remedial classes, Kari spent his time in the library. The monks of the temple did not pursue the art of fighting, neither with their bare hands nor any weapon, but there were books, lots of them. By that time, despite the prejudice the monks and many of the village people had against him, Kari was known to be obedient and studious, well-mannered, with a friendly disposition. And so the monks granted him full admission to the library.

He studied the books, took meticulous notes, and practised what he had learned in his secret little hiding place in the woods behind the temple. Once he had understood the general idea behind it, he soon figured out the moves.

No, Kari didn't need Jin's protection, but he needed Jin's friendship and love. And Jin... well... Jin needed to be needed. Kari had felt it from the start, although he hadn't understood it then. He did so now, and whatever Jin needed, Kari would give him. Which was why he had to keep so many things about himself a secret, even from Jin.

It was a lovely spring day when eleven years old Kari was sent down into the village on an errand. Like many of the monks now, a lot of the village people were rather fond of Kari, that sweet little boy. Jin had been detained by Brother Shige for falling asleep in class – again – and so Kari went alone to take Brother Hanjo's precious cooking knives to the smith for a decent sharpening. Kari enjoyed the opportunity to go into the village, see what was new, listen to the gossip and chatter of the village folk, and sneak back sweets for Jin and him.

He had just left the knives in the capable hands of the blacksmith, when he was grabbed by more than one pair of hands and dragged behind the workshop.

Steren, the village bully, and his two cronies loomed over Kari. The metallic concert of anvil and hammer from within the workshop was loud enough no-one would hear Kari scream. Frankly, Kari hadn't thought Steren capable of such foresight.

"Well, look who we have here," Steren sneered. "All alone, are you? Where's your little guard dog? Trouble in paradise?" Steren's friends snickered. Kari didn't react; he had known it would come to this sooner or later, given Steren's proclivity for tormenting those weaker than him – which, to be fair, was pretty much every other child. Even at fourteen Steren was tall and packed with muscle from working the fields and chopping wood. His friends, whose names Kari didn't know and could honestly not remember ever having heard, were only marginally smaller and less brawny. By all rights, Kari had no chance against them. However… "*Don't forget, Tsukiko, being underestimated can be a huge advantage.*"

"Aww, am I right? Are you going to cry now?" Growing tired of this already, Kari looked up straight into Steren's mocking face. Whatever the older boy saw in Kari's eyes, and it certainly were no tears, made him hesitate, if only for a moment. Quickly, Steren's confusion was replaced with pure malice. "You know, I've always wondered if those rumours that Ethereals have tails are true?" Steren's cronies obligingly roared with laughter. Kari, however, could barely stop himself from rolling his eyes. He had enough of this.

When Steren made a grab for him, Kari was ready, dodging the big calloused hand and stepping into Steren's space. His own, so much smaller hand, rigid, his fingers pressed tightly together, forming the shape of a spear tip, shot forward like a striking serpent. Throwing all of his weight behind it, Kari drove his fingertips into Steren's sternum. With a loud gasp the older boy folded at the waist. Losing no time, Kari next rammed his knee into the older boy's groin. Steren went down, curling up into himself, wheezing. His friends gaped, dumbfounded, at their leader and the weak little boy who had just struck him down.

"You'll pay for this," Steren wheezed. Kari had no doubt the bully would try and make Kari's life hell if he got the chance. The only problem was that if Steren took things too far – and he would eventually – Kari's secret would also come to light. There was only one thing he could do to make sure Steren left him alone and keep his secret safe: he had to impinge on Steren's pride. It was a gamble.

"Damn it," Steren growled, slowly sitting up. His face was red, tears streaming down his cheeks, but his bloodshot eyes were hard. Anger, more than pain, distorting his face. "You little piece of shit, I'll –" Neither Kari nor Steren's friends ever found out how that sentence ended, for precisely at that moment the heel of Kari's hand collided with Steren's nose. A sickening crunching sound preceded Steren's howl. Blood gushed from his broken nose. His friends cried out in shock, hurried to crouch beside their leader, but all they did was to look with big round eyes from Steren to Kari and back.

"Language," Kari chided. It was the same reprimand several of the monks gave the older boy every day at school. "You better not think to ever mess with me again... or any of my friends."

"We... we'll tell Brother Shige about this," Steren's friend, the one Kari had always thought looked like a scarecrow, but less friendly, sputtered.

"Oh? Tell him what, exactly? How a boy half your size beat the shit out of you?"

"Th-that's –"

"How about we tell everyone what a little shit you really are?" Steren mumbled thickly, blood still trickling out of his nostrils and over his lips. His nose was already swollen and purple like a ripe plum. His beady eyes glinted maliciously.

"You think anyone will believe you?" Kari laughed derisively. "Let me tell you something: no-one will believe you, and why should they. Everyone knows you love to bully those who are weaker than you. The only reason you haven't gotten punished till now is because the monks have no proof. Because everyone is too afraid to speak up against you. And you think they'll believe that I – what? Attacked you, out of the blue? Or are you going to admit that you and your cronies came at me?"

"Fine!" Steren snapped. Although his friends looked ready to run up the hill to the temple and find the next best monk they could tell tales about Kari to, Kari could tell his gamble was paying off. The humiliation Steren would have to suffer, if he admitted having been defeated by Kari. The blow to his reputation... "What the hell do you want?" he demanded, glaring, slowly pushing himself to his feet with the help of his friends.

"I told you: leave my friends and me alone, and today never happened."

"You better not go running to your little friend to tell him then."

"You should rather worry that your cronies don't blab."

"Oh they won't if they know what's good for them." The threat and the steel in Steren's voice made his friends flinch. They quickly shook their heads, promising profusely never to tell a living soul.

They parted ways then, both parties wary of the other, but assured to know they had a hold on the other. It wasn't until years later that Kari realised that encounter had been his undoing, for while some grudges fade in time, others fester until, one day, they find the means to burn you down.

Jin pushed a folded piece of paper across the floor, stoically looking straight ahead, his face impassive in an attempt to pretend to pay attention. Kari, his eyes never leaving Brother Shige either, quickly snatched it before their teacher could notice.

Jin's handwriting, messy at the best of times, was nearly unintelligible. *Let's go looking for shooting-stars tonight.* Kari smiled to himself. Jin could have asked him at any time all day, without risking getting in trouble with Brother Shige, but once Jin had an idea in his head, he got utterly fixated on it. It drove others mad, Suzu, however, quite liked that about his friend.

Kari chanced a glance at Jin, and found him, in turn, casting quick glances at Kari in what he no doubt thought was a surreptitious way. He gave a curt nod. Jin's answering smile was radiant. It made Kari's heart skip a beat.

"Jin!" Brother Shige snapped suddenly, making both boys jump. "The principles of Hôjô's Path," the monk demanded. Jin gulped. He wasn't good at having questions thrown at him all of a sudden. Kari noticed him rubbing his sweaty palms on his trousers. Brother Shige raised an eyebrow at Jin – not a good sign.

"Um..." Jin turned to Kari, helplessly. Looking back at his friend, Kari tried to convey encouragement and confidence. Jin took a deep breath, turned back to look up at Brother Shige, and enumerated, "Give charity. Do not seek riches for your own greed. Do not lust for power nor the flesh of another."

Brother Shige huffed and gave a curt nod of acknowledgement. It was as much praise as Jin was likely ever going to get from the monk. He smiled proudly at Kari.

"And who can explain what each of those principles entails? Torben." A boy, a couple of years older than Kari and Jin, sitting in the front row, tensed as if he had been hit by lightning. Torben was a kind-hearted boy, big and strong, but his mind tended to drift. It was difficult for him to concentrate on one thing, or to understand complex matters, and he was slow to learn. Two years ago, Torben's father had left him in the monks' care, fed up with having to explain things over and over again, exclaiming that he had had enough of the boy's uselessness. It was then that Kari finally understood why Jin was so desperate to be needed by someone. Until he witnessed it, Kari had not been able to believe there were parents who didn't want their children, who considered them useless.

"Ch-charity means... um... to give..." Torben mumbled, "to give food to someone who has nothing and is hungry?"

Brother Shige considered the boy for a moment before relenting with a "Good enough. Well done, Torben." Torben slumped in relief. "Saya, how about you continue?" The girl sitting right in front of Kari sat up straighter. She was one of the village children the monks offered an education to, and she was among the first friends Kari and Jin had made – or perhaps she was only Jin's friend. Saya was pretty and clever, she enjoyed being the centre of attention. And she loved being the best. No wonder she was Brother Shige's favourite.

Kari knew Jin liked her, but he was glad when she wasn't around. She seemed to think of Kari as a rival.

Now, Saya flipped her long, glossy hair over her shoulder and dutifully began to recite. "Charity means to help those in need, to feed them, to clothe them, to give them shelter. Which is why the temples of Hôjô are a refuge for orphans and unwanted children – those most in need. It also means to share knowledge with everyone, so they learn to take care of themselves, which is why the temples also function as schools." Saya paused. Probably to let the information sink in, in an imitation of Brother Shige, but Kari was certain she just took a moment to revel in the undivided attention she got. "The second principle: Do not seek riches for your own greed," Saya continued. "Although the Brotherhood and the Sisterhood have not made a vow of poverty, the Path dictates a simple life. One shall only want what one needs, and not stow away riches or seek unnecessary luxuries. In short, don't be greedy.

"The third principle is actually two principles: Do not lust for power, means that one shall not seek a position that gives one power over others. That is why Followers of the Path cannot be found in councils or the like. And finally..." Saya faltered, a blush creeping up the back of her neck. She cleared her throat, quickly looking over her shoulder at Jin, before she continued with a slight stammer: "Finally: Do not lust for the flesh of another. What it means is... is that... well, Hôjô says..." Barely suppressed snicker from their classmates let Saya's soft blush deepen into a furious red. "Hôjô says, s-s-s-- intercourse shall only serve to create new life, else it's but an act of lust and therefore a sin."

Brother Shige glared at the room at large, silencing the not so suppressed snicker once and for all. "Very good, Saya." Saya looked back at Kari, beaming proudly. Kari humoured her and smiled back. He hoped she wouldn't boast about being praised at every opportunity, as she had a tendency to do.

Out of the corner of his eyes, Kari noticed Jin leaning towards the boy sitting on the other side of him. They had their heads together, whispering rather urgently. Kari frowned. And unfortunately he wasn't the only one who had noticed. Brother Shige's long shadow fell over them. The monk stood in front of Jin, hands on his hips, glaring down at the boy as if he had affronted him. Slowly, Jin sat back and looked up at the man's dark expression.

"Brother?" Jin asked with an air of nonchalance that made Kari wince. There was hardly a day on which Jin didn't receive some kind of punishment – usually from Brother Shige.

"Jin, why don't you share your discussion with the rest of the class?"

"It wasn't really a discussion."

"You –" Brother Shige hissed, but at the sight of Miki's raised hand, he stopped, riveting on the other boy. "What?" the monk snapped, irritated.

"Um... it's just... you know... it's my fault, I... well... you know that m-my uncle is married to a man, so... well they can't create life, now, can they... and I was... I'm scared that... does the Brotherhood think they are sinners?" Miki looked close to tears. Everyone knew how much Miki adored his uncle and his uncle's husband, they were his family, they had raised him every since Miki's parents had died. It was also true that there were some in the village who looked at them askance.

"Well," Brother Shige sighed. "I see why you'd be worried. But no, we do not. Love never is. It is... well... solely a question of how they express their love. In a physical way? Well – that would indeed be a sin in the eyes of Hôjô, for nothing can ever grow from a union between two men, or two women. Therefore this would be a mere act of lust and a sin. But then again, that is something between your uncles and their conscience. We do not pry into the lives of those outside the Brotherhood, nor do we judge them."

Miki worried his bottom lip between his teeth. Kari could tell he wasn't assured. The rest of the world may be different, but the village so very often felt like a mere extension of the temple. It was hard to say if the villagers were true believers of Hôjô, but they sure loved to present themselves as such. Which was to say, Miki's uncles didn't have the best of standing. Being the only smiths in town was probably all that kept them safe.

"I think that's all nonsense anyway," Jin blurted suddenly. This time, Kari wasn't the only one wincing. Sometimes it was as if Jin was begging for punishment. Brother Askr not only accepted but encouraged his charges to have a mind of their own, he enjoyed discussions with them. But Brother Shige was another story, as everybody knew. "Who cares what anyone does or does not do, as long as they don't hurt other people."

"And pray tell what makes you an expert," the monk snapped, his face red with anger.

"You just said so," Jin replied matter-of-factly, "love is no sin. And lots of people want to have sex when they love each other, don't they? But they don't necessarily want to a child. Like most of our parents, or we wouldn't have ended up here."

There was a collective intake of breath. It was a sore topic: parents, those dead and those who had thrown away their own children. Jin had a point, though, and no-one could deny it, not even Brother Shige. For a moment the monk was quiet, his hard expression softening a tiny bit. "It is unfortunate that some people do not value the gifts the gods have given them," he sighed at last. "But see, Jin, many of the children, whose parents don't want them, were... well... they were often conceived in an act of sin. Do you understand? That is why Hôjô tells us that a husband and wife should only lie with each other for the sake of creating life."

Jin deflated slightly. "But, Brother, do you think that's fair? Miki's uncles, they love each other, and perhaps they would like to create life, but they can't. That's not their fault. Isn't it rather the gods' fault?"

Brother Shige threw his hands up with a disgusted sound. "We are not discussing this any further. Miki's uncles are not Followers of the Path anyway, ergo it is on their own conscience and their own business how they live their lives."

"Wait, so that means, even if they do sin, you don't care?" Jin wondered.

"It's not that we don't care, but it is not our place to judge them. I've said that already. If we did, we'd have our work cut out for us. There are few who follow the Path in this empire." Miki relaxed in relief and he smiled at Jin, who grinned back. "However!" Brother Shige thundered, wiping the grin from Jin's face. "Remember this, all of you, who are the children of our temple. Hôjô has taken you in, shelters you, gives you food, education. You owe him fealty until the day you leave this temple and find your own way. Which means, until you are of age, for as long as you live under our roof, you will abide by our laws, you are Followers of the Path. Break our laws and you will be punished accordingly, initiated or not." A shocked gasp ran through the room. "Your name will be stripped from the records," Brother Shige continued mercilessly. "You will be beaten with canes to purify the evil, so that your sins will not infest the temple. You will be cast out, left with nothing, not even a name. no-one will offer you help, the Path forbids it." Brother Shige let his gaze wander over the shocked faces of the children. He lingered on Kari and Jin, and Kari felt a shudder run down his spine. "I hope you have all understood this."

"Yes, sir," the class answered in one voice.

"Why do you have to provoke Brother Shige all the time?" Kari scolded. Classes were finally over and they had a moment of freedom from their duties. Jin threw his arm around Kari's shoulders and steered his friend towards the garden, laughing.

"You say that as if I do it on purpose. My entire existence is a provocation to Brother Shige. And I was only pointing out facts."

Kari sighed. "Yes, and how, may I ask, did you come by these facts?"

Jin looked at him in surprise. "Y-you don't agree with Brother Shige, do you? You don't think I am a child of sin, do you?"

"A child of sin? Where in the world did you hear that nonsense? Of course I don't!"

Tears swam in Jin's dark eyes, he rapidly blinked them away. Kari's chest felt tight. Even now, so many years after his parents had abandoned him, Jin was so full of doubt, so anxious to not be discarded again. It was why Kari could never let him find out he wasn't the sweet innocent boy Jin needed to protect and take care of. Jin needed this, he needed to be needed. Kari didn't want his friend to hurt anymore, he wanted him to be happy. And if Jin being happy meant he had to be 'Kari', than that's who he would be.

"All right, but really now. You didn't come up with that all by yourself."

"Fine. I've been talking to some of the villagers, and some of the pedlars, and —"

"You really do talk to everybody, don't you?"

Jin grinned broadly. "You know me. Anyway, they all said that the only ones who think that way are the Followers of the Path. They said, otherwise Miki's uncles wouldn't even be able to be married. So there! Oh, and Fumihito-tan, he told me that he and Masao-tan always wanted a child. Well, they have Miki now, but... you know... it's not so nice how they got Miki. I mean..." Jin trailed off. He glanced at Kari anxiously. It's been six years, but — Jin wasn't the only one who still wasn't over his parents. Because Jin didn't want to upset Kari, he tried to avoid all talk of dead parents, which, in an orphanage, was an unavoidable topic. "W-well, anyway," Jin hastily continued, trying to steer the conversation back to safe ground. "So, I was curious about a few things, and Fumihito-tan and his husband are really nice, you know, they said we can come by and ask them anything at any time. They gave me cookies, and –"

"Wait!" Kari cried, grabbing Jin's arm and spinning his friend around to face him. "You got cookies?" Kari demanded, indignantly. "And you didn't bring me any?"

Jin blinked like an owl at him before he burst out laughing so hard, tears pooled at the corners of his eyes and he had to hold his belly. Kari gave his friend a half-hearted push, but Jin's laughter was infectious.

In good humour, they strolled down the garden path, enjoying the bursts of colour declaring the resurgence of nature. Yellow narcissus and a wild variety of tulips stood out vividly amidst a sea of white snow drops. Soft fragile cherry blossoms, tender vibrant plum blossoms were only just unfurling. The big old camellia tree was a blaze of red, as if it stood engulfed in flames.

The snow drops had a special place in Kari's heart, for they were the harbingers of spring. Despite their size, despite their apparent fragility they persevered, year after year, winter after winter. Where others faltered they pushed forward, against all odds. But the camellia would always remind him of his mother: her gentle smile, her tender touch. The way she had made him laugh. How she hadn't needed words to tell him just how much she loved him.

The tender touch of fingers brushing his cheek startled Kari out of his thoughts. He turned from the vibrant red to look into the dark eyes of his best friend. Eyes so dark they were almost black – in them Kari saw the warmth and love he had only ever known from his mother. He smiled, and was just about to suggest they go beg some tea of the monks on kitchen duty, when Saya's voice came from the garden entrance.

"Jin," she called, breathless as if she had run all the way here, ignoring Kari. "The candy man is in the village. Let's go watch the kamishibai. He said it's a new one."

Excitement lit Jin's face at once, eyes twinkling. The boy loved the kamishibai so much that he could sit and listen to a story he had heard a thousand times before with the exact same enthusiasm he'd had the first time.

The moment Saya reached them, she grabbed Jin's arm. "Let's go, hurry!" She managed to drag him along for about two steps before Jin stopped and whirled around.

"Kari, what are you waiting for, come." Jin held out a hand. "I'll buy you some sweets to make up for the cookies." It took Kari a moment to recall what cookies Jin was talking about. Chuckling, he at last grabbed the other boy's outstretched hand.

On their way down to the village, Kari caught Saya glaring at him. It wasn't just anger that burned in her eyes – it was hate. The shock of it cut Kari to the bone, cold and searing. It made him falter in his steps. But in the blink of an eye, the hateful glare was gone and Saya was running alongside Kari and Jin, laughing, face flushed from excitement and anticipation.

But Kari knew what he had seen, what he had felt. Saya wasn't his friend.

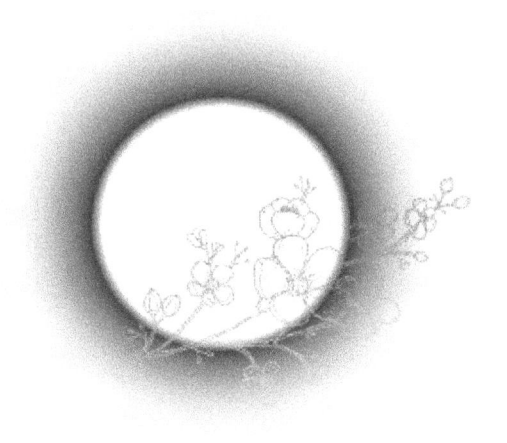

Chapter 11

The new story was hilarious, the picture slides of the kamishibai exquisitely drawn, and the candy man himself as funny and kind as always. He even gave Jin a discount so he could buy Kari the sweets he had promised him. The monks didn't give the children an allowance, of course, the temple didn't have that kind of money, and it was against the Path. Instead, to earn a little pocket money they had to help out in the village, on the fields or in one of the workshops. Jin, however, seldom had the time between punishments and his chores at the temple, so his funding was limited – and gone by the time he had paid for the sweets. Kari would have gladly paid for his own sweets, but the expression on Jin's face – a blissful mixture of joy and pride – when he presented them to him was worth more than any money could ever buy.

They shared the spoils with their friends – Miki, Saya, and Saya's brother, Satoru – before hurrying back to the temple. In the end they cut it close and Jin rushed to the kitchen just in time for his extra chores – Brother Shigeru's punishment of the day.

Kari was left to fill his free time on his own. At first he aimlessly wandered the garden, but with the sun descending behind the hills and the shadows lengthening, the air grew chill. Already shivering, Kari changed course and headed in the direction of the dormitory, passing the corner of the school. A door stood open, light and voices spilling out into the twilit garden. Curious, Kari slowed down. When he recognised the lanky figure of Nobu, he stopped. He was a novice now, but Kari was still wary of the young man. And lately he had noticed he wasn't the only one – even though most people seemed to be inexplicably charmed by the young monk. One person, in particular, didn't seem to be fooled by Nobu's easy smile and charisma: Brother Anri, Nobu's mentor.

As Kari crept quietly closer into the shadows of the building, he could hear the monk's angry voice. "... have to tell you? A devotee of Hôjô seeks neither power nor money. So stop your foolish little power games, will you?"

"Power games?" Nobu snapped. "I'm only demanding what is rightfully mine. You know who my father is. He –"

"He's not your father! He never acknowledged you, Nobu. The moment your mother died he got rid of you. He made it exceedingly clear that he wanted nothing to do with you. So stop torturing yourself by trying to get hold of a birthright you never had in the first place."

Kari could only see Nobu's back, but the rigidity of his posture, his clenched fists, the way he hung his head... He was furious.

"Nobu," Brother Anri said more gently, putting a hand on the other's shoulder. "Come, let it go. You've already made your decision anyway, haven't you? Don't stray from the Path. You know what the consequences would be. As your mentor I implore you, take your vows serious and let go of your past." Nobu didn't answer. Brother Anri sighed and dropped his hand from Nobu's shoulder. "All right. I want you to go to your room and reflect on your behaviour. You need to choose once and for all which path you want to follow. Go."

Kari hastily took a few steps deeper into the shadows. Only a heartbeat later, Nobu bolted from the room. He leapt from the porch, but instead of rushing onwards, he stopped and looked back over his shoulder – straight at Kari, standing silent as stone and hoping the shadows were deep enough to hide him. For one breathless moment they stared at each other, then Nobu turned and was gone. Relieved, Kari retreated the way he had come and took the long way back to the living quarters.

The next day, while Jin once more had to do extra chores, Kari met with Torben in the library. One of his duties was to practice reading and writing with the other boy.

The library's shelves were twice the height of a grown man, built of sturdy, dark wood, and arranged in what at first glance was utter chaos. Exploring the library, however, one soon found out it was on design, a clever way of creating nooks that served as working spaces. They were only big enough for a table and chairs for two. Most of the nooks were permanently reserved by one monk or the other, but there were enough unoccupied ones for the students and novices to use.

Kari – as he did whenever possible - chose his favourite nook. It was nestled between shelves full of folk tales and myths. While Torben got settled and readied his ink and paper, Kari perused the shelves. He decided on a collection of legends from the north. Just as the heavy book fell on the table with a thud, Kari, out of the corner of his eyes, caught movement on the other side of the shelf. Curious as to who was on the other side, he took a peek through the gap where the tome had been. There was another row of books blocking his view. Carefully he tried to push them apart, and found that there was just enough room to create a gap wide enough to see the desk, stood at an angle towards the bookshelf. The seat was empty, but the desk was strewn with papers and stacks of books. A small figure of Hôjô declared this to be a reserved space. Reserved for whom, Kari had no idea, but he knew it wasn't Nobu, who was presently rifling through the papers. As Kari watched, the young novice cast a nervous glance over his shoulder, pulled something out of his sleeve, and put it beneath an open scroll. Then he quickly left.

Puzzled by Nobu's strange behaviour, Kari sat down. Although he wondered what Nobu was up to, he told himself it was none of his business and he'd better keep out of it. Instead he tried to focus on the legend of the Wolf Brothers, to no avail. At last, he put the book aside and got to correcting Torben's squiggly writing.

The pitter-patter of bare feet on the wooden floor announced the arrival of several monks. One of them peered around the shelves, scrutinising the two boys for a moment, before he disappeared again. Kari, his curiosity rekindled, stood up quietly and went back to peer through the gap between the books, holding a finger up to his lips to tell Torben to stay quiet.

From his vantage point, he could only see their backs, but there appeared to be at least five of them, crammed into the small nook. There was the rustle of paper, then a voice Kari didn't recognise demanded, "Whose workspace is this?"

"Mine," a voice Kari recognised as Brother Anri replied. Torben was now standing beside Kari, tugging nervously at the hem of his shirt. Kari patted the boy's arm reassuringly.

"Care to explain this?" the voice from before snapped, holding something up. As the monks in front of Kari shifted slightly, he could see it was a golden seal.

"I..." Brother Anri stammered bewildered. "I don't know how –"

"You don't know how this came to be on your desk?" Brother Anri was cut off. "This is your desk, isn't it? Do you want to make us believe you have no idea how the Head Priest's seal ended up hidden beneath a scroll on your desk? What were you planning to do with it?"

"Nothing! I didn't take it," Brother Anri implored.

"What were you doing with it?"

"I told you, nothing. I didn't --"

But Brother Anri wasn't even given a chance to explain himself. In a babel of voices they demanded to know how he had gotten the seal and what he had planned to do with it. Brother Anri's denials and pleas to listen to him were drowned in a sea of angry accusations. Just then, Kari spotted the brown robe of a novice amongst the sunflower yellow of the monks'. Nobu was standing against the opposite bookshelf, hugging himself and letting his head hang as if he was sad and anxious. But Kari could see the smile on the young man's face.

Anger welled in Kari's chest. Brother Anri's despair, the feeling of betrayal. Nobu's smug smile. The monks' refusal to listen to what the accused, one of their own brothers, had to say for himself. Kari's anger turned into a need for justice. Perhaps it was none of his business, perhaps he ought to stay out of it – he couldn't. Kari didn't know Brother Anri well, but he knew the man didn't deserve this.

"Excuse me!" he called over the din of angry voices, stepping around the corner of the bookshelf. The monks fell silent and turned to him almost immediately, so quick and sudden, it made Kari shudder.

"What is it, child?" the Head Priest asked, not unkindly. It surprised Kari that he was here as well.

"Umm..." Kari fidgeted. He was taking a gamble with the lie he was about to tell. And hoping that Torben, who probably didn't understand what was going on, would play along. "The thing is... um... T-Torben found it lying on the floor... somewhere. And well, I didn't know what it was, but it looked important, so we... we... thought one of the monks would know what to do with it, but there was no-one around, so we just put it on the desk... and forgot about it..." Kari let his voice trail off, not quite looking at the Head Priest or any of the other monks, wringing his hands in the hem of his shirt. Then he abruptly looked around and beckoned to Torben, standing uncertainly at the corner of the shelf. "Is-isn't that right, Torben?" he asked. Torben took a step back when everyone's attention turned on him. He hit his shoulder on the shelf. Looking wide-eyed at Kari, who held his gaze steadily, he nodded his head emphatically. Kari suppressed a relieved sigh.

A moment of stunned silence was followed by the monks talking over each other, each with an urge to voice his opinion. The Head Priest quietened them with a simple gesture.

"Thank you, young men," he said to Kari and Torben. "You did right in coming forward and telling us. It would have been a truly dreadful thing to punish an innocent man." At his words the other monks, with the exception of Nobu, Brother Anri, who looked close to fainting with relief, and Brother Askr, grumbled. "It seems once again that my own clumsiness is to blame. I guess I'm getting old," the Head Priest chuckled. Brother Askr winked at Kari. "Thank you, my children. Now, it's getting late, you should get ready for supper. Go on, now." Though the Head Priest sounded cheerful, it was a clear dismissal. Kari bowed to the man, smiled at Brother Askr and, dragging Torben along, gathered his belongings and left the library.

He left his friend at the door to the dormitory. Contrary to what the Head Priest had claimed, it was still a while till dinner and the sun had yet to set. It was a beautiful day, so Kari decided to take a stroll through the garden to see what he could discover today. That was the best thing about spring, that one could discover something new every day: a new blossom here, fresh green there, a pair of birds nesting in one of the trees, a chubby bumblebee, still clumsy after the long months of winter.

But just as he rounded the corner of a hedge someone fell in step beside him.

"That was a clever trick," Nobu said, his tone conversationally and friendly, but Kari wasn't deceived. "To use the Head Priest's own forgetfulness and your dimwitted friend to back your tale – clever."

"Don't call him that," Kari hissed. It made him furious, the way people treated Torben, only because the boy didn't meet all their expectations. Not even Torben's parents had recognised their son for what he truly was: gentle, empathic, creative. So what if he was a little slow at learning, he was a better person than most.

"Whatever." Nobu suddenly grabbed Kari's arm and pulled him to a stop, leaning down, his face close to Kari's, brown eyes glittering menacingly. "My point is: I don't know what you're playing at, but little children should keep their noses out of things they don't understand. Should I ever catch you messing with my affairs again, I'll make your life a living hell, do you understand?"

Kari should have felt scared perhaps. Intimidated at the very least. But unlike others he had always known Nobu to be false. To see the young man's true face at last was no shock to him. So instead he stared straight back into those hard hateful eyes, that held nothing of the easy smile and kindness that Nobu usually presented to the world, and let the novice know how unimpressed he was.

"How about – just as a little lesson for you – we go and tell the Head Priest that you lied," Nobu continued in a voice dripping with venom.

Kari raised an eyebrow. "Oh? You're sure you want to do that? I mean, if you insist. But then he would want to know how you knew I had lied. So are you actually going to tell him that it was you who stole the seal in order to frame Brother Anri?" Kari exclaimed in mock astonishment. The shock on Nobu's face was a welcome reward.

"What?" Nobu gasped, letting go of Kari's arm, and took a step back. "I don't know what you mean." There was an audible waver in his voice.

"I saw you, you know, when you put the seal on Brother Anri's desk. So you might have noticed that I didn't tell on you either – yet. You better don't make me change my mind."

Nobu's initial shock turned into useless rage. He clenched and unclenched his fists repeatedly, breathing faster than normal. The usual placid handsomeness of his face was distorted with anger and hate. For a moment Kari wondered if he had pushed the young man too far, but then Nobu took a deep, deep breath and visibly pulled himself together.

"What's in this for you?" Nobu hissed. "None of this is any of your business."

"True, and I don't care about what you do. But Brother Anri hasn't done anything wrong. He doesn't deserve the harsh punishment that would have awaited him, just because you have a quarrel with him."

"Hmm?" Nobu took another step back. "Well, let's hope you won't regret your righteousness one day." And with that he turned around and left the way they had come, leaving Kari alone in the suddenly chilly spring garden.

Someone was shaking Kari's shoulder. He slowly cracked his eyes open. In the week light that filtered in through the high windows he could just make out the silhouette of Jin.

"What is it?" Kari mumbled sleepily.

"Come," Jin whispered, "let's go look for shooting-stars."

Kari sat up and rubbed the sleep from his eyes. The night before their stargazing plans had been literally blown away by a storm, today the sky was clear. They tiptoed out of the dormitory, careful not to accidentally step on any of the other boys. It wasn't that uncommon for someone to leave the room in the middle of the night, usually in search of a cup of water or to visit the outhouse. But getting out into the courtyard was trickier, for not only did they have to pass several other rooms, the entrance door creaked. However, Kari and Jin had done this a hundred times before. Within minutes they had slipped through the door, out into the wide, open courtyard. They headed for the great stone lion, greeted their stony friend, and sat down on its pedestal. It was their favourite stargazing spot, for here, in the middle of the empty courtyard, the sky opened up to them with nothing to mar their view. A sea of stars. A myriad of tiny twinkling lights. The moon was showing only half her face, but she was no less beautiful. And there – flashes of light, here and gone within the blink of an eye, adding movement to the stillness of the stars.

The night still held a breath of winter, and soon Kari was shivering, hugging himself against the chill. Noticing, Jin scooted closer and put his arms around his friend. Kari huddled close.

"This is nice," Jin sighed. "Sometimes I wish it were only you and me – for ever."

"Wouldn't you miss Miki and Brother Askr – and Saya?"

"Hmm... not as long as I have you."

"Do you mean it?" Kari turned his head to look into his friend's face, although the darkness hid his expression.

"I do. Kari, let's be together always, you and me. I don't mean just now, I mean when we are old enough to leave the temple. Let's go and live together somewhere. In the capital. Or we could travel, or – wait! You don't plan on staying here and joining the Brotherhood, do you?"

The mixture of disgust and despair in Jin's voice made Kari laugh. "No," he chuckled.

"Oh, good," Jin sighed in relief. "So let's stay together, you and me. It doesn't matter what we'll be doing or where we will go, as long as we are together."

"Like Miki's uncles?"

Jin hesitated before he asked in a small voice: "Would that be bad? Is that something you don't want?"

But Kari shook his head. "No, I'd... I'd like that." He could feel his face heating. If he was being honest with himself, thinking about Miki's uncles always made him imagine himself and Jin in their stead. He liked the idea of them sharing a home, being a real family together.

Even in the darkness Jin's smile was dazzling. But the smile vanished too soon. Before Kari could ask what was wrong, Jin took a deep breath as if to steel himself, leaned forward – and pressed his lips against Kari's.

The cold vanished from Kari's bones and heat rushed through him as if he drank it from Jin's lips. His heart began to race; it felt as if there were butterflies trapped in his belly, fluttering wildly.

The kiss lasted a mere second – too long, too short, he couldn't say – and yet it left him breathless. They stared at each other wide-eyed, uncertain, overwhelmed, until a smile tugged first at the lips of one boy, then the other's. It was a silent promise. An oath, witnessed only by the Goddess and Her silent stars.

A few days later Brother Anri suddenly left the temple. no-one gave an explanation or a reason, Kari never found out why. He simply walked out the door with a pack over his shoulder. Went down the thousand stone steps. And never came back.

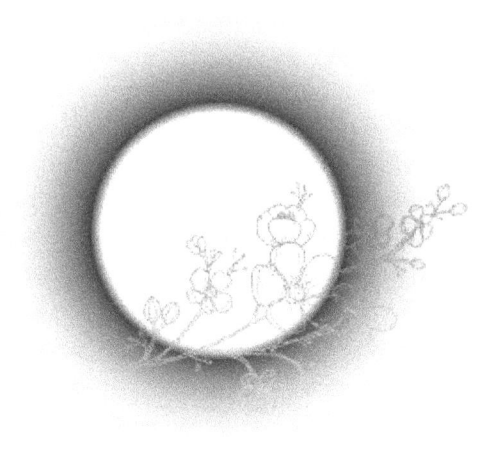

Chapter 12

It began with an innocent kiss. A promise between friends. Brothers. But as the years passed and the boys grew from child to adolescent new emotions, new and strange desires, intertwined with the bond between them. Something that hadn't been there before blossomed between them. Something that knew no reason, something fierce and fearless. And with it came a reckless curiosity about the forbidden, an urge to explore and discover. And to find wonder in a touch. To marvel at the beauty of the other. The surprise of unexpected pleasure and reactions even more unexpected.

Deep in the woods behind the temple, far from the monks and the village, they had found a private refuge in the form of an old abandoned hut. It was a place to hide away from the world, a place where no-one existed but them.

A single beam of sunlight fell through the broken roof. A pattern of light and shadow dappled their tangled bodies. The song of birds joined the music of Jin's heartbeat as Kari listened to it, his head on his friend's chest. He had never felt so content in his life. He wished they could remain like this forever. Jin's fingers drew lazy swirls on Kari's back. A gentle breeze dried the sweat on their skin.

Eventually Kari shifted, put his arms across Jin's chest, and rested his chin on his forearm. His curiosity had finally caught up with him. "How did you know that?"

Jin's eyes drifted to the roof above them, a faint pinkish hue colouring his cheeks. "Know what?"

"You know... what we just did... that."

"I didn't. I just thought... perhaps? I was experimenting." Jin was a terrible liar.

"Tell me," Kari pestered, and Jin mumbled something incoherent. "What?"

"Masao-tan, all right? Masao-tan kind of... well... I was curious, all right. I asked him."

"Asked him?" Kari asked, puzzled. He had a pretty good idea exactly what that conversation had been about, but he enjoyed Jin, blushing redder by the second, squirming beneath him.

"You know... I asked him to... t-tell me how to... um... make you feel r-really g-g-good..." Jin's face was now beet red and he kept his gaze fixed on the roof. Kari had to suppress his laughter. "Well." Jin cleared his throat. "It was... embarrassing... like really embarrassing. But Masao-tan – he tried to explain, and then he gave me books to read."

"Books?"

"You know... *that kind of* books... ah! Can we please stop talking about this now?" Jin whined. Kari could suppress his laughter no longer. And although Jin tried to look offended he was soon laughing, too.

Amongst a flood of giggles, tickle attacks, and rolling around on their makeshift bed so much they ended up tangled in the sheets, their lips found each other, again, and again, sweet and gentle, hungry and demanding. Until at last the lay breathless, gazing at each other, eyes reflecting affection – a perfect mirror.

"Kari," Jin said softly, "let's just leave?"

"Leave? What do you mean?"

"I mean, we should leave the temple, go somewhere, anywhere. I dunno... let's go to the capital."

"Run away, you mean."

Jin sighed, rolled onto his back, eyes once again fastened on the straw thatched roof. It wasn't the first time they had this conversation. During the last months Jin had grown more and more restless. The closer and more intimate their relationship had become the more often Jin had suggested running away together. At first Kari hadn't taken him seriously. Until the weather had warmed and spring had arrived, and with it Jin had grown more and more insistent.

Indulging in their relationship was a risk, a very big risk, but Kari knew they'd have an equally hard time should they leave the temple before it was their time to leave.

"Jin, it's only two years until –"

"That's an eternity," Jin protested. "Do you really want to keep sneaking around like this, always afraid someone might catch us? For two more years? Because I don't. I want to be with you, really be with you, let the world know that I love you. Like Miki's uncles. Like everyone else who's not stuck in this bloody temple with its bigoted Brotherhood and stupid rules."

„Jin, be reasonable," Kari pleaded. "We would have no money, no shelter, no food – and no experience of the world outside this village. How would we survive?"

"We'd have us," Jin insisted stubbornly.

Kari sighed. He hated being the voice of reason, but Jin was too reckless, too stubborn. Kari didn't feel any less caged, trapped in a cosmos he didn't belong in, never had, and slowly suffocating. But he wasn't going to be stupid about it. The world was a vast and harsh place if you couldn't take care of yourself. Abiding by the Brotherhood's rules for a foreseeable period of time wasn't that bad compared to what situation they might find themselves in if they ran away now with nothing but the clothes on their backs. When they turned eighteen the monks would provide them with enough to start a new life – not a luxurious one, but it would be enough, so they wouldn't have to starve for a while.

And one thing Jin always seemed to forget: Brother Askr was like a father to them. Even though it was a long time ago now that they had been the old monk's responsibility, they still had a special bond. Brother Askr often turned a blind eye to a little bit of mischief, secretly gave them sweets, and personally took care of them whenever they were ill. And he had never looked at Kari with suspicion, scrutinising his every action only because he was Ethereal, like many of the others did. It would break Brother Askr's heart if they ran away like this.

"We could ask one of the travelling salesmen to let us tag along for a while, learn from them, perhaps even earn some money." Jin didn't seem inclined to abandon the idea yet. "Or we can earn money in the village and buy what we need little by little, hide it away here."

"To earn enough money and get all we needed would take us at least two years, so we can just as well wait till then," Kari countered. He knew Jin was out of arguments, when he saw his friend's crestfallen expression. He didn't like to do it, but Kari decided to smother the debate once and for all. "Besides, you know that if we run away we can never ever come back. No matter how bad things might be for us, we'd be refused help at any Temple of Hôjô. We would never be able to see any of our friends again, or Brother Askr... it would break his heart, you know that."

Jin threw his arms across his eyes and growled in frustration. Of course he knew, he just liked to forget about it. Although Jin liked to pretend that he didn't care for Brother Askr, Kari knew that he, like Kari, saw a father in the old man. Running away would mean losing everything, including the only father either of them had ever known. The Path of Hôjô wasn't quite as charitable as the Brotherhood would like the world to believe, nor was it forgiving. And for an orphan to run away was an irremissible act of ingratitude towards the god's mercy and generosity.

"But you are months younger than me," Jin grumbled. "What do you expect me to do? Sit around in the village waiting for you?"

"We could talk to the monks. I'm sure Brother Askr would rather we left the temple together. I am sure he'd help us convince the High Priest to let me go with you a few months earlier."

Jin made some non-committal and entirely unconvinced sound. Kari slapped his friend's thigh. He loved Jin with every fibre of his being, but the other boy's pigheadedness regularly drove him mad.

"Stop pouting. You know I'm right!" he snapped. In answer, Jin suddenly rolled right on top of him, his mouth hungrily claiming Kari's, stifling any protest.

"Fine, I'll stop pouting," Jin whispered against Kari's lips. And just like that, their debate seemed forgotten, blown away by a storm of passion.

A tiny voice in Kari's head, feeble and half-hearted, warned him that they had already spent too much of the afternoon in their own little world, and soon someone might notice their absence. But sensation expelled everything but Jin's touch from his mind, the feeling of Jin's skin against his own, Jin's lips on his, trailing down the side of his neck, across his chest... And the tiny voice was lost in the roar of the storm.

The more Kari and Jin had begun to spend their time alone together, the more they had drifted apart from their friends. Kari knew he should feel sad about it, but the truth was, he wasn't. Miki – out of all of them – was the only one Kari even considered a friend. Saya, her brother Satoru, and the others – they might have been Jin's friends, but he knew they weren't his. The monks, the village people, the other children, even after all those years, had never fully accepted him. Kari was Ethereal, and their prejudices against the god blessed were too ingrained in their minds. He was tired of pretending to be obedient, demur, timid. It was exhausting. Terribly, terribly exhausting.

It was one thing to try and be the person Jin needed him to be. After all, Kari loved Jin, so he wanted to be that person – for Jin. When he had been younger he he had thought nothing of being what people wanted him to be, what they wanted to see. To pretend. To put on a mask. Now Kari saw the error in it. For the only time he could ever just be himself, no pretence, the only time he could loosen the iron grip on his mind, his thoughts, his heart, was when he was alone. It took a greater toll on him than he had thought possible. What was even worse was that no matter how much he wanted to be Jin's Kari, losing himself to that mask frightened him. He wasn't sure he even liked 'Kari'.

And so, Kari had eventually begun to seek solitude, to relax and to regain his strength. It wasn't too difficult. He was quick and efficient in doing his chores and unlike Jin he didn't get punished on a regular basis. Kari had time to spare. It was like balm for his soul, his mind.

Until he began to notice that many of Jin's errands led the boy down into the village. And clearly he didn't just run his errands, for he always took his sweet time coming back.

A little bit of spying on him – Kari wasn't proud of it – quickly revealed that Jin retained a much better relationship with their old friends than Kari had known. It felt like a physical blow, to realise that while Kari's entire world revolved around Jin, it didn't seem to be the same for Jin. Still, perhaps it wouldn't have hurt so much if it hadn't been for Saya. Kari had always known they were rivals for Jin's affection, but in the last year Saya had finally dropped all pretence of being Kari's friend. She had made it quite clear she didn't like him. The only one who didn't seem to know this for a fact was Jin. Worse, he even insisted Kari was only imagining Saya's animosity. It had become a sore point between them.

A few days after their latest debate about running away from the temple, Kari was on his way back from one of his walks, when he saw Jin and Saya alone at the foot of the temple stair. The sight stopped him dead in his tracks. Although Kari was too far away and they spoke too quietly for him to make out what they were saying, the way they behaved towards each other infuriated him: standing far too close to each other for a simple conversation. Laughing flirtatiously. Casually touching each other. Saya, coyly brushing a lock of hair behind her ear, her eyes downcast, a pretty blush on her cheeks. Jin, leaning down, whispering into her ear. It made her laugh and playfully smack his arm. Then she suddenly stood on the tip of her toes – and kissed Jin.

Fury, bright and hot and unbridled, rushed through Kari, white noise filled his ears. He clenched his fists so tightly his fingernails cut into his palms. His heart was hammering against his rib cage. A voice inside his head screamed at him to move, to tear Saya away from Jin, to scratch her eyes out, to make it clear to her once and for all what would happen if she ever so much as looked in Jin's direction again. But Kari didn't move; he stood rooted to the spot. Watched as Saya quickly turned, a smile on her pretty face, and hurried down the path towards the village. Watched as Jin stood staring after her for a while longer before he, too, turned and began to climb the many stone steps, a light spring in his step.

Kari took a deep breath. And another. And another, forcing air into his lungs, forcing his heart to calm down. Forcing the fury to subside. He told himself that Jin would never betray him – never. He could trust Jin, like he always had, like he always would. But Kari couldn't get the picture of Saya kissing Jin out of his mind. What if Jin decided he didn't want to wait for Kari to agree to running away together anymore? What if Jin decided he didn't want Kari after all? No no no – Jin wouldn't do that to him. He could be an idiot sometimes, not thinking about what he was doing and the consequences of his actions, but he would never betray Kari.

At last, his heart calmed down, his breathing came easier, and Kari once more had a grip on his anger, so he slowly began the tedious ascend to the temple.

He was dragging his feet so much he was almost late for supper. It wasn't lost on Jin, and neither was his bad mood. After supper Jin drew his friend aside. "What's wrong?"

"Nothing." Kari evaded Jin's searching look and quickly stepped through the door and out into the small pleasure garden. Jin followed him.

"Something must be. First, you were almost late for supper, which is not like you. Second, you are in a terrible mood – and that's not like you either."

What do you know what's like me? Kari bit his tongue. His anger hadn't fully abated yet, it was dangerous not to keep it in check, but he was tired of never being able to speak his mind, of always being the understanding one, the placid one, the kind one. And for once he had enough.

"So what? I'm not allowed to be in a bad mood?" he snapped before he even realised what he was doing. "I'm only allowed to be nice and well-behaved, and never complain? What? You can do whatever you want and I have to smile and accept it. Well, what if I don't? What if I complain, or don't smile? You won't like me anymore then, is that it?" Kari fell silent, shocked at his own outburst. He hadn't meant to say any of those things, he was ruining everything. He didn't need to see Jin's face to know his friend was at least as shocked as Kari was. Was that it? The moment Kari had dreaded all his life, when he made a stupid mistake and Jin would realise Kari was not the person he had thought him to be – not the person Jin said he loved. He couldn't lose Jin, but... Kari didn't know how to save the situation, so instead he let his instinct take over. He bolted.

He didn't get far before Jin caught up to him, grabbing his arm and pulling him to a stop.

"Kari, wait! I'm sorry, that's not what I meant," Jin said, his voice low but urgent. "You know I love you, I'll always love you. Of course you are allowed to be in a bad mood, that doesn't mean I'd stop loving you."

"Doesn't it?" Kari's voice wavered.

"Of course not," Jin insisted with all that terrible sincerity and honesty that made Kari believe and forgive anything. "Kari, tell me what's wrong."

"I saw you and Saya."

"You saw... You mean in the village? You were in the village? Why didn't you come join us?"

"No, not in the village. Down at the foot of the stairs. And I don't think I would have been welcome to join you." Kari heard the sharp bite in his voice but he couldn't help it, he had his hands full, reigning in his anger as it was. Jin flinched from the edge in Kari's voice, but instead of guilty he looked confused.

"Why wouldn't you have been?"

"You two seemed rather busy – flirting."

"Oh." Jin had the audacity to smile then, indulgently, infuriatingly. "Kari that –"

"No," Kari cut him off. "Don't you dare. I saw you. It wasn't just Saya, it was you, Jin, you kept encouraging her, touching her, whispering in her ear. I saw how much you enjoyed it, her flirting... and... her kissing you." Jin's smile faltered. There it was at last: the guilt. Kari's anger screamed inside him, demanded him to be merciless, to punish Jin, to hurt him. But he would only end up hurting himself. At that moment, however, Kari didn't care. He was so tired, the edges of his soul felt flayed, his heart felt leaden. Day after day after day wearing a mask, acting, being whatever, whoever he was required to be. People only saw what they wanted to see, Jin wasn't any different. If Kari didn't love the other boy so much, if Kari could imagine a life without Jin, would it be easier? Would he feel less like a ghost? Would anyone actually see him? For once someone else needed to hurt like he did.

"Just be honest, Jin," Kari continued, harsh and cold. "You'd rather be with Saya, wouldn't you. I can't really fault you. She is pretty and clever, and it would be so much easier being with her. So fine, do as you wish, I've had enough of her glaring and snapping at me, and watching you flirt. Go and be happy with her!"

Kari had not expected the glitter of tears in Jin's eyes. Neither had he expected how rapidly the shock that was so plainly on Jin's face twisted and turned into anger. He had clearly miscalculated, blinded by his own rage. An angry Jin was a force of nature, rare, and all the more terrifying for it. Kari cursed inwardly. Now he really had done it, he had destroyed the best thing in his life, and he only had himself to blame. He slowly backed away from Jin, but the other boy was taller and considerably stronger. He grabbed Kari's arms hard enough to bruise.

"What the hell, Kari," Jin hissed. "How can you say that, how can you even think... I... what the hell? By the gods, Kari, do you have any idea how much I love you?"

Heart pounding in his chest, Kari snarled, "Do you? Then why do you have to keep flirting with Saya every opportunity you get? You know she has set her eyes on you from the day she first met you, and you keep encouraging her. You enjoy it."

"All right, fine, perhaps I do enjoy it. It's flattering. But it doesn't mean anything."

"It does to her! And how long until you realise that you prefer her."

"That won't ever happen! There isn't anyone in this world I could ever love more than I love you, Kari. Believe me. Have I ever lied to? I haven't, right? Listen, I'm sorry about that thing with Saya, and I promise, I really really promise that I won't do it again and that I will make it clear to her that I'm not interested. All right?" Jin's anger had evaporated as quickly as it had come, a mere shadow, a glimpse of what it could be, without the teeth to bite. A single tear rolled down his cheek, catching the last of the day's light. The sight of it doused the heat of Kari's rage. "Please," Jin pleaded, "forgive me, all right?" And there it was, that vulnerability, that need to be needed, to not be alone, abandoned. Kari remembered it well, he had seen it in the boy's eyes that very first day. He hadn't had the words for what he saw and what he felt then. He did now.

Not trusting his voice, Kari nodded. The change in Jin was immediate: relief, joy, an abundance of affection. He leaned forward, his lips close to Kari's ear. His words, a soft whisper, rang with emotion loud enough to shatter walls.

"I love you so so much, my Kari." And Kari believed every word.

After their confrontation Jin distanced himself from Saya. He was still friendly with her, occasionally complimenting her cleverness in class, other than that, he put up a wall between them. As a result Saya did not only storm off after class on more than one occasion, she became outright hostile towards

Kari, glowering at him, snapping at him, huffing irritatedly whenever Kari answered a question in class, clicking her tongue when he received a "Well done" from their teachers. Kari tried to excuse her behaviour, to feel bad for her, tried to imagine how he would have reacted, had Jin chosen Saya. It was a futile attempt. If there was one thing in this world Kari could not imagine, it was Jin not being with him, no matter what he had said when he was angry. They were meant to be together. Perhaps Saya had always known so, too, but chosen not to believe it. As much as Kari tried to sympathise with her, he could not.

Instead, however, he was vexed all the time, to a point where he not only lost his patience more than once with Torben – apologising profusely to the boy afterwards – but also got into heated arguments with Jin about running away from the temple. In the time he spent alone Kari began to worry that he might end up driving Jin away.

"Idiot!" Kari growled at his reflection. He was sitting on the bank of a brook running down the hill, and staring into its crystal clear water. Why was it that after so many years of wearing the persona of 'Kari' with ease, it now became more and more of a burden? It didn't feel natural anymore, but like a cage in which he was trapped. He didn't really believe Jin would leave him over a few arguments or because they had a different opinion, but what if Jin found out Kari wasn't who Jin wanted, needed him to be?

There was a storm brewing inside Kari. He firmly walled it in. It was an almost ridiculous attempt at stifling it. For every time he argued with Jin, every time Saya glowered at him or made cow eyes at Jin, Kari felt his control slip.

Perhaps Jin was right after all, perhaps they should leave now and damn the consequences. But Kari was certain they would only doom themselves. They knew nothing about the world, they had no money, they didn't know hardship. There was also the strong sense of ungratefulness the thought of running away brought with it – if not towards Hôjô or the other monks then at least towards Brother Askr.

Two years weren't that long a time – but Jin was right, it felt like an eternity.

Kari angrily rubbed a hand through his hair. He needed to blow off some steam, that was all. Something to get rid of the restless energy, the frustration. He needed something he could put his mind to instead of fretting about Jin and Saya and all the little things that kept him up at night. Perhaps Brother Askr could use his help tending the herb garden and preparing medicine. In fact, Suzu realised with a jolt as if he'd been hit by lightning, he ought to ask Brother Askr to teach him all about herbs and making medicine. This way, by the time he and Jin were ready to go out into the world, Kari would have the means to earn money.

With new determination, Kari sprang to his feet and hurried back up the hill. But his enthusiasm was short-lived. The moment he entered the gardens, he ran straight into Jin, laughing and chattering with Nobu of all people.

"... doesn't he though?" Jin laughed. He turned around at Kari's approach, his face alight with merriment. Kari hadn't seen him like this in a long time. He felt a stab of jealousy and anger at the fact that Nobu had been the one to make Jin laugh like this. "Oh hey, Kari. Where have you been?"

"On a walk," Kari replied flatly. An awkward silence descended between the three of them.

Until Nobu cleared his throat and announced, "Well, I have to get back to my studies. See you two at supper." And just like that, the young monk left.

"Didn't know you were so friendly with Nobu," Kari said, wincing at the petulant tone in his voice. Jin didn't seem to notice, he just smiled and nodded.

"He's really nice. We have been talking a lot lately. He knows a lot of stuff. You should join us some time, I'm sure you'd find him interesting. He's not as stuffy as the other monks."

"I don't like him," Kari blurted, and could have bit his tongue for it.

Jin stared at him in shock. "You don't like him? You like everybody."

"Well obviously not," Kari snapped. He had to get out of this conversation and away before he said or did something he would end up regretting. Desperately he tried to rein in the storm of anger that seemed to be raging inside him all the time these days.

"Is something wrong? You're being weird."

Kari shook his head. "I... I'm just tired a-and cranky... I guess." Jin's expression softened. He threw an arm around Kari's shoulders and drew him closer.

"I guess you really didn't get much sleep last night. That storm was horrible." Kari made an agreeable sound. It wasn't really true. After Jin had pulled Kari's futon close and put his arm around him, Kari had listened to his friend's even breathing and steady heartbeat and soon fallen asleep. No matter how bad a storm was, as long as he had Jin with him, Kari felt safe.

"You are out on walks a lot lately." Kari could hear the question hidden beneath the remark. He laid his head on Jin's shoulder. It was as close as they could allow themselves to be here under the watchful eyes of the monks. Perhaps even this was too much, but everyone knew the two boys were very close, as close as brothers, so they usually turned a blind eye to anything that wasn't a clear transgression.

"I just have a lot to think about."

"For example?"

"For example..." Kari couldn't tell Jin that he was spending a lot of his quiet contemplations raging inwardly – against Saya, about Jin being flirty – or fretting that one day soon his carefully construed persona would crumble like a sandcastle and Kari would end up alone and hated. "I've been thinking, I should ask Brother Askr to teach me about medicine."

"Do you want to be an apothecary?"

"Well, why not? Or a medicine seller. Think about it, we could travel the entire empire – and it's a sure way to earn money anywhere."

A grin spread across Jin's face, his dark eyes sparkling. "And what would I be doing?"

"I'm sure we'll find something. And just in case... you could be my bodyguard," Kari teased with a shrug of one shoulder. He was delighted to hear Jin chuckle.

"I can see that you need one – to protect you from thunderstorms," Jin laughed. Then he leaned in and whispered, "And because you are too damn pretty."

Kari blushed, a pleasant shiver running through him. He was aware of his looks, always had been. It was one of the traits of the Ethereal, the gift of beauty – and also one of the reasons there were so many ridiculous prejudices about them. Shigeru had used to say it was because people were jealous. To Kari his beauty was meaningless, as were the compliments he received occasionally. He didn't care about any of it – unless it was Jin who complimented him.

Jin had a quick look around the garden, then suddenly pulled Kari even closer and kissed him. It was a chaste kiss, as fleeting as the brush of butterfly wings, but it left Kari breathless nonetheless. He wished with all his heart that Jin's love would never wane.

Brother Askr was delighted to take Kari under his wings and teach him all he knew about herbs and how to make medicine out of them.

Kari quickly found that he enjoyed working with the old man. He loved the warm fragrance of the herbs, and was fascinated by how a dangerously poisonous weed, if treated correctly and administered in small doses, could save a life.

By staying so much at the temple instead of wandering around, Kari soon began to notice a lot of things he hadn't before – mainly about the relationships between the temple's inhabitants. There were some rather unexpected friendships as well as animosities, and to his delight, Kari discovered that Jin and he might not be the only ones with a secret. Two of the older monks were never far from each other. Kari recognised the way they looked at each other, the casual touches that lingered just a bit too long. He wondered if they had hidden the true nature of their relationship all their lives, or if theirs was a love in accordance with the strictness of the Path.

Apart from exciting, interesting, and curious discoveries, however, Kari only now noticed just how much time Jin spent with Nobu and how well they seemed to get along. Somehow it had never occurred to him that Jin could enjoy the company of the novice, nor did he understand why he would. Did Jin not see the falseness behind Nobu's pleasant mien? The kindness that bristled with thorns? The presumptuousness that left a bitter taste in Kari's mouth every time he had to listen to the young man. The assumption of being superior that crackled like static in the air around Nobu.

Seeing Jin in deep conversation with him, laughing together, felt like a punch in the gut. Kari soon couldn't shake the feeling that something bad was about to happen. He felt taut, his every nerve raw. Kari's entire life was built around Jin, his very being was. What if Nobu took it all away?

Kari's anxiety didn't stay unnoticed for long. He was distracted and irritable, dark shadows beneath his eyes showed his lack of sleep; he made mistakes, even dropped an expensive ceremonial tea cup. Worried, Brother Askr sent him to the infirmary and made him drink herbal concoctions that were meant to cleanse his blood. In the end, Kari slipped away and hid in their little hut in the woods.

It was there that Jin found him an hour later. "Kari, what is it?" Jin asked, gently pushing a lock of hair behind Kari's ear. "Everybody's worried about you. You're going to give poor Brother Askr a heart attack. And *I* am worried."

"Sorry," Kari mumbled.

"You don't need to apologise, just tell me what's going on."

Kari took a deep breath. "Do you have enough of me?" he blurted before the courage to do so left him.

"What?"

Kari looked up into his friend's anxious face, dark eyes wide and worried. Tears blurred Kari's vision, the tension of the last weeks finally broke, and as if from a wound that had been lanced, all his anxiety and fears poured out of him. "You're going to leave me, aren't you? You're tired of me, and rather want to have other friends, be with some one else... I don't know... N-Nobu or Saya. I know I'm holding you back, and... and –"

"Kari, stop!" Jin cupped Kari's face between his hands, their gazes locked. A deep frown drew Jin's brows together. "What in the world made you think I'd ever tire of you? Kari! I love you."

Kari closed his eyes. Tears slipped from beneath his lashes. Those words, those wonderful words – weren't they supposed to be like balm to a wounded heart? If only Kari could believe them, could trust them. But doubt had its iron claws buried deep inside his heart. Jin seemed to notice Kari's insecurity. He wrapped his arms around the smaller boy and held Kari as tightly as he could.

"Kari, listen to me," he said quietly. "I know lately it seems like we were drifting apart, and I know you don't like me being friends with Nobu. But I promise you, I'll never leave you. Never. I don't have the words to tell you how much I love you, and perhaps I'm not good at showing it. I'm sorry I pressured you into running away from here. I've been too rash and inconsiderate. But look, I haven't distanced myself from you because I don't want to be with you anymore. By the gods, Kari, do you have any idea how hard it is for me to do this? Some of the monks are suspicious about us, I'm trying to protect you. Do you understand?" Kari was taken aback. Who were those monks? He had never noticed anything, no sidelong glances nor whispered words besides the usual he had gotten all his time at the temple. But why would Jin make this up? It did explain why he had been so insistent they'd run away, and his behaviour lately. So Kari slowly nodded his head against Jin's shoulder. "All right. Please Kari, don't ever forget just how much I love you. Everything I do, I do for you, so that we can be together. I swear."

Gently, Jin pulled away from Kari, so he could look at him. Tears still glittered in Kari's emerald green eyes. "Kari, you trust me, don't you?"

In the dim light Jin's eyes were as black as a starless night, but in their infinite depth Kari saw nothing but the love he was promised. In the silence in their little hut, deep in the woods behind the temple, those words, spoken softly, rang with unshakable truth. Kari wanted to believe them, he wanted to believe the boy he loved, the boy who was his entire world, who held his fragile heart in his strong hands.

"I trust you," Kari whispered, and with each syllable the claws of doubt retreated and released him.

Jin smiled his brilliant, captivating smile before his lips met Kari's, burning away the last of Kari's fears. Kisses so full of promises.

Three days later Kari's world came crashing down on him.

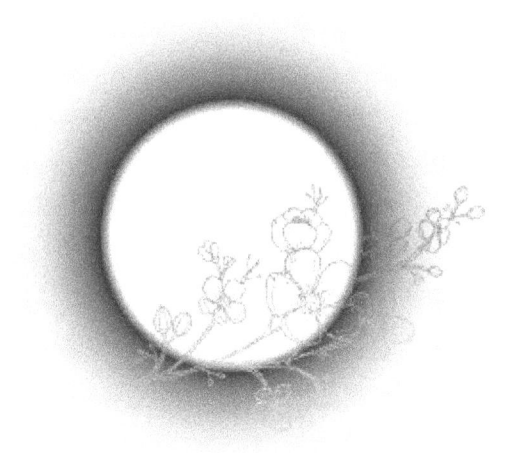

Chapter 13

Since that afternoon, only three days ago, Jin had been acting strange. Not in ways most people would notice, but Kari did. They had hardly spoken all day, and now, lying side by side in the dormitory, Kari was staring at the back of his friend in the dark, wide awake and not sure what he ought to do. There was an awkwardness between them that had never existed before, a hesitancy.

Just when Kari had finally made up his mind and was about to reach out for his friend's shoulder, Jin suddenly stood up from his futon. For a moment he only stood there, looking down at Kari. It was too dark for him to notice Kari was awake. Kari's heart was racing. Something was wrong, he could feel it.

After a while Jin turned and carefully made his way between the other sleeping boys to the door and left the room.

Kari didn't hesitate, scrambling to follow, nearly tripping over some of the other orphans.

In the courtyard, beneath a sky strewn with stars, he finally caught up with Jin. The moon was already past her zenith – a silver sickle in the western sky. As Kari approached Jin turned to him. Although there was hardly any more light to see by than in the dormitory, Kari could see his friend's smile. Relief flooded through him; he hadn't been sure about Jin's reaction. But there he was, smiling and holding out his hand – and Kari was glad to take it.

They crossed the yard to the statue of the giant lion guardian, where they had spent so many sleepless nights gazing at the stars, only the two of them in their own little world. It was a mild night despite the crispness that still lingered in the air. As they settled at the guardian's feet Jin drew Kari close and kissed him. It was a tender, lingering kiss that filled Kari with a strange sadness.

"You don't think the guardian is going to strike us down, doing this right in front of him?" Kari whispered against Jin's lips, desperate to chase those strange feelings away.

"I don't think he cares as much as the monks do."

Kari nestled into Jin's arms, his head on the other boy's shoulder. "Is something wrong, Jin? You were acting strange these last few days."

"Was I? It's nothing... Brother Shige was yelling at me over stupid little things again, and... I don't know. I'm just being moody, don't think too much of it."

"I see... so you came out here to be alone... and I ruined it."

"Nonsense," Jin chuckled. "I was hoping you'd follow me."

"Really?"

"Really."

They fell silent then and just sat there, at the feet of the stone guardian, beneath a star-strewn sky, holding each other tight. For how long, Kari didn't know, but he wished the night would never end.

Eventually, however, Jin reached into the darkness beside the stone pedestal and miraculously brought forth a bamboo flask.

"Where did you get that?"

"I put it there earlier this evening," Jin replied with a wink and Kari laughed.

"So you had this all planned out, hm?"

"Guilty as charged." Jin opened the flask and offered it to Kari. "Here, it's Brother Hanjo's sacred strawberry wine."

Kari's eyes widened in surprise. "How...? Brother Hanjo guards that with his life."

"I have my ways," Jin said mysteriously, his grin growing a little wider. Kari accepted the flask and took a sip. The sweetness of wild strawberries washed over his tongue, a hint of bitterness hidden beneath the burn of the alcohol.

"Go on," Jin encouraged him. "You can drink as much as you like, I got it for you." Kari, sharing the monk's fondness of it, didn't need to be told twice. He took a couple of swigs before handing the flask back. Licking his lips, Kari wondered at the strange underlying bitterness. It hadn't been there when he had drunk the wine last. Perhaps the wine was too old already. Before he could mention it, however, Jin pulled him back into his arms, stroking his hair, and whispered into his ear.

"One day, we will have our own little house – in the capital or wherever you want. Just the two of us. And each night before we go to bed –" Kari suddenly felt like a weight had settled on him, his eyelids grew heavy – "we will sit together like this, looking up at the stars, the moon smiling down on us." Sleep was dragging him under, but he didn't want to sleep, he wanted to be here with Jin, listening to him talk about their future. "We could..." Jin's voice became the susurrus of the wind, the gurgling of a brook, words flowing into each other, undistinguishable. He could feel Jin's fingers combing through his hair, felt the boy's warmth like a blanket around him. He tried to keep his eyes open, to stay in the here and now with his friend, his lover. He tried –

And then he knew no more.

Kari awoke to a cacophony of bird voices. A single beam of light fell across his face. He squinted, shading his eyes with his arm. The ceiling was all wrong. It wasn't the panelled ceiling of the dormitories, it was higher, wooden beams and straw thatching. And yet it was oddly familiar. Kari rubbed his eyes. The last tendrils of sleep were leaving him only slowly, but his mind cleared enough for him to recognise his surroundings: He was in their hut.

Surprised Kari sat up too quickly. His vision spun and his head was pounding dreadfully. It took a moment and several deep breaths for the dizziness to recede and the pain to lessen enough that he didn't fear his head would burst.

Kari carefully opened his eyes again and took a look around. He was alone, no sign of Jin. He tried to remember how he had gotten here and failed. All he could recall of the night before was that he had been stargazing with Jin. Had they come here

Stumbling back to his feet, he turned to the monks, tears streaming down his face, shaking like leaves in a storm.

"P-please, I d-don't understand," he sobbed. "Why are you doing this? Please!"

"You need to ask, filthy scum?" one of them sneered. The disgust in his eyes left Kari speechless. A moment later they slammed the door shut and threw the lock, its click unreasonably loud, giving a sense of finality.

Panicking, Kari threw himself at the door, banging his fists against the thick wood, screaming for someone, anyone, to let him out. To explain what was going on. no-one came. Eventually Kari gave up. He curled in on himself, arms tight around his legs, forehead pressed against his knees. Quietly, almost soundlessly he cried. He was scared, hurt, and confused. He couldn't remember what had happened after he had followed Jin outside. They had sat beneath the stone guardian, watching the stars. How had Kari gotten to the hut? Why had he been alone? Where was Jin? Kari needed answers. He needed Jin, he needed his friend by his side, to hold him, to tell him everything was going to be all right. The need to be with Jin at that moment was so strong it became a physical ache, strong enough to tear his heart in two.

Hours passed – and no-one came to him. Too exhausted from crying and being afraid, Kari lay one the stone floor, cold and miserable, and stared unseeingly at the ceiling. There wasn't much in the room to look at anyway: an old thin futon, a small table, a single chair. The small rectangular windows, set too high for Kari to reach, were barred, the heavy door had no handle on this side. The little sunlight that made it through the windows created patterns of light and shadow but couldn't chase away the gloom. The floor was so cold Kari's limbs went numb after a while, but he didn't have the energy to get up.

It must have been long past noon, when the door finally opened and Brother Askr entered. Kari scrambled to his feet. The old monk stood in the door for a moment longer, then went to the table and set down a tray, bearing a pitcher of water and a single slice of bread. A young monk closed the door after him.

"Brother Askr, I..." Kari began, his voice scratchy. The sight of the pitcher reminded him how parched he was, he hadn't had anything to drink since... since last night? He didn't dare reach for it, however.

The old man heaved a sigh and sat down heavily in the rickety chair. It squeaked a protest at the monk's weight. "Oh Kari, what have you done?"

"I... but I don't even know what is going on. Why am I here? Where is Jin?"

"Jin is gone, Kari."

"Gone? What do you mean 'gone'?" Kari's heart was pounding loudly in his ears, vertigo made the room spin, his lungs refused to fill with enough air. How could Jin be gone? Hadn't he promised they'd always be together? That he'd never leave Kari?

Brother Askr was talking, Kari could see the man's lips form words but it took him a moment to hear them over the roaring in his ears.

"... letter explaining why he had to leave. Kari, I don't understand. I thought you were better than this. How could I have been so wrong about you? To do this to your best friend, your brother – the sin... I... don't even know you. I don't know what you are, is it truly your Ethereal blood or some other inherent wickedness inside you...?" The old monk shook his head, ruefully rubbing a hand over his bald head.

"Brother... I... why are you saying that? I don't understand," Kari murmured, his voice thick with tears. "Why did Jin leave? Why do you say such hateful things? I don't understand what is happening. Please."

Brother Askr shoved himself to his feet, took a step towards Kari. Towering over the boy, he opened his mouth to speak again, but seemed to change his mind and sighed. He looked suddenly so very tired and years older.

"Tomorrow," he said at last, his voice flat and void of emotion, "you will be tried. We don't carelessly cast someone out and declare them a sinner. There will be witnesses called forth, evidence... To be honest, none of it is really necessary, Jin's letter is damning enough. But it is the custom... You will be convicted of transgressing against the Path by seducing another boy, by forcing him to... let you have your way with him. You will be cast out, Kari."

It was as if the floor beneath his feet had suddenly fallen away. Kari's knees buckled, his vision darkened. He tried to breathe and found he could not, his heart was hammering so hard against his ribs he was sure they'd break. This wasn't real, it couldn't be. A nightmare – it had to be a nightmare, if only he could wake up. What was Brother Askr saying? That Jin had run away – because of him? That he had left Kari – no, that he blamed him for...? Jin would never do that. This had to be a mistake, a terrible mistake. They loved each other, they hadn't done anything wrong, even if the monks didn't see it. No. No. No! This wasn't real, it wasn't!

The door opened again. Light streamed into the dark room, illuminating Kari's wretched form, crouched on the floor, gasping desperately for air.

"I wish I could be sorry, boy," Brother Askr's voice reached his ears, dull as if they were deep underwater. "But you brought shame and misery to this temple, you only have yourself to blame."

Then the door fell shut, leaving Kari alone in the dark with his panic and his pain.

For the rest of the day Kari was left alone with his thoughts. He couldn't believe that Jin would abandon him. Throw him away. And yet, Jin wasn't here. He wasn't here in this cell with him, an accused sinner. Was that it? Had someone found out about them? But how? He thought they had always been so careful. But Jin would never leave him to face the consequences alone... would he?

Jin's words from only days ago came back to his mind. *"Some of the monks are suspicious of us."* Had someone warned Jin? If so, why hadn't he told Kari, why hadn't they run away together? And what letter had Brother Askr been talking about?

Kari's head was spinning with questions he found no answers to. Fear and pain mingled with the confusion. He was scared of what was to come, and hurt that the man who had raised and adored him could turn on him so quickly, so viciously. And beneath it all lurked something darker, something ugly he didn't want to acknowledge: suspicion. As much as he didn't want to believe that Jin would intentionally hurt him, abandon him, Jin wasn't here. Jin had left him all alone. What did that letter say? Was it really written by Jin? Why hadn't Jin left him any letters explaining what was going on? Had he really put all the blame on Kari?

In the cracks of Kari's broken heart something new slowly grew, something dark, something nourished by the flame of anger that had always burnt inside him: betrayal.

It was early the next morning when they came for him. There were three of them, monks with stony, unsympathetic faces. One carried a lamp, another a bundle of rough spun cloth and a shaving knife. The third remained at the door, vigilant.

"Sit down," the monk with the lamp ordered. Trembling, Kari did as he was told. The second monk put the bundle of cloth on the table and moved to stand behind Kari, shaving knife in hand. For one moment of blind, irrational panic Kari thought the monk was going to simply slit his throat. Instead, the man roughly grabbed a fistful of Kari's hair with unnecessary force, and a second later locks of glossy black hair fell to the floor. A short time later, Kari was sitting in a little pool of black silken hair. Then the monk stepped away, pointing at the cloth, and barked, "Put that on. And be quick about it."

Shaking like a leaf, Kari stood up and fumbled with the strings of his jinbei, earning himself a clout to the head when he wasn't quick enough. It wasn't until he shook out the bundle of cloth that he realised what they had given him: a Sinner's Robe. A simple rough-spun dirty white robe, almost like a yukata, but barely reaching past his knees. Shocked, Kari stood in the cold and stared at the robe in his hands.

"I said to be quick about it!" the monk snapped, and slapped Kari.

Startled, Kari hurried to put the robe on, clumsily tying the thin belt. Then he tentatively put a shaking hand to his head. His hair had been hacked off unevenly. The last flicker of hope he had had died. This was real. Jin was truly gone, had truly abandoned him. He was really going to be cast out. He was alone. All alone. He had nothing left, no friends, no family, no home.

He felt sick. The room was spinning. Kari fell to his knees and threw up what little he had in his stomach. The monks made noises of disgust and derision. Kari was grabbed roughly by the arm and dragged up and out of the cell.

"That's right," the man holding him sneered. "You have reason enough to be scared, abomination. You deserve all that's coming for you. Something like you should have never been allowed into this temple in the first place. Now move!"

The monk that had been waiting by the door grabbed Kari's other arm, and together they marched him towards the main building. If they hadn't kept such a tight hold on him, Kari would have stumbled and fallen before he had taken even two steps, for his legs refused to work properly. His heart was pounding hard, his vision blurry at the edges, sweat beaded his brow. He couldn't tell where they were taking him. The paths he had walked almost all of his life were suddenly strange and unfamiliar to him. The altar room, once welcoming and bright, was cold and hostile. The air was thick, suffocating. Monks, novices, and the orphan boys were sitting along the walls. In front of the statue of Hôjô, sitting on high backed chairs Kari had never seen before, were the Head Priest, Brother Shige, and Brother Askr. The latter looked old and sick, smaller, a shadow of the once strong big man. Brother Shige and the Head Priest, on the other hand, wore matching expressions of derision and anger.

Kari was dragged into the middle of the room and forced down on his knees. He was panting, his heart racing. Nervously he looked about, hoping to find a friendly face in the tableau of disgust, hostility, and anger, but he found none.

The entire room was silent, waiting; Kari's quick breath the only noise in the stifling quietness. Then the great temple bell rang. Kari felt each stroke vibrate through his body – the sound of impending doom.

As the last bell stroke faded, a figure stepped out from the line of monks and slowly made his way into the middle, coming to stand between the three elder monks and Kari. Kari looked up and saw it was Nobu, a sober expression on his face. For a moment he simply looked at Kari, indifferently, neither derisive nor angry – nor pitying. At last he turned to the elders and bowed low.

Brother Shige got to his feet and let his gaze sweep the room before his eyes fell on Kari and sent a new wave of terror through the boy. Never before had anyone looked at Kari with so much cold fury and hate.

"Today," Brother Shige began, his voice booming and full of authority, "we will judge one of our own for he has sinned – against our temple, against the Path, against Hôjô himself. He has brought shame to our sacred home, defiled it, mocked our faith, our mercy, all that we have given him with his wantonness, his wickedness." Each word hit him like a blow. Kari wanted to deny it all – and found he couldn't. He had always known what Jin and he were doing was against the Path. But they hadn't hurt anyone – he hadn't hurt anyone. He had never meant to disrespect the monks who had raised him, given him food and shelter and education. Kari was no monk, he wasn't even a novice, he shouldn't be treated so harshly.

Break our laws and you will be punished accordingly, initiated or not. Brother Shige had warned them once. But Kari had asked Brother Askr and the older monk had amended that while it was true that the uninitiated would be exiled from the temple, they would not receive as harsh a treatment as the initiated. So what was this? Why this trial? Why the Sinner's Robe? Why not just throw him out and be done with it?

"However!" Brother Shige continued. "Before we make a verdict, we will give the accused a chance to defend himself, and we will have witnesses and evidence against and in defence of the accused be brought forth, for we do not judge based on rumours and hearsay. Brother Nobu, you may begin with the witnesses."

Nobu gave a curt nod of acknowledgement, then beckoned to someone standing in the shadows behind the assembled. As the person came to stand before Nobu, Kari's heart sank. Saya. Why was she here? This couldn't be good, Kari had no illusions that Saya felt inclined to help him.

"Saya," Nobu casually addressed her. "You've been attending classes here with Jin and Kari, is that correct?" Saya nodded. "Would you say you are friends?"

"Well," Saya said shyly. "I am... was friends with Jin. But wherever Jin went, Kari was always tagging along, they used to be inseparable."

"Used to be? But not anymore?"

"Oh, when we were little they were. But..."

"But? It's all right, Saya, just tell us what you know."

Saya threw a quick glance at Kari. Too quick for him to read the look on her face, but enough for the bad feeling he had to solidify. Saya had always been jealous of Kari – of his relationship with Jin. And the older they had gotten the worse it had become, to a point at which it had been clear even to outsiders that they were no friends. She had never been good at hiding her hostility towards Kari.

Kari's mind wandered back to that moment, weeks ago, at the foot of the temple hill: Jin and Saya, laughing together... flirting. That dark feeling inside Kari, the one he didn't want to acknowledge, the one that held the pieces of his heart together yet, grew.

"Well, at first Jin... he felt kinda responsible for Kari, like a big brother," Saya reported. "But Kari... he became really possessive, and Jin... well... for a while now Jin felt suffocated by their relationship. And Kari only got more demanding. He didn't want me around Jin." Saya stopped there, as if for effect, to let the question that had to logically follow that statement linger in the air. *Lies, lies, lies*, a voice in Kari's head repeated over and over again.

"And why was that?" Nobu obligingly asked.

"Because..." Saya blushed, and with her eyes demurely cast down she said softly, "Because Jin and I – we were in love." Words like knives.

"Lie!" Kari cried, unable to remain silent any longer. He tried to stand up, but his guards pushed him back down. "That's not true. She's lying! She –" A blow to the side of his head knocked him down. He fell onto his side, ears ringing.

"Silence!" Brother Shige roared. "The accused will not utter a single word unless he is granted permission to speak! If he won't comply, he will be gagged and restraint. Have I made myself clear?"

Kari didn't answer. He slowly pushed himself back onto his knees and lifted his pounding head, glaring defiantly at Saya. For a second she looked shocked, at his defiance or at the blow he had received Kari couldn't tell. It didn't last long. She threw her head back haughtily and exclaimed, "There, see? He always wanted Jin all for himself. He didn't care how Jin felt or what Jin wanted. He's hated me ever since we were children because he knew the one Jin loves is me! We wanted to get married." Saya's voice broke on the last word and suddenly there were tears in her eyes. Kari had never known she was such an accomplished actress. If she hadn't been set hard on destroying his life out of pure spite because she hadn't gotten what she wanted, he would have applauded her. How masterfully she was spinning delusions and wishes into weapons. Or was she? Kari's mind was still screaming *Lies! All lies!*, but beyond that, quiet but persistent, a new voice: *Are you so sure it's all lies? Then what is this? Why are you being put on trial? Where is Jin? He promised to always be with you – and yet he has abandoned you. What other lies did he tell?*

"Married?" Nobu was clearly as surprised as everyone else, given the sudden excited whisperings.

"Yes, we had planned to get married as soon as Jin was of age... but... but that... that monster ruined everything!" Saya screeched, pointing an accusing finger at Kari. "He just couldn't stand seeing Jin happy. And Jin was suffering – because of *that thing*. Suffering! Do you have any idea how desperate he was? He even thought about ending his life, and... oh gods, I am so scared that he has hurt himself." The tears were streaming down Saya's rosy cheeks now, the whisperings became louder, more excited. "I kept begging him to tell me what was wrong... but... but Jin, he... was too ashamed... he thought I'd... I'd find him disgusting if I knew... I kn-knew it had something t-to do with him, but... but... Jin c-confided in my brother, and now that Jin... my brother told me, and it's... Oh gods, my poor Jin!" Saya wailed, dropping to her knees, sobbing hysterically. Nobu went to her, trying to comfort her, a second later Saya's brother was at her side as well.

Kari stared at them, aghast. What was this? Saya couldn't be that good an actress. This... No, no, that... it couldn't... But Jin had loved him, Kari. Jin had told him so. Over and over again. He had loved to imagine their life together, away from the restrictions of the temple and the Path. Jin had... he had... *He has abandoned you. And look, look at that girl. He has played you for a fool, and then he threw you away.* Kari gritted his teeth. No, he knew Jin better than anyone, none of this was true.

Nobu helped Saya to her feet. She clung to him, still sobbing. Satoru, her brother, stood beside her, his expression thunderous. He had never been the cheerful kind, but with the years Satoru had only become more morose. He didn't like people, but his protectiveness of his sister was well known.

"Satoru, can you tell us what Jin confided to you?" Nobu bid the boy gently.

"Jin... well, he told me he had done something bad," Satoru recited monotonously. "Said he'd understand if I didn't want him near my sister once he's told me. Said he had sinned and that he was filthy. He said he... he couldn't refuse him. Kari, I mean."

Kari bit his tongue. It was so obvious that the boy was repeating something he had memorised. Unlike his sister, Satoru was a horrible actor, and it seemed a lousy liar as well.

"He... Jin, he... um... said that Kari had used his Ethereal charm on him... s-seduced him, then... then blackmailed him to... continue." Satoru's voice wavered on the last word. He cast a quick glance at his sister, who was still clinging to Nobu, although she had stopped her wailing and sobbing. She gave him a scarcely perceptible nod. This was a farce! Why did no-one stop them? Why was every word they spoke taken at face value?

"Seduced him?" Nobu urged. "Could you please elaborate?"

Satoru at least had the decency to blush furiously and keep his head down as he stammered, embarrassed, "He seduced him... you know... to... h-have s-s-sex with him."

A grumble went through the assembled crowd, until Brother Shige demanded silence and order. Nobu thanked the siblings, and they slunk away, but not before Saya, one last time, caught Kari's eyes. A triumphant sneer on her lips, malice glinting in her doe eyes. Kari gritted his teeth. His fingernails were digging into the palms of his hands, he clenched his fists so tightly. Oh how he wanted to expose them for the liars they were – but he could already see that the crowd was more than willing to believe them. And how could he convince them it were all lies, when Kari himself wasn't even so sure about the truth anymore. Perhaps his truth was different to Saya and Satoru's truth. Perhaps the only liar was Jin.

Kari was still struggling with the mayhem of his emotions when he suddenly noticed that someone else had taken Saya's place, smirking like someone who finally gotten what they had wished for: Steren.

What had happened years ago was clearly never far from the bully's mind. The way Steren glared at Kari every time they passed on the street was proof of the grudge the young man still held. And now Steren had finally been presented with the perfect opportunity to exact his revenge. Kari had no intention of giving Steren the satisfaction and cower in fear, so he kept his head up and glowered at him. If getting his revenge was important enough for Steren to tell the world how a boy nearly five years his junior and half his size had bested him, fine, he was welcome to make a fool of himself.

But Steren didn't tell the story Kari had expected, instead what Steren did say was far worse. "Yeah, that little minx, knows exactly how to get what he wants. He's always acting all innocent but he's not. He's been selling his sweet little arse to travellers for years. Used his unnatural charms on them. There's this old hut in the woods behind the temple – that's where he takes them."

Kari felt as if he was trapped in a nightmare. It all felt so bizarre, so surreal. Lie after lie after lie – and no-one to question them. The willingness with which everyone believed the very worst of him was as much a blow to Kari as the growing certainty that Jin had used him, abandoned him, betrayed him.

"And how do you know this?"

"Oh," Steren's grin grew large, wolfish. "He tried his tricks on me and my friends. But, well, doesn't matter how pretty he is, Ethereal or not, I don't like boys – if you know what I mean. Some of those travelling folk, though… give them a nice cool drink and they like to talk. Told me all about it."

"You fucking liar!" came a sudden roar. Miki pushed his way through the crowd.

"Watch your language, young man!" Brother Shige admonished. "What kind of behaviour is this? I think you were taught better."

"Sorry, Brother Shige," Miki said breathlessly, "I really tried to stay quiet and wait my turn, but I can't listen to all those lies anymore. Especially all those lies that just came out of his filthy mouth!" Miki pointed at Steren, glaring so ferociously, even the young man, easily a head taller than Miki, looked taken aback.

Kari, too, was shocked by this rather unexpected side of Miki, who was usually so mild-mannered. Hope blossomed in Kari's heart, a tiny, fragile blossom. Perhaps he wasn't quite as alone as he had feared, perhaps he had a friend yet.

"It's all lies! Kari never... did any of this! And he definitely never forced or threatened Jin into anything. Jin loves Kari – no matter what Saya claims. She's just jealous, she always has been, because she's in love with Jin, but he only has eyes for Kari. What is all of this anyway?" Miki spread his arms and slowly turned, indicating the elders sitting up front, the rest of the assembled crowd, the tribunal as a whole. "You know Kari even longer than I, you should know better what kind of person he is, you've watched him grow up! But you are ready to believe the worst of him! And why? Because he's Ethereal? That one," Miki spat, redirecting his glower at Steren. "He just likes the attention, and he finally spotted the opportunity to get his revenge on Kari."

"Revenge?" Brother Askr asked. For the first time since the trial had started, the old monk looked up, and for a moment he seemed a little bit more like his usual self.

"For getting humiliated in front of his minions. I saw what happened that day – oh it's been how many years now? Never mind. But Steren, he and his cronies dragged Kari behind the smithy and ganged up on him. Too bad for our village bully, but he got his arse handed to him instead. By a little boy."

Kari gaped at Miki. He had had no idea anyone, least of all Miki, had witnessed that scene; the other boy had never said anything. But Kari wasn't sure mentioning it now was such a good idea, however much he appreciated Miki trying to help him. But Miki, at least, had succeeded in flustering and embarrassing Steren and eliciting a heated discussion amongst the attendees.

It was Brother Shige, who once more called for order and silence. He let his stern gaze wander the room before turning on Kari. "Accused," he snapped, and Kari flinched, as much from the monk's tone of voice as from the form of address. It was as if they were strangers. As if the time in which Brother Shige had been his teacher, had praised him for his clever mind and diligence, had never happened. "What do you have to say for yourself?"

Kari swallowed. He felt trapped. Countering lies with lies would not save him. And the truth? He was doomed either way, but perhaps the truth could mitigate his punishment, perhaps the others wouldn't believe all those lies about him anymore.

"Miki... Miki's telling the truth. I used violence against Steren – in defence. But I didn't do any of those things Steren accused me of. And... and J-Jin and I... that is... I love Jin, and he loves me."

"So, you want to say that this... *relationship* was mutual?"

"Yes."

"And you have never done anything sinful, anything in violation of the Path?"

Kari was aware that strictly speaking he and Jin had done quite a few things that weren't in accordance with the Path, but he also believed with all his heart, that their love was no sin. Surely Hôjô, too, would not claim otherwise. And so Kari spoke the truth, his truth. "We haven't."

It was the nasty sneer that slowly spread across Brother Shige's narrow face that killed even the last spark of hope Kari had still harboured. "Really. Well, we'll see about that. Brother Nobu," the monk turned to the younger man, "isn't it correct that you have been rather close to Jin?"

"Correct."

"And he confided in you. We are all aware of the betrayal of trust should you tell us what the boy told you, and yet I must ask you to. For the sake of justice."

Nobu nodded solemnly. "I understand. Well, it is true, we have been friends. I noticed that something was troubling him and merely wished to offer help or counsel. Of course he didn't want to tell me, all he said was that he didn't know what to do anymore. I think it was about two weeks ago, when he finally asked for my help. He told me how his relationship to Kari had changed from when they were children, that Kari had become increasingly demanding and possessive. How, in the end, Kari had bewitched him, bent him to his will to commit sinful acts against Jin's better judgement and will. Afterwards he felt ashamed and scared. He didn't dare confess out of fear of what would happen if he did. And Kari used that fear to blackmail Jin into obedience. Jin was too afraid to deny Kari. It nearly broke him. He... he indeed spoke of taking his own life, that's how desperate he was."

Word by single word Nobu dismantled Kari's world. Word by word the last shreds of hope died. Words like shards of glass, cutting and stabbing – hurt and betrayal. Words like hammer and chisel, chipping off pieces of his heart. There was his truth: He had been betrayed and abandoned.

"Of course I tried to calm him down. I told him we ought to tell the Head Priest about it, that Hôjô, in his mercy and wisdom, would not judge him, that he was the victim. Yet despite the pain and despair his childhood friend had caused him, Jin could not bring himself to damn the boy he had once loved like a brother."

"You didn't report this either. Why?"

Nobu hung his head, ashamed. "To be honest, at first I simply couldn't – no, I didn't want to believe that Kari was capable of such atrocity. I've known both boys almost all their lives, as have all of you. But it seems we all have been fooled by his innocent face, the gentleness, the kindness. Who would have thought such a tender youth to be capable of such duplicity? None of us wanted to believe any of the tales people tell about Ethereals, none of us saw the darkness within him." He paused. Dimly, Kari was aware of the agreement Nobu's words received from all around them. "But I saw just how broken Jin was, how troubled. Still, I didn't want to betray his trust. I thought it better to try and persuade him to come forward himself. Now, however, I wish I had not waited, I wish I had reported it, then, at least, the poor boy hadn't seen it necessary to run away."

Silence – louder and more damning than the roar of thunder. And into the silence Kari found himself mumbling over and over again, "It's a lie. It's a lie. Jin wouldn't do this." Wouldn't he? Kari had no trust in Jin anymore, yet still he couldn't let go. If he let go, it would all become reality. It would become true. Why? Why had Jin done this to him?

"Well, if it is so hard for you to believe it from us, perhaps you'll believe it from the boy himself," Brother Shige taunted. "Brother Nobu, you found a letter under your door this morning. This was how you knew the boy had run away, isn't it? And you have shown the letter to the Head Priest, Brother Askr, and me. We can all attest that Brother Nobu's report is in accordance with the contents of said letter, Brother Askr and I can also attest to the authenticity of it. It has clearly been written by Jin.

"I assume that the assembled are satisfied with the proof they were given. Although it seems there is one person left here who still isn't. Brother Nobu, show the accused the letter."

Kari barely registered Nobu coming to stand in front of him, until Nobu waved a piece of paper in front of Kari's face. Slowly, Kari took it and stared at it, his eyes slow to focus on the black ink on the paper, his brain struggling to decipher what he was looking at, to form words out of lines. Single, damning words sprang out at Kari, vicious and hurtful, accusing. But Kari didn't care about the content. It were the brush strokes, untidy, clumsy, it were the mistakes, the crooked lines, the missing signs, the lack of punctuation that gave him the final blow. What was left of his heart shattered into a thousand tiny pieces.

"You can tell that Jin wrote it, can't you?"

Kari didn't answer, he had nothing left to say. The one person in the entire world he had trusted more than anyone, whom he had loved more than life itself, whom he had given his heart and soul, had betrayed him and thrown him to the wolves.

When the verdict was announced Kari heard the words, but they meant nothing to him.

"The accused is guilty of transgression against the Path and for using his unnatural gifts to force an innocent into committing sin. For his wicked behaviour, his treason, and his heinous acts, we declare him a sinner and cast him out. His name shall be erased from the books and never mentioned again, he shall be forgotten. For the unspeakable shame that he has brought upon this temple, for defiling it, he will be driven out with a hundred strokes of the cane – to cleanse this holy ground and its inhabitants from the vileness of this sinner."

Words had lost all meaning, punishment had lost all dread. None of it could compare to the sea of pain he was drowning in.

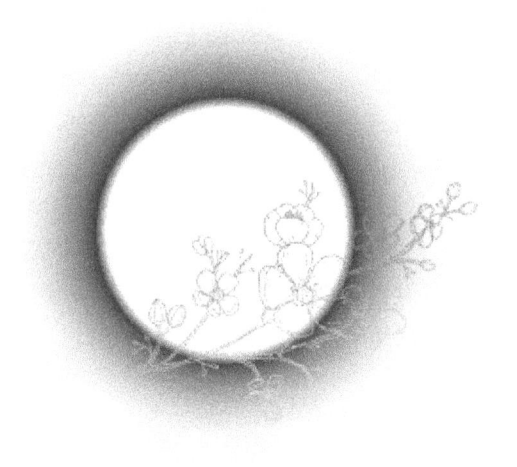

Chapter 14

They took him back to his cell. Dimly he noticed Nobu there as well. Strange, Kari thought, he had always expected Nobu to be over the moon of Kari's fall from grace. But here he was, and instead of gloating he looked inexplicably sad.

"I know we had our differences," Nobu said quietly, "but I truly didn't want it to come to this. Such a waste. It isn't often that one finds a possible equal. I think we could have achieved great things together, but alas... Still, I guess I should thank you. I don't enjoy wasting such potential, but you have been a great help." Kari's head jerked up. Only now did he realise he was alone with Nobu. Seeing his bewilderment, Nobu's lips spread into a vulpine grin. "You... and Jin, both. Ah, I really hope that boy finds his way. Oh, don't worry," Nobu leaned forwards, as if confiding a secret. "He should be fine for a couple of months at least, I've provided him with enough money." Nobu winked, and before Kari had time to process what Nobu had said, the young monk had already left. The heavy door fell shut, plunging the single room into shadow, the lock clicked. And Kari was all alone.

He stood there, in the middle of the room, taking deliberate breaths, his head reeling. A flood of emotions and confused thoughts was drowning him. Jin had abandoned him. Jin had used him. Jin had betrayed him. Jin –

Kari's breath hitched, his chest felt so tight, his throat so constricted, he could hardly breathe. Almost all of his life he had only ever wanted to make Jin happy. He had been willing to become someone he wasn't, to pay any price. And this was where it had gotten him. This was what Jin's pledges of love amounted to: he had sold him out.

The pain was unbearable. As if his very being, every atom of it, was being torn apart. The abandonment – a thousand wicked nails. The betrayal – serrated blades clawing at him. Too much. Too much. He could take no more.

Kari fell to his knees, screaming. And he screamed, and screamed. He screamed his pain to the heavens, forced the gods to witness his agony. He screamed long after his voice had broken, his throat raw. And still he screamed even when his voice died, for his pain seemed endless.

Yet there, amongst the ashes of what once was his heart – a tiny ember. It caught and grew into a new flame. And the new flame grew into a fire. And the fire became an inferno – savage, wild, and all-consuming: rage.

No-one came in answer to his screams. Not until early evening the following day. No-one spoke as they led him out through the big double doors of the temple. The monks stood in two lines, forming a straight path across the courtyard to the steps leading down from the temple hill. Each monk held a wooden cane. Behind them, craning their necks, were the temple's children, eager to see the spectacle, glad it wasn't them. All these people had once been Kari's friends. His family even. Now they were strangers, looking down on him with hostility and revulsion.

Out of the corner of his eyes, Kari saw Torben trying to get to him. Tears were streaming down his round cheeks. Two of the older boys were trying to restrain him, talking to him in low urgent voices, but Torben shook his head, strangled noises giving voice to his distress. A tall monk stopped the boy's progress at last and the led him away, back inside.

Amidst the fiery storm of fury raging inside Kari, he felt a stab of pity and sadness for his friend, Torben did not understand what was happening.

Kari stood up straight, head held high in defiance – and for the first time noticed that the monks' eyes were not on him but on the ground. Only Brother Shige, when he stepped out of the row, looked straight at him.

"You are hereby expelled. Your name has been erased from our books as it has been erased from our minds. No follower of the Path will offer you help, lest their very souls be tainted by your wickedness. As you are expelled from this temple, so shall your sins be driven out, for this sacred house of Hôjô to be cleansed and purified." Brother Shige slowly and very deliberately turned his back on Kari before, with a curt nod of his head, he stepped back into line.

Kari was pushed forward. He stumbled and nearly fell, but caught his balance at the last moment. So this was the end of the life he had lived, of the bonds he had had. From this very moment on, all of it was gone.

Slowly, keeping his eyes on the small stone guardians flanking the stairs, he took a step forward, then another, and another – and finally came at him. He caught their movement at the edges of his vision. Like a tidal wave the monks surged towards him. There was nowhere for him to go, except forward. They hit his shoulders, his back, his legs. One caught him in the stomach and made him double over. He tried to shield his head with his arms and push on, but the beatings were relentless. A heavy blow collided with his ribs and he heard a crack, but couldn't say if it was the cane that broke or his ribs. He was hurting all over, couldn't even say anymore where a blow landed. Some broke his skin, thin rivulets of blood running down his arms, his legs, his back. Breathing hurt, walking hurt. Being hurt. There was nothing but blinding pain.

He thought he had finally reached the stairs and looked up, when an old, battered cane glanced off his brow, making him stagger. A burning pain, more intense than anything before, ran through the right side of his face, blood ran into his eye, tingeing the world red. A strangled cry escaped him, irritating his sore vocal cords, his sore throat.

Kari stumbled onward, only wanting to escape. In his haste he slipped on the first step and just barely kept himself from tumbling down all the way to the foot of the hill.

When he was finally out of the monks' reach, Kari allowed himself a short break, sitting on the stone steps, beneath the canopy of the budding trees. He knew he couldn't stay for long, but his ribs, if not broken, badly bruised, made it hard to breathe. His right eye was already swelling shut. He desperately wanted to wash out the wound, take a look at the damage. It felt like he had a splinter in his eye, a line of fire ran from his brow to his cheekbone, hot blood dripped from his chin.

After too short a time, Kari got painfully to his feet and began his long, laborious descent. More than once he lost his footing. Strange, for he had walked these steps uncountable times and never had they felt so long or so treacherous.

Finally, at the bottom of the stairs, he stood still for a moment, catching his breath. He couldn't tell what was worse, the physical pain or the agony of his shattered heart, his torn soul. The gathering darkness had never felt so hostile. He needed to get away from here. Kari pondered his options. Following the road eastward would take him straight through the village, but the capital lay in that direction and so did a multitude of villages and hamlets between here and the Getsuro. In the opposite direction was nothing but wilderness for miles and miles. Despite what else it might cost him, Kari decided to go east.

His steps were slow and heavy, a bone-deep tiredness dragging on him. His throat, raw from all his screaming, was dry like sandpaper.

In the village the lights were already lit, but Kari could see people lining the street, pretending to be out on some business or other. Some, however, didn't even make the effort to hide why they were here. What a spectacle, scandal, something to talk about for weeks. It was probably the most excitement the village had had in years, and they hadn't been allowed to witness either the trial nor the punishment, so who was going to miss his walk of shame through the village now?

Kari gritted his teeth, kept his eyes on the ground and kept walking as fast as his battered body was able to. Anger, so unfathomably deep it threatened to swallow him whole, lent him new strength. Anger at these people, who only pretended to follow the laws of a god they didn't truly worship. Anger that his pain should serve as their entertainment. He tried to ignore the insults, the stones thrown at him, and pushed on, despite his laboured breathing, despite the pain and the fatigue.

From time to time Kari looked up to get his bearings. Familiar faces wherever he looked. He had known these people almost all his life. They, too, were strangers now. Strangers, sneering at him, gleeful, disgusted, gloating. At this moment Kari felt nothing but hate.

"Kari!" a familiar voice made Kari look up. He could make out Miki struggling against the hold of his uncles. "Kari," he cried again in a tear-filled voice, straining towards his friend, but he had no chance against his uncles' hold.

As he got close, Kari saw all the three of them were crying – for him. Miki had risked everything for him at the trial. He and his uncles had never had an easy life in this village. If they hadn't been the best smiths in many many miles, who knew whether they would have ever been accepted here. And yet they stood by him, shed tears for him publicly. Gratitude slipped through the thorns of Kari's anger like sunlight through a hedge. But in its shadow lurked fear – for his friends. Miki's loyalty might have already cost them their standing in the village, Kari could not allow his friend to make it worse. He locked eyes with Miki and gave him a quick shake of his head. Miki almost at once ceased his struggle and slumped against his uncles, wailing. The two men regarded Kari with such sorrow, Kari had to gasp for air. He forced a wavering smile on his lips for their sake, then quickly turned away and continued on his way. A sob escaped him, but he forced himself not to cry. He wouldn't show these people any weakness, wouldn't give them the satisfaction.

The sun had truly set by the time Kari was almost out of the village, but he wasn't surprised to see Saya and her brother loitering next to the stone lantern marking the village boundary. Of course Saya had come to gloat. The last house at the end of the street belonged to Saya and Satoru's family, but Kari couldn't tell if anyone else besides the siblings was there, watching him from the shadows.

When they noticed him coming, Saya stood so the light from the lantern would clearly show him her triumphant expression. The banked fire inside Kari flared. Although it cost him a lot, he pulled himself to his full height and held his head high. He made sure to walk close by, to let the light from the lantern fall on him, to let her see his defiance, let her see that he would not be broken.

As the sparse light illuminated the extend of Kari's abuse, the triumphant sneer fell from Saya's face. She covered her mouth, gasping in shock, and stumbled back against her brother. Her eyes were wide, tears glittering in the lamp light. Those were no tears for Kari, he was sure of it, those were tears of shock about what she had done, what she had been accomplice to. *What did you expect would happen?* Kari thought angrily. At least Satoru had the decency to look ashamed. It was a small victory at least – and for a while it was what kept him going. But for how long, Kari could not say.

Half blind, in agony, gasping for painful breath after painful breath, he stumbled on, through exhaustion and thirst. Until, in the middle of the night, he heard the soft gurgle of water and followed its sound through the darkness to a brook. Weeping willows lined its banks, the long boughs dipping into the water. Kari collapsed beside it. Every movement sent a fresh wave of pain through him. The cool water, as he scooped some up in his cupped hands, felt like liquid fire to his raw nerves. Nevertheless he splashed some of it into his face, gritting his teeth, whimpering. He needed to clean the blood from his face, but he gave up quickly. The blood had already dried and rubbing at it hurt so much he nearly fainted. His eye was swollen shut and there was nothing he could do about that. So instead he slowly drank a few mouthfuls, then let himself fall back on the grass, moist with dew. He had never felt so tired in his life. It would have been so easy now to just close his eyes and let sleep drag him under, but he knew he would never wake again if he did. The pounding in his head and the heaviness in his bones told him so. For a moment he entertained the idea of it. No more pain. But the raging wildfire of anger inside him wouldn't allow it. Not like this. Not now.

After only a little rest Kari struggled to his feet again. He looked up at the sky. The moon hid her face behind thick clouds as if she could not bear to watch his struggle.

Kari had lost all sense of time and distance. He stoically kept moving by sheer force of will and an all-consuming rage. If he had thought he might find help eventually, he was thoroughly disappointed. Travellers cast him curious glances as they passed him. Farmers and villagers scowled at him before hastily turning their backs on him and ignoring his very existence. Only when he found a small stream or well with no people in sight did Kari risk to take a break. He didn't sleep, he could not for fear of never waking again. He had no food. His vision was cut in half and blurry. He felt frayed, as if walking in a never-ending nightmare. Was any of this even real? Kari had no way to tell.

 He walked for hours, for days... for years... for ages. Eventually not even his rage could keep his body moving any longer. He stumbled and fell, only just barley catching himself on his forearms. His cracked rib sent a stab of nauseating pain through him. He had no more strength left and collapsed face down in the middle of the dusty road. His breath came quick but shallow. His anger screamed at him to get up, to keep fighting, but he was too exhausted and in too much pain. He had even forgotten the source of his devastating anger. Why had he defied death for so long, why not just give in? Let it all end.

 He let go. Of his consciousness. Of his pain. His rage. Of who he had been and who he had tried to be. And just like that, the boy who used to be Kari was gone.

Part 3

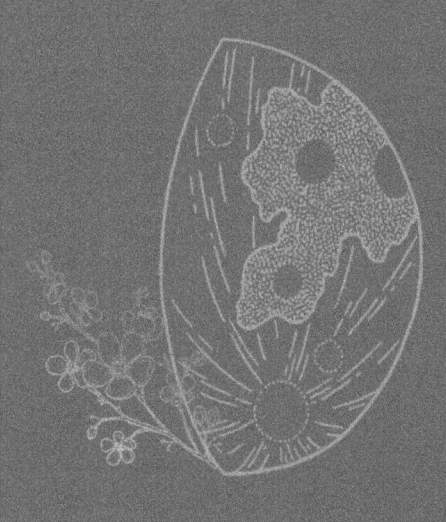

Loss

Chapter 15

Jin was staring at him with an expression of shock that bordered on horror. And there was something, something very familiar that lurked beneath it. Betrayal. But why should Jin feel betrayed?

"Of course," Suzu continued with deliberate nonchalance, "I hadn't been walking for days, only for about one and a half. Though if Mother and Haldor hadn't happened to be on that road and decided to pick me up..." He let the rest of the sentence unspoken, no need to spell it out.

"Ka– Suzu –"

"Even found me a good doctor who was able to save my eye. Well mostly."

"Please, Suzu!"

Suzu fell silent, glaring icily at his former friend. The young man was visibly shaken, his face a pale, horror-stricken grimace. Another man – a better man perhaps, or a weaker one – might have taken pity on him. But Suzu was merciless, his anger burnt too hot, the betrayal had gone too deep.

"Don't you dare and say you never wanted this to happen," Suzu hissed when Jin didn't speak. His voice was dripping with venom. He could barely restrain himself from leaping at Jin and strangling the traitor. "Do not tell me you didn't know what would happen when you wrote those lies and ran."

"But I didn't!" Jin cried at last. "I didn't write that letter," he continued urgently, imploringly. "I didn't say those awful things. Not in a letter, not to anyone. I never promised Saya to marry her, or –"

"I've seen that letter! It was your writing. Do you understand? Yours! Down to the last crooked and wrong brushstroke."

"That... I – I did write a letter. All right, yes, I did. But I – those lies, I didn't write those. The letter I wrote was to you. Only to you. I was explaining why I had to leave and that I would soon sent for you. Really. I swear that was all I wrote. I never lied to you, I –"

"How did you survive on the road, in town?"

"What?"

"How did you get by? How did you find food and shelter?"

Jin fidgeted, clearly noticing he couldn't talk himself out of this. "Nobu gave me money."

"Did he now?"

"But that wasn't... it wasn't like that. Please, Kari –"

Before that hated name had fully left Jin's mouth, Suzu sprang to his feet, grabbed the next best object – a dainty porcelain vase – and hurled it at Jin. Jin dodged it just in time and the vase smashed into the wall behind him, shattering, shards of porcelain raining down on the tatami mat. Aghast, Jin, too, got to his feet – and took an involuntary step back. Suzu's eyes were ablaze with hatred. He was an avenging angel, a demon, a wrathful god, relishing the look of fear on Jin's face.

"Don't ever call me by that name again," Suzu snarled. "That boy is dead, and you killed him. Do you understand? He's gone. I don't want any of your fucking excuses, I want you out of my life. I want the very memory of you erased from my mind."

Eyes so dark they were almost black. Once they had looked at Suzu with affection and warmth, now they only spoke of pain, of heartbreak. And still it wasn't enough. Every fibre of his body screamed for him to inflict more pain. More. More. To make him suffer as Suzu had suffered. Yet when Jin suddenly brushed past him and fled the room, Suzu didn't move or call after him.

Slowly, Suzu sank to his knees, exhausted in a more profound way than physical exhaustion. He didn't cry, he didn't scream, he did – nothing. He just sat there, breathing in and out, until his heart calmed down.

Jin fled from the room, from Suzu and his abysmal anger, the hate in the young man's mismatched eyes. He felt as if it was suffocating him, crushing him beneath its weight. How had this happened? This was not what he had expected their reunion to be like. Suzu's suffering, the pain, mentally and physical, the betrayal – Jin had intended none of it. It hadn't been supposed to end like that.

His head was spinning, he couldn't think. He had to get out of here. Jin dashed through the first door he found that let him out of the house and found himself back in the lush garden. Opposite from him was the room where Kazue had received them. He saw Niall lounging on the verandah. She sat up, smiling, when she saw him cross the garden. Jin couldn't do this here, he couldn't break down here in front of Suzu's family, but he couldn't pretend nothing was wrong either. Instead of going to his friend, Jin quickly turned right, through the gap between the two buildings. Niall called after him, but Jin did neither look back nor slow down and hurried towards the front gate, glad there was no-one else around, and out into the street.

At the next corner Jin sank down in the shade of a high wall, leaning his back against the cool stone. This time of the day the streets were blessedly deserted. He buried his face in his hands. How had everything gone so wrong?

The sound of running feet announced Niall before she almost threw herself down next to him. "Gods, Jin, what the hell? What happened?"

Jin lifted his head and looked at his friend. He swallowed around the thickness in his throat, the shame he felt. Tears pricked his eyes. It took a few moments, in which Niall waited patiently, for him to admit, "Niall... I... I think I did something horrible." And then he pressed a fist against his mouth as the tears just spilled from his eyes and heavy sobs shook him.

He felt empty. It was a strange feeling after years of working hard to contain his rage. Catharsis – right, that's what it was. Suzu hadn't believed Kazue, hadn't wanted to believe, that confronting his past would be good for him. All he had longed for was oblivion.

He looked at the sad remains of the vase and felt a pang of regret. Not for having thrown it, but for breaking one of the pretty porcelain vases Mother liked so much. He'd have to buy her a new one. Luckily the vase had been empty, Suzu would have felt bad about destroying one of Miharu's flower arrangements.

With a sigh Suzu pushed himself to his feet and left the room. In the hallway he found one of the younger boys staring at him with big eyes, unsure what to do. Suzu smiled at the boy and ruffled his hair affectionately.

"Sorry, I broke a vase. Could you clean it up?" The boy nodded. "Good boy, thank you. But be careful not to cut yourself, you hear?"

He left the boy to his task and made his way back to Mother's room, dragging his feet. He needed a smoke and a drink – perhaps several. And he would ask Mother for the evening off. He wasn't good company today.

But when he reached Kazue's room Naloc was still there. Suzu had never interacted much with the man before, save for a quick greeting and a few fleeting words. He was aware that Naloc and Kazue had history, had probably been lovers at some time, but Suzu didn't like the man much. Right now, he liked him even less. Why was he even still here, sitting in Kazue's room, drinking tea, looking for all the world like he belonged here.

Suzu sat down on the verandah, not wanting to be in the same room as the man. Perhaps it was childish, but he didn't care.

The conversation inside the room ceased, Mother and Naloc both turned to look at him. Ryū came to sit beside him, Rani, who had just finished pouring tea, began to fidget.

"Rani," Suzu said, proud of how calm and nonchalant he sounded, "could you please bring me my pipe and a drink? Not tea. Bring me..." He caught a glimpse out of the corner of his eye of Naloc sipping his tea. "Bring me some of that wine the General brought," he finished with a smirk, and felt an immense satisfaction when Naloc choked on his tea. The rivalry between the two men was legendary, everyone in town knew about it.

"Don't you think it's a little early to start drinking?" Mother criticised.

"No. It's exactly the right time. Thank you."

Rani uncertainly looked from Suzu to Mother, until Mother, with an exasperated sigh, waved a hand at the boy.

"So, you're still here," Suzu commented waspishly. "Your boy has already fled with his tail between his legs. And it seems Niall ran after him. Are you sure you don't want to follow and lend him a big strong fatherly shoulder to cry on?"

"Suzu!" Kazue snapped, but Naloc merely smiled.

"It's all right, Kazue. To answer your question, no, I don't think I need to do that. Niall can handle this on her own. As for why I am still here, apart from enjoying the company, I have a favour to ask of you."

Suzu scowled. Naloc didn't ask for favours – he snapped his fingers and everyone jumped and did his bidding. "Sorry, I think you must have mistaken me for one of your lackeys. I don't grant favours – as you call it."

Naloc was about to speak when Rani came bustling around the corner, struggling with a heavy tray laden with an ash pot, a pipe, a glass, and a decanter of wine. They watched in silence as the boy put down his burden, set out the glass, filled it with a wine of such a deep red it seemed black, put the ash pot next to it, and presented Suzu with the pipe. Rani leaned in and whispered conspiratorially, "I filled it with the really good tobacco." Despite his dark mood, Suzu found himself smiling. He patted Rani's cheek and whispered a 'thank you'. Rani blushed, but he looked unusually pleased with himself.

When Rani had been sent off again – to the kitchen to find himself a snack – Suzu lit his pipe and took a deep drag. Glowering at Naloc, he banged the pipe unnecessarily hard against the ash pot, which emitted a deep, foreboding clang. "If that was all you wanted, I think we are done here. I gather you know the way out?"

"Suzu!"

"Don't you think you should listen to what I have to say first?" Naloc asked unperturbed.

"No." Mother shook her head at Suzu's mulishness.

"Not even if I told you that I have reason to believe the Earl of Tsukikage is a murderer?"

Suzu slammed his pipe down onto the ash pot and glared at Naloc. "Bullshit!" he growled. "How dare you. I won't have you slander him!"

And there it was again, the equilibrium broken, the rage flaring. A devastating fire – and it had a new target. Suzu distantly took notice of Ryū plucking the pipe from his fingers. Mother was saying something he couldn't hear over the roaring in his ears. Slowly, Suzu got to his feet and stalked towards Naloc. A predator and his prey. The way Naloc involuntarily leaned away from him was immensely gratifying.

"Hurt him in any way, and I swear you will regret it." Suzu's husky voice was low, almost seductive, dripping with dark promises of violence. Naloc swallowed. A bead of sweat glistened on his brow, but he held his place, held Suzu's gaze, eyes grey as burnished steel – cold, unyielding.

"Then do me this favour and prove me wrong," Naloc said. "Two young people have gone missing. Both were in his employ, and both vanished without a trace – together."

"Sounds like they've run off together."

"They are not the types to do that, they have family to take care of. Far stranger yet is the Earl's reaction to his servants just vanishing on him. His entire household pretends there is nothing wrong at all – or rather as if those two had never been there in the first place. Don't you find this suspicious? Why would they do that if they had nothing to hide? Servants like gossip. Had those two eloped, they wouldn't stop talking about it."

"First of all, they are not his servants, they are his employees. And second, your view of service staff is quite prejudiced, I have to say. The Earl's employees are loyal."

"And because of that loyalty they would lie for their master – pardon, their employer. Wouldn't they?"

"Why in the world would the Earl kill two of his own employees? This is ridiculous. You know nothing about him. You just want him to be a horrible person and a degenerate because he's a noble. Oh, and let me guess, you can't stand him, because he is close to the General. Perhaps you would do well to keep out of things that are none of your business –"

"Those two, Numie and Genta, they are my business," Naloc snapped and finally pushed himself to his feet. He was only slightly taller than Suzu, but he drew himself to his full height and put on an air of authority. Anyone else might have been intimidated, but Suzu wasn't impressed. "The people of Kigetsu are my business. It is my responsibility to take care of their needs, to make sure that even if those bastards in their mansions and palaces across the river don't care about them, they don't get forgotten. And when two young people do not come home from their work, and neither their employer nor their colleagues deem it necessary to do something about it, and their families seem too frightened to ask for help, then yes, that is my business! So either you help me find out what happened to them, or I'm afraid I'll have to use other methods – and I doubt you'll like those. The Earl, certainly, won't."

Suzu took another menacing step towards Naloc. He was barely holding himself back. His rage was screaming for him to tear the man apart. "That's what you call asking for a favour? I call this blackmail."

"Call it whatever you want. But know this: I didn't have to come to you, or even ask nicely. I'm doing this out of courtesy towards the Singing Dragon, and because he's a valued customer."

Suzu was about to punch Naloc, and the man knew it, for he gritted his teeth and planted his feet, either not intending to defend himself or knowing it was no use. Ryū's hand closed around Suzu's wrist. Kazue stepped between them.

"Enough!" she ordered. "Naloc, I will not allow you to threaten one of my boys or slander our patrons. You've said your piece. I think it is time for you to leave."

Naloc nodded and sighed heavily. As he walked past them, however, keeping his gaze straight ahead, he said, "Don't think I like ruining a man's reputation by throwing unproven allegations of murder at his feet, because I don't, but I will do it."

A growl escaped Suzu's throat. He tried to break free of Ryū's hold, almost blind with rage, but Ryū was taller and stronger than him. In this very instant there seemed to be only two things of importance in this world: to rip Naloc to pieces, and to protect Toshi at all cost. Despite his struggles, Ryū held on tight, and Naloc was quickly out of the door, slipping his feet into his sandals. Fine, if he couldn't do the first, he could still do the latter. Suzu ceased his struggle.

"Fine," he said sharply. Naloc looked back over his shoulder at him, almost as surprised as Kazue and Ryū, whose grip finally loosened. "But don't be too happy just yet. I will prove to you that Toshi has nothing to do with people going missing or has killed anyone. And then I will make you apologise – and trust me, you will not like it."

Chapter 16

Jin held his cup so tightly one might have thought it was all that anchored him to the here and now. The tea inside had long since gone cold. Tears stung his eyes, his throat was raw from talking. Niall had dragged him out of that alley and home, not once letting go of his arm, where she had made him tea and waited patiently until he told her what had happened. And Jin had told her everything.

"Did you know, my parents deposited me at the temple because they hadn't wanted another mouth to feed. In parting they told me that my siblings at least were useful. I was only four… but I still remember that. Have I ever told you?" Niall shook her head. She wore that sympathetic yet distanced expression on her face she usually reserved for her patients. Jin didn't know what it meant. "Kari… Suzu – he needed me, to him I wasn't useless. Even though he has always been so much cleverer than I..." he trailed off.

They lapsed into silence. Jin sipped his cold tea, his shoulders tense, awaiting judgement. It would be harsh, he knew Niall too well. As caring and kind as Niall was, what she could never forgive was betrayal – and Jin had betrayed Kari, even if he hadn't meant to. Niall scrutinised him for another few minutes.

"I have questions," she said at last, her voice professionally curt. "Running away is regarded as an act of ungratefulness against Hôjô and against the Brotherhood, which is why the temple refuses any further help towards the runaway. Correct?" Jin nodded. "All right." She didn't elaborate, but instead became pensive again. And after another while: "But if you were a victim of... harassment, abuse... desperate enough to take your chance – the Brotherhood would forgive you, wouldn't they?" Jin's death grip on his cup tightened. He forced himself to put it down before he broke it. With a sinking feeling he gave a curt nod in affirmation. "I see." It was a blunt and damning statement. She was going to hate him, and he deserved it. He deserved to be hated. "What you've just told me – that was from Suzu's perspective, wasn't it? So, did it really happen like that?"

"No!" Jin exclaimed before he could stop himself. No, it hadn't happened exactly like this but what difference did it make? He had caused this, he had caused Kari – no, Suzu, so much suffering and pain. What difference did it make that he had never intended any of it? "I mean... it's undeniable that it happened... that it happened like this to Ka-- Suzu, it's just... I... it's..." he faltered, searching helplessly for words that wouldn't come, for a way to explain himself that didn't sound like a cheap excuse. "I didn't write that letter, I never said such horrible things about Kari... Suzu," he said at last in a small voice, hanging his head. It was the truth, even if it didn't matter.

"Jin," Niall said, softly, her voice gentle, almost tentative, and Jin looked up at his friend. The shut off expression was gone, she wasn't the doctor who, although sympathetic, distanced herself from her patient anymore, but Niall, his best friend, his sister. Her eyes were sad but full of warmth. "Tell me what happened those last weeks at the temple – from your perspective."

His perspective...

"All right." Jin took a deep, steadying breath.

It had begun at the end of winter that year. Jin had been trapped in one of the classrooms until late one day – doing impositions again – when Nobu had found him there. The young monk had taken pity on him, given the late hour, and helped him finish the rest quickly.

The next day Jin looked for Nobu to thank him, and they ended up deep in conversation. It was strange how easy the young man was to talk to, so very different to the other monks. Nobu wasn't as rigid, as narrow-minded, as bound up in strict laws and rules. He showed a lot of understanding for Jin, often feeling as if he couldn't breathe in the confines of the temple and his need to escape into the wider world.

Some weeks later Jin confessed Nobu his love for Kari. Of course he didn't tell his new friend exactly how far their relationship had progressed, he wasn't certain Nobu's sympathy would go so far. What he told him, however, was enough – and a risk. Nobu was quiet for a long while, and Jin grew more and more anxious.

"This is dangerous, Jin," Nobu said at last. "Some of the monks already don't like how close you two are, if you give them any reason to suspect your closeness is anything other than brotherly love..."

"I know!" Jin cried, throwing his hands up in a gesture of as much frustration as it was despair. "But I just can't not be with him. I know Kari would understand and probably tell me that it's only two years, but I can't – I can't see him everyday, be in his presence, and keep my distance from him. It's simply impossible."

"Then you need to go. Leave the temple."

"Run away, you mean? Don't think I haven't thought about it, but Kari is against it, he – "

"No, Jin, you, and only you, need to leave."

Jin stared at the young monk, taken aback. He didn't know if he ought to be shocked, angry, or hurt. Nobu had presented him with what he clearly considered the obvious solution to the problem, and he had done so in a very emotionless, rational way. But emotionless and rational weren't exactly Jin's strength. He swallowed around the sudden thickness in his throat and blinked against the tears, welling up in his eyes.

Nobu saw his distress and immediately relented. "Oh. Jin, don't... I didn't mean it like this. It's not that I want you to go. But I honestly think that it might be the only way to keep both you and Kari safe. Look, I can imagine why Kari is against the idea of running away, and he is right. I can provide you with money, but not with a lot. For you alone it's enough to last you a few months. You can use it to find a home and work, get settled. And as soon as you're ready, you send for Kari. In the meantime he's safe here."

Jin admitted that the young monk was making a lot of sense. And yet – Kari was right, too. It were only two years, perhaps even less. They could talk to Brother Askr. Two years. It seemed like an eternity. Self-discipline was not something Jin had ever been very good at, but for Kari he'd do anything. And so, Jin rejected Nobu's suggestion and made the decision to try harder, to do whatever it took for Kari and him to remain safely here at the temple until their time to leave had come.

However, over the next few days every conversation he had with Nobu ultimately came back to Jin leaving the temple now – without Kari. Nobu explained, assured, planned, promised. In the end, Jin had no doubt there was only one right decision: He would leave Kari in Nobu's care and go ahead alone to lay the foundations of their future life. Only one problem remained: There was no way Kari would ever accept that plan, and not only because he had already made his stance clear. Just the other day, he and Jin had gotten into an argument over Jin, spending so much time with Nobu lately. Jin couldn't say why, but Kari – and that in itself was rather shocking – seemed to honestly dislike the young monk. Despite his gentle nature, Kari had a stubborn streak. No persuading, no explaining, no argumentation would convince him of a plan Nobu had devised.

"Then don't tell him," Nobu said with an exasperated edge to his voice.

"I can't just disappear on him."

Nobu sighed. So at last, his new friend, too, was about to lose his patience with him. Jin had wondered how long it would take. But instead of snapping at him, Nobu put a hand on Jin's shoulder and said, kindly and understanding, "I know this is hard. And I won't claim to know how Kari will react to it. It seems the only way, though."

"He will not listen to you," Jin admitted. "No matter how you try to explain it to him, he will not listen. He can be very stubborn."

"Then you will do it."

"What? But –"

"After you've left. Write him a letter, explain why you had to leave, your plans, and that you're going to send for him as soon as possible. If he won't listen to me, he will listen to you, won't he?" Jin nodded. It wasn't ideal, but it was better than nothing. Kari was going to be so angry.

Making preparations took them another few days to ensure Jin's departure remained a secret from anyone but the two of them. The final obstacle was for Jin to sneak away unnoticed – especially from Kari. Easier said then done. He couldn't leave during the day for his absence would be noticed too soon. Leaving in the depth of the night seemed the only possibility, yet Jin and Kari had slept next to each other for almost all of their lives. It was like a natural instinct to wake when the other woke, a special sense that told them when the other had a nightmare or couldn't sleep in the first place.

"Here," Nobu said holding out a tiny paper triangle to Jin.

"What is that?" Jin asked. He recognised the neat triangle, it was one of Brother Askr's medicine sachets.

"Just slip it in Kari's tea at supper or later. Oh, don't worry, it's harmless enough. It's a sleeping draught, nothing more."

Jin accepted the sachet, dubious. He didn't like the idea of drugging Kari. The draught in his pocket was making him more nervous than running away. All day long it felt as if it was burning a hole in his shirt.

That evening, after curfew, Nobu would take Jin's pack and stow it beneath the stone guardian in the courtyard. All Jin had to do was to sneak out of the dormitories as he had done so many times before, grab his pack and leave. Nobu would be the one who would have to deal with the aftermath. Why the young monk was going so far for him, Jin had no idea, but he was grateful to him nonetheless.

But supper came and went and Jin had not found the opportunity nor the courage to slip the sleeping draught into Kari's drink. He was running out of time. And mixing with his indecisiveness about the draught was his nervousness about running away – about actually and truly running away from the temple. It was a clenching ache around his heart that outshone even his anxiousness. Heartache. Leaving Kari was the single most difficult thing Jin had ever done, but he hadn't expected it to hurt so much.

One could call it a strike of inspiration or pure selfishness that made him head off Nobu shortly before curfew and ask him for one last favour. Nobu raised his eyebrows at the request, but only a heartbeat later a smile tucked at the corners of his lips and he agreed. Now, Jin would at least be able to properly say goodbye to Kari.

"So," Niall said slowly, "you went stargazing with Kari, just like you've been doing hundreds of times before. And you put a drug into the wine – on the words of that Nobu bloke that it was a harmless sleeping draught. Seriously? Do you have any idea how dangerous that is? Mixing some drug with alcohol, you have no idea how those might react to each other. Not to mention the dosage, what if –"

"Niall!" Jin cut his friend off. Of course she would latch onto this in particular. "I get it, all right. Now I know how reckless that was, but I didn't know then. And I trusted Nobu. He wouldn't have hurt Kari – at least I thought he wouldn't. I don't know anymore."

Niall relented. "Fine. I guess that's beside the point now anyway. So you said your sweet goodbyes to the boy and just left him out there in the courtyard?"

"Of course not. Nobu had promised me he'd take care of Kari. That included taking him back inside when I was gone."

Niall pinched the bridge of her nose. She was either getting a headache or she was having strong feelings – about Jin. "Jin," Niall said tightly. "You just trusted someone you had barely known until a few weeks before then with the love of your life? You trusted that man – someone your love, who was apparently incapable of disliking anyone, detested – to take care of him, to explain to him what was going on, to console him? Use your bloody head, Jin! What the hell?" Niall's voice had steadily risen in volume until, in the end, she was yelling at Jin. She hadn't yelled at him since Jin and Issei had gone for a swim in the river in the middle of the night in winter, drunk. Jin ducked his head. He deserved it. Hell, he deserved a lot more than this. "And the letter?" Niall snapped. "The letter you wrote."

"I gave it to Nobu," Jin admitted in a small voice.

"Of course you did." Niall gritted her teeth, her hands, like claws, gripping her knees. Jin didn't know what he would do if she hated him now as well, but how could he pity himself, he had brought this unto himself. He deserved it. Niall valued loyalty above all else, she would not be able to overlook or forgive this. Jin could not forgive this. What had he been thinking. Then. All those years since then. Why had he never, not once, questioned Nobu, questioned his own actions? Kari – Suzu – hated him for what he had done, and Jin deserved it. Niall was going to hate him. And he deserved it. She would tell Naloc, Risa, Durin – Issei. They, too, were going to hate him. And that he deserved as well. Jin hated himself for what he had done.

Eventually Niall took a deep breath and exhaled sharply. "Jin. Jin, look at me," she demanded, but her voice had lost its edge, she sounded almost gentle. Slowly, Jin lifted his head and looked at his friend. Niall's eyes, the colour of deep water, were filled not with hate but sadness. "Jin, I know you. You have not a drop of malice in your body. And you are a terrible liar. I think if Suzu really thought about it he'd see that, too, but his pain and anger won't let him. And fact remains that you abandoned him, even if you didn't mean to. You didn't intend to betray him, to harm him, to cause him all this pain – but still, you enabled someone else to do this to him. You are not a bad person, Jin. But you are too gullible, too easy to manipulate, too trusting – and a fucking idiot!" Leave it to Niall to throw the harsh and ugly truth straight into your face, to prod at every sore spot. Niall, unlike Jin, had the ability to see right through a person, she wasn't easily fooled, and she had no patience for those who were.

"But... but why? Why would Nobu –?" Jin was grasping at straws, he was aware of that. Yet he didn't understand why the young monk, his friend – or so he had thought – would do that.

"Who knows. Does it even matter? It doesn't change what happened."

"No. You are right. Nor does the fact that I didn't do it."

Niall sighed and patted Jin's arm. "No. I fear it doesn't."

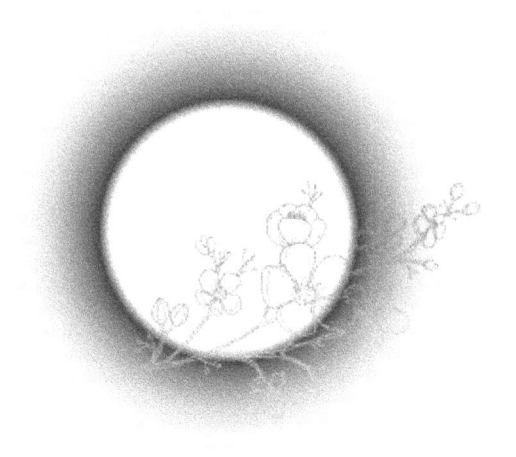

Chapter 17

It had been two very strange days that followed Suzu's confrontation with Jin. On the one hand he felt a lightness that had not been there before, as if for the last five years he had lugged around a heavy weight that was finally gone. At the same time the eternal flame of anger residing in his heart, his very soul, had been stoked anew by Naloc's outrageous accusations, the demands that bordered on blackmail. Therefore, Suzu had been irritable, his mood volatile. He had spent his free time in the dojo working himself to exhaustion under the worried observation of Haldor and Ryū. Kazue had tried to appease him several times, but each time she had thrown up her hands in defeat, clucked her tongue, and retreated to her parlour after mere minutes.

And before he knew it, the day of Suzu's stay at the Earl's mansion had come. Suzu stood in front of the rather ornate travel chest Mother had presented him with – already packed. She and Rani had taken it upon themselves to oversee Suzu's luggage.

"Don't you think this is a bit much?" Suzu asked, raising an eyebrow at the big chest. "I'm back by tomorrow evening!"

"So? You need to be prepared for all eventualities," Kazue retorted.

Ryū, sitting cross-legged on the floor next to Suzu and peering into the chest, snickered. "Really? I don't think the 'eventualities' the Earl has planned require any clothes at all." Suzu jabbed him between the ribs, but it made Ryū only laugh harder. Kazue rolled her eyes at Ryū.

"Take this serious, Ryū. You are my heir after all."

Ryū bowed his head, although he didn't quite manage to wipe the smirk off his face. "Yes, Mother."

Kazue huffed, exasperated. "Go. Help Suzu get dressed. Off you with you two. Go. Shoo!" They scrambled to their feet as Kazue shooed them out of her room like little boys and slid the door closed with a thud. Suzu and Ryū exchanged a glance, fighting to suppress their laughter and barely succeeding. They flew down the hall to Suzu's room, where, the moment the door closed behind them, they collapsed, laughing, in each other's arms.

When at last they had calmed down, they were lying on the floor, gasping for breath. Ryū turned onto his side, looking at Suzu with sudden sobriety.

"Are you really going to be back by tomorrow evening?" he asked quietly. Something in his voice made Suzu's heart clench.

"What do you mean? Of course!"

"But, once you are there, in his mansion, with him, and you get a taste of what life with him could be like, perhaps you decide to finally accept his proposal."

"I won't," Suzu snapped. The lightness and the silliness of only a moment ago had evaporated like fog in the sun.

"Suzu, stop being so damn stubborn. I know that you love him, you –"

"Don't. I don't love him. I enjoy being with him, I do like him. I do not love him. You, Mother, Rani, Akito, Haldor, Miharu, the others – you are the ones I love. That's more than enough love, isn't it?"

Ryū sat up, cocked his head, a small, almost sad smile on his lips. His amber eyes burned with affection. "I know, Little Moon," he said softly. "And you know how much we love you. But it's a different kind of love, and you know that."

"It's the only kind of love I want and need."

"Suzu," Ryū began, but Suzu launched himself at his friend, arms tight around the young man's middle, his face buried in his chest.

"No," Suzu hissed viciously. "I don't want it. And I don't need it. So... please."

Ryū gaped speechlessly at his friend. He had known, of course, that Suzu had been hurt badly by his first love, but he had underestimated just how desperately, ferociously the boy rejected and denied his own feelings. It broke Ryū's heart. As hard as it would be for him – for all of them – to let Suzu go, Ryū knew the Earl truly loved the boy. Suzu deserved to be loved, to be happy – to know that he would never be betrayed again. The Earl could give him all of that and more. But Ryū had no idea how to make Suzu see and believe it. Instead, he did the only thing he could do. He wrapped his arms around

Suzu and whispered, "Hey Little Moon, make sure you come home quickly, all right? It's boring without you."

There wasn't any need, helping Suzu get dressed. Unlike to the General's party, Suzu wore a simple, dark red yukata, his hair simply bound back with a matching ribbon. Half an hour later he was already sitting in the carriage the Earl had sent, heading towards Mangetsu.

Crossing the River Opal via one of the many bridges that spanned the crystal clear waters, was like crossing into an altogether different town. The noise, the bustle of lively Kigetsu fell away in favour of Mangetsu's serenity, the wide streets that seemed almost deserted in comparison.

Suzu had never been to the Earl's mansion before and he couldn't help but gape as the carriage swung onto the driveway, lined with big old cherry trees. The breeze carried the gentle fragrance of wisteria. They stopped in the half-moon courtyard in front of the main house. Suzu jumped out of the carriage before it had even fully pulled to a stop, and marvelled at the strange but magnificent building. Whereas the General's mansion was built entirely in the northern style, the Earl of Tsukikage's estate was an interesting blend of both, northern and southern styles. Sitting at the end of a long driveway as was so typical for northern manor houses, stood a very distinctly southern style manor, not unlike the Singing Dragon, with a gabled roof and dark wood beams and pillars instead of marble.

The wide sliding doors stood open, Toshi was already waiting for him on the porch. Suzu had never seen him look so relaxed, wearing a simple grey yukata and a gentle smile.

"Suzu," he called in greeting, and Suzu felt his knees go weak. He hesitated a moment, chiding himself for such a silly and useless reaction. "What is it? Are you nervous?" Toshi asked.

"What? No... I... why should I be nervous?" Too late Suzu realised that the soft-spoken, coy Suzu, who was the Earl's Suzu, wouldn't splutter like this. But Toshi chuckled and led Suzu inside.

The inside of the house, much like the estate as a whole, also was an unexpected mixture of northern and southern style. They were standing in a wide, open hall. To the left and to the right a staircase led to the upper floor. Opposite the entrance hall open doors revealed a smaller room. A family shrine, bigger and more beautiful than any Suzu had ever seen, occupied the room.

Suzu took a moment to get a feeling for the place. The wooden floor was polished to a warm sheen. The banisters – exquisitely carved dragons, winding their ways upwards. A single calligraphy, a masterpiece in black and golden ink, accentuated with humble splashes of vermilion, adorned the eastern wall. Beneath it stood an artful arrangement of a hydrangea blossom, peonies, and lush greens. Like its master, the house had an aura of simple elegance and beauty – and hidden secrets.

Suzu followed Toshi past the family shrine and down the hallway to a parlour. The open shori doors across the room revealed a glimpse of the enormous garden. A glass bell swung gently in the breeze, giving a chime of serene beauty. The room was sparsely furnished: another flower arrangement, and a low table, already bearing cups and a tea pot. Toshi motioned Suzu to take a seat, sat down on the opposite side, and poured the tea.

"I thought a cold barley tea would be more refreshing in this heat," he said. "I hope you're not disappointed."

A surprised but relieved laugh escaped Suzu, the tension he had felt since he had arrived, snapped. "Do I really strike you as so materialistic?" Suzu asked with laughter in his husky voice.

Toshi grinned. "One can never be too sure. And I wouldn't want to ruin the image you have of me."

"What am I to do with you? You keep dazzling me with all your riches, when I'm telling you, I am a simple boy from the boons. It doesn't take much to impress me."

Toshi cocked an eyebrow at him. "Is that so? I don't think I've ever seen you impressed by anything. Certainly not by any riches." Suzu smiled and shrugged. "And there is nothing simple about you, Suzu." Suzu felt pinned to the spot by Toshi's intense gaze, hardly able to breathe. Those eyes, like chips of agate – not for the first time Suzu felt as if those piercing eyes were able to see through all his layers, all his masks, and into the depth of his soul. Suzu shivered. The thought of being truly seen sent as much dread as excitement through him. Oh how he longed for Toshi to know him, see him – all of him, the good and the bad, the ugly and the beautiful. To see him – the real him. Yet at the same time he feared nothing more.

To cover his uncertainty, Suzu smiled and lifted the cup to his lips, lowering his eyes demurely. It was time to change the topic.

Suzu took swallowed his tea – which was admittedly very refreshing – and said, "So, you prepared the tea yourself? Isn't that what rich people have servants for?"

"I guess, but what's the fun in having someone else do everything for you?" And there it was, the opening Suzu hadn't been looking for. Asking about the seemingly absent servants had been nothing but a cheap trick to get out of an awkward situation, but now that it had come to it, Suzu might as well pry a little. He hadn't forgotten about Naloc's lousy threats, and he had no doubt the man would make good on them. Suzu would find a way to pay him back later.

"And what does your maid say about you stealing her work?"

"I don't have a maid."

"What?" Suzu only half feigned his surprise. It wasn't the answer he had expected. "Everyone this side of the River Opal has a maid."

"I guess this is normally the case, yes."

"Ah, but you are not normal," Suzu teased and was rewarded with a rakish grin and a wink. "All right, no maid. What about... well, you obviously have a driver, he picked me up earlier. That means there's also a groom and perhaps a stable boy?"

"The groom is the driver, no stable boy."

"Fine. A butler?"

"If by butler you mean a certain someone who has taken it upon himself to fill the roles of butler, footman, valet, and personal secretary, just so he can annoy and pester me with boring paperwork – then yes, I have one."

Suzu laughed. He knew Toshi was speaking about Kagetora. Suzu had met the man before, although only briefly. no-one really knew what the relationship between the Earl of Tsukikage and the quiet man, who shadowed him wherever he went, truly was. Was he the Earl's valet, his secretary? A friend? no-one knew, and no-one dared to inquire.

"I get it, I get it," Suzu chuckled. "Your household is a little unusual. But please don't try and tell me that gardening is your favourite pastime. There is no way you can care for all of this on your own." Suzu gestured outside, where the garden stretched away from the house, more park than garden.

This time Toshi was laughing, too. "Gods no. If I did it would be the most desolate place in all of the empire. I have a gardener – well, I usually do."

"You usually do?" Suzu raised an eyebrow in question. Toshi said nothing for a moment, and Suzu wondered if the man was trying to come up with a lie or evade the topic altogether.

But then: "He left with the maid."

Suzu burst out laughing, he couldn't help it. It was a strange kind of relief, and only then did Suzu realise that he had been afraid Toshi might make up lies and excuses, anything that might give a reason for doubt, that might prove Naloc right.

"He left with the *maid*? So you *did* have a maid!" Suzu said. "And what? The gardener stole her?"

"You could say so," Toshi chuckled. "They were planning on getting married – I guess they decided to elope."

"Doesn't that make you angry?"

"They are young, their family situations aren't the best. They probably just wanted time for themselves for a change. I'm sure they'll be back eventually."

Suzu latched onto that last sentence like a predator onto prey. Toshi wouldn't believe they'd come back if he had done away with them, he'd be looking for replacements. Suzu smiled – and smothered the tiny voice in his head that murmured that it might be a ruse, that that was exactly what Toshi wanted him to believe. No, Suzu wasn't going to let Naloc into his head, he wouldn't let the man poison him against the man he –

against Toshi. Naloc was prejudiced and he didn't know the Earl as Suzu did.

"You seem a very forgiving employer if you are ready to take them back, considering."

"I choose my employees very carefully. They are all people I know I can put my absolute trust in. I would not necessarily call them my friends, but in a strange way they are family to me. I know it doesn't make any sense. And please don't tell anyone, people already consider me eccentric. But... this is what my home is like." *And it could be yours, too.* The words were left unspoken, yet rang so clearly through the air. They tugged at Suzu's heart, trying to draw him in. He resisted, instead imagining the look on Naloc's face when Suzu, triumphantly, told him just how wrong he had been.

"Come," Toshi said, getting to his feet, invitingly holding a hand out to Suzu. "I want to show you the garden."

The garden, as Toshi called it, was a conglomeration of a variety of gardens, separated by cleverly placed high hedges and rows of trees, which created the illusion of suddenly stepping from one world into another simply by rounding a corner or stepping through an arch.

From the house one entered a traditional southern garden: serene, well-defined, elegant, and beautiful. A bowed bridge spanned a koi pond, stone lanterns lined the gravelled path. A maple gazed at its reflection in the clear water of the pond. Big old hydrangea bushes in hues from a vibrant red to a gentle blue and soft pink were splashes of colour. A bamboo grove formed the first border, a path leading into the cool green tinged shadows.

After only a few steps the path diverged. Toshi took them down the left-hand path – and into an entirely different world. Gnarled old trees, a riot of wildflowers – had it not been for the well-kept earthen path, it would have seemed as if nature reigned freely here. A hidden archway in a hedge, overgrown with rambling roses, was a portal into the stark contrast of a rose garden with its elegant order. The air was heavy with the sumptuous fragrance of hundreds of different kinds of roses.

Next they passed through a neat and fragrant herb garden, followed by a small orchard, and finally they came to what Toshi called his fairy garden, with a pond and a small stream. The stream ran through yet another hedge and came out on the other side as a small, artificial waterfall in a water garden, filled with lotus. Dragonflies flitted across the surface of the water, competing with its glitter in their sparkling colours.

Coming around in a circle they came to the last garden, which was more like a small refuge, hidden from the world. A tall gazebo of white stone stood in the centre of a lawn strewn with daisies. Wisteria fell like a curtain from the eaves. Inside, sitting cushion were arranged around a low table laid with food. A man stood beside the gazebo, impassive and still like a statue. His thin face was a neutral yet pleasant and utterly unreadable mask, his black eyes, however, were sharp, and seemed to perceive everything. The hyper-awareness with which he took in his surroundings, the strength and power that radiated from him – this man was no secretary or valet, no matter what he and his master claimed.

"My Lord," Kagetora said with a bow. He turned to Suzu and bowed to him as well. Something in his gaze softened;

Suzu could have sworn there was a smile lingering at the corners of the man's lips.

"Ah, Suzu, I think you have met Kagetora before but you two haven't been officially introduced, yet," Toshi remarked. "Well, Kagetora is my... hmmm." Toshi fell quiet with a pensive hum. It surprised Suzu that Toshi had to think about it and didn't just give Suzu the official version of who Kagetora was.

And so it was Kagetora who suddenly answered instead, in a dry, emotionless voice. "I'm his butler, his bodyguard, his spy, his drinking buddy, his sparring partner, his conscience, his advisor, his shoulder to cry on. Have I forgotten anything?" Suzu gaped at the man, incredulous.

"Yes, you idiot!" Toshi retorted. "You forgot that you are my best friend, that we are like brothers." Toshi actually rolled his eyes at his friend, then burst out laughing when he noticed the bewildered expression on Suzu's face. He threw an arm around Suzu's shoulders. "What? Is that so hard to believe?"

"Yes – I mean, no. I'm surprised that you are telling me this. It's not something that's supposed to be common knowledge, is it?"

"True. But I wanted you to know, and I trust you not to tell anyone."

A blush heated Suzu's cheeks, happiness bubbled in his chest. Kagetora, genuinely smiling this time, gestured at the small feast he had laid out for them. "I'll leave you to it then." He bowed – winked at Suzu – and left them alone.

The food was sumptuous. Graved salmon, various side dishes, chilled watermelon. The water, cold like fresh spring water, was infused with slices of lemon, ginger, and sprigs of rosemary. A soft breeze carried the scent of the wisteria, the gentle chime of a summer bell.

"Is that really all right? Telling me about Kagetora?" Suzu asked eventually.

Toshi smiled and took a sip of water. "Of course it is. I told you, I trust you."

"Must be difficult, maintaining that facade."

"Perhaps it is harder for me than it is for him."

"What do you mean?"

"Kagetora – he is very... aware of his duties, always has been. When we were children all I wanted was for him to be my friend, and it frustrated me to no end when he kept his distance and was always so servile and correct, calling me "young master". That changed only when my mother finally took pity on me. She sat us down and explained very clearly that there was nothing wrong with us being friends. That, in fact, it would be better, that it would make our bond stronger. But she also imparted that it was necessary for us to keep it secret from the world. Finding out then just how much Kagetora had wanted to be my friend, too, made me ridiculously happy. So we became friends, best friends. We worked hard on the picture of master and servant we show to the world, but I wish there was no need for it."

Suzu understood only too well. He, too, had been wearing masks all his life, and even though he mostly didn't mind, there were times they exhausted him, and times in which he wished there were no masks. Once he had believed that if he wore one long enough he could become that person. He had been wrong. Only after it had been ripped off of him had he realised how suffocating it had become. Now he could take them off, replenish his energy, was allowed time to be himself. No masks that slowly suffocated him anymore – none but one. When had the one he wore towards Toshi become so heavy to bear. So painful. When had he started wanting Toshi to see him, just him? When had he become so scared of finding out what would happen if he dropped the mask?

Yet the longer he was with Toshi, the closer they got, the more relaxed Suzu found himself in the man's company – and the more his mask had begun to slip. And Toshi? He hadn't seemed to mind, not once. Was it possible? Could it be? Could Toshi really love him, accept him as he really was? The beauty of him and his ugly side. The uncontrollable anger, and his thirst for knowledge. His independence and his need to call someone his home. His shattered and badly mended heart.

The idea sent a flash of joy on a wave of anxiety through him. He shouldn't be wanting this. No, Suzu had all he needed – the family he found for himself. That was enough, he needed nothing else. And most of all, he didn't need that kind of love – he didn't want it. It only led to pain and misery and he wanted none of it. He hated that a part of him still craved for it nonetheless, after everything.

"Well, anyway," Toshi continued, interrupting Suzu's rumination. "My sister and her family know of course. And Jarick and Akari, who are basically family. What I'm trying to say is... Suzu, I wanted you to know, because..." Toshi reached across the table and took Suzu's hand in his, his light grey eyes locked with Suzu's. "I know – and I won't push. I know you have your reasons. All I want is for you to know that I meant what I said. I want to be with you – now and till the end of my days. That won't change, even if I have to wait decades for an answer. You know I'm not good with this... with people. You're the only one... Just... spend some time here every once in a while, whenever you want."

A compromise, that was what Toshi was offering him, and it said more than any oath of love. For this man, who usually seemed so aloof, so cold, to bare his vulnerability and gentleness to Suzu like this – why couldn't Suzu just follow suit? He wanted to, he didn't want to. He wanted to flee Toshi's presence, and he wanted to throw himself into the man's arms and beg him never to let go. He wanted to yell and scream, to tear at his hair and slap himself for being so... weak. Oh how he hated this weakness, this indecisiveness, this desire of him to be loved by this man when love had destroyed his life once already. But Toshi was throwing him a lifeline. One he could accept.

Suzu smiled and squeezed Toshi's hand. "I'd love that," he said. Toshi stood up, and pulled Suzu to his feet and into his arms. A light touch, no more than the tip of a finger beneath his chin, gently tilted Suzu's head back. "Thank you," Toshi whispered before he leaned down and kissed Suzu. Softly, gently, susurrating a promise of delights. Suzu couldn't help the tiny sound of protest when Toshi pulled away. Chuckling, Toshi dragged him through the curtain of wisteria and into the twilight. Lanterns had been lit – and Suzu marvelled at Kagetora's skills, he hadn't even once noticed the man.

They made their way back into the fairy garden where they took a seat on the high backed bench by the pond, leaning against each other in companionable silence. Fireflies were already flitting through the air, twinkling like tiny stars among the bushes and flowers, blinking amongst the reflection of the first true stars on the pond's still waters. The wind had picked up, rustling through the trees, the evening serenade of birds the only other sound.

"Toshi," Suzu whispered eventually.
"Hm?"
"Thank you."
"What for?"

Suzu took a fortifying breath. "For understanding. For not pressuring me. For being so impossibly patient with me. It's not that I don't want to be with you – you know that I do. But… it's difficult to explain…" How did you explain that you hated the idea of loving someone with all your heart? How to explain that you were still fighting against it although you knew you had already fallen deep enough to never get out of it again. How did you explain this? To the person who had opened their heart and filled it with you. If it even was you they had filled it with and not an illusion. Suzu didn't want to risk breaking something that was as precious as the moon. "I… I'd really like to stay with you more often… here… perhaps once a month? And… and I'll try…" Try – try to explain? Try to become that ideal that Toshi loved?

"It's all right, Suzu," Toshi replied, ending Suzu's stammering. "I'll wait until you are ready – I'll always be waiting for you." The gentleness in his voice, the way he looked at him stole Suzu's breath, sent a tingling sensation through his body, and if he hadn't been sitting already, his knees would have buckled. Being with Toshi, Suzu had no idea if the Moon Goddess loved him, as everyone else claimed, or if she hated him.

"You are too good for me, I don't deserve you." Suzu hadn't meant to say this out loud, but he wouldn't take it back either.

Toshi sighed. "How can you be so sure? Perhaps it's me who doesn't deserve you."

Suzu frowned. What an odd thing to say. But before he could ponder it further, Toshi's lips claimed his in a kiss so very different to the one before. It was deep, demanding, with a hunger behind it. Speaking a language of desire. Suzu moaned as Toshi pressed him back against the bench, one hand slipping beneath the hem of Suzu's yukata, describing a trail of fire along his inner thigh, slowly, oh so very slowly moving upwards. Suzu tangled a hand in Toshi's hair, and bared his neck for him, allowing the man to paint a path of kisses along his jawline. Toshi's fingers were a butterfly touch, agonisingly teasing, a mere brush against –

Thunder rumbled overhead. Suzu jumped, pushing Toshi away in reflex. "Th-thunder," he stammered – and could have slapped himself for sounding so stupid.

Toshi raised an eyebrow. "It's all right, it's still far away." And he leaned in again, kissing the spot beneath Suzu's earlobe. But Suzu's mind was on the oncoming thunderstorm now. It didn't matter how far away it was, the fact remained that it was coming.

"Ne, Toshi, let's go inside."

"We still have lots of time before –" A sudden squall, lightning forking across the sky, for an instance illuminating enormous portentous clouds, proved Toshi's words wrong. Thunder followed only seconds later.

Suzu jumped to his feet, trembling. "T-Toshi, let's go inside," he said more urgently.

"Are you scared?" Toshi asked, startled.

"No! Just..."

"All right, let's go." Toshi grabbed his hand and led him back through the maze of gardens. They were going too slow. Suzu wanted to run, to sprint back to the house, the quicker the better. But Toshi was still calmly walking along the path. Just once he glanced down at their clasped hands; Suzu's grip was tight enough to grind the fine bones of Toshi's hand. He didn't comment. Above them the clouds raced across the sky, the sudden gale chasing them relentlessly. Lightning flashed and thunder roared.

"Can we run, please?" Suzu pleaded, raising his voice over the wind.

"You *are* scared, aren't you?"

"No! I just think... it's going to start raining any moment now." What a lame excuse, but as if the sky had heard him and decided that if rain was what he wanted, rain he would get, a sudden downpour followed on another roar of thunder.

Hand in hand they sprinted towards the house. They didn't stop to kick their shoes off but burst straight into the parlour, heedless of the tatami mat. For a moment they just stood looking at each other, dripping.

"Huh, that came a lot quicker than I thought," Toshi admitted at last, laughter colouring his voice. Another roll of thunder, close enough now to shake the ground, made Suzu yelp. Unconsciously, he flung himself at Toshi, burying his face against the man's chest, his arms tightly around his middle, hands grabbing fistfuls of Toshi's yukata. It took Suzu a second to notice what this reaction must look like, but when he tried to step away quickly, Toshi's arms were already around him. Slowly he lifted his head – and found the man looking at him with what he had to assume was an amused expression, he couldn't be sure in the dark. Outside the rain had turned into a deluge, the torrent whipping the trees. Toshi, not letting go of Suzu, shuffled around, until he could reach the edge of the sliding door and pulled it closed.

"Shouldn't we also close the verandah?" Suzu asked, not that he was very enthusiastic about it. Toshi shook his head.

"Kagetora will do that if necessary. He's much quicker at it anyway. So... afraid of thunderstorms, eh?"

Suzu felt his face flush. "What?" He was trying to sound indignant and failed. Flinching violently at another flash of lightning and the clap of thunder, did not help. He could feel the soft vibrations of Toshi quietly chuckling in the man's broad chest. "That's not funny," Suzu snapped, then bit his tongue. Gods damn it, why was it so difficult to keep his mask on when he was with this man? Toshi, however, didn't seem to notice or didn't mind, he only squeezed Suzu tighter.

"I'm sorry," he said softly into Suzu's ear. "It's all right. I won't let anything happen to you. You are safe here."

And Suzu did feel safe – here, in Toshi's arms, while outside the storm raged, and the storm inside him never abated. It was dangerous, this kind of safety. Treacherous. If his mended heart broke again, he didn't think there'd be anything left to salvage this time. And yet... and yet... and yet...

"Toshi," he whispered, "distract me?" In answer Toshi's arms around him loosened, yet their contact never broke as Toshi took him by the hand and led him through the house and upstairs. The warm yellow light of lamps illuminated their way.

Suzu didn't see much of the bedroom. As soon as the doors shut behind them Toshi pulled him into a kiss as fierce and wild as the raging storm.

And Suzu hated how he let himself be guided, getting swept away by the exhilaration of Toshi's passion. He hated the way he allowed the man to worship him, how he let him drive him, oh so slowly, to ecstasy.

He wanted more. He wanted Toshi to abandon all restraint, all care, wanted the man to ravage him. He wanted to show him pleasure he had never known existed.

Yet even in throes of passion Suzu held on to his mask, as tightly as if he'd drown without it – and he hated *this*! This person who curled up against Toshi afterwards, that fell asleep in the man's arms as if it was his right. He wanted that person gone, he wanted to be that person. He wanted the man lying next to him all for himself. For himself – Suzu.

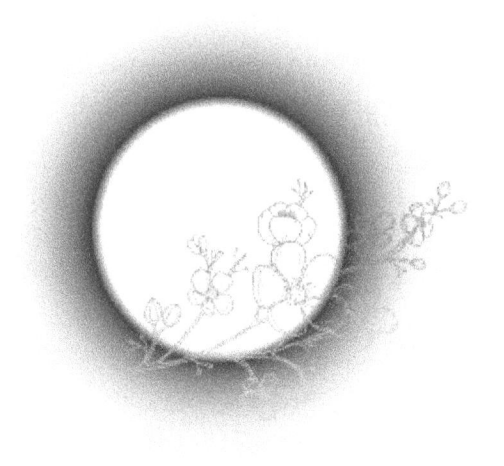

Chapter 18

Suzu woke the next morning to the songs of birds and sunlight. Opening his eyes, he blinked at the unfamiliar ceiling, momentarily confused, until the last tendrils of sleep evaporated like mist in morning light. He turned his head and a smile tugged at the corners of his lips.

"Good morning," Toshi said softly. He was propped up on his arm, chin resting on his hand, regarding Suzu with that miraculous secret warmth in his eyes that seemed to be reserved for Suzu alone.

"Morning," Suzu replied, feeling suddenly shy. It was a strange feeling, but something about waking up next to this man, feeling his affection like the sun on his skin, made Suzu realise he had been given an ineffably precious gift, and he didn't want to break it. "Were you watching me sleep?"

"I was."

"Weirdo," Suzu chuckled, feeling a rush of fondness.

"Takes one to know one," Toshi retorted and rolled onto Suzu, pressing him back into the mattress, and kissed him, deep and lingering, before Suzu had a chance to wonder about that comment.

They remained in bed for a while longer, luxuriating in the intimacy. When they finally emerged from the bedroom, they found breakfast waiting for them in the parlour. The doors had been thrown wide once more, revealing the view of the garden, lush green and vibrant colours. Raindrops were still glittering in the sun, soon to be gone, victims to the relentless heat. As soon as they had sat down, Kagetora appeared with a fresh pot of tea – and vanished again at once, like a shadow flitting across the wall. It was strange to know someone was always close by, watching for hidden dangers, yet being unable to perceive that person unless they wanted you to. Because his vision was limited, Suzu had trained hard – with Haldor's help – to 'feel' the presence of other people, to anticipate their moves. It wasn't that his right eye was completely blind, he could still perceive light and shadow, and therefore broader movement. He had had to learn to be more observant, and thus had become quite proficient at reading small, subtle movements that allowed him to predict what a person would do next. Despite the scar and colour of his right eye, not many people knew that he was almost blind in one eye. And he was proud of having accomplished this. Yet Kagetora completely eluded him.

Toshi must have noticed his discomfort, for he asked, "Does he scare you? Kagetora?"

"No, that's not it," Suzu replied honestly. "It's just... well, you know I can't see with my right eye. It used to freak me out, not knowing if someone approached me from the side, if something came at me, all that. It got bad enough that I panicked every time I wasn't able to cling to a wall or have someone I trusted shield my side. Until Haldor started training me, he made me learn to listen more closely to my senses and my instinct. Not many people can sneak up on me anymore, but Kagetora… he certainly lives up to his name, he's like a shadow."

"That he is. I'm sorry, I didn't realise… I'll tell him to stop sneaking around."

Suzu laughed. "No, it's all right, let him sneak. We can make a game of it, see how long it takes me to catch him."

After breakfast they decided to go for a walk and take a look at what damage the storm had caused. They had just come from the gardens and were rounding the corner of the house when they saw a carriage coming up the driveway. It swept into the courtyard and pulled to a stop next to them. The carriage was small, without a crest adorning its sides, the curtain was drawn across the window. For a moment nothing happened. Suzu could see the curtain twitch, but that was all. He glanced at Toshi and the man's face darken – he, at least, seemed to have an inkling as to who was sitting inside.

Then the door creaked open and a man jumped out: tall, brawny, dirty blond hair bound back messily in his neck. The left side of his face was a landscape of scars, pulling the corner of his mouth into a permanent sneer, his beady eyes glittered maliciously.

The moment the man had emerged from the carriage, Toshi stepped in front of Suzu. His posture was tense, the merriment and gentleness from only moments before now locked tightly behind ice and steel. Toshi was gone and in his place stood one of the most powerful and redoubtable men in Tsukiyama – the Earl of Tsukikage.

Suzu's instincts kicked in. He shifted slightly so he had a good view from behind the Earl's back of their unexpected guest, and which also allowed him to react quickly if necessary. To the stranger, on the other hand, his movement seemed as if he shrank back, uncertain, perhaps even scared.

"Heya, Earl," the man drawled, cocking his head to leer at Suzu. "Sorry to interrupt your fun time."

"What do you want?" the Earl snapped.

"Got a message from my master."

"Then deliver it and be gone." The Earl held his hand out expectantly.

"Aww, don't you want to introduce me to your pretty friend?"

A low growl came from the Earl's throat, the air around him growing heavy with the threat of violence. The man raised his hands and took a step back, laughing. He cast a glance over his shoulder back at the carriage. Suzu wasn't sure, but he thought he saw the curtain twitch again, yet what caught his attention was the stranger's profile – the unblemished side of his face. It looked oddly familiar. Before Suzu could think of where he might have seen him before, the man continued, and Suzu, though pretending not to, paid close attention.

"All right, all right. Here." But instead of handing a letter or a note to the Earl, the man said, "When day holds dominion over night, the moon and all his stars will fall into a dreamless sleep, and a new moon will rise in his stead." For a long moment the man and the Earl stared at each other, until, suddenly, the stranger winked at Suzu, the scars twisting his grin into a grotesque face. He jumped into the carriage, slammed the door, and the carriage rattled back the way it had come.

Suzu suppressed a shiver. That man made his skin crawl. But the strange familiarity of him was nagging at Suzu's mind. He watched the carriage trundle down the driveway, and just before it was out of sight, someone leaned out of the carriage window and looked back at them – and it wasn't the man, but they were already too far away for Suzu to make out their features. So Suzu turned to the Earl.

He was livid. Rage radiated off him in cold, violent intensity, his face set in a dark grimace. "T-Toshi?" Suzu asked, disquieted, taking an involuntary step back from the man. The Earl whirled around, the full force of his cold furious gaze made Suzu gasp. He froze. Suzu didn't frighten easily, and there was hardly anyone who truly intimidated him. Yet in this moment, he realised, he was honestly, truly scared of the Earl.

The Earl saw him flinch, saw Suzu's fear, and the ice and steel broke, fell away from him like leaves in a storm. The tension left his body, the grey eyes warmed. He was only Toshi once more.

"Suzu," Toshi said quietly, as if Suzu might bolt, and held a hand out, but didn't reach for him. "I'm sorry. I'm so sorry... I... I didn't mean to scare you."

"You didn't," Suzu lied and tried to smile, though it felt strained and wobbly. He didn't take Toshi's hand. Instead he went to him and slung his arms around the man's middle. Toshi returned the embrace – perhaps a bit too fiercely – and planted a kiss on Suzu's temple.

"Sorry," he whispered again.

"It's all right." And then, because Suzu couldn't stop himself: "Who was that thug?"

"no-one. The associate of a business parter. Don't worry about it. But he should know better than... I don't know what he was thinking... That is... Suzu, I'm sorry, but I need you to forget what you've just heard."

Suzu scowled, but nodded. His guts twisted uncomfortably. Naloc's accusations rang in his head, mocking his trust, his certainty of Toshi. What if Naloc was right? No! Absolutely not! Suzu knew Toshi better, he knew the side of him he hid from the world, his gentleness, his kindness, his passion, and his vulnerability. What did Naloc know? Rumours and assumptions.

An echo of the fear he had felt just heartbeats ago washed through Suzu like a wave. To suppress the shudder he hugged Toshi tighter. He hadn't known that side of the man. Neither had he known Toshi would have any business with such dubious personages.

Still. That anger, that rage – Suzu was familiar with those, felt a certain kind of kinship. That had not been the anger of having someone inconvenient interrupt one's time with one's lover. It burnt much brighter than that, fiercer. Protective. Yes. It was the kind of anger he felt when someone dared threaten his family, his loved ones. The kind of anger he had felt at Naloc for threatening Toshi.

Whoever this alleged business parter and their associate were, they were bad news. But Suzu was certain that whatever had happened to the maid and the gardener wasn't Toshi's fault. Rather, it seemed that Toshi was tangled up in something dangerous – and he was the kind of man who did whatever necessary to protect the people he cared about. Oh, Naloc was not going to like that... That thought gave Suzu an idea. He would give Naloc something to gnaw on: that strange man and his even stranger message. Naloc was on the hunt, so let him hunt. Who knew, he might inadvertently help Toshi.

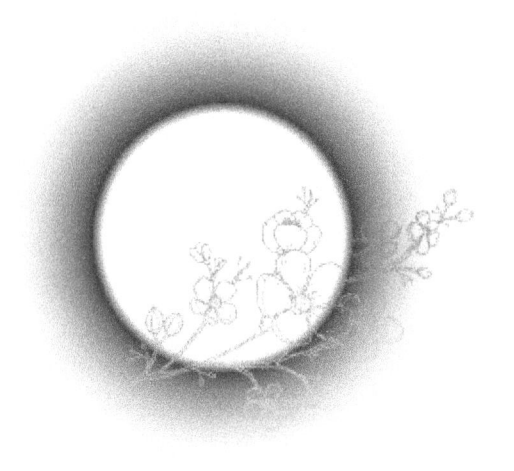

Chapter 19

Deep breath, Jin told himself. It didn't help, his lungs wouldn't fill with air, and his feet seemed to have decided to take root – right in front of the Singing Dragon. Gods, not even a week ago he would have given anything just to see Kari again, but now... First things first, he really needed to drill it into his head that the boy was not Kari but Suzu – though they also were the same, weren't they? Jin groaned and furiously rubbed his head, making his hair look like he had just walked out of a typhoon. In all honesty, Suzu and Kari were two completely different people – if they hadn't been – *argh*! Jin was certain he was going mad – any day now... It would be easier if he just stayed as far away from the young Furyusha as possible. But here he was.

Had he done something wrong? Why was Naloc punishing him? Why couldn't Risa or Durin or Niall or anyone, really, have come to get the information Suzu was supposed to have gathered while at the Earl's? Besides, Jin had issues with that as well. If the Earl was dangerous, it wasn't safe for Suzu to be snooping around, no matter if the Earl loved him or not. Which, again, was another matter Jin couldn't wrap his head around. The few times he had seen the Earl, the man hadn't struck him as the loving and caring type.

But there was no arguing with Naloc when he had the bit between his teeth. He commanded, everyone else obeyed. And Jin wasn't in any position to argue in the first place. He was practically dead weight, a ne'er-do-well who couldn't even write one sentence without ten mistakes, who had been refused one apprenticeship after the other. If there was something, anything he could do to repay Naloc for all the man had done for him, Jin would do it. Even if torture would have been the kinder option. Aside from that, there were still two young people missing.

Jin took a deep breath, forcing the air into his lungs. He could do it, he just needed to be professional about it. Yes, be professional, his feelings had nothing do with it. Right.

"Are you coming in or not?" asked a voice, sounding exceedingly bored. Jin nearly jumped out of his skin. Two teenage boys were standing in the doorway, glaring at him. Seeing as they would never dare treat a potential customer this rudely, Jin gathered they knew who he was. The daggers they were glaring at him also told him that they knew he was the source for Suzu's distress. This day just couldn't get any better.

"Naloc sent me. I need to speak to Suzu," Jin stated in his most professional and confident voice. He wasn't going to let some little boys intimidate him.

"We know," the right one retorted and rolled his eyes at Jin. He actually rolled his eyes at him – Jin felt the sudden urge to strangle the kid. The other boy looked slightly familiar... Ah! Jin remembered he had been there last time. Great. Jin had thought the youth meek and shy, but although he wasn't saying a single word, he was glowering fiercely at Jin.

"Suzu has just finished his daily training. You know, he is an amazing swordsman, Haldor says he's the best student he's ever had, and Haldor knows what he's talking about."

"Hmm." Jin hummed, disinterested. He wasn't sure why the boy was telling him this, but he could make an educated guess.

"Oh, but Suzu is also really good in hand to hand combat," the youth continued with a smirk. "He could probably take you down without even breaking a sweat. Right, Rani?" The other boy – Rani – nodded emphatically. Yes, Jin thought, that's what he had thought. They were trying to scare him. As if he needed any more reason to be scared witless of another confrontation with Suzu.

"All right," Jin drawled. It wasn't the reaction the boys had hoped for. The older boy huffed indignantly and Rani's expression became downright murderous.

"Akito?" Rani said quietly, his voice tight. "Shouldn't we tell Ryū that this... that he is here. To see Suzu."

"Guess you are right."

Fabulous. So they weren't satisfied with making him feel as unwelcome as a cockroach in the kitchen – as if he needed their help for that – now they were calling for reinforcements of the worst kind. Granted, he had met Ryū only once, had exchanged not a single word with him, and the situation had probably been even worse than today, but something about him... Ryū – tall, handsome, built like a young god, basically exuding masculinity – was the type of man that made Jin itch for a fight. To punch this perfect visage, make him a little less perfect. Ryū was the kind of person who seemed to just get anything he wanted, who was able to do anything – while Jin... well... there had been a time Jin had thought he could do anything, become anything. He had been wrong, and he was not above admitting that he felt bitter towards those who had everything. Jin was probably being unfair to the young man, but he couldn't help it. And he thanked the gods once more that the Singing Dragon only entertained male customers for Niall had a very unhealthy crush on the guy.

"I'm pretty sure that you were told to expect me today, weren't you?" Jin pointed out and was rewarded with the youths looking chagrined, if only for a moment.

"Fine," Akito snapped. "Rani, go and fetch Suzu. I'll take care of that one. And then I'll go and find Ryū," he added with a vicious grin. Damn that little minx. Jin hoped Ryū was too busy to find the time to pick a fight with him.

Jin followed Akito. They passed by Kazue's parlour, down the hallway-like verandah. From behind the many closed doors Jin could hear voices, laughter, the hectic sounds of people getting ready for their working day. Akito stopped in front of the last room at the far end of the verandah.

"There. Sit!" the boy ordered, pointing to a spot on the wooden floor as if Jin was a dog. Irritated, Jin crossed his arms in front of his chest and gave the boy a hard stare. It didn't have the desired effect. The boy merely huffed and shrugged his shoulders. "Whatever. But don't you dare move. I don't want you wandering around. Suzu will be here shortly." With that, Akito turned and left, leaving Jin to his own devices – and feeling stupid. He shouldn't let the hostility of a boy several years his junior get to him like this. Jin understood only too well. Had he been in Akito's position, he'd be the same. It used to be him, getting angry at other people for daring to hurt Suzu. Being on the opposite side was a horrible feeling.

Dejected, Jin sat down and leaned against a wooden beam. So many years – so many nights he had dreamt of finding his Kari again. Of Kari falling into his arms, crying tears of joy at being reunited. Swearing to the Moon Goddess that he'd never ever let go of him again, if only she brought Kari back to him. Nothing was as he had wished for, imagined – not even Kari. Suzu – it wasn't only the name that was different. Perhaps he hadn't found Kari after all.

The door behind him slid open. Jin turned around, and his breath hitched. He was dumbstruck by the young man's beauty. No memory, no mental image, no fantasy could ever compare to the real Suzu. He was wearing a simple black yukata, bound loosely at the waist, so it fell open wide enough to reveal hard, defined muscles beneath a skin like white jade. His wet hair was a midnight cascade down to the small of his back. He was almost unreal, otherworldly, ethereal, an artist's masterpiece. Not the thin silver scar that ran from his brow to his cheekbone, nor the opaque haze of his right eye could mar his grace.

Wordlessly Suzu sat down and leaned back against the frame of his door. He scrutinised Jin with a haughty expression that made Jin squirm. He would have given anything to break the tension, the electrified silence, but his brain felt empty, his mouth dry and uncooperative. Sweat beaded his brow, his heartbeat quickened. He felt like a fly caught in a spider's net, prey cornered by a predator. He stood no chance against this divine being, never had.

"Didn't think you'd dare show your face here again," Suzu said after an eternity.

Jin cleared his throat and tried to collect himself. "W-well... I didn't have much of a choice. Naloc's orders."

"And since when do you follow orders so obediently?"

Jin had no answer to this. On the contrary it took him by surprise, it poked at something deep inside of him. When had he become so obedient? There had been a time he had baulked at every tiny order and had revelled in being contradictory. His urge to be free from a life of strictness and rules had been so strong, he had been blind and too stupid to see he was being manipulated.

While Jin was lost in thought, Rani had followed Suzu out onto the verandah, carrying a small ash pot and a pipe. He passed the pipe to Suzu and lit it for him. Jin watched Suzu exhale a cloud of smoke.

"You smoke," he stated stupidly.

"I thought it better to have something to do with my hands – keeps me from strangling you."

Ouch, well, he might have deserved that. Jin caught Rani's smirk, the boy didn't even try to hide it, and clenched his jaw. Gods, he wanted this over with.

"Thanks, Rani," Suzu said, pulled the boy to him and planted a gentle kiss on Rani's forehead. "Run along now. We have business to talk."

"All right. Call if you need anything." Rani stood up and turned to leave, but not before he had once more glared at Jin. Then he was gone. Jin sighed.

"You are really loved," he remarked, surprised by how much it stung.

"I am." There was no smugness in Suzu's voice, it was a simple, honest confirmation. Yet Jin's heart constricted painfully. I *love you* – the words were on the tip of his tongue. He swallowed them. He had no right to say them – nor was he sure they were true. Kari – he loved Kari, he missed Kari with every fibre of his being. But he didn't know this young man, sitting across from him. Yes, Jin was fascinated by the Furyusha, drawn to him like a moth to a flame. However, being here in the presence of him, no-one would have mistaken Suzu for Kari. Jin wanted to flee from him and be closer to him at the same time. In his mind Suzu was like a palimpsest – if he could just find the right angle, the right light, perhaps he could find the hazy remnants of Kari.

As the silence dragged on, Jin finally became aware of Suzu watching him intently, studying him as if he were some interesting specimen. Jin cleared his throat and said – trying and probably failing to sound business like. "So, were you able to find out anything about the missing servants?"

Suzu took a deep drag from his pipe. Cocking his head slightly, he exhaled another plum of white smoke, not taking his eyes off Jin. Jin was again reminded of a predator cornering its prey. It sent a shiver down his spine.

"Indeed," Suzu drawled. "I found out that the Earl is sad and worried about the disappearance of his employees."

"So?"

"So what? Did you just listen? He's got nothing to do with their disappearance. He's just as worried."

"Could be an act."

"It's not."

"What makes you so sure? Because that's what he told you? Come now, you aren't naïve, you know those noblemen don't give a damn about their servants. He claims to be worried? Oh please."

"And what do you know?" Suzu snapped. "Do you even know any of 'those noblemen' personally? Or are these all just assumptions based on envy? Granted, there are enough of them around who are heartless and greedy and consider themselves superior. But there are as many who genuinely care about other people, who know that their status and their money comes with a responsibility to society and those who don't have as much as they do. Perhaps you first ought to learn not to judge a book by its covers. So yes, I am damn sure when I tell you that Toshi cares about the people he employs and would never harm them."

The fervour with which Suzu spoke for the Earl irritated Jin. *Toshi?* Jin had the sudden urge to punch something. Fine, perhaps he was a little prejudiced, what had those high born across the river ever done for him? But if the Earl of Tsukikage, Mori no Toshiaki, was so concerned about his lost 'employees', why was he acting as if nothing was amiss?

"I still don't see what makes you so sure that this is not all an act," Jin grumbled.

"Because I know him!" Suzu retorted sharply, his eyes blazing.

"Oh, you know him. How convenient."

Suzu slammed his pipe down. "Yes, I know him. Unlike you. Unlike your beloved Naloc. Unlike most of Getsuro. You may think him cold, aloof, and harsh – I know him better. I know the sides of him he doesn't show the public." Suddenly, a vicious, nasty snarl appeared on Suzu's lovely lips. He leaned forward, his husky voice became quieter but all the more cutting. "I know his gentleness, his generosity – he never takes his pleasure without giving in return." Oh gods, Jin did not want to hear this. He didn't want to know, didn't want to imagine the two of them together. But instead of cutting this off, he just sat there, petrified, letting each word cut him like a knife. "You can't imagine the passion burning inside that man,"

Suzu continued mercilessly, "or how he abandons all restraint when lust overcomes him."

Slowly, Suzu sat back, took up his pipe again, and brought it to his lips, satisfied with the blows he had dealt. Jin stared at the wooden floorboards in front of him, trying to get himself back under control. He wanted to purge the images Suzu's words had conjured from his mind. He wanted to silence the voice that kept screaming that *he* should be the one the young man spoke about like this – he should be the only man allowed to touch him. No, he had no right to even think so, not any more. Jin felt angry, not with Suzu, not even with the Earl. With himself. So he welcomed the pain, for he deserved it.

"I think we can agree that I am the only one here who is at all qualified to judge the Earl's character," Suzu said after a long while. His voice was oddly calm, almost emotionless now. Jin only inclined his head in agreement. He just wanted to get out of here. Naloc was not going to like it, but Jin had gotten what he had come for, and it was as it was. Yes, he should just go now. If only his body would cooperate. Instead, Jin lifted his head, looked at Suzu, and froze. His heart was a well of painful yearning. He wanted to be close to Suzu, to hold the young man in his arms, to feel him, smell him, taste him. He wanted to erase the last five years, he wanted back what he had lost because of his own stupidity.

Eventually, Jin managed to push himself to his feet. Suzu, in all those long minutes had just mutely stared back at him. "Well... thank you. I'll be go –"

"Wait!" Suzu cut him off, and when Jin looked at him in surprise, Suzu, not looking at Jin anymore, wore a pensive expression. "Wait," he repeated. "While I am certain that the Earl has done no harm to the missing two... that is... well...

whatever has happened to them, it might not have been Toshi, but possibly *because* of him."

"Because of him?"

"I'm not sure, but..." Suzu looked up at Jin then, and there was something akin to pleading in his eyes. "I think Toshi might be in trouble."

"These are the exact words of the message?" Naloc asked again, frowning at the piece of paper in his hand. Jin nodded. "How accurate do you think this really is?"

"Ka-- Suzu has always had an exceptional memory. I believe him when he says those were the exact words."

"'Scuse me, but if his memory is that good," Durin interjected, "why in the Goddess's name did he write it down? It's obviously too dangerous to have written evidence of."

"Well..." Jin hesitated, his gaze flitting about, landing everywhere but on any of his companions.

"Let me guess," Niall said as if it should have been obvious, "he didn't trust you to remember it correctly."

Feeling his face heating with embarrassment, Jin grumbled some unintelligible affirmation, and tried to ignore the knowing grins and nodding heads. "Anyway," he raised his voice over the snickers, "what does it mean? Is it something of importance?"

"Hard to say," Naloc replied, his voice serious. "But if it weren't, and if its contents weren't dangerous, why go to the length of making a damned cryptic poem out of it."

The room was quiet while everyone seemed to try to figure out the meaning of it. Eventually, and to no-one's surprise, it was Durin who spoke up. "To be frank, I don't think this is the most elaborate cypher. Some parts are even pretty straightforward. Such as this: 'When day triumphs over night' – it's the summer solstice during Tsuki no Matsuri. That means whatever it is, it's going to happen in three weeks."

"Hmm, I think Durin is right. Suzu told you the message was delivered verbally, not in a letter? That means it can't be that hard to figure out."

"But does this even concern us?" They all turned in surprise to the man who had spoken. Kuroto, Risa's right hand and almost father-in-law, usually preferred to be quiet, unless he had something important to say. Older than Risa by thirty years, Kuroto had never been an ambitious man, leading a good life and being able to provide for his wife and daughter had always been his priority. He thought nothing of having younger people ordering him around – *if* they deserved his respect. In turn, not only Naloc but all of them valued Kuroto's input and advise.

A low murmur filled the room. Even if they were looking for two missing people, even if they thought the Earl was acting suspicious about their disappearance, prying into the man's private business might go too far.

Naloc pensively stroked his beard. "There is only one way to find out, and that is by deciphering this message. Should it turn out to be something private, something that concerns only the Earl, we will drop the issue and focus on our search for the youngsters. However... how shall I put this... I have a bad feeling about this. Jin, didn't Suzu say he was afraid that the Earl might be in some kind of trouble? And look here, this part." Naloc put the piece of paper on the table for all to see and stabbed a finger at a particular word. "'The moon and his stars' – *his?* That's too odd to be a simple mistake. I think they aren't speaking about the Goddess, or her celestial avatar, but about the emperor – the Moon Emperor and his Moon Council."

The silence that followed was absolute. It seemed as if even the birds outside had ceased their singing. no-one needed to ask what 'dreamless sleep' meant if Naloc's interpretation was correct. But it was preposterous, inconceivable, outrageous. In the thousand years the empire had existed, through natural disasters, disputes, clan wars, the institution of the Moon Emperor of Tsukiyama had never been threatened. The history of the empire had seen emperors die before their time of illness or disaster, emperors abdicating, and in one instance there had even been a public outcry and general demand for a new election. But never in a thousand years had there been a plot to assassinate the emperor or their council. It was unthinkable.

"Well," Durin sighed. "I had really hoped I was reading something into this that wasn't there. Knowing and not doing anything against it... What if they succeed?"

"I think," Risa finally spoke up, "I got a hunch what happened to that maid and her gardener. Guess they heard or saw something they shouldn't have." Risa shrugged. "Doesn't tell us what the Earl did or didn't do, though."

"What?" Jin burst out. "Isn't it obvious that he did something to them, those were his servants, I mean..." He trailed off at the sight of Niall shaking her head with a slightly exasperated expression, Durin scowling at him, and Risa raising an eyebrow. Anger was like a stone in his belly. Why didn't they see something that glaringly obvious? Why was everyone suddenly trying to make excuses for the blasted Earl of Tsukikage? Jin was so fed up with everyone treating him like some kind of idiot.

A heavy hand landed on his shoulder. Jin turned his head and found Naloc looking at him with his most fatherly expression – a mixture of patience, exasperation, and warmth. "Jin." The patronising sound of Naloc's voice made Jin cringe. "I understand, but you cannot let your personal feelings cloud your judgement. Granted, no-one – with the exception of your little Furyusha, I guess – really knows much about the Earl, but one thing is indisputable: He is unfailingly loyal to this empire, and he knows the burden of power too well. He's the last person who'd make a grab for power like this."

Jin gaped at the man in disbelief. "Until just half an hour ago you were out for this man's blood. You fully intended to pin the disappearance and possible death of two people on him!"

"You are right and I won't apologise for it. Though that accusation would have never stuck. It might have hurt his reputation a little – if even that, given that most people are afraid of him anyway. But this, this is something else entirely. And yes, we will stick our noses in it, because this concerns us as well, perhaps even more than that rich folk across the river. If you think we are leading a nice and calm life and whatever happens in Mangetsu doesn't affect us, you are wrong. And if some power hungry, selfish bastards, who do not shy away from murdering people, get what they want, you can bet that your carefree life will be over as well. So putting a stop to this is in our own best interest."

Jin stared morosely at the meticulously kept garden. What had happened to searching for missing persons? When had this turned into a dark conspiracy and matters of national security. Jin didn't feel up to something this big, nor did he think that any of them should meddle with this. They ought to tell... whom? Someone who had the power to actually do something about it. The General? But if the Earl was mixed up in all of this, who was to say the General wasn't. After all the two men were practically family. So then... the Silver Guard? Jin snorted. Right, as if anyone at the palace would believe them.

"Jin." Naloc stepped out onto the verandah. "I need you to go back to the Singing Dragon and talk with that boy again."

"About what? He's already told me everything there was to tell. It's not like we're going to reminisce about the good old times. And I doubt he will grant any of us any more favours. In case you haven't noticed, he doesn't like you much either."

"Oh I did notice." Naloc put a hand on Jin's shoulder with a stern look. "Listen, lad, our personal issues are meaningless compared to what's at stake. We need to know who they are and how many, and what they are planning if we want to stop them."

"But why us? Come on, boss, that's way bigger than some power struggle between gangs. It's too big for us."

"Perhaps it is, but we might also be the only ones who are at least trying. Who would you want to trust with this in the first place? It is obvious that there are some very powerful people involved. And you can't just stroll up to the palace and tell them you believe someone is planning to assassinate the emperor. They'd either throw you out on the street or into an asylum."

"But your words have weight. You are, after all, the First Seat of the Crescent." But Naloc was already shaking his head before Jin had even finished speaking.

"We need more than some cryptic message that might not even be correct. Which is why you will go back to the Dragon and talk to Suzu. Anything he can give us: the Earl's business partners, are any new acquaintances. Have there been any threats against his person or his family? What does the Earl know about the plans of the conspirators."

"Wait. You want Suzu to spy for you... No!" Jin snapped, taking a step back from his boss, shaking off the hand on his shoulder. "No," he repeated. "I'm not going to ask Suzu to put himself into danger."

"By the Goddess, Jin, enough now! The Earl is completely besotted with that boy, he wouldn't harm him even if he found him snooping around."

"Perhaps, but have you forgotten that two people close to the Earl have already vanished because of this business? He might not hurt Suzu, but who's to say he'd be able to protect him."

Naloc sneered. "I think you're underestimating your little friend." There was a mean glint in the man's cold grey eyes, a harshness to his voice that Jin had only ever heard directed at someone else. He flinched from it like a child flinching from a father's raised hand, and hung his head. Jin had disappointed Naloc so many times, but the man had never given up on him, had never once blamed him for his failures, or made Jin feel like a lost cause – even though Jin thought he would have deserved it. Today, however, Jin realised that Naloc was finally at the end of his patience with him.

"What if Suzu refuses?" Jin mumbled.

"Well, then you better make it clear to him that I am not asking. For now – as I see it – the Earl is complicit in a conspiracy to murder our emperor, unless he can prove otherwise." Naloc turned and stalked back into the house, leaving Jin stupefied. He hadn't thought his boss, mentor, the man who was like a father to him, would ever go so far. Jin exhaled a shaky breath and crouched down, putting his head into his hands. He had a very bad feeling about this.

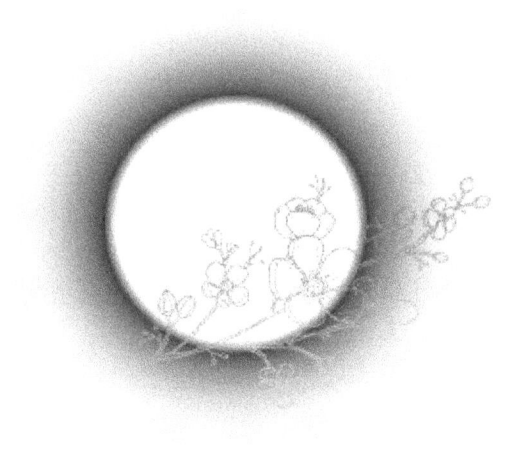

Chapter 20

For the second time this day Jin found himself in front of the ornate gate of the Singing Dragon estate. He drew a number of amused looks from passing patrons as he paced in front of the gate trying to rally his courage. A few called out advice and encouragement, their laughter still audible even after they had vanished behind the high walls. Jin didn't pay them any mind. He was even more reluctant to go inside than earlier that day.

Meeting Suzu again was one thing. Bullying the young man into spying on his lover was another. What was Naloc thinking? First, he chided Jin for being unreasonably suspicious of the Earl, convinced the man would never commit treason. But then he was more than willing to accuse the Earl of exactly that to force Suzu to comply. It wasn't right. It wasn't right at all. Not to mention that Jin was sure they were in way over their heads.

The night was getting deeper, the first patrons left the establishment, their gait languid, the expressions on their faces one of tired joviality. Jin had wasted enough time.

If he had thought the estate quite the sight during the day, he couldn't help but marvel at the magical transformation it had undergone. It felt like stepping into a hidden world. A myriad of stone lanterns lit the winding way. Fireflies danced beneath the cherry tree and across the little stream. The house itself was ablaze with light, spilling through the latticework windows and creating intricate patterns of dark and light on the lawn. Laughter and music came from inside. Jin stopped short, taken aback. This was not what he had expected – and, frankly, feared. Jin flushed with embarrassment. Gods, no wonder Issei had kept calling him an ignorant little temple boy whenever he had tried and failed to drag Jin to Yūgao.

Jin slapped his own cheeks and shook his head, then he took a deep breath and went inside. Left to the entrance was a small sitting area with a low table filled with refreshments and delicate sweets. On the right a huge flower arrangement hid the view of the hallway and the staircase beyond. Other than that, the entrance was empty. Uncertain what to do, Jin decided to just wait. He kicked his shoes off and was just about to put them with all the other neatly arranged shoes, when he heard the patter of bare feet on the hardwood floor.

"Wel– ugh, it's you again," a youthful voice groaned, displeased. Jin unbent, leaving his shoes as they were, and found himself face to face with Akito. Jin sighed. Wasn't that just his luck. Of course it was Akito, Getsuro's most stroppy and obnoxious youth.

"What do you want?" Akito snapped.

"I need to talk to Suzu. Urgently."

"Urgently, is it? Well, too bad. He's working."

"Working?" Jin asked stupidly, before a barrage of very unwanted pictures attacked his mind. He quickly banished them.

"Yes, working," Akito repeated, very slowly and enunciated as if Jin's brain capacity wasn't up to par. This time, Jin thought, cringing, he had deserved it. "It's what we do here, you know. We entertain people."

Jin ignored him. He stepped up into the entrance hall and went straight for the sitting area. "Nevertheless, I need to speak with him – tonight. So, I guess I'll just have to wait."

"You... what? Here?" Akito sputtered. "No! Absolutely not." He grabbed Jin's arm before he could sit down and tried to drag him out of the house. Although he pulled with all his might, Jin didn't budge. He was easily a head taller and had three times as much muscle on him as the youth, so all Akito achieved was to keep Jin out of reach of the plate of flower-shaped nerikiri. Jin looked longingly at the confection.

"You can't wait here," Akito hissed through clenched teeth. "This is for customers only." He yanked on Jin's arm, but Jin didn't move. He was getting thoroughly fed up with this snotty child, though. Akito, frustrated and angry, cried, "Go! Away!"

Jin wrested himself free of the boy's hold, crossed his arms in front of his chest and looked down his nose at Akito. "No," he refused succinctly. Akito's face turned an unflattering shade of red. In the end he was still more child than grown-up. Angry tears filled the boy's eyes, he clenched his hands into fists, and began to tremble, forcing himself not to scream and throw himself at Jin as he so obviously wanted to.

"You," Akito began, pointing a shaking finger at Jin, eyes flashing. But it was as far as he got, for at that moment Kazue swept into the hall, graceful, formidable, imperious.

"What's going on here?" she demanded.

"Mother, he –" Akito said, only to be cut off again, this time by Jin.

"I need to speak with Suzu, it's urgent."

"Did Naloc send you?" Kazue asked, her elegant brows drawn down into a frown. Jin nodded curtly. "Fine. But you'll have to wait. He's still with a patron." If Kazue noticed Jin's involuntary flinch at the words, she mercifully ignored it. Instead she turned to Akito. "Akito, take him to Suzu's room, he can wait on the verandah. And bring him something to drink and a snack for the wait."

"What? But, Mother!" Akito sputtered.

"Do as you are told!" Kazue snapped, brooking no argument.

"Yes, Mother," the boy mumbled, deflating. Passing Jin, he hissed a quiet "Come" and vanished down the hall without waiting to see if Jin followed. Jin swiftly bowed to Kazue and hurried after him, although he wouldn't have needed a guide to find Suzu's room again.

Akito snarled a "Wait here" at him, left, and reappeared only minutes later with a tray in his hands, bearing a cup of tea and two of the colourful, flower-shaped nerikiri. With an heroic effort he kept himself from slamming the tray down. Then he threw a last glare at Jin and stalked off.

With nothing better to do, Jin sipped his tea, nibbled on a sweet in the shape of a lotus flower and looked out across the nightly garden. He had, of course, already seen it in daylight and thought it even more exquisite than the front garden. But now it was simply magical. The air was filled with the flickering lights of fireflies, like blinking stars amongst the trees and flowers. The few stone lanterns provided only a meagre light, little points of orientation along the winding path. The gurgling sound of water, the wooden clack of a water feature. The song of nightbirds mixed with the laughter and the music, the chirping of crickets underlining it. The breeze carried the fresh scent of dew and the heavy sweetness of jasmine.

It would have been a scene of tranquillity if it hadn't been for Furyusha and younger boys hurrying to and fro. Occasionally one of the Furyusha would come out of the main house and cross the gardens, only to vanish inside one of the dark rooms down from where Jin was still sitting and waiting on the verandah.

He had no idea how long he had been waiting. His tea had long since been drunken, when he spotted Suzu coming out onto the verandah of the main house. He was lit from behind, and for a moment he just stood there, unmoving, a shadow, but Jin would know him anywhere. Jin's heart ached with yearning. There he was, the boy Jin had loved for as long as he could remember, who was his first and last thought every day. A small boy approached Suzu and he turned to him. He straightened suddenly, turned his head in Jin's direction – and the useless little bubble of hope Jin had nurtured still burst. His heart broke a little more. Jin swallowed the tears that threatened to spill all of a sudden. He couldn't be like this now, he couldn't show that kind of weakness – not here, and not in front of Suzu.

As he watched Suzu on his way over, however, Jin noticed a certain... clumsiness to his motions, very unlike his usual grace. As he came closer, Jin could make out the bottle in Suzu's hand.

"So," Suzu drawled, slinging and arm around a wooden beam and leaning precariously against it. "You're back – again. And here I thought, I had finally seen the last of you. Hadn't thought you were that much of a masochist... or is it a sadist... I don't know... are you torturing me or yourself? Which one is it?"

"Sorry I'm here again," Jin grumbled, slowly getting to his feet. "There –"

"You know, the General and I had such a great time just now!" Suzu talked right over him, excitedly. "We were playing this drinking game... what's it... it's hilarious. You have to drink whenever... oh I won, by the way. So... wait. Did you know that the General has a pet peacock? Had. He had. Your lousy Naloc stole it!" He gestured wildly with the bottle in his hand, spilling some of its contents.

Jin sighed. This was a disaster. What was he supposed to do? Wait for the boy to sober up? He didn't know how much Suzu had been drinking, or how he reacted to alcohol. He didn't think Suzu was a mean drunk, he was a Furyusha after all, but... "Naloc didn't steal the bird," he said. It was an automatic reflex.

Suzu snorted. "He didn't? Then what do you call it when someone just takes something that isn't theirs?"

"It followed him home."

Suzu roared with laughter. Jin couldn't fault him, he had never given that shoddy excuse much credit himself. "Right," Suzu chuckled. "And you believe everything Naloc tells you and do everything he asks of you. Like an obedient little puppy." That stab had been delivered so deliberately, Jin amended his earlier estimate – Suzu probably was a mean drunk, he only hid it well. Now, however, there was a rather malicious glint in his mismatched eyes.

"Suzu –"

"Oh, do you want me to tell you what the General and I usually get up to together? Ah, but that wouldn't interest you. I bet you are far more interested in what the Earl likes... You know... between the sheets..."

And there it was. Jin had expected Suzu to play dirty, but damn it, he knew exactly how to get to Jin. "Suzu," Jin sighed, hoping that if he didn't let it show, if he feigned disinterest, nonchalance, Suzu would stop.

But Suzu continued. "So one time, while he was inside me, he –"

"SUZU!"

Suzu fell silent, a venomous sneer on his lovely lips. He straightened up, letting go of the beam. All of a sudden he didn't seem drunk anymore.

"Well," his voice was hard and cold, "if you aren't here to learn some salacious little secrets about my sex life, you really have no reason to be here at all, now do you? So I suggest you leave."

"We think the Earl is involved in a conspiracy against the emperor," Jin blurted when Suzu turned to leave. The young man stopped and scowled at him.

"What?"

"That message – we think there will be an attempt on the emperor's life – and possibly the Moon Council – during the Tsuki no Matsuri celebrations."

"And you think the Earl is involved in that? Ridiculous!"

"He did receive that message, didn't he? From some shady thug – your words."

"So what? That could have a thousand reasons, including it being a threat or a warning. He is a member of the Moon Council, after all. Have you thought about that? Or were you just too happy painting him the villain because you are jealous of him?"

"Yes, he's a council member – what better position to plan and execute an assassination?" Jin retorted, ignoring Suzu's jibe.

"You did not just say that," Suzu hissed, his face darkening.

"Well, we just don't know, do we?" Jin relented, before adding, "Which is why we need you to find out."

"No," Suzu refused.

"You are the only one who can find out if he is involved or not and in which way."

"Do you have any idea what you are asking of me?"

Jin knew. He knew, which was why he hadn't wanted to do this. Of course, Jin was worried about Suzu's well-being, but perhaps even worse, they were asking him to betray the trust of a man who loved him. The man Suzu loved? Jin didn't know about that, but it was plain as day that the young man cared a lot about the Earl. But what choice did they have? There was no time to try and plant someone inside the Earl's household, and his staff was too loyal as that any of them would be worth a try.

Naloc's men were all over the town, looking for clues wherever they could, sussing out any kind of strange happenings, rumours, hearsay. How this conspiracy had gotten so far without them knowing was anyone's guess, but chances were slim that they'd suddenly have better luck catching them within the three weeks they had left. So what else could they do?

"I do know," Jin said quietly. "I know, and I am sorry, but we have no choice. This is important."

"I don't care."

"Suzu, this could impact all of our lives – and not in a good way."

"So?" Suzu shrugged. "Oh right, it's much better to just ruin my life then... again."

"That's not –"

"Why don't you just ask the Earl yourselves? Tell Naloc to go and knock on the Earl's door and accuse him of whatever the hell he's accusing him of – see how that turns out for him. Who knows, perhaps he'll even get an answer?"

"Come now, no-one is just throwing around baseless accusations. Admit it, all of this... the missing servants, the message... it's suspicious."

"No."

"Are you really that blind towards the man?"

"What's that supposed to mean?"

And then Jin said the words he had held in his heart ever since he had first seen Suzu with the Earl. Words, he knew he should not say. Words, unfounded. Words, he regretted the moment they left his mouth, and yet he could not stop himself, for they were words born of hurt, anger, and jealousy. "Oh, please. The Earl is just another rich, privileged, arrogant prick who thinks he's better than anyone. He's nothing but a power hungry bastard. And you, you are nothing but a pretty ornament everyone's jealous of, but eventually he'll tire of you."

Dimly, he noticed the bottle in Suzu's hand. Suzu lifting his arm. The contents of the bottle spilling. Yet he didn't understand what was happening until the bottle smashed into the beam beside him, just inches from his face. He flinched violently as shards of glass and wine rained down. A shallow cut on his cheek stung from the alcohol. In utter shock Jin looked from the glittering remains of the bottle to Suzu. The young man was livid, his rage like an aura around him. His eyes glittered dangerously. His body was coiled, ready to strike.

In this very moment Jin was scared of him, more than he had ever been afraid of anyone ever before. Suzu was like a raging god – and Jin felt on the verge of falling to his knees and begging for forgiveness.

"How dare you?" Suzu hissed, taking a single step towards Jin. It was enough for Jin to back away.

Then Ryū was suddenly there, grabbing Suzu's arm before the young man could take another step. Jin hadn't even noticed him and Rani hurrying towards them. He had never been so happy to see the man.

Suzu turned on Ryū with a snarl, trying to yank his arm free, but Ryū held on, not even flinching. Beside him, however, little Rani quickly hid.

"You should leave," Ryū said, and Jin agreed wholeheartedly. But as he passed a still seething Suzu, Naloc's words rang in his ears. Almost as if in trance, he stopped next to him and said in a low voice, "If you don't want everyone believing your Earl is part of a conspiracy against the emperor, you better prove his innocence." He rather felt than saw Suzu tense. Without another word Jin left the Singing Dragon.

He was at the border between Yūgao and Kigetsu when his feet finally stopped. Behind him was the glittering pleasure district, in front of him a dark alley. He felt dirty and disgusted with himself. Jin couldn't even blame Suzu for getting so furious after having riled him up like that. But the intensity of that rage still shocked him – and it hurt.

His hands were shaking. Jin could feel the adrenaline in his veins ebbing, but he was too agitated to go home and sleep. So instead he changed directions and went to the next best tavern that came to his mind – and got royally drunk.

Suzu was still breathing hard. His hands clenched and unclenched unconsciously. His eyes were fixed on the mess of broken glass and spilled wine. Inside him his rage was howling, demanding release, threatening to burst forth and devour the nearest possible victim. As if from very far away he could hear someone call his name.

"Suzu!" Ryū's voice finally broke through to him, shattering the red haze surrounding him. Suzu slowly wrested his eyes away from the broken bottle and turned to Ryū. By all appearances his friend was as calm and collected as always, but the scowl on his handsome face and the storm of emotions reflected in his amber eyes betrayed his anxiety and worry.

"I need to go to the dojo," Suzu murmured, freed himself from Ryū's grasp, and hurried into his room. Ryū followed him like a shadow. He didn't comment on what had happened, nor did he say a single word when Suzu carelessly yanked his expensive kimono off and let it fall to the floor. And just as quietly he followed Suzu to the dojo. He did not try to hold him back, he did not point out that it was the middle of the night, he did not offer any assistance. Ryū only stood and watched over him, while Suzu lit a single lamp and vented all of his rage on a helpless straw dummy, until it was battered beyond repair, and his wooden training sword was cracked.

Chapter 21

Jin woke up, feeling as if he had been kicked in the head by a horse, which then had used his body as a comfortable mattress. After a moment he realised the warm weight pinning him effectively down on the futon was, in fact, another human being. Two human beings, to be precise. He carefully lifted his pounding head, unable to quite suppress the groan the movement elicited.

A dark head rested on his chest, a slender arm across Jin's hips, a leg across his thigh. Black hair spilled like ink over porcelain skin. Pressed against his other side lay what seemed at first glance the mirror image of that person – leg thrown across Jin's, hand resting possessively... a little too low. As identical as they seemed, as different they felt against him – edginess compared to rounder shapes, hardness compared to softness. The Hibiki twins.

Jin had a hazy recollection of running into them in front of a crummy tavern last night. He had been surprised to find them there, the sibling's tastes normally ran to more expensive establishments. By then he had already drunken enough to forget that he had sworn to avoid the twins. Niall was going to kill him – if his head didn't do it first.

Unfortunately, a while later, when the twins had woken and dressed, and he was hoping to quickly and quietly see them off, Jin was still very much alive. And Niall was sitting outside her house, leisurely sipping a cup of tea, a very pointed look on her face.

The very moment the twins had vanished through the front gate, Niall pounced. "So," she drawled. "Arata and Asuka, eh?"

"Well..."

"Don't you ever learn?"

"I was drunk," Jin blurted. As excuses went it was the oldest and lamest in the book, but also the only one he had. "Really, really drunk. And..." He had no 'and'. He had been heartbroken, angry, shocked, disgusted with himself. It made him sound only more pathetic, so he decided to retain what little dignity he still had and shut up.

Niall sighed. "Come here." She picked up the tea pot and another cup from the little tea table next to her and offered both to Jin. "I know things must have been really bad for you to break your promise." Jin shrugged.

A few months ago Niall had made Jin promise to stay as far away from the Hibiki twins as possible. Before that, Arata and his sister, Asuko, had tumbled into Jin's bed on a number of occasions. The twins were strikingly beautiful: black glossy hair, flawless silken skin, faces as sweet and delicate as those of celestial beings. Their personalities, on the other hand, were less celestial being, and more vicious demons.

The siblings knew they were beautiful, and they knew how to use their charm to wrap even the most stoic soul around their little fingers. For as long as they got whatever they wanted, they, in turn, kept their hapless victims happy. But when they didn't... To call them demanding was an understatement. It had been anyone's guess what in the world they wanted with Jin in the first place. He wasn't their preferred type of prey. Jin had no money, no power.

What Niall – smart, clever Niall – had known from the very beginning, however, soon became apparent, even to Jin: He was but a toy to them.

"You do have a type," Niall commented suddenly.

"A type?"

"I always thought the picture of Kari you had in your head was some sort of idealised version – too pretty to be true. Then I saw the boys and girls you chose as lovers and I started wondering if perhaps they all resembled your Kari. Which is why eventually I thought to myself: 'Gee, Niall, if Jin ever gets to see Suzu he'll be head over heels for him.' I don't know if it's irony or destiny or whatever that it turned out Suzu is, in fact, your lost Kari."

Jin snorted. "Only he isn't, is he? In the end I did idealise Kari, just not the way everyone thought I was. I don't know him at all."

"Suzu is..." Niall trailed off, searching for the right words. Although she had known Suzu for several years now, she couldn't claim to know him well. On the other hand, what she did know of him, she was confident was the truth of him. Niall wasn't a potential patron, so the boys didn't face her with their masks on. "I don't know him well," she admitted. "But I know he is fierce – his entire being is a force to be reckoned with. I've seen him around Rani, Akito, Miharu – he certainly has a sweet side. But if you ask me, he isn't someone you should mess with. I think the Earl – or any of his patrons – has no idea how dangerous he can be."

Jin laughed humourlessly. "Ah, well, I certainly do now."

"What happened?"

"Made him angry. He threw a wine bottle at me... To be honest, I don't know what would have happened if Ryū hadn't shown up. Gods," he sighed, running a hand through his messy hair. "He was scary. Really scary."

"And that's why you crawled into a bottle last night?"

"Maybe." Niall waited patiently for him to elaborate, so Jin, hesitantly, did. "I didn't want to involve Suzu in whatever this is – but I did. Worse, I forced him into cooperating... I had sworn I wouldn't do it, no matter what Naloc said, but..." He was still disgusted with himself, no amount of alcohol could drown that feeling. Emotional blackmail was as low as it got, in Jin's opinion. Naloc was probably going to scoff at his weakness. And even though he had merely parroted Naloc's words, it had been he who had thrown the threat like a knife at Suzu. Jin, who had witnessed Suzu's reaction. The sudden stillness, the tension, the expression of rage, tinged with shock and defeat. It was enough for Jin to know that Suzu would do as asked, reluctantly, reproachfully. Suzu was not going to stand by and let the Earl be slandered and accused of a crime that would see the man executed or exiled. Jin didn't know what bothered him more: the way they had compelled the young Furyusha's cooperation, or that Suzu seemed to genuinely have feelings for the Earl.

Jin put his cup down to massage his temples. His head felt as if it was about to split open. Perhaps he deserved it – no, scratch that, he definitely did. For a moment, a single short moment, no more than the length of a breath, he had enjoyed it. For an instant he had wished with all his heart that the Earl proved to be a greedy, ruthless traitor.

He didn't tell Niall this, too ashamed. His friend sat quietly, waiting, pondering, her gaze on something that wasn't there. Eventually, she blinked and returned to the presence.

"Do you want something for your head?" she asked.

"Please," Jin replied with heartfelt gratitude.

It only took her a moment to go inside and come back with a cup in her hand. "Drink this. And then go and lie down again. Try to sleep. We have work to do, but it can wait till later."

"Work?" Jin grimaced, both at the thought of having to do anything other than lying on the ground and the bitterness of the concoction Niall had given him.

"We will go and visit a handful of apothecaries."

"What for?"

"Because last night, while you were off getting pissed – and shagged," Jin winced, Niall wasn't going to let this go any time soon. "Aika pointed out, that 'dreamless sleep' might not just be some fancy metaphor, but that it is also, in fact, a droll monicker of a very rare and very deadly poison called Deva's Breath."

Jin gaped at her. Poison? So this was how it was going to happen. But how? You didn't just wander up to the emperor and chuck poison into his drink – or the drinks of the Moon Council for that matter. There were security protocols, guards. Didn't this mean that this whole conspiracy was far bigger than they had thought, the people behind it even more influential than anticipated.

"Stop gaping like a fish on land. Drink your medicine and go to bed," Niall ordered impatiently. Jin obeyed and drank the rest of his bitter brew in one go.

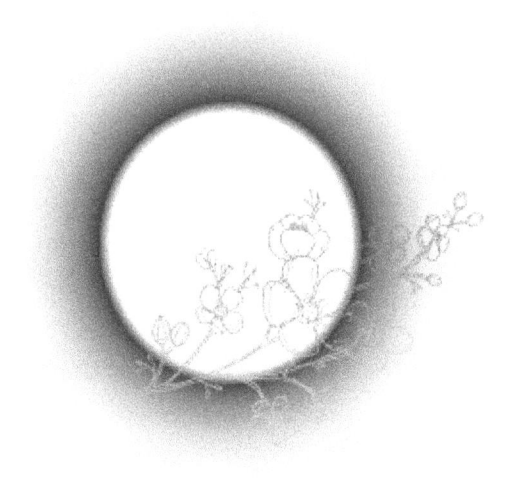

Chapter 22

Suzu listlessly sorted through a collection of kanzashi. The box was full of delicate strings of flowers, sparkling butterflies, birds, dragonflies. He picked up one of the hair sticks, moving it this and that way, as if scrutinising the phoenix in mid-flight, hanging on a thin golden chain. The truth was that Suzu didn't feel like entertaining anyone today. After the confrontation with Jin the night before, he felt out of sorts. He didn't regret it – his outburst. Not one tiny bit. Jin had had it coming. Just thinking about him made Suzu's blood boil. Well, perhaps now that bastard would know better and stay away. How dare he even insinuate Toshi could be a traitor. Jin and this blasted Naloc. If only the man wasn't that close to Mother. What was it between them anyway? Suzu didn't quite understand their relationship. Had they been in love once? Were they still?

Why was Mother doing Naloc any favours in the first place? If it had been anyone else, asking her to spy on the Earl of Tsukikage, she would have buried them alive in an ant hill.

No, Suzu didn't regret his fit of temper – he only regretted that the bottle had missed.

"Suzu? Blue or... what is that? Yellow?" Suzu looked around at Rani, sitting cross-legged on the floor in front of two boxes. He had folded back the thin paper to reveal the kimono it protected. Rani... well, that was the one thing Suzu did regret – that Rani had witnessed it. How often had the boy been the victim of his father's drunken rampages until the man had finally sold him to the Singing Dragon to buy more booze? Suzu sincerely hoped he had drunken himself into an early grave. Bringing Rani here had been the only decent thing that man had ever done. It had taken years for Rani to stop flinching whenever someone moved too suddenly in his proximity. He had been doing so well – until last night.

Last night, shocked and scared witless, Rani had been cowering in a corner of his room, crying for hours with no-one able to calm him down. Suzu was only told that Rani had witnessed the whole unseemly scene after he had vented his rage at the dojo. He had hurried to the boy at once, apologised a thousand times. He had tried to explain, without making excuses. Most of all, he had tried to make Rani understand that it hadn't been directed at him.

Eventually Rani had crawled into Suzu's lap, clinging to the older boy, and cried himself to sleep. And now he was sitting here as if nothing had happened, trying to decide on the colour of Suzu's kimono for the day. But his eyes were still red and puffy.

"Rani," Suzu said softly and the boy looked up from the boxes. "You do know that I would never, ever, hurt you or any of the other boys, don't you? I –"

"I know," Rani cut him off with a shy smile. "I know that, Suzu. Everyone here knows. You may have the temper of a demon, but you are our Little Moon. We all know you'd rather die than see any of us hurt."

Little Moon. It was a nickname that seemed to follow him wherever he went. Had his parents called him that as well?

"Th-that's how you see me?" Suzu asked quietly.

Rani nodded and beamed. "The Moon Goddess Herself must have sent you to us. She graced you with Her beauty and Her heart, but also with the fierceness and strength of Her warriors."

Suzu chuckled. "You really love the stories about the Moon Goddess and Her loyal warriors, don't you?"

"You can laugh. But they are real, I know they are." Rani grinned.

Suzu smiled and shook his head. Who was he to deny the boy his fantasies.

"So," Rani prompted. "Blue or... um... yellow?"

Suzu sighed. "I think I'm going to ask Mother to give me the night off."

"Are you moping because the Earl hasn't been here since your visit at his place?"

"I don't mope... but yes," Suzu grumbled, pushing the box full of kanzashi away from him. Toshi had indeed not come to see him since. It made him anxious. It was ridiculous, of course, it had only been two days. Still, Suzu was certain it had something to do with that message and the people it had come from. What if Toshi was in trouble? And then there were Naloc's threats hanging over them like a portentous cloud.

Suzu had to give the man something that proved Toshi's innocence once and for all. How was he to do that, however, if Toshi all but vanished on him. It would be too suspicious to just suddenly show up on the man's doorstep unannounced.

More than anything – as difficult as it was for Suzu to admit, even to himself – he missed Toshi. Every day Suzu did not see him, talk to him, touch him, was a day that was lacking something he could not name. It felt like a whisper, too quiet to make out the words; like a thought, there and gone too quickly to catch; a feeling, so fleeting it could not be grasped. It left Suzu with a phantom itch, nerves tingling.

"So," Rani asked, cocking his head. "Do you want me to go and ask Mother?" Suzu hesitated. He shouldn't do that. Nowadays he was entertaining hardly anyone else apart from Toshi and occasionally the General, and yet he was still the most popular Furyusha in Yūgao – sometimes it didn't make sense to him at all.

Before Rani had gotten to his feet, the door opened. Ryū came in, a wicked grin on his face. "What was that? You want the night off? Are you sure? If I were you, I'd reconsider." He paused dramatically, obviously waiting for either Suzu or Rani to ask him why. When they didn't oblige him, he shrugged and announced brightly, "The Earl is here to see you."

Suzu brightened instantly. He grabbed a leather string from his dressing table and bound his hair in a simple, high ponytail.

"Well, I guess I really shouldn't let him wait then, should I?" he blurted, aware that he sounded far too eager and not caring, not even when Ryū started laughing. Rani frowned at Suzu, binding his hair with a string.

"Um... do you... want the blue or –"

"Neither, I'll stay as I am."

Suzu knelt in front of the door. He slid it open, slowly but fluidly, then touched his fingertips to the floor and bowed. "Welcome back, my lord." In the end it was all about keeping up appearances; it wouldn't do to storm into the room and throw himself at the man, much as he'd have liked to. So instead, he stood up gracefully, took a single step inside the room before kneeling again – sideways to the door so he never showed his back to his customer – and sliding the door softly shut. Only then did he look around and raise his eyes.

Toshi was sitting in the window seat, a cup in one hand, one leg up on the seat, his arm resting on his bent knee. He looked more relaxed than Suzu had ever seen him in this place, wearing a yukata instead of the usual bespoke suit. The suits made Toshi a striking appearance, exuding authority and sincerity. Suzu found he preferred this simple linen robe, it suited Toshi in a more natural way.

Suzu slowly stepped forward, perhaps he was hesitating, perhaps he was simply too taken with the picture of this breathtakingly handsome man, he couldn't say. But Toshi put his cup on the floor and stood up – and then he was there. Their bodies collided like stars – inevitable, devastating, a force greater than the will of gods drawing them to each other. They were starved, desperate, as if they could only breathe in the presence of the other.

"Gods, I missed you," Toshi breathed against Suzu's lips, panting. They held on to each other as if fearing one might suddenly vanish. Toshi leaned his forehead against Suzu's, tightening his arms around the smaller man.

"I missed you, too," Suzu whispered, closing his eyes, enveloped in the closeness of Toshi. They remained like this for a while, drawing out this single perfect moment.

Eventually, Toshi drew him back to the window seat. Smiling, Suzu sat astride him and gently cupped the man's face between his hands. There was a tightness around those light grey eyes, a frown seemed to have permanently dug a line between his brows, he looked unbearably tired, worried, as if he carried the weight of the entire world upon his shoulders. Suzu's stomach twisted.

"You seem exhausted," he remarked quietly.

"It's just business," Toshi replied with a sigh as deep as the unfathomable depth of the sea.

"Do you want to talk about it?"

"I'd rather not involve you in this, Suzu."

"Why? Is it something bad? Does it have anything to do with that strange message that thug delivered?"

A shadow rushed across Toshi's face. Anger, regret... self-chastisement? Suzu couldn't quite grasp it, but for a moment he felt Toshi tense and wondered if it was he Toshi was angry with.

"That bastard," Toshi snarled. "He shouldn't have said that in front of you. Suzu, I'm so sorry, this is not something I want to drag you into. Please, I know it's difficult, but please forget what you heard and saw then. Please."

Yes, that morning at Toshi's house, after they had been alone again, Toshi had asked him to forget what he had heard. Not asked, pleaded, just as he was doing now. This, more than that strange message and its dodgy bearer, had convinced Suzu that Toshi had become embroiled in something very troublesome.

"Toshi, are you in trouble?" Suzu asked. He wasn't sure why he asked, he doubted he could be of any help. But perhaps Naloc could. As much as Suzu would have liked nothing better than to rip the man apart, limb by limb, if there was a chance that he could help Toshi than Suzu had to grasp it. Even if that meant he had to give Naloc what he wanted. For now.

But Toshi shook his head. "Don't worry about me, love. I'll be fine. No matter how many headaches it gives me, how onerous it may be, I have a duty, which I have accepted and sworn to fulfil when I became Earl of Tsukikage. So I'll be fine. Promise."

Suzu frowned. Confused, he wondered how being part of a conspiracy could be the duty of an earl. No, Naloc and Jin were planting doubt when Suzu should know better. With the tip of his fingers he gently smoothed the lines of worry and fatigue away from Toshi's face, felt the man relax only fractionally beneath him. Suzu finally understood. It wasn't the weight of the world but the weight of the title Toshi bore. Sometimes a title was the heavier burden.

"Have you ever wished to be someone else? Anyone but the Earl of Tsukikage?"

Toshi smiled, a melancholy little smile. "Suzu, have I ever told you why I inherited the title and not my sister?" Suzu shook his head. "It should have been Kikka's by all rights, but she chose love over her inheritance. She was twenty, I think.... yes, she was twenty, I was eleven. At that time I was obsessed with becoming an Umbrage like Kagetora – oh, I take it you've already guessed that's what Kagetora is. Anyway, I remember that Kagetora and I were practising stealth, so we were trailing my sister. Who in turn was having a clandestine meeting with a young man. Ito no Atsushi – my now brother-in-law." Toshi chuckled. His eyes had a far-away look to them as if he was looking into the past. "Of course we couldn't not eavesdrop. We were eleven years old, after all. And it turned out that Kikka had been seeing Atsushi for quite a while already, and even to an eleven year old it was obvious that those two were madly in love. See, Atsushi is from a minor noble family. Marrying my sister would have suddenly turned him from a minor lord into an earl, so you can imagine that many would have been accusing him of wanting my sister's hand for his personal gain if their relationship had become public. However, Atsushi was the sole heir of his family, there was no-one else, and he didn't want to let his line die. So when he asked my sister for her hand, he told her so. He told her he'd rather be a lord than an earl, to keep his family line alive. But if Kikka decided she didn't want to give up her title, he'd accept that – and still choose her. It was for this, Atsushi's honesty and genuine love for my sister, that my parents agreed to the wedding – and to Kikka stepping away from her inheritance. She was, in fact, rather glad to do so. And that's how I suddenly became heir to the earldom." He fell silent, his smile slowly dying, before he quietly added, "When my parents died a few years later and I became earl... I think, even now, she feels guilty about it." And she would, wouldn't she? Suzu had met Ito no Kikka only a handful of times, each time for only a moment, but her affection towards her brother shone as strong and bright as the sun for the whole world to see. It wasn't difficult to imagine her regret when their parents died in an accident and Toshi, a mere fourteen years old, had to take up the mantle of the Earl of Tsukikage.

"Is that why her son is your heir? Although that means the end of the Ito line?"

"Perhaps it's why Kikka and Atsushi agreed to it so readily." A smile tugged up the corners of Toshi's mouth, crinkled his nose. It was something Suzu had found out the first time he had seen Toshi interact with other people – if his smile was genuine, it made his nose crinkle in the most adorable way that never failed to make Suzu's heart happily skip a beat. "You don't need to worry about the Ito line, though. Sachie will inherit it."

"Sachie?"

Toshi chuckled at Suzu's quizzical expression. "My niece. You haven't met her yet. She's only ten years old and too young for social events."

"I didn't know you had a niece," Suzu pouted. Not having known such an important fact about Toshi's life had an unexpected sting to it.

"Sorry. Does it make it any better when I tell you that she knows all about you and can't wait to meet you? I think she already likes you more than she likes her uncle," Toshi soothed, amused by Suzu's reaction.

"Perhaps... a tiny bit." Suzu wasn't ready to forgive that easily. But Toshi laughed, pulled him closer, and plastered kisses all over Suzu's face and neck until Suzu's pouting dissolved into helpless laughter.

"Did you know," Toshi said quietly, the laughter suddenly gone from his voice. "After my parents died, there were rumours that I was cursed. They said the white streak in my hair was a sign."

Suzu frowned. How painful it must have been for fourteen years old Toshi to hear those malicious whispers, laying the blame for his parents' untimely death at his feet. Sometimes people's cruelty knew no boundaries.

He gently ran his fingers through Toshi's hair. "It wasn't your fault. You're not cursed, Toshi. Fate has its own rules, which we mere mortals will never understand. Believe me, I should know. You were just unlucky – or perhaps your parents were. Don't ever listen to what people whisper behind your back. They don't know you, they have no idea how wonderful you are."

Perhaps there were tears in Toshi's eyes, or perhaps they shone with love, but when he kissed Suzu, the message was unmistakable and filled Suzu's heart with warmth.

He laid his head on Toshi's shoulder and breathed in the man's comforting scent of fresh linen and sandalwood. He could stay like this forever, forget the rest of the world. Let them play their games of power and deceit, Suzu couldn't care less if Jin and Naloc and whoever else there was drowned in their conspiracies, their desire to attain distinction. All he needed was this – this man, and his motley family.

"Suzu," Toshi said, so soft it was but a mere whisper. "I want you to know, that no matter what happens, no matter what you might hear – you and my family are what is most important to me and I would never do anything that would endanger either of you or cause you any kind of harm. Do you believe me?"

Suzu lifted his head, taken aback by the sudden change of mood. As he looked into those familiar agate eyes he felt a shiver down his spine. A sense of foreboding he couldn't explain. Yet with it came a certainty as unshakable as the Goddess's will: Toshi would never commit treason – if only to protect the ones he loved.

"I believe you," Suzu answered, but it sounded like a vow. And he sealed it with a kiss.

Chapter 23

Their search had begun promising. The very first apothecary had been able to provide them with ample information about *Dreamless Sleep*: its gruesome effects, its lethality, and its excessively difficult production and rarity. After that, however, Jin and Niall had hit a wall.

It wasn't for a lack of helpfulness. The apothecaries in Kigetsu were all just too eager to give Naloc a helping hand. Some owed him a debt, others had been trusted business partners for years. They hadn't expected to find the conspirators' ally amongst them, but they had hoped for a little more information besides a generic description of the poison's effects.

They dragged themselves into the last apothecary on their list, listless and without much hope of learning anything new. And their premonitions proved true until...

"You should try the apothecaries in Mangetsu. It's not just difficult to distil, the main ingredient costs more than I or any of my colleagues make in a year. You won't find anyone in Kigetsu who can make that stuff."

And so, armed with the name of a potions master who was well-known to supply the rich with whatever they desired, Jin and Niall headed across the river – after donning their best clothes for the occasion. They didn't have the advantage of people falling over themselves trying to be useful to Naloc on the other side of the Opal, so they needed to at least look like they had every right to be there. And because neither of them could ever possibly pass as nobility, Niall had decided posing as well-off members of the Academy would be their best bet.

Jin glanced appreciatively at Niall. She wore an ankle length dark green skirt, a white shirt, sleeves rolled up to the elbows, and a tight fitting brown vest. She had even put on her physician's badge, which Jin had only ever seen once before. But in Kigetsu everyone knew her as a talented young doctor, despite her not having a surgery of her own. Her father's old surgery was run by an old family friend from the north. What had been supposed to be only a temporary arrangement did still persist fifteen years later.

When her father had died, Niall had only been thirteen years old. Naloc – a good friend of her father's – had become her guardian and made sure she finished her education. To Niall Naloc was more of a surrogate father than he had ever been to Jin. Perhaps it was that she felt she owed Naloc why she remained in his employ instead of taking over the surgery, perhaps she simply didn't feel ready yet. Or perhaps – as she insisted – it wouldn't be fair to make Fiete give up the surgery after he had dedicated so many years of his life to continue his friend's work.

They crossed the river into the Academic Quarter. The university and its myriad of different colleges, spread out over a space almost twice the size of the emperor's estates, was a sight to behold. Stone buildings, larger than any building, that wasn't a temple, Jin had ever seen, built in the northern style with turrets and bay windows, gables, stucco, and – so Niall told him – frescoes. Some buildings even housed effigies of patron gods and guardian spirits in vestibules above the entrances, from whence they benignly looked down upon the passers-by.

The Academic Quarter was a small town of its own. Little greens and parks divided the different faculties as if there was a need to keep them apart from one another. Next to the physician's college, towering over all the other buildings, was the hospital. Despite its huge capacity hardly anyone from the other side of the river received treatment here. Except for the free treatments the students offered once a week.

Niall halted, wistfully looking at the white building of the Academy of Medical Arts. Students were milling about, hurrying to and fro between the buildings, talking and laughing, in rapt debate. She had always dreamt of attending the academy. But as with so many things in life, this was the prerogative of the rich and the highborn. The only day Niall had ever set foot inside the white marble halls had been the day she had taken the exam to earn her doctor's badge. It was more than some physicians in Kigetsu or outside the capital had to show for, which was why she was so proud of it. And yet she hid it away in a box at home.

Jin looked at his friend and felt an overwhelming pride and affection for her. She stood tall with her head held high, her auburn hair shimmering in copper hues in the sunlight, her cobalt blue eyes sparkling. She didn't need any academy, she had earned her badge on her own through hard work and diligence. And in the end she had bested them all and passed the exams with flying colours.

Niall turned her back on the building and sighed. "Ah, but I really would like to have their library."

In a quiet side street on the edge of the Academic Quarter, just shy of the more humble part of Mangetsu – if one could call it humble – they finally found their quarry. "Azhar's" read the sign above the door in elaborate flowing script. Just below it, a lot smaller, it said, "Apothecary."

"Right," Niall said. "Follow my lead. And don't forget, you are my assistant." She didn't wait for Jin to reply before she pushed the door open. The merry tinkle of a silver bell, hung above the door, announced their entrance. The warm, fresh scent of herbs and spices greeted them.

"Welcome," a dark, strangely accented voice called from the other end of the shop. Beyond a plethora of little flasks of potions, pots of creams, jars of spices, teas, and herbal mixtures, all neatly arranged on dark wooden shelves, behind a counter of the same dark wood stood a man, tall and slender, smiling at them. Niall returned his smile and strode purposefully towards him. Jin followed a little slower, marvelling at the packed shelves. This wasn't at all like the apothecaries he knew.

"Welcome," the man – Azhar, Jin presumed – repeated. "How may I be of service?" Azhar was an unusually tall man, but unlike so many very tall people, he did not stoop. There was an elegance and grace about him that reminded Jin of a dancer. His slender face was handsome with fine features and high cheekbones. A dark blue head scarf hid his hair, his graceful hands rested on top of the counter. His most striking feature, however, were his eyes, which were of such a unique light shade of brown they shone like burnished gold against the darker brown of his skin.

"Good day to you, sir," Niall answered brightly. "My name is Niall ax Corbin, I'm a doctor over in Kigetsu, and I was wondering if you might be able to help me. See, it seems your colleagues on our side of the river are rather flummoxed – as am I, to be honest." Niall laughed, embarrassed.

"Oh, well, I shall do my best to shed light on whatever the mystery may be," Azhar said. If he was looking down on them for being from Kigetsu, he hid it well. The musical lilt of his voice was so golden and gentle it was hard to imagine it ever being filled with something as ugly and harsh as derision.

"A couple of my patients have been asking me about this weed. Apparently it can heal arthritis and other inflammations, but I must confess, I have never heard of it before. Ah... what... something..." Niall waved a hand around, looking up at the ceiling, down at the counter top, as if it might present her with the answer she was looking for. Then she turned sharply around, snapping her fingers at Jin's face. "There now. What was the name of that weed?" Jin jumped and at once rummaged through his sleeve from whence – after a few hectic seconds – he pulled out a piece of paper.

"Deva's Breath," Jin read aloud.

Azhar's eyebrows shot up. "Deva's Breath?" he exclaimed. "Yes, I know it. And I can assure you, it is no cure for inflammation. I don't know where your patients have heard such nonsense. This is a dangerous rumour."

"Oh dear," Niall cried, sounding so genuinely distressed, Jin got worried for a moment she wasn't pretending. Her acting skills were truly impressive. "May I ask, what it is then?"

"A rather unremarkable little weed. But the poison that can be derived from it is one of the most dangerous substances known to humans. Luckily it doesn't grow in these parts of the world and is thus very costly to obtain."

"Oh, but you seem to know a lot about it," Jin blurted – according to plan, but also because he found himself curious about that mysterious deadly plant.

Niall rounded on him and snapped, "You! Don't be insolent" and winked at him. Azhar raised his hands in a soothing gesture and smiled. "Please, that is quite all right. Your assistant is right to wonder. Well. You have probably noticed that my origins are not within this empire," he laughed. "In my country Deva's Breath grows like every other wild weed. It is everywhere. Every child knows it and knows to leave it alone. It won't harm you by touch or by smell as some poisonous plants do, and we thank our gods for that, and for the fact that it is so difficult to distil its poison. But once you have, you are left with one of the most deadly poisons in the world – a few drops are enough to kill a grown man almost instantly."

"How difficult? Could you do it, say, with the right instructions and a knowledge in distilling poisons?" Niall inquired.

"No. It takes years to master the process."

"And you have – mastered it."

"Of course. In my country a pharmacist is required to be able to do it."

Well, and that was that. In the end finding their man had been easier than expected – if what Azhar had told them was true. Jin suppressed the glee bubbling inside him and forced his face into a neutral expression. He glanced sideways at Niall. There was a glint in her eyes, one he always associated with her having her quarry exactly where she wanted it, getting ready for the killing strike.

"I wonder," she said. "You don't happen to have some Deva's Breath here, do you? I'd really like to inspect such a strange plant."

"I'm sorry, I don't," Azhar replied – too quickly. For the fraction of a second his golden eyes flitted to the side, his elegant fingers twitched involuntarily. Jin would have missed all of it had he not been looking for signs the man was lying. Niall and Issei had taught him well. "I might have a picture I can show you. One moment, please." Azhar turned on his heels and left through a doorway to his right. When he pushed the curtain aside to pass through, Jin caught a fleeting image of what looked like a workroom.

Jin tensed, listening for any tell-tale sounds that the poisons master was making a run for it. Next to him, Niall was slowly gathering her long skirt, just in case. Only a moment later, however, Azhar returned, a heavy tome in his hands. Slowly relaxing, they looked down at the book as he laid it on the counter and flicked through the pages. It was a beautiful book: leather bound, with magnificent drawings of plants. The script was unfamiliar, beautiful and ornate, flowing and gentle like the waves of a babbling brook.

"Ah, here it is," Azhar announced and turned the book around for Niall to see. Jin leaned in to get a better look. The picture was drawn with so much skill, in such minute detail, it seemed almost real. It was indeed an unremarkable little plant. It's stem and leaves much like any other plant Jin had ever seen. It's only distinguishing feature were the tiny vermilion blossoms that sat on top of the stem like a huge red cloud.

"Amazing how something so seemingly harmless can be so dangerous," Niall said softly, staring at the picture as if trying to burn it into her mind.

"Hmm, yes." Azhar nodded. "It is why we call it Deva's Breath. Deva is a demon in the guise of a small child. Small, harmless. Unremarkable. But get too close and Deva will steal your breath – and with it your soul."

Heavy silence filled the room. Dust motes glittered here and there, dancing in the air. At last, Niall cleared her throat. "Well. You have been most helpful. Thank you." Azhar smiled and bowed his head. Niall followed suit, but she had only just started the motion when her head snapped up again. "Ah! Before we leave I must take advantage of this myriad of herbal mixtures you have here. Say, you wouldn't – by chance – have something to..." She cleared her throat again and glanced at Jin. "To soothe a broken heart." Jin bit his tongue, stifling the urge to strangle his friend. Oh, they were going to have words later.

Azhar's golden eyes focused on Jin. There was so much understanding and gentleness in his gaze, in his smile, Jin had to swallow the sudden lump in his throat and blink his eyes rapidly a few times. "I have a lovely herbal tea to lift the spirits. Just a moment."

A few minutes later they were out in the street, Niall clutching a jar and looking very smug.

"So?" Naloc demanded the moment they set foot on the verandah. The mournful calls of the peacock filled the garden, the animal itself strutting restlessly across the grass. Niall

plopped down next to Naloc, trying to lure the bird to her. She gave their boss a quick report of their search.

"Well, he lied when he said he had none of that weed in store," Jin said.

"It doesn't matter," Niall said, "he told us plenty else. He not only admitted to basically being the only person in town who can distil the poison, he also told us that the weed doesn't grow in our country. It has to be imported. You can imagine how expensive it must be."

"And yet, someone is willing to pay for it."

"Indeed. And unless they have imported another poisons master along with it... Well done, I guess you've found our man. Remains the question, what we do about it."

Neither Niall nor Jin had an immediate answer to that. For the moment, however, Jin was glad and a little proud of the day's work. It wasn't often that he got a taste of success and praise. It was better medicine than Azhar's tea.

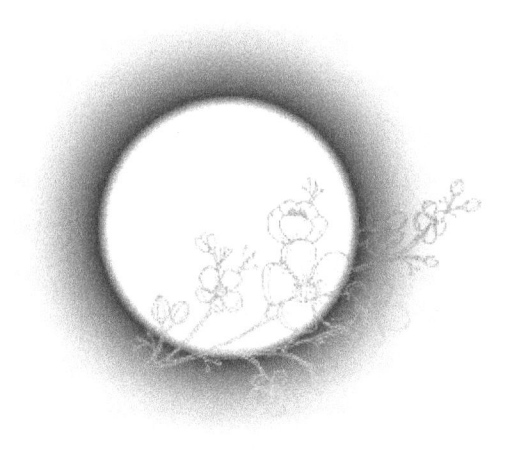

Chapter 24

It was still early, the time of reaching shadows and golden light. Suzu carefully arranged his long, trailing kimono and sat down on the cushion Rani had put for him on the verandah. He picked up his pipe, let Rani light it for him, and leaned back against the wooden beam, exhaling a plum of smoke.

"Rani," Ryū called, coming their way, "go and help Akito prepare the waiting area. Make sure he doesn't sneak any of the sweets." Chuckling, for everyone knew Akito was keen on working the waiting area only because of the sweets, Rani ran across the grass and vanished into the main building.

"You look good," Ryū said and sat down.

"Only good?" Suzu raised an eyebrow, which made Ryū laugh.

"You know exactly that you're stunning. You always are. You could probably wear a rice sack and still be radiant."

"All right, now you are just stroking my ego." Suzu laughed. He took another drag of his pipe and a closer look at his friend. Ryū was slouching, rubbing his eyes. There was a tightness to his jaw that told Suzu he had been clenching his teeth all day, a crease between his brows. "You look exhausted. Has something happened?"

Ryū sighed. "No, I just didn't get much sleep."

"Did you have nightmares again?" Ryū didn't remember much of his life before the Singing Dragon. He was born to parents who couldn't even take care of themselves, yet he remembered them trying their best. The only memory he had left of them was a happy one. They died, like so many others, the year a fever had ravaged the town, and Eigetsu, getting the worst of it, had turned from an already desolate place into a mass grave.

Eigetsu, the oldest part of the capital, where once the nobility and the rich had resided. Eventually the town had grown, more and more people moving in from the countryside. Kigetsu had grown from an afterthought into a town of its own, until Yūgao, the pleasure quarter that had once graced the edges of the capital, had suddenly been imbedded between the two halves. The nobility, however, hadn't like rubbing shoulders with plebeians. In the end the reigning empress of the time had granted them land on her side of the river.

Eigetsu had been abandoned, and into the void had moved the desperate, the forgotten, the very bottom of society. The former glory had vanished, the splendour had been reduced to filth, the genteel had been ground down to harshness.

Into this place of despair and suffering Ryū had been born. A life of misery, hunger, and violence. Until, at the age of thirteen, he had somehow found his way into Yūgao and through the first gate he saw: the Singing Dragon's. They could have thrown him out at once, perhaps shown him some kindness and feed him first. Instead, Kazue and Aoi, the Dragon's former owner, had decided to take the feral boy in. It was the day Ryū's life had truly begun.

"No." Ryū shook his head. "No dreams, just... I don't know... a feeling."

"What kind of feeling?"

"I can't explain it. But if feels like something bad is going to happen. Or perhaps I'm just feeling melancholic... I don't know."

"Melancholic?"

Ryū didn't answer. He took a deep breath and let his gaze drift over the twilit garden. One of the boys was already busy lighting the lanterns. The air was filled with the songs of birds and the chirping of crickets; from a distance they could hear the typical sounds of Yūgao awakening.

"Do you remember when you first came here?" Ryū asked suddenly. "When the fever finally broke and you asked where you were – do you remember?" Suzu nodded his head. Of course he remembered, it wasn't something he'd ever forget. "And Mother told you that you were in Getsuro, in a part of town called Yūgao – the pleasure quarter. She told you, you were in a house of Furyusha. And you took it all in calmly, contemplated it for a little while. And then, suddenly, you burst out laughing. You laughed so long and so hard we thought you were hysteric – or mad. But eventually you calmed down, and you said something I never forgot: 'So that's how you want to play? Fine, then I'll play your game.'" Ryū turned his eyes on Suzu. "At that moment I was certain you were mad. Then you turned to look at Mother and said, 'I'm going to work for you.' Just like that. We had no idea what to make of you. But you kept insisting that you would work as a

Furyusha – although you seemed to have no idea what that even was. You kept calling us whores."

Suzu blew out a cloud of smoke with a smirk, then tapped the ash out of his pipe. "What did you expect? I grew up in a Temple of Hôjô. I assumed they were one and the same."

"Which made it all the more curious why you were so intend on working here."

Suzu shrugged one shoulder. "But you let me."

"How could we not? Have you ever looked into a mirror? And let's be honest, if you wanted you could charm the moon from the sky." Ryū chuckled, but his mirth was short lived. Only a heartbeat later he asked in a sombre, serious tone, "Suzu, what game were you talking about back then? Who was the 'you' you were talking to?"

After a final drag from his pipe, Suzu tapped it on the ash bowl and set it down. He had never spoken to anyone about this. To be honest, he didn't want to say it out loud, afraid it might make him look conceited. "The gods," he said at last, quietly. "I told you what had happened at the temple I grew up in, how I had ended up the way Mother and Haldor found me. And then I learned that it was the proprietor of a brothel – yes, yes, shut up, I know it's not. I know that now, I didn't know it then – so anyway, that I was saved by the owner of a brothel, it felt like the gods just had a good laugh on my expenses. So I thought, all right, fine! That's how they want it? Then I'll show them I can play this game as well." He shrugged again, a crooked grin on his lips.

Ryū shook his head, smiling. "Ah, Suzu, don't you know? The Moon sent you to us. You are our Little Moon."

Ryū's words, spoken with so much pride and affection, hit Suzu deep in the heart. For a moment he could hardly breathe. How – when had it happened that he, who had tried so hard to deny himself love, became so beloved? What had he ever done to deserve all of this?

And suddenly, out of nowhere, unbidden, slicing through the golden warmth of love that filled him like a shard of ice, came an uneasiness, a feeling of foreboding he could not name. Intangible. Formless. He shook it off quickly, not wanting it to ruin the moment.

"Ryū," he began and faltered, his words failing him.

"Suzu, I want you to know, that whatever you do, wherever you go, how ever long you might be gone, this will always be your home."

The uneasiness was not to be shaken off so easily. "What is this, Ryū?" Suzu asked. "Why do you sound like you're saying good-bye? You know that I plan on growing old here with you, being grumpy and complaining about the youth. Annoying them with never-ending 'In my time we didn't...'" He tried for levity and gained a small smile in return. But Ryū wasn't to be deterred.

"And we can still do that. Accepting the Earl's proposal doesn't mean you'd have to leave for good. You know he isn't the kind of man who would keep you away from us. We are family, and always will be. So for fuck's sake, Suzu, stop ignoring what your heart tells you to do."

Suzu shook his head, stubborn. "You know Toshi loves an idea, a fantasy, not the real me."

"Oh, you'd be surprised. I think you're underestimating your earl."

The comment left Suzu dizzy, as if the ground beneath his feet had suddenly fallen away. A tingling sensation accompanied the fuzziness in his head, the confusion. He thought back to the myriads of time he had let himself relax too much in Toshi's presence, the times his mask had slipped.

Each time Toshi had acted as if he hadn't noticed anything – no, that wasn't true, if anything Toshi had seemed a fraction happier each time it happened. Suzu had been too busy reigning in his self-control and berating himself to notice, but now that he thought about it... Before he had a chance to ask Ryū to explain, however, Kazue stepped out of her room and, seeing them, came to join them.

"My boys," she said fondly. "What are you two up to?"

"I was just explaining to Suzu that this is his home, now and for ever, no matter what," Ryū expounded.

Kazue crouched down between the two young men, looking from one to the other. "Of course it is! Suzu, we are a family. I know all the houses claim to be, what with all that 'mother' and 'father' nonsense. But we are, we truly are. And I thank the gods for it every day. My sweet Little Moon, nothing will ever change that."

Suzu swallowed the sudden thickness in his throat and had to blink quickly a few times. There were no words to express the gratitude he felt, the warmth of their love. So, he merely smiled at them, but their answering smiles were like the gentlest of embraces.

With a sigh, Kazue heaved herself to her feet again. "Well, unfortunately I have to call an end to your sweet togetherness, but we have a guest who asked specifically for you, Suzu. Or should I say, he insisted."

"Who?"

"Never seen him before. He was *very* insistent, paid up front... I don't know, but he gives me the creeps." Suzu raised his eyebrows at that. It wasn't like Kazue to be either impressed or intimidated by anyone. "I have Haldor lurking in the hall, just to be save. I would have rejected him, but something tells me that would only cause more trouble."

"It's all right, I'll handle this. Where is he?"

"The Grey Room."

The Grey Room was the room closest to the entry – and the least comfortable. They seldom entertained guests in that specific room unless they wanted to get rid of them as quickly as possible. "I'll be fine, don't worry," Suzu said and got to his feet. Kazue nodded in a way that said she wasn't convinced, but she turned and left ahead of him. "Hey, Ryū," Suzu drawled, "we're a family, and we do call Kazue 'mother', and Haldor is...at least an overprotective uncle. But what does that make us? And please don't say brothers, because... well... you know... some of the things we do together... that would be... hmm really awkward, you know?"

"Devil," Ryū laughed with a slap on Suzu's behind. In return Suzu put on his most wicked smile and purred, "Tonight, I'll make sure there are no bad dreams bothering you." Ryū rolled his eyes at him, his laughter chasing Suzu down the hall.

Suzu knelt in front of the sliding doors, fingertips lightly touching the hardwood floor, his head bowed. At a nod from him, Rani, positioned to the side so he would not be visible, slid the door open.

"Welcome to the Singing Dragon," Suzu said. "My name is Yūzuki no Suzu." He stood up gracefully and stepped into the room, keeping his eyes downcast. The door slid quietly shut behind him. Slowly, Suzu raised his head – and the blood in his veins froze.

Standing in front of him was a young man, a few years older than Toshi. A sneer contorted his gentle face, his dark eyes glittered with hidden malevolence.

"You look well, little sinner," he greeted Suzu.

"Nobu," Suzu growled, his rage awakening like a dragon from its idle slumber. Only barely did he resist the urge to throw himself at the man and tear him to pieces.

"How nice of you to still remember me." Nobu chuckled. "I admit, this is a surprise. I hadn't thought you'd survive."

"So sorry to disappoint you," Suzu snarled.

"Ah, but I should have known better, shouldn't I? You've never been the helpless fragile little flower you've had everyone believe."

"Why the hell are you here?"

"Haven't you figured that out yet? But then, how could you? However, imagine my surprise seeing you standing with the Earl of Tsukikage in front of his house, looking all happy and cosy together. And look at you. There's hardly any of the damage left – well, that eye, I guess. I take it you have some trouble seeing with it."

"You were there, in that carriage," Suzu noted, ignoring the remarks. His hands were balled into fists.

"Indeed. I've heard of the Earl's infatuation with some Furyusha, of course." Nobu nonchalantly, slowly began circling Suzu, inspecting him like a horse he might decide to buy. "And it turns out, it's you. You do see the irony in your chosen profession, don't you?" Nobu laughed. "Oh and don't give me that 'Furyusha are no prostitutes' speech – you sleep with your customers for money, so I really can't see the difference. Never mind. Granted, though, you are gorgeous, even more so than in the past."

"If you can't tell the difference between a Furyusha and a prostitute... well, are you sure you should be here?" Suzu asked in sweet mock concern. "If the Brotherhood finds out one of theirs... I don't even want to think about it." He fluttered his eyelashes at Nobu, who huffed in response. That lousy monk wanted to play games with him? Fine then, they would play.

"Do I look like a monk to you?" Nobu stopped his slow circling in front of Suzu, gesturing at himself. A spark of doubt – Nobu didn't wear the well-known yellow robes of the Brotherhood but an expensive indigo blue kimono. Nor was his head shaven but his black hair was kept short and neat.

"You obviously wouldn't walk into Yūgao wearing your robes. The hair is a bit confusing, but I seem to recall that there was no rule that said a monk had to shave his head. Or are you telling me that they've finally found out what a hypocrite you are and kicked you out?"

Nobu smiled radiantly, taking just a single step towards Suzu. "Not at all. In fact, I am their High Priest now."

Suzu choked. "You? High Priest?" he sputtered. "You are but one step away from being a bloody novice. You'd have to skip a hundred steps at least, and then Brother Askr would still be in your way. He was next in line."

Nobu nodded, acknowledging Suzu's arguments. "True. Ah, but see, Brother Askr... the old fool – he was just too heartbroken after... well, you know. Chose to retire to one of the monasteries in the far north." It felt like Nobu had punched him in the guts. Suzu wouldn't have thought it possible, but he still did care about the old man – after all, he had been the only father Suzu had ever known. To learn how hard he had taken what had happened, brought an unexpected sadness and regret with it. "As for skipping a hundred steps," Nobu continued.

"What shall I say? I always get what I want, you should know that by now."

"What's that supposed to mean?"

"What... Oh, wait, you don't actually think Jin... back then...?" Nobu burst out laughing.

"Shut up," Suzu snapped. "He obviously couldn't have come up with all of that on his own, he's not cunning enough. And you were too obviously enjoying yourself during that farce of a trial." He meant what he said – and only now realised that he had never really believed Jin capable of such duplicity. Though it didn't change the fact that Jin had abandoned and betrayed him.

"You are right, Jin doesn't have the brains – he is too... what is the word I am looking for? Honest. Yes, he's too honest – and too gullible. Gods, even I was taken aback by how easy it was to make him do whatever I wanted."

Ever since Jin had shown up at the Singing Dragon, overjoyed, believing he had finally found his beloved Kari, Suzu had known for certain that Jin hadn't known, he just hadn't wanted to admit it, not even to himself. And from where Suzu was standing, being foolish enough to be so thoroughly manipulated didn't excuse anything.

"Oh, Saya and Steren, on the other hand, now they didn't need any persuasion at all. They practically fell all over themselves for a chance to have a go at you," Nobu continued gleefully.

The monk's taunts didn't reach Suzu, however, for his mind was filled with only one question, a question he had been asking for five years: Why? Here was his chance at last to get answers. So he asked. "Why?"

Nobu frowned, his delight at taunting Suzu evaporated. "Because they hated you. You would have noticed if you hadn't been so full of yourself."

"Not they, you. Why did you do it?" Suzu hissed, glowering at the man.

"Because you were a nuisance to me," Nobu stated as if it was the most obvious thing.

"A nuisance... we... Jin and I, we would have been gone as soon as we were old enough. We would have been out of your hair in no time."

"Yes, but where would have been the fun in that?" Nobu laughed. It took all the self-restraint Suzu possessed not to beat him to a pulp right there and then. If they hadn't been at the Singing Dragon, where there was always the risk of a customer witnessing it, Suzu would have already broken several of the monk's bones. Nobu, no doubt, had anticipated this and therefore chosen to confront Suzu at a time and place where he could do the least damage.

Suddenly, Nobu's laughter snapped off, like a taut thread cut in half, the expression on his face darkened. The usual malevolent glitter in his eyes turned into a menacing glint. Suzu forced himself not to flinch at the threat that emanated from the man.

"I remember telling you once that you'd regret standing in my way. Do you remember?" Nobu hissed quietly. "What happened five years ago was only a taste of what will happen, should I ever again get the feeling that you are opposing me."

"You're insane," Suzu gasped, stunned.

"Am I? Do you want to find out? You are this close already... It's a strange coincidence that you seem to have suddenly reconciled with Jin, isn't it? Oh, sure, you would think that it's of no matter – that is, if Jin wasn't working for

Murasaki no Naloc. I know all about that man. How could I not. After all, one should always know one's potential allies and even more so one's potential enemies. And you, being so close to the Earl – I know you've heard my little message. Of course you did, I told my man to make sure to deliver it in your presence. Call it a little test. Well... it seems, my little sinner, that you've been a naughty boy." Suzu fought to keep any expression off his face. If Nobu was fishing for confirmation of what he thought to know, Suzu wouldn't give it to him. Suzu had meant it when he had called the monk insane. And now, looking straight into the eyes of the man before him, the franticness that seemed to simmer just below the monk's surface, Suzu wondered if it might actually be true.

"Ah, but I might be willing to forgive you one last time," Nobu continued. "After all, it would be a shame wasting such a well-honed sword as yourself. We are quite similar, you and I."

"I am nothing like you," Suzu spat.

Nobu dismissed the comment with a wave of his hand. "Think whatever you want. But you are just as manipulative as I am. You wear a thousand masks as if they were your true self for your own gain. So here's the deal: Join me, and you can have whatever it is you want."

"No thanks."

"I'm not offering twice. And by now, you should know what happens if you cross me."

Suzu drew himself to his full height, looking Nobu square in the face. "I'm not a traitor. I'm not a lunatic. And you are the last person on earth I'd ever join hands with. I remember having told you so before, haven't I."

"You are making a grave mistake," Nobu hissed through clenched teeth. Suzu had the feeling that for the first time he saw the real Nobu – unadorned with smiles that never reached his eyes; without an armour of pleasantness and courtesy. What he saw repulsed him and made him pity the man in equal parts. Suzu had always seen the maliciousness, the deviousness beneath the mask, barely visible under the polished surface – a person like a palimpsest. Was Suzu like that, too? Could others see what lay beneath if only they looked at him in the right light? Perhaps they were more similar than he cared to admit, perhaps that was why he felt so revolted by Nobu. But this frenetic, obsessive streak – had this been there all along?

"You better leave now," Suzu snarled. Nobu didn't move. The rage living inside Suzu was like a coiled snake, ready to strike, screaming at him to kill this man. Kill him now! And he knew he could do it. It would be easy. Nobu was a monk, not a fighter, and he was unarmed.

But before Suzu could move, the door behind him slammed open and Haldor stomped into the room – tall, broad, and menacing.

"You!" he growled, pointing a finger at Nobu. "You leave right now. You can do it on your own two feet, or I will drag you out."

"How dare –" Nobu had no chance to finish the sentence before Haldor was behind him, quicker than a man his size had any right to be, and clamped one huge hand around Nobu's neck, with the other he twisted one of Nobu's arms behind his back. Nobu gasped in pain and shock, futilely attempting to free himself. Haldor pushed him out of the room and down the hall where Kazue and Ryū where waiting. Rani and Akito hidden behind them.

"How dare you! Let go of me this instance," Nobu screeched, only to be ignored.

"You are no longer welcome in this house," Kazue declared haughtily, regarding Nobu as if he were a mere insect, not even worth the effort to be squashed. "Now – or ever again."

"You will regret treating me like this," Nobu yelled, trying to twist his head around to look at Suzu, but Haldor had an iron grip on him. "You... sinner. Mark my words, you'll regret refusing my offer. And the rest of you – I'll make you pay for your insolence!"

"And you!" Ryū growled, more angry than Suzu had ever seen him. "You will not set foot in Yūgao ever again. I'll see to that."

Haldor didn't give Nobu the chance to make more threats. He pushed the man forward, out of the door, and marched him down the path to the gate, past a small group of confused and shocked looking patrons, who had just arrived.

"Are you all right, Suzu?" Ryū asked, grabbing Suzu by the shoulders, anger replaced with worry in the blink of an eye. Suzu took a deep breath and nodded.

"Damn it, I knew there was something fishy about that guy. I shouldn't have let him in in the first place." Kazue pinched the bridge of her nose, shaking her head angrily. "You sure, you're all right?"

"Yes,"Suzu confirmed again. "But I need to get a message to Jin – at once."

What Suzu didn't tell his family, however, was that he couldn't shake the terrible feeling that Nobu didn't make idle threats.

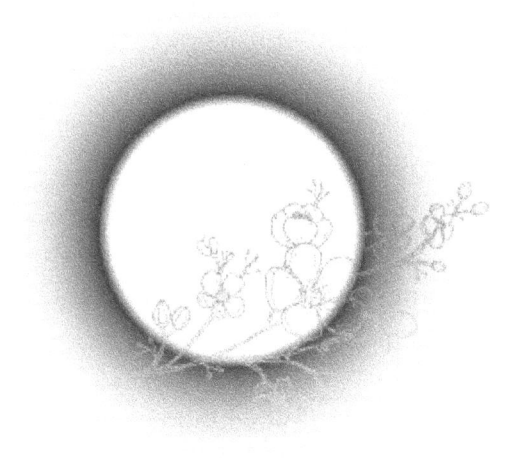

Chapter 23

Suzu was pacing the hallway, abuzz with angry energy. Kazue and Ryū had long since given up trying to calm him down and sat in quiet, watching him warily. He longed to go to the dojo and imagine the training dummy to be Nobu. Instead, he had to wait for Jin – who seemed to be taking his sweet time. When he finally did arrive, he wasn't alone. Suzu had expected Niall and even Naloc to accompany him, given the urgency of the message Suzu had sent. But he had no idea who the tall, fierce looking woman or the small older man were.

Jin pushed his way through his entourage and hurried towards Suzu. "What do you mean, it's Nobu?" He fired the question at Suzu. "How can it be Nobu? That doesn't make any sense. He –"

"Calm down, lad," Naloc admonished him, ushering both Jin and Suzu ahead of him into the room where Kazue and Ryū were waiting. But Suzu understood Jin's confusion. He only took a couple of steps into the room, before he whirled around, facing his former friend.

"He came here, Jin. This evening. He all but told me that he was behind... whatever it is. He's pulling the strings, it's what he does best: manipulating others to get what he wants. And he knows you are snooping around and that I gave you information."

"What?" It was the small man, his exclamation sounding curiously affronted.

"All right, everyone, calm down now!" Naloc snapped. "Let's sit down and have the whole story, shall we?"

While Suzu recounted the evening's events, Ryū handed out cups of saké. Suzu downed his in one swallow.

"So this Nobu," Naloc said after Suzu had finished. "Who is he and why would he want to assassinate the emperor?"

Suzu opened his mouth to answer, but Jin pre-empted him, "We grew up together. Well, actually he's older, he... he was like an older brother. He understood me... I thought... I..." His eyes flitted to Suzu, shame, hurt, confusion warring on his face. Suzu couldn't blame him for that, until only recently Jin had believed Nobu to be this older brother figure who had supported and understood him. What Suzu could blame him for, however, was for being so damn gullible in the first place.

"Nobu is," Suzu interjected thus, before Jin continued stammering nonsense, "a manipulative, presumptuous, delusional, and self-aggrandising bastard." Not feeling like laying his entire life bare in front of Naloc and his goons, but seeing he needed to further explain, Suzu reluctantly told them what had happened at the temple five years ago. To Jin's apparent wonder, Suzu also made it clear that Nobu had manipulated Jin. When he was done he gave Jin a sardonic smile. Having a clearer picture of what had happened all these years ago didn't mean Jin was off the hook.

"But... why? To what end?" Naloc asked eventually.

Suzu gestured for Ryū to refill his cup. It wasn't until after he had downed another cup of saké that he answered. "I've been thinking about this. Apparently, or so he claims, because I was a nuisance to him, and waiting until I left by my myself would have been no fun." A few raised eyebrows told Suzu he wasn't the only one who thought that explanation weak. "We are talking about Nobu, so I'd not put it past him this was part of the reason. It was probably what put the cherry on the cake for him. But he did it with a certain intention, I'm sure of it."

"You said, Nobu was high priest now? But how can that be?" Jin tossed in, and it hit Suzu like lightning. Of course, Nobu had practically told him why he'd really done it.

"Brother Askr," he said. "He told me that what happened broke the old man's heart and he retired to one of the northern monasteries, seeking seclusion. Brother Askr had been next in line. And he was a very steadfast man with an instinct for falsehood. He wasn't keen on Nobu."

"In short," the tall fierce looking woman spoke up, "getting rid of you also ditched his biggest obstacle. All part of his plan to... eh... what?"

"To become high priest. Have enough power to pull something off as ridiculous as killing the emperor?" Suzu shrugged.

"Right. And then what?"

A memory, blurry as if seen through a rain-washed window, colours bleeding into each other, fragments of sound, words spoken in anger. Nobu in novice colours; the face of another young monk, expression angry – no, worried. Suzu tried to catch hold of the memory but it evaded him, flitting through his mental fingers like a tiny bird. He shook his head and shrugged, he had no insight into Nobu's mind to offer.

"Whatever," the woman dismissed it, unconcerned. "Who cares why he does what he does, we just have to find him and stop him, right? Boss?" Naloc gave a curt nod but no reply, he seemed lost in thought. "All right, how difficult can it be to find a monk of the Brotherhood in this town. A high priest to boot."

"You shouldn't underestimate him," Suzu retorted at the same time as the small man sitting almost hidden behind Jin interjected, "You said he knew about us sniffing about." Suzu had completely forgotten about the man. It wasn't just that until now he had been so quiet, not making a single sound, no shift, no gasp, no murmur or hum, but it was as if he had hardly any presence of his own, blending into the background. Unseen and unperceived. It was unnerving, and yet familiar. It reminded Suzu of Kagetora.

He focused on the man. The intensity of Suzu's gaze made him squirm; it gave Suzu an odd kind of satisfaction, Kagetora wouldn't even have blinked. "He knows," he confirmed. "Nobu did his research, he knows all there is to know about Naloc-tan, and has planned ahead accordingly. It's how he found out I had passed on information."

"Oh, but other than that? He doesn't know anything specific. Does he?"

Suzu raised an eyebrow, the man seemed unreasonably smug about this. "I guess so," Suzu said slowly. "But as I was saying, Nobu isn't stupid. He didn't wear his monk's robes when he came here, and I doubt he will as long as he's in town unless it serves a purpose."

While the others around him fell into speculation and summarising what they knew and what they didn't knew, Suzu was occupied by his own contemplations. Nobu was too certain of himself, but that was nothing knew. The monk had never once doubted that he would get whatever he wanted, achieve whatever he strove for. In a way it was admirable, yet this out of proportion confidence was a sign of the monk's hubris. And where there was hubris, there was recklessness, there were flaws. They only had to find them.

Suzu fiddled with the dainty little cup in his hands. There was one more thing nagging at his mind ever since that morning at Toshi's: Nobu's henchman. He looked so familiar, but perhaps it were his generic thug like looks. He had the build of a tree trunk, big in a way that spoke of masses of muscles beneath a softer padding, the strength of an ox; moving with the grace of a wet towel. A readiness for violence radiated off him, lopsided smile promising a world of pain.

Suzu tried to imagine the face younger, without that scar – but before he got even started, Naloc rudely interrupted him. Suzu looked up, annoyed. From the way everyone else was looking at him expectantly, it seemed Naloc had called his name more than once. So, reluctantly, Suzu turned to look at him.

"I was asking," Naloc said – and Suzu enjoyed his irritation at having to repeat himself – "if it is this Nobu who pulls the strings, or rather the Earl."

Suzu had forgotten he was still holding the saké cup in his hand until he shattered it with force on the tatami mat, shards of broken porcelain biting into his hand. Through the haze of anger, he heard surprised yelling, felt his hand being yanked away from the broken cup.

"I swear," Suzu hissed, voice dangerously low, "if you accuse Toshi" – he used the familiar nickname deliberately – "one more time, dare to insult him just one more time, it will be the last thing you'll ever say. I will rip your bloody tongue out of your fucking mouth. And if you think your she-ogre or anyone else can stop me – think again."

The silence was absolute. From just behind Naloc Suzu could make out the tall woman mouthing the words "she-ogre" with a dejected expression that would have been funny if not for the momentary situation.

"I have no idea how or why Toshi is involved in this, but I know that he's got a good reason for it. He's not a traitor."

"And I still don't see how you can be so certain of this," Naloc snapped. He seemed to have overcome his initial shock and replaced it with irritation. Clearly, he was not used to being spoken to like that – it was high time someone took him down a peg, in Suzu's opinion.

"Because, unlike you, I know the man," Suzu replied slowly, enunciating each word carefully. Naloc leaned back, his nostrils flaring as he took a deep breath, his jaw tightening in anger. But he didn't try to argue the point, he knew Suzu was right. What did Naloc or any of them really know about the Earl of Tsukikage? A public image. A tragic past. A young man burdened too early with the weight of an illustrious title and its history. Legends. Rumours. Lies. Of all of them, Suzu was the only one who had a right to judge the man's character, the only one who had seen behind the mask.

And so, Naloc relented – not completely ungraciously. "Fine. So. We need to rethink our current strategy, how best to move on. There's a lot we... well, but that is none of your concern, is it? I think we can all agree that the information you have given us is more than enough. We won't be troubling you again. Kazue, I take it you've made sure that monk won't set foot into Yūgao again?"

"Of course I did, who do you think I am?"

"But Nobu doesn't have to come here himself, he can just send his henchman or someone else, can't he?" Jin pointed out, and Suzu mentally commended him for it. After all, now that Jin had gotten his perspective straightened out, he seemed to see some things a lot clearer.

"Right. I'll have Risa and her men patrol the streets around the Dragon." Naloc cast a quick glance at the woman behind him, who gave a curt nod in reply.

A short while later, when Naloc and his entourage where about to leave, Suzu pulled Jin aside.

"Look," he said quietly, "I'm not forgiving you for being a gullible idiot who could even be persuaded the sky was a sparkly green. Nor am I going to forgive you for trusting a blasted madman instead of using your own bloody head, or at least talking to me. But for what it's worth, I might forgive you for what happened after you were gone. A bit, at least. I know you wouldn't have let any of it happen had you known. Perhaps I knew it all along but didn't want to acknowledge it – and Nobu did put a lot of effort into being convincing, we should at least appreciate that." Jin huffed a surprised laugh. He had been staring at Suzu wide-eyed for the entire speech, now it seemed like a weight had dropped off of him. The tension in his shoulders lessened, and a smile spread across his face. That smile – damn the gods, but how had Suzu forgotten about that smile. So bright, so dazzling – like sunshine after a storm. Suzu had to admit to himself that he had missed it.

"Does that mean you are not going to throw bottles at me anymore?" Jin asked. Even his voice sounded different – a golden, rich baritone whereas it had been tarnished with a patina of forlornness before.

Suzu cocked his head. "Are you going to insult Toshi again?"

"No?"

"Then I guess I won't."

Jin smiled at the floor, shifting his weight from one foot to the other. And just when Suzu was beginning to wonder why he was suddenly so shy, Jin asked, "Can... I mean... um... if it's all right, can I... come visit you sometimes... to talk...?"

Suzu stared at the young man. Five years had passed. Five years full of agony, full of rage. Five years he had tried his best to forget the past – and failed. The rage was still there, and so was the pain. But it had changed its course, found a better target, a more deserving one. Now he looked at that young man who had become a stranger to him, and he saw that small boy who had only wished to be needed, to be loved, to have a place in this world. The boy who had saved him from his grief, his loneliness, his fears, who had held him tight through every storm. Who had given him his first kiss. Who had embraced him. Who had loved him. And Suzu couldn't find it in his heart to hate him any longer.

"All right," he said at last.

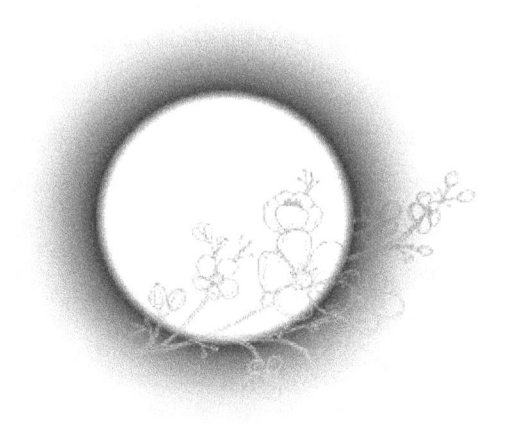

Chapter 26

The following day was so ordinary and uneventful it grated on Suzu's nerves. It felt like the unnatural calm before a storm, the air so charged it made his nerves tingle. He had heard neither from Toshi nor from Jin. The uncertainty and the wait for something, anything, to happen felt like walls slowly crushing Suzu between them.

So when the next day a message from Toshi arrived, asking Suzu to be ready to be picked up only two hours later, he was so relieved he didn't even wonder about a message arriving at a time too early for the nocturnal Singing Dragon. A confusion of emotions made him impatient for action. Dread of Toshi's reaction to the confrontation with Nobu, his disappointment in Suzu about passing on information. And what if Toshi was yet a willing part of the conspiracy? No. No, no, no. Never.

He felt nervous and impatient, relieved and glad; he was fidgeting so much Ryū had to take over braiding his hair in the end.

"Why are you so nervous? Are you really going to tell him about everything? Do you think the Earl might –"

"No! No, Toshi would never hurt me," Suzu intercepted his friend's worries. "Trust me, I know he wouldn't. The worst thing that could happen is that he never wants to see me again."

Ryū smiled. "Well, and that, I can assure you, will never happen." Suzu shrugged. Ryū tied off Suzu's braid, put his arms around his shoulders and hid his face in the crook between Suzu's neck and shoulder.

"Ryū?" Suzu asked gently. "What is it? Do you still have that bad feeling?" Ryū nodded. "Hey, Naloc has his men patrolling the streets and searching the town for Nobu. You know I don't trust Naloc, but that Risa and the other one, they seem like competent people." A small smile tugged at the corners of Ryū's mouth. It wasn't much. But Suzu had no comfort to offer his friend, no assurances. There was only one thing Suzu could do to make sure his family was safe: he'd have to ask Toshi for help. He couldn't say how the man would react to Suzu's admission of having passed on information and knowing more than he should have – unless, of course, Nobu had already told him – but he hoped most urgently that his trust in Toshi was justified.

Suzu was half-way out of his room already when, for reasons he couldn't name, he hurried back to his washstand, opened the little jewellery box, and grabbed the necklace Ryū and Rani had given him. He felt he needed it as a kind of tether between him and his family.

Ryū, Kazue, and Haldor were waiting for him at the gate. "What is this?" he asked with a mixture of amusement and puzzlement.

"I think it best if Haldor accompanied you," Kazue said, and Haldor grunted assent.

If their worry hadn't been etched into their faces, into every tight line, every frown, every tensed muscle, Suzu would have thought they were joking. He sighed. "Mother, Haldor, please, it's Toshi we are talking about here. You know he'd never hurt me – besides, you don't seem to put a lot of trust in my abilities to defend myself."

"I know that you could best the Earl if you were serious," Haldor rumbled with obvious pride in his voice. "But he's not alone either, is he. What about that so-called valet of his?"

Suzu smiled. Leave it to Haldor to immediately see through Kagetora. The man was like a bloodhound when it came to sniffing out fighters, there was no fooling him.

"I don't know," he answered honestly. "I am not sure I could beat him. But it doesn't matter because I'll be fine. Nothing is going to happen."

Kazue exhaled loudly, her shoulders slumping, and Suzu knew he had won the argument. "Fine, I trust your judgement, and I've known the Earl long enough to know better. It's this whole nonsense with that conspiracy and that shifty monk." Suzu put his arms around her and kissed her on the cheek. She smelled of lavender – dark and warm, familiar, calming. She hugged him back and whispered into his ear, "I love you, my beautiful, clever boy."

"I love you, too. Don't worry, I'll be back before you know it."

One last squeeze and she let go of him, gifting him instead with one of her rare smiles. Suzu noticed Haldor still scowling and couldn't help but tease the man. "You need a hug, too, my big bear?" Haldor snorted and rolled his eyes at him. But then he suddenly pressed a tantō into Suzu's hand.

"Take it," he growled.

"What? I can't –"

"You take it, you keep it, and you won't ever leave the house without it again." The order sent a chill down Suzu's spine. Feeling slightly unsettled, he stuffed the short sword into the sash of his yukata. Trying to argue would have been futile, Haldor was not the kind of man you talked back to when given an order. Nor did he ever give unreasonable orders. Satisfied, Haldor clapped Suzu on the shoulder and then stepped back.

Ryū had stood by, keeping silent. Now he grabbed Suzu in a fierce hug. There were no words necessary between them, they knew each other's darkest secrets, their nightmares, the lies they told themselves, the hidden truths. But before he let him go, Ryū kissed him – it wasn't passionate, not even very gentle, but determined and insistent – a promise, an oath. To stay safe. To come back.

Within seconds the nondescript hansom that had been waiting in front of the Singing Dragon pulled away, with Suzu sitting inside, looking back at the people he loved.

They were not going the right way. Mangetsu lay in the opposite direction. Instead they left Yūgao through the west gate, sitting on the boundary between Eigetsu and Kigetsu. Suzu felt the first flutter of anxiety. He banged his fist on the roof and called, "Kagetora? I know it's you. Where are we going?" He received no answer. Nervous, he gripped the hilt of the tantō Haldor had given him.

They reached the outskirts of Kigetsu, close to the town wall, home of smithies, tanneries, and an assortment of different kinds of workshops people preferred not to have in their direct neighbourhood. It wasn't an area of the town Suzu had had much opportunity to visit in the five years he had been living in Getsuro. It was noisy and busy, people hurrying to and fro, smoke and steam from the smithies and the tanneries adding to the sweltering heat.

The hansom pulled up behind a blacksmith's. Suzu didn't move, the grip on his short sword so tight the white of his knuckles showed. A heartbeat later Toshi emerged from the shadows of a shed. He looked tired and drawn. Slowly, Suzu got out of the hansom and walked towards the man. Toshi's gaze only briefly flickered to the weapon at Suzu's hip.

"I'm sorry about this," he said. "I'll explain, but let's go inside first." He ushered Suzu into the dim coolness of the shed, cast a glance back over his shoulder, and pulled the door closed. "The smith is a friend of mine," he blurted, uncharacteristically nervous. "He'll hide you here until I can get you out of town safely."

"What? To--"

"I'll take you to my country house, you'll be safe there. Don't worry, I'll talk to Kazue and Ryū, I'll explain everything to them – and to you... later... when this is all over... right now – I can't tell you everything right now, it's..." Toshi was babbling; Toshi didn't babble.

"Toshi!" Suzu's voice held enough authority to end Toshi's ramblings and catch the man's attention. "What the hell is going on?" For a second Suzu acknowledged the fact that his carefully created persona was absent, then he decided he didn't care. Not now. Something bad was going on, something more important than maintaining a mask. Toshi was never like this, he was never such a nervous, hardly controlled wreck.

"Gods." Toshi exhaled hard. "Suzu, I am so sorry. You should have never gotten involved in this. I'm so, so sorry." He rubbed a hand angrily through his hair. "If only they had never seen you with me. It was so stupid of me to indulge myself before this was all over."

"Stop! All of this? What is all of this? Toshi, you're not making any sense. You didn't involve me in anything. Never seen me – are you talking about Nobu?"

Toshi's eyes widened in surprise. So Nobu had not told him about Suzu and his little visit – or their past. Interesting. He could have sworn the first thing Nobu did was trying to sow dissent between Toshi and him. So why hadn't he?

"He means to kill you, Suzu," came the answer to his unspoken question. It should have been a shock, but the only thing that shocked Suzu about it was the finality of it. He had thought Nobu to be more creative and more sadistic, finding ways to draw out Suzu's suffering for as long as possible. Ending Suzu's life seemed almost... trite.

"Kagetora followed him last night. He heard Nobu give the order to go after you. It was all I could do right now, getting you away from the Singing Dragon before his men arrive –"

"Wait! Before they... you mean they are there? Now?" Suzu's heart skipped a few beats before it began furiously hammering against his rib cage like a trapped bird. The floor beneath his feet seemed to move, almost throwing him off balance. In his mind he could hear Nobu's voice, as clear as if the man himself was speaking them into his ears: *You will regret treating me like this. I'll make you pay for your insolence.* "By the gods, he's going to kill them all."

"No, Suzu, that's insane. He's after you, he wouldn't –"

"You have no idea what he is capable of!" Suzu yelled. He only noticed Toshi flinch with half his brain, the other half was screaming at him to run! Back to the Singing Dragon – back home and to the people he called family. He had to warn them, help them, protect them. He was half-way to the door when Toshi grabbed his arm and pulled him to a stop.

"Please, Suzu listen. It's you he's after," Toshi repeated urgently. "He doesn't care about the others. With you gone he won't... he gains nothing from hurting them."

"You don't know him. Don't underestimate his madness. Now let me go!"

"I can't."

Gods, there was no time to discuss, explain, convince. With a skilful twist of his arm he broke free from Toshi. He didn't give him a chance to react, the moment Toshi lost his grip on his arm, Suzu bolted. He burst through the door and ran down the street as fast as he could. Toshi's frantic voice chased after him but was quickly lost in the din from the forges and workshops. And then the only thing Suzu could hear was his blood pounding in his ears, his hard breathing, the slap of his feet on the ground as he ran faster than ever before in his life.

His thigh muscles were on fire, screaming for him to stop. He had long since lost his sandals, the hot dirt and cobblestones of the roads burning the soles of his feet, carrying him onwards. Onwards and onwards, no time to stop. Not enough air in his lungs, but the adrenaline fuelled his urgency, pushing him to go beyond his limits. Onwards. A single thought in his mind – *Please, please don't let it be too late.* Onwards – to his home, to the people he loved, to his life. Onwards.

At first he didn't notice he wasn't the only one running towards the Dragon anymore, or people yelling at each other to hurry. Hurry! It wasn't until he rounded a corner – and the sight stopped him dead in his tracks.

There, at the end of the alley, where it had stood, proud and magnificent, for decades, the Singing Dragon was ablaze. Tongues of fire licking the sky. The popping and bursting sound of burning wood as loud as thunder.

For a moment Suzu stood, petrified, staring at the scene and not comprehending what he saw. People were yelling at each other, running to and fro, forming a line and handing down buckets full of sloshing water. Over the din Suzu heard the disharmonious clanging of the fire bell. Black clouds of smoke rose to the sky, dimming the sun, flakes of hot ash fell like snow to the ground, ember sparks like malicious fireflies. And the Dragon – the house, the gardens – a raging inferno. It was like a scene from a nightmare; it didn't feel real. And yet, the acid burn of the smoke in his air-deprived lungs, the roar of the fire in his ears, the heat against his skin, aggressive, painful, intensifying the already scorching heat of the day...

Suzu pushed through the throng of people, hardly aware of doing so, driven by single-minded determination. He needed to get to the house – to his home, to his family. Where was his family? He needed to know they were safe. Hands were grabbing at him, trying to hold him back, but he shook them off, evaded them. And suddenly his cut feet wouldn't move anymore, the muscles in his legs cramping, a weight pulling him to a stop. He tore his eyes away from the rampaging conflagration and looked down at what hindered his progress.

Skinny arms were wrapped around his middle. A soot and tear streaked face stared up at him with red, swollen eyes. The left side of the face was one angry blistering wound, once fine black hair burnt away, replaced by red and raw skin.

"Akito," Suzu gasped.

"S-Suzu, they... Rani... they... d-d-dead," the boy stammered through great, heaving sobs racking his small frame. Howling, he pressed himself against Suzu. Almost mechanically Suzu put his arms around him. Too late. He was too late. His legs were trembling, threatening to not hold his weight for much longer. A terrible cold had settled in his veins, replacing his blood with ice. He felt disassociated from himself, from the present. His eyes stung, his throat burnt. Suzu let his gaze wander over the pandemonium around them. The hectic, almost panicking crowd, still throwing one futile bucketful of water after the other onto all-consuming flames. The fire, burning unhindered, devouring all Suzu had loved.

A tiny group of people caught his eye, leaning against the wall of the Lotus Flower, friend and neighbour of the Singing Dragon for so many happy years, shell-shocked expressions on their faces, blood, soot, and tears covering their skins and singed clothes.

Suzu wrested himself free of Akito's hold, grabbed the boy's hand, and fought his way though the crowd to the small group by the wall. His heart was hammering against his ribcage. Mother wasn't amongst the group... nor Rani... nor... Ryū... Haldor...

"Suzu, thank the gods." Tomiko. Suzu reached with his free hand for her, but the Dragon's seamstress shied back, holding both her hands up for Suzu to see. They were so red, so black, so blistered they were unrecognisable as the fine boned, clever hands that had made so many of the exquisite garments they had worn.

Bile rose in his throat, Suzu swallowed convulsively, blinking hard against the tears that threatened to undo him. *No, not now.* "Tomiko, what happened?" he forced himself to ask.

She shook her head. "I don't know. There... there was screaming, horrible screaming... then Ryū... yelling for us all to get out. I... then... then I heard some kind of... bang... and fire, fire everywhere... w-we ran... but outside... outside were men with swords, and they... oh gods, Suzu... I-I saw Mother lying in a p-pool of b-blood, Rani... in her arms... they were so still... and... and..." Tomiko's voice broke. She fell to her knees, her ruined hands pressed against her chest as she screamed out all her pain and horror.

Suzu stared at her, frozen, Akito still clinging to him, shaking with sobs. He couldn't breathe. He looked at the pitiful ragged little group that was all that was left of his family – horror-stricken, wounded. He looked at Tomiko's hands. He looked at Akito's burnt face. At Hayate's wild eyes, his yukata drenched in blood from an unseen wound, at Aurin cradling a broken arm, his handsome face marred by bloody cuts. At Sabia's empty eyes as she sat slumped against the wall. The cook's arms and legs were badly burnt. Tomiko's words echoed in his head, painting visions of terror and pain.

And then something inside Suzu cracked. Something inside him began to scream – loud and fierce. Louder than the roaring fire and so much fiercer yet. His fingernails dug into his palms, hard enough to draw blood. He didn't even notice.

A sudden tab on his shoulder made him whirl around with a snarl, expecting an enemy. But it was one of the Lotus's girls. She flinched but stood her ground. In a voice as sad as it was musical she said, "Suzu, thank the gods you are here. Ryū needs you."

Ryū – he was alive! Suzu felt a heady rush of relief. Yet when he saw the expression on the young woman's face his relief died instantly.

"You better come quick," she said, the tone of her voice foreboding. Suzu turned to Akito, pleading the boy to stay with the others. Wordlessly, Akito gave a curt nod and went into the waiting arms of Tomiko.

The girl – why couldn't he remember her name? – led him quickly through the gates and into the small bamboo grove beyond that hid the rest of the Lotus Flower's estate. For now at least it seemed safe enough, the estates in this corner of Yūgao big enough and far enough apart from each other.

They didn't go far. In the middle of the winding path, blankets spread beneath him, lay Ryū, surrounded by a small group of people. And as he got closer something inside Suzu died along with his hope. The entire left side of Ryū's body was a charred bleeding wound. Almost all of his once lustrous hair was gone. Half of his beautiful face had been ravaged by the flames. The one remaining golden eye void of its usual light; no humour, no joy, instead it was dull and filled with pain. Laboriously drawing a breath, his lungs emitted a horrible wheezing sound.

Suzu fell to his knees beside his friend. His vision went dark around the edges, the cacophony, the chaos, the confusion on the other side of the walls grew distant, his focus, his entire world narrowed in on Ryū: his best friend, his brother, his sometimes lover. A person whose presence was larger than life in Suzu's heart and in his mind. Who had patiently dragged him out of the darkness, who weathered every storm for him, with him, who had brought back Suzu's smile, who always had his back, and never let him fall. Suzu tentatively touched Ryū's good hand, felt his friend's fingers twitch against his, and gently took Ryū's hand in his.

"Suzu." A whisper, hardly more than a breath. Suzu leaned down to his friend so he could hear him better – and perhaps so that Ryū could feel his presence.

"I'm here," he said, his voice wavering.

"I tried... failed... Haldor is... dojo... d-dead." A single tear fell from the corner of Ryū's eye. "Someth--... wro--... thunder... fire... ran to get back...waiting out--... th-the gates were sealed."

"Hush, Ryū," Suzu pleaded, he didn't want Ryū to exhaust himself, to relive those moments in what most probably were his last ones. It was enough for Suzu to piece together what must have happened.

From what Ryū had told him and Tomiko's account Suzu gathered that Ryū had for some reason been looking for Haldor, only to find the man dead in his dojo. Haldor had been an experienced fighter, tall and burly, not an easy target. They must have taken him by surprise, perhaps even overwhelmed him in numbers. Knowing something terrible was happening, Ryū had run back to warn the others, but it was too late. A crash, a roar – fire broke out, hungry and indiscriminate. Ryū, oh valiant Ryū – of course he would have run back inside to help whomever he could help, save as many as he could. But instead of safety, what they found outside were the sharp edges of swords, waiting only to cut them down. To die on the blade or to die in the fierce embrace of a roaring fire. In the end, it was a wonder there were any survivors at all.

"Some of the others dragged him out from under a fallen beam," said the man kneeling opposite Suzu. Suzu spared him a quick glance. He was a white haired older man who Suzu knew to be one of Yūgao's doctors, but he had no name to put to the face. "His burns are too severe, and it seems his spine was injured. We couldn't even get him into the house. I feared the pain would kill him. But still... I'm so sorry, there's nothing I can do."

Suzu clenched his teeth and closed his eyes for a moment. *Not now, not yet.* He couldn't break, he couldn't cry, if he allowed himself to cry he would break. *Not now, not until...*

"Apart from the Akito, Tomiko, Sabia, Aurin, and Hayate – who else made it out?" he asked, although he already knew the answer.

"Suzu –" Ah, he knew that voice, it belonged to Astrid, the Lotus's owner.

"Who else?"

"no-one," came the answer, soft and gentle as if it would make a difference. Suzu's chest felt as if a giant hand had him in an iron grip, squeezing harder and harder. It felt as if fissures had opened, spiderwebbing his heart and soul. Any moment now he was going to be torn asunder.

But Ryū was still fighting to hang on, his breath wheezing in his lungs, his dulled golden eye fixed on Suzu's face. Waiting for Suzu on the other side of the wall were Akito, Tomiko, Sabia, Aurin and Hayate, wounded and scared. He had to be strong – for their sake. He had to keep himself together, couldn't let himself fall apart now. *Not now, not yet.* He knew exactly what he had to do.

And there it was, like an old familiar friend, filling in the cracks in his heart, his soul, like molten metal, red hot and searing. Its intensity consumed him, burnt away the shock, the grief, the pain like the conflagration claiming his home, until it was all that was left. Rage. A rage unlike any he had ever felt before.

A feverishly hot hand brushed against his cheek and Suzu flinched, jolted back to the moment, the terrible present. Ryū's hand. Suzu quickly caught it, held it in place against his cheek.

"Suzu, don't... be... want yo-- hap--" Ryū's voice was growing weaker.

"Hush. It's all right. Don't speak. I promise I will make him pay."

"Su--"

"I swear, Ryū, by my name, by the goddess above. I will hunt him down and kill him."

Tears fell from Ryū's good eye, ran down his temple. "Pl...ease... hap-- need you...be-- I--" And then Ryū fell silent and would never speak again. A last breath left his once smiling lips, the light in his eyes went out. His arm sagged, fingers slipping from Suzu's grasp. All that Ryū had been, the very essence of him, his gentleness, his laughter – gone forever.

And Suzu? He sat beside the broken husk that had been his friend, his brother, his teacher, the other half of his soul, frozen and still. Inside his head he was screaming, like he had once screamed until his voice had broken. The pain, the agony became a physical sensation, yet he could neither move nor voice his pain. He just sat there for hours, days, aeons.

Eventually someone grabbed him beneath his arms and heaved him to his feet.

"Suzu? Hey, lad, do you remember me? We met the other day... my name is Durin. Naloc sent me. Come, come with me now." The stranger's grip was strong and yet tender as if he was afraid Suzu might break. But Suzu wouldn't break, not yet. He had made an oath and he was intent to keep it. He was a piece of broken pottery put together – a piece of *kintsugi*, mended not with gold but rage.

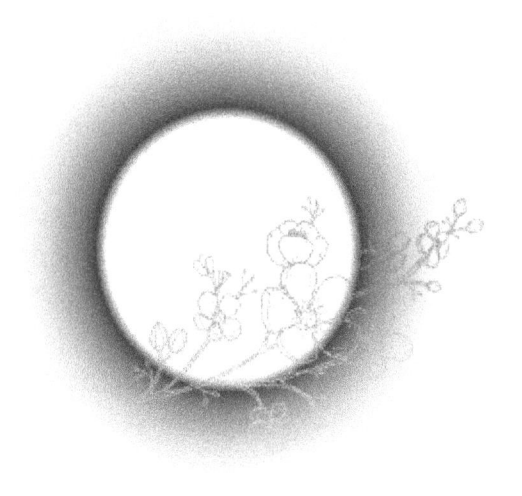

Chapter 27

"Damn it! Where is that blasted monk hiding?" Risa savagely kicked the door frame, which earned her a scathing glower from Naloc.

"Calm down, will you," Aika tried to sooth her. She grabbed the hem of Risa's yukata and tugged. Risa got the hint at last and sat down next to her lover.

Jin shared Risa's frustration. It was as if they were hunting a ghost. Not only had they found neither hide nor hair of him so far, there was not a whisper of the monk or his men. Not a single soul in town seemed to have seen anyone matching either Nobu's or his lackey's description.

"I am telling you, he's not in Kigetsu," Risa continued. "And obviously he is not hiding in Mangetsu. So there is only one place he can hide, and I have been saying so from the start!"

Naloc sighed, rubbing his temples. "And I have been telling you, that I sent men to look for him in Eigetsu – with just as much success as you."

"Yes, because you were only looking in the inhabited parts of Eigetsu. If I had something big planned and needed to go to ground, I'd hole up in Ghost Town. And as this sorry excuse of a monk is obviously a rather clever little bastard, that's where he'll be. As I have said – repeatedly."

"And I have told you – repeatedly – that searching Ghost Town takes a lot of time and is easier said than done," Naloc retorted. "The fact that it is deserted makes it a tad more difficult to go in there with a search party unnoticed."

Jin's head was pounding, he felt they'd had that very discussion a thousand times over the last two days. Risa was right, of course, but Naloc had a point. Ghost Town, the abandoned part of Eigetsu, was a warren of overgrown, dilapidated old mansions and town houses. Some were little more than ruins, others defied time and neglect – to a degree. Whereas nowadays the western parts of Eigetsu were home to the displaced, the poorest of the poor, the unwanted and the forgotten, the former home of Getsuro's elite was deserted. Eigetsu's inhabitants shied away from the light and glory of the empirical seat just across the river and chose to put as much distance between them as possible. It wasn't just the ideal place to disappear in, it gave Nobu all kinds of advantages.

And so the last two days they had spent searching in places no-one seriously believed would yield any clues, knowing where they should be looking instead. Which was why every time they reconvened they had the same useless discussion.

Aika was trying her hardest to calm down Risa, who looked more than ready to punch some faces, while on Risa's other side Aika's father, Kuroto, shook his head, exasperated, and

Naloc opened his mouth to say something, when suddenly the door slammed open. Daisuke, Durin's youngest son, stood sweating and panting in the hallway, his eyes huge and wild, his small hands shaking.

"The Dragon... t-the Singing D-Dragon is burning!"

The tension was stifling. Jin couldn't sit still and wait. He had an urge to flee the house, to run all the way to Yūgao – to see for himself... to help. To do something, anything other but wait. But Naloc had ordered Niall and him to stay put, while the others had followed Daisuke. Jin could tell Niall wasn't happy about it either. She was, after all, a doctor, and where there were casualties they'd need doctors.

Instead here they were, cooped up with their boss, tense and anxious. They hadn't spoken a single word since the moment the others had left. Any second now Jin was going to explode, he was too wound up. He was certain his excessive pacing had already ruined Naloc's tatami mats. Why was this taking so long, what was going on in Yūgao?

Just when he had finally had enough and was ready to burst out the door, Naloc's orders be damned, they heard agitated voices and the sound of feet on the hardwood floor. The door opened, Risa and Kuroto entered, covered in soot and grime, dishevelled, exhausted. They bowed to Naloc, faces sombre.

"Boss... I'm... I'm so sorry," Risa began haltingly – and Jin's breath caught, his heart stumbling painfully. "The Singing Dragon... is no more."

The words fell like a hammer on an anvil, heavy and merciless. Jin's knees buckled. Niall was suddenly beside him, gripping his hand hard enough that it hurt. She was trembling.

"Kazue?" Naloc asked, his voice flat and quiet. Risa dropped her gaze and shook her head. A ragged sob shook Niall's body, her grip tightened. The floor was moving, heaving like the deck of a ship on high seas. There was only one thought going through Jin's mind: *no no no nononnonono.*

"O-only a handful s-survived," Risa continued, struggling visibly to keep her composure. Jin had always thought of her as a hardened warrior, someone who could walk onto a battlefield and still be able to sleep a good night's sleep. But perhaps what cracked even Risa's tough shell was that those had been no warriors, this had been no battlefield. Innocent blood had been spilt for nothing more than a bruised ego. Young vibrant lives – snuffed out like candles. Dreams forever shattered. Laughter forever become silent. Strings of fate cut short.

The Singing Dragon had been more than just another pleasure house, it had been an institution, one of the corner stones of Yūgao, it had been, first and foremost, its inhabitants. Neither could ever be repaired.

"Durin is bringing Suzu here," Kuroto added quietly, and Jin finally drew a breath. Although he felt guilty for feeling relieved when so many had been lost.

While they waited, Risa and Kuroto drank cups of water to soothe their parched and smoke burnt throats. Niall was crying softly against Jin's shoulder. Naloc... Naloc was sitting in unnatural silence, staring at something only he could see. When, at last, there came a knock on the door and Durin entered, leading Suzu by the arm, Naloc took a deep breath and shook himself out of it before getting laboriously to his feet.

Jin took a single step towards Suzu – and stopped. The boy looked like a ghost. His mismatched eyes were empty, bare feet and hands bloody, his yukata dirty and ripped, his expression blank. Jin felt his heart break in two at the sight. Only a couple of minutes ago he had been relieved that Suzu had survived, but seeing him like this Jin wasn't sure he truly had.

"Suzu," Naloc said when the silence stretched too long. His voice carried an uncharacteristic quaver of uncertainty. Slowly, Suzu lifted his head. At first it didn't seem like he even recognised Naloc – until suddenly his blank expression turned into a snarling grimace of pure hatred, his empty eyes filled with burning rage. Before any of them had a chance to react to the sudden change, Suzu sprang at Naloc with a savage growl. His hands closed around the older man's throat as he dragged him to the ground.

"This is all your fault!" Suzu screamed. Naloc's eyes bulged, he tried in vain to prise Suzu's hands off of his throat. "Where were you? Where were your damn people?"

Momentary shock had stalled the others, now they rushed forward, crying for Suzu to stop, to let go, but Suzu ignored them all. Jin stepped over the prone and convulsing body of his boss, grabbed Suzu beneath the arms and yanked, at the same moment as Niall hit a nerve in the young man's wrist. His grip slackened, Jin pulled him away from Naloc.

But Suzu didn't give up yet. He growled and screamed, rage robbing him of words. He kicked and thrashed about, his hands reaching for the object of his fury. Jin had a hard time trying to hold on to him. Suzu was like a feral beast, intent only on reaching its prey.

All of a sudden, however, Suzu went limp in Jin's arms, his hateful cries cut off. Light glinted off the long silver needle stuck in his neck. Panting, Jin turned his head. Niall, wide-eyed and trembling, stared at the unconscious young man in Jin's arms. "Sorry," she said helplessly.

Chapter 28

Waking up felt like he was fighting his way through syrup. The first time he had woken up, Suzu had had murder on his mind – but the object of his rage was gone. Instead, he had been lying on a futon in an unfamiliar room, Niall sitting beside him, a long glinting needle in her hand, poised as if she might stab him with it any second. Hovering by the door had been Jin, looking unsettled, worried. Suzu's cuts had been cleaned and dressed, the stringent smell of ointment still lingering in the air.

Niall had narrowed her eyes at him, but at last put the needle aside and instead picked up a cup which she pressed into his hands, ordering him to drink. Suzu's throat felt parched so he hadn't argued. But it had been neither water nor tea. Before he had been able to ask what the bitter concoction was, however, Niall had put her hand over the bottom of the cup, tipped it back against Suzu's lips, and forced him to drink it all.

Spluttering, he had had just enough time to curse her before his limbs grew heavy and numb and darkness claimed him.

Fighting his way out of a second involuntary slumber now, his mind was full of cobwebs. It took him a little while to put together the pieces and understand what had happened and where he was. He turned his head and found Jin still lurking by the door, although by now he had sat down. His black eyes, looking steadily at Suzu, were filled with sadness.

"So it wasn't all a bad dream," Suzu croaked. His throat was as dry as a desert. Whatever Niall had given him had left a lingering bitter taste and numbness on his tongue.

"I'm so sorry." A whisper, no more. The words alone, however, rang louder than a temple bell, the tightness of his chest felt as if an anvil had been placed on top of him. Suzu stared up at the ceiling, blinking his eyes against the sting of tears, and forced air into his lungs, one deep breath at a time. *Not yet.* Two words, quickly becoming his mantra. He couldn't break down now, he had a promise to keep and there were still Akito and the others, who counted on him. But a single tear would be enough to unravel his resolve; a single tear would start a flood, washing him away, drowning him in a sea of grief. Thus he fought down the tears and drew on the one thing that had always given him strength when all else had failed: his anger. It burst forth with an intensity that even shocked Suzu before he could take a firm hold of its reins. Grief and pain were once again securely locked up behind a wall of flames.

He slowly sat up with a grunt and turned to Jin, intending to ask him for a cup of water, only to find Jin already beside him, holding out a cup. Suzu took it and sniffed it suspiciously.

"It's only water, I promise," Jin said. "But if you want, I can try it first." In reply Suzu downed the whole cup in one go and held it out for more. "Take it slow," Jin admonished, refilling the cup.

"What the hell did Niall give me?"

"Just a simple sedative. She said you needed sleep – without nightmares."

"How very kind of her. Sure she didn't just want to knock me out so I wouldn't go on a rampage?"

"A little, perhaps," Jin admitted sheepishly. "Why did you attack Naloc?"

"You really need to ask? Because none of this would have happened if not for Naloc and his ambitions."

"That's not fair."

"Is it? Then is it fair that my family got mixed up in this mess, that they had to pay with their lives, and all because Naloc wouldn't take no for an answer. How is that fair? I won't ever get them back, do you understand?"

"Of course I do, and I am so, so sorry. But Suzu, how could Naloc have known what would happen? How could any of us have known?"

But Suzu stubbornly shook his head. A part of him knew he was unfair and unreasonable, but he just couldn't help himself. The pain was so raw, the anger so wild – he needed someone to lash out on, he didn't care if it was right or wrong. *And you just don't want to admit that it's all your fault.* No, he could punish himself later, when he had fulfilled the promised he had made to Ryū and the others.

"Suzu, come on, you know it's not his fault," Jin continued, unaware of Suzu's inner struggle. "You said yourself that Nobu saw you at the Earl's. He –"

"Don't you dare!" Suzu cut him off, grabbing the front of Jin's shirt. "Don't you dare pin this on Toshi." Yes, he was undoubtedly biased, but he refused to lay the blame at Toshi's feet. If there was one thing he could still be certain of, it was that Toshi would have never wittingly allowed any harm to come to him or his family.

"What I'm trying to say is, that neither can you blame Naloc for what happened. Nobu is the one who did this. He and his lackeys."

"Oh, trust me, I'm going to make him pay for this." Suzu's voice was low and dangerous enough to seem to have an effect on Jin, for the young man could not hide his shudder. "I'm going to make all of them pay for this, even if I have to tear this world apart to do so."

"Suzu –"

"Do not stand in my way." Suzu's two-coloured jade eyes bored into Jin's. Cold, and hard, and very very determined. After a long moment Suzu pushed Jin away, not even looking at him anymore.

Silence followed. Stretching from seconds to minutes, growing heavier each passing moment. It became uncomfortable. Stifling. Until, at last, Jin didn't seem able to stand it any longer. At the door, however, he turned. Suzu ignored him, looking straight ahead. His face was a mask hiding the storm of emotions brewing inside him. None of the grief, the pain showed. None of the rage. A perfectly emotionless, yet dignified countenance – the face of an indifferent god.

"Naloc mourns, too, you know," Jin said quietly. "He and Kazue... she was his wife, after all." A fraction of a flinch, the tiniest reaction. Suzu would not give Jin the satisfaction of

"Hotaru was three years younger than me and the sweetest, prettiest little thing. I was so proud to be her big sister. I wanted to be with her every moment of the day. She was perfect, and precious, and everybody loved her. But she couldn't hear or speak. Don't get me wrong, no-one in their right mind would have considered that a flaw. And Hotaru just had to smile at you to completely wrap you around her little finger," Niall chuckled. For a short moment she was lost in happy memories, than her mirth died. "But... I was about eleven, Hotaru just nine... there was an accident. I don't remember what exactly happened, but a pair of horses pulling a cart panicked – and ran. In their panic they barrelled down the road, blind to everything and everyone in their way. The driver had been thrown off, there was nothing to stop them. People were screaming and running, making way as fast as they could. We..." Niall paused, blinking against the tears in her eyes. "We heard the commotion before we could see the carriage. Everyone was yelling to get off the road – but Hotaru couldn't hear them. She was playing with a puppy in front of the neighbour's, three houses up the road. Naloc started running towards her, but almost at the same time, the puppy got scared and ran, and Hotaru ran after it. She... she ran... and when she noticed the horses, it was... it was already too late, they..." Niall's voice broke. It took her a moment before she said, "I had nightmares for years. Even now I... I don't think I'll ever forget the terror in Kazue's scream, the despair." Her voice trailed off, she rubbed at her eyes, taking slow, deep breaths.

Suzu felt something wet on his cheek, and, brushing it away, was astonished to find that he was shedding tears – for Kazue and her little girl. For Niall. Perhaps even for Naloc. But the sympathy was quickly drowned in the vastness of Suzu's anger. Already having lost the most precious thing in the world, Naloc should have known better. He should not have put Kazue at such risk.

Niall seemed to have read some of it on Suzu's face, for she vehemently shook her head. "No, he would have never put Kazue in any real danger. Not knowingly. Yes, he bought information from her, but honestly, Suzu, you are not the naïve type, you must know that every pleasure house is as much entertainment as it is a treasure trove of information sold for the right price. If Naloc had... if he had known... I mean... he would have never pushed –"

And then Suzu broke out laughing. Because suddenly he was hit with a revelation. Of course, why had he not seen it earlier. Niall was staring at him as if he had lost his mind – who knew, perhaps he had – and raised an eyebrow. "Of course," Suzu laughed. "Of course, my bad. Naloc would have never put *Kazue* in danger – the only one who was in danger, or so he thought, was I." Niall's eyes went wide, her mouth opened in protest, but Suzu, the laughter in his voice replaced with venom, spoke right over her. "Because who gives a damn about some little Furyusha, right? We're easy to replace, isn't that so?"

"No! That's not –"

"Oh, he must be so disappointed then that I didn't even have the decency to die with the others."

"That's not true. Suzu, he –"

"Do you think I care what he wanted?" Suzu barked, harsh enough to make Niall flinch. "Do you expect me to forgive him because he never intended to hurt Mother? I won't. Nor do I have any sympathy for him. He lost his daughter and now his wife? I don't care. I lost my entire family. They are dead. Those that are left? They are badly wounded, broken, traumatised. And it is all his fault."

Niall opened and closed her mouth a few times more, but whatever she tried to say, it wouldn't come out. Perhaps she realised the futility of her words. In the end, she got up and left.

It was possible that he should have been nicer to Niall. It was also possible that he was indeed unfair to Naloc. Not just possible, he knew he was, and yet...

He should have asked Niall to send Jin back in – but she probably wouldn't have done it, afraid Suzu would end up doing irreparable damage to her friend. But being alone in an unfamiliar room, suppressing his grief and pain, was slowly driving him mad. After a while he would have even welcomed a visit from Naloc. Fed up, he carefully stood up. The cuts on his bandaged feet stung for a moment, but it wasn't so bad he couldn't stand and walk. Only now did he notice he was wearing fresh clothes – probably also Niall's doing.

Wondering if they had locked him in or posted a guard outside the room, Suzu tried the door. It slid open without resistance, the hallway was empty. He could take the chance and leave and... And then what? He had no place to go, no way of finding Nobu, he didn't even have a weapon. Suzu remembered the tantō Haldor had given him – Niall, or Naloc, or anyone else had probably taken it so he wouldn't start a murder spree, cutting down everyone in his way. Admittedly, the idea had its appeal, but he wasn't Nobu, he didn't just indiscriminately kill people on a whim. But he had meant to kill Naloc – or at least hurt the man. What idiocy, to try and strangle the man when he had had a perfectly fine weapon on him. It spoke volumes of his mental state at the time.

Yesterday – only one day ago. One day ago he had had a family, a home. One day ago he had lost everything. Which one was dream and which reality?

By now Suzu had already done what he did best: he had built walls. Around the pain, the darkness. Even around the rage, to keep it contained for the right moment. Thick walls. Thick, but brittle. A fresh wave of grief washed over him, stole his breath, brought tears to his eyes, thorns, long and wicked, burrowing deep into his heart. He stomped it down ruthlessly. Build the walls higher, thicker. Fortified them with a single purpose: revenge. A single promise: soon. It left him feeling numb, yet his mind was crystal clear.

For a while he wandered the empty hallways, wondering where everyone was. Until, at last, he could hear voices, a dull clang he only knew too well – wooden practice swords – followed by the occasional hoots and laughter. Curious, he followed the sound to the front courtyard.

About ten men and women sat in the shade of two big maple trees. Jin and the tall, mean looking woman, Risa, were circling each other in the middle of the courtyard, each armed with a wooden sword. It took a single glance for Suzu to see that Jin stood no chance against Risa. She held her sword low, almost mockingly nonchalant, but there was not a single opening, she knew what she was doing. Jin, on the other hand, looked like he was holding a sword for the first time.

"Come on, Jin, we've practised this a thousand times," the woman discounted that impression. "You have to get better eventually!"

"I'm telling you, it's no use. Sorry to disappoint you, Risa."

"Nonsense!" she snapped. "It is basically impossible not to improve at least a little with practise. Everyone does. So you won't become the greatest swordsman of our generation?

Boohoo. But you should at least be able to defend yourself, don't you think?"

"Or he could just turn tail and run like the wind," one of the men called and guffawed. His friends snickered, and Jin – well, Jin shrugged as if he was saying they had a point.

"Oi! You! Enzo! Shut your stupid fly trap or I'll stuff it for you," Risa barked, pointing her sword at the man, who fell quiet at once with a chagrined look on his face.

Suzu slipped his feet into the next best sandals, lying scattered in the entrance hall – Mother would have had hysterics if she had seen this – and made his way to Risa and Jin. "You need to relax, you are too stiff," Suzu told Jin. "And your stance is all wrong. What are you trying to do anyway? Skewer your opponent? Because I can tell you it won't end well for you." Blushing furiously, Jin let his sword sink. Risa raised an eyebrow at him, tapping her sword against her shoulder.

"Sorry, beautiful, but we're not doing any fancy swordplay here, we're doing real fighting." Enzo again. Seemed like he was the sort who just always had to open his big mouth.

"Oh, I see," Suzu replied. "So in a real fight, it's all right to just use your sword as a club and bludgeon your enemy with it?" A few snickers followed, but Suzu's sarcasm seemed lost on Enzo.

"I guess you've never seen a real fight. Why would you. Nah, reckon all you've ever seen of a fight is a nice little sparring between some of your lordlings. Might be pretty to look at, but, no offence, that's not real fighting. Better stick to pretty clothes and hair ornaments."

Next to Suzu Jin winced and shook his head. It seemed he had a pretty good idea what was going to happen now for he wordlessly held out his wooden sword. Suzu took it, quickly smothering the smirk tugging at the corners of his lips, and said nonchalantly, "How about we test that theory of yours?" Like Jin, the others must have picked up on something, some of them sat up straighter all of a sudden, Risa's raised eyebrow rose even higher, and Jin sighed, resigned. Enzo, however, was oblivious to all of that.

"Oh, no. No. That wouldn't be a fair fight now, would it? I might end up hurting you, and –"

"Enzo, shut up," Risa cut him off, not even looking at the man. Her eyes were on Suzu, shining with excitement, hunger. "Do it." She held her own sword out for him to take. Enzo slowly got to his feet.

"Boss, you can't be serious."

"Do it."

"But, Boss –" Risa finally turned to look at Enzo. It was enough to silence the man. Uncertain, he took the sword. "Sh- shall I go eas--"

"Don't you dare go easy on him, Enzo," Risa warned. "If you do, I'll know it, and you will regret it." Enzo swallowed hard. The courtyard was suddenly very quiet. Suzu nodded at Risa, who grinned back at him. He was pretty certain that she had never seen him fight, but perhaps she knew that Haldor had trained all of them. Perhaps it was Risa's instinct as a swordswoman that recognised Suzu as a fighter.

Scowling at the pity in Enzo's eyes, Suzu took his position. "I'll make it quick," Enzo whispered as if he was showing Suzu mercy. On Risa's cry of "Fight!", the man rushed Suzu.

It was over quickly, just as Enzo had promised. Suzu laid him flat on his back in the time it took him to take a deep breath, though if he was being honest, Suzu had used a really dirty trick on the poor man and taken him by surprise.

A collective gasp went through the crowd. Enzo, lying wheezing on the ground, stared wide-eyed at the tip of Suzu's sword. A single silent moment later Risa burst out laughing. Loud, full-bodied laughter that nearly doubled her over. It was infectuous. Within seconds the courtyard rang with laughter. Even Enzo, slowly getting to his feet again, joined in, albeit it with a hint of sheepishness. Suzu was the only one who didn't laugh, for he wasn't sure what was happening.

"That," Risa gasped, slapping Enzo on the back, "was the best thing ever. Hope it teaches you not to underestimate a pretty face."

"You know that he never learns," came the reply from amongst the others, followed by a fresh wave of laughter.

Eventually, the laughter puttered out, and Risa caught her breath. She bent to pick up the wooden sword Enzo had dropped. When she looked up, her dark brown eyes glittered with excitement. "All right. You're up for a real fight?" she challenged – it was what Suzu had been hoping for. He was brimming with unspent energy, the need for action. With a wicked grin on his face, he adjusted his stance. It was all the answer Risa needed.

She came at him unceremoniously. A lesser swordsman might have been taken by surprise, but Suzu had been trained by Haldor. Sneak attacks had been the man's favourite pastime. Suzu's parry elicited a gasp from their audience, and delighted laughter from his opponent as she jumped back to avoid his retaliation. They drove each other across the courtyard. Relentless. Merciless. A perfectly choreographed dance, beautiful in its intensity; breathtaking in its intransigence. Until – a final parry, a final break, a final spin – wooden blade resting against slender neck, just a breath away from touching skin. And it was over. Silence, stillness, broken only by the harsh breathing of the fighters and the distant cry of a peacock.

"Damn," Risa exhaled. Her gaze travelled from her sword against Suzu's neck to the one resting against her own. "Do you have any idea when someone last beat me?"

"No," Suzu panted. "It's not today, though."

"Neither did I win."

"No, you didn't."

As they slowly let their swords drop, matching grins brightening their faces, their audience woke from their bafflement. A babel of excited voices filled the air. Enzo, rejoining them, clasped Suzu's shoulder, laughing, full of praise for Suzu's skills. Suzu marvelled at the easy and affable nature of the man, when only moments ago he had taken him for a bully and a prick.

Suddenly, Suzu felt a presence on his blind side. Although a rational part of his brain told him it was unlikely anyone would attack him here and now, he couldn't help but tense, nor his quick sidestep. Shifting into a position that allowed him to react to any possible attack as well as see what was coming at him, Suzu glowered at whoever dared approach him thus.

Jin held up his hands placatingly, mouthing an apology. Suzu forced himself to relax.

"That was amazing!" Risa crowed, still caught up in the euphoria of the fight. Not taking his eyes off of Jin, Suzu couldn't help but smile. The woman's enthusiasm was as infectious as her laughter.

And then Jin smiled back. Dazzling, brighter than the sun, illuminating. That smile, Suzu had really tried to forget it, but it was hard to do so. Jin didn't just smile with his lips and his eyes, he smiled with his soul. It was a force of its own, it had power.

"Oi, oi, oi! What the hell is this?" They turned to find Niall standing on the porch, hands on her hips, a thunderous expression on her face. Naloc stood next to her, looking into the distance and pretending not to notice anything. "Who said you were allowed to get up and move around? Never mind playing with swords!"

"Playing with –" Risa exclaimed at the same time Suzu retorted, "no-one said I wasn't!"

"Oh? You might have noticed those bandages on your feet? It's common sense not to run around with bandaged feet!" Niall's voice had taken on a very distinct, irate screech, which caused everyone else to look anywhere but at her or Suzu. Even Jin found his sandals fascinating all of a sudden.

"Please, it's just a few scratches, it doesn't even hurt," Suzu dismissed. He was taken aback by the collective wince that followed his words, but he stood his ground, even when Niall's expression turned positively murderous.

"You!" she hissed. "Are you a doctor? No? Didn't think so. You get back to your room at once! I'll be the judge if those are just a few scratches, not you!"

Suzu opened his mouth to protest, but Jin quickly shook his head. "You better do as she says," he whispered. Risa and Enzo nodded emphatically in agreement. Sighing, Suzu threw up his hands in surrender and went quietly. Niall followed to make sure he went back to his room. He could feel her glaring at his back the entire way.

With nothing else interesting happening, and Risa calling it a day on their training session, her gang quickly scattered, leaving her alone with Jin and Naloc.

"And?" Naloc asked. He didn't need to elaborate for Jin to know what he was asking, neither did Risa. "Haldor had every reason to be proud of that boy," she said.

"He's that good?"

"As good as Risa," Jin supplied, but Risa shook her head.

"Better, I think," she corrected, much to both Jin's and Naloc's surprise. She gave the wooden sword in her hand a little twirl. "It was a standoff, but it wasn't easy. He made me fight seriously and he's not even in top form. Or else, I'm not too proud to admit I'm not sure he wouldn't have beaten me."

Jin lacked the knowledge to judge a fight. To him they had seemed evenly matched, but Risa wasn't one for idle praise.

Naloc nodded his head slowly. "I see. But don't tell him, I don't want the boy getting ideas."

"You think he wants to take revenge?" Jin blurted. It was what he was afraid of. No good could come from taking revenge.

"Of course he does," Naloc confirmed Jin's worries. "And he's got quite the temper... anyway, I have confiscated his *tantō*. Make sure he doesn't get his hands on any other weapons."

"What are we supposed to do? Lock him up? I don't think he'll just stay put if we ask nicely... And he hates you."

"I'm aware. And yes, if it comes to it, I will lock him up myself. It doesn't matter if he hates me, Kazue loved that boy, and I'll be damned if I let anything happen to him." Naloc had hardly finished the sentence before he whirled around and strode back inside, leaving Jin and Risa to stare after him. It spoke for itself, Naloc getting snappish with them. Despite appearances, Suzu wasn't the only one grieving.

One last look around, one more reassurance he was alone – then Suzu sprinted for the gate. Within seconds he was out in the street, the gate falling shut behind him. It would have been stupid to linger, even to get his bearings, so for the moment, Suzu simply turned left, headed down the street, then ducked into a small alley. He couldn't remember how he had gotten to Naloc's house the other day, and he had never been in this particular area of Kigetsu. The easiest way to get back to Yūgao would be to follow the river upstream. But which way was the river?

In the end Suzu decided to simply let his feet carry him whichever way his gut was telling him looked promising. Hopefully he had something like a homing instinct.

Not long and he was rewarded with the sight of the River Opal and its myriad of bridges. It seemed that perhaps the ghosts of his lost home were guiding him back to it.

Jin was nursing a cup of saké, his mind filled with thoughts of Suzu. Was he asleep? Awake? Sitting there in the dark, all alone with his pain and grief? Jin felt he should be with him. Or was it perhaps better that he wasn't? He didn't know anymore. There was too much hurt between them, too much misunderstanding, too many things that had gone too wrong. These past days Jin had worked hard to accept that Suzu was not Kari, and that he, Jin, had no place in the young man's life. And then tragedy had struck.

Who could have ever expected anything like this to happen, here, right in the heart of Getsuro. In broad daylight.

Jin could not reconcile the Nobu he had known growing up, who had been like an older brother to him, always listening patiently, giving advice, with the Nobu of Suzu's accounts. The Nobu who'd have a dozen innocent people slaughtered just because he felt slighted. But the Singing Dragon was gone, only a handful of its inhabitants had survived. And Suzu – Suzu was alone, had lost everything. How could Jin leave him alone now? Even if Suzu threw things at him, yelled at him, cussed him, hit him – Jin would not leave. He could not.

"You're aware your cup's been empty for at least ten minutes." Jin looked up at Risa, regarding him with a raised eyebrow. Frowning, he lowered the cup from his lips and put it down. It was indeed empty. "If you're that worried about him, why don't you just go to him?"

"It's not that simple."

"Of course it is. You get up, go down the hall, knock, and enter the room. See? Simple."

"You know what I mean."

"No, I really don't. You –" Risa stopped mid-sentence when the door burst open and a small scruffy boy dashed inside and straight for Durin. Jin got a very bad sense of deja-vu. The small boy, though slightly taller and older than the last one, was unmistakably his brother. He whispered urgently into Durin's ear. Jin saw the man tense.

"Someone go and check the guest room," Durin commanded. He didn't usually order people around, so they all knew this was serious. Without hesitation Kuroto sprang to his feet and went. Jin's stomach clenched.

"Why? What's wrong?" he asked. But before he got an answer Kuroto returned with the guard Naloc had stationed outside the guest room.

"He's gone," Kuroto announced. Panic washed over Jin in a wave of dizziness. Suzu was out there all on his own and for all that they knew, Nobu was looking for him.

"What is going on?" Naloc stood in the open door to the garden, frowning. Niall, who had arrived with him, took one look at Jin and it was enough to make her ask more urgently, "What happened?"

"Boss." Durin stood up, the small boy clinging to his arm. "My boys have been keeping an eye on the area around... the Singing Dragon. It seems that a bunch of unsavoury looking people are lurking about. And apparently Suzu is heading straight there."

"I see. And you think they might be lying in wait for the boy?"

"It's a fair assumption."

Naloc nodded, tiredly rubbing his face. Jin's heart was racing. He was close to just bursting through the door and running after Suzu, but he had been told repeatedly in the last few days not to lose his head and rush into potentially dangerous situations. So instead, he stood up, tried hard to appear collected, and pressed in an admittedly strangled voice, "Boss." It sounded like pleading, he didn't care.

Naloc's gaze flicked to him before landing on Risa. "Gather your people, go after the boy and bring him back. Do not engage in any fights unless absolutely necessary."

"Yes, boss," she replied, jumping to her feet, sword in hand. She headed for the door without hesitation. "Well, you've heard him. Let's move!"

Within seconds the room cleared, Risa's usually boisterous crew suddenly serious and focused. Jin wanted to follow them, no, he needed to. He knew he was no good in a sword-fight if it came to that, but he couldn't stay behind – again. He'd go mad.

Niall, as always, knew exactly what he was thinking. She grabbed his arm and pulled him along. With a quick look over her shoulder she called, "We go, too", before hurrying to catch up with Risa and the others, not waiting for Naloc to give his permission.

Risa spared them only a sidelong glance. "You stay behind us. If things get ugly, you hide, or you run. Do not do anything stupid or I will kill you myself. You do exactly as you are told when you are told, you do not question me." And neither of them had any doubt Risa would follow through on her threats, not that they were stupid enough not to obey her command in the first place. So all they said was a curt "Yes, sir" as they ran down the dark streets.

It really was gone, it hadn't been a nightmare. The once proud Singing Dragon, one of the oldest and most renowned establishments of Yūgao, was gone. All that remained of its former splendour was the gate – blackened and crumbling. The rest lay in ruins, burnt to the very ground, every single building, from the main house to the bathhouse, the dojo, the storage house. Burnt, crumbling wood and ashes. The once lush trees now black, twisted corpses, grotesque silhouettes in the meagre light that spilled over from the other estates, miraculously unharmed. A ghostly stillness lay over the place, interrupted only by the occasional creak and crack of the still settling ruins.

Suzu was glad it was dark, for he doubted he could have stood the sight of what was left of his home in the light of day.

Even without seeing it, the absence of what should have been here was devastating. And it wasn't just this place, Yūgao had felt different – wrong. There had been hardly any people out in the streets, which should have been alight with hundreds of lanterns and bustling. Yūgao should have been singing, a song it had been singing for as long as it existed, a harmony of voices, laughter, and music. Instead it was draped in a hush – oppressive, stifling. The lanterns remained unlit, the shutters closed. Yūgao was in shock, it was deeply wounded. It was in mourning.

Trembling, Suzu stepped through the charred remains of the once splendid gate and slowly made his way across the burnt lawn, past the rubble and the ashes of the two main houses to what had been the garden. There he stood and waited. For what, he could not say. His heart was hammering against his ribcage, his breath too shallow. He closed his eyes against the sting of tears, reminding himself once more: *Not yet! You cannot break yet.*

If he wished for it strongly enough, if he willed it with all his heart and soul and being – could he open his eyes and vanquish the dark? Dispel the nightmare? Could he find himself once more surrounded by those precious to him? Laughing and full of life? Slowly, he opened his eyes with bated breath. Ruin and death, swathed in darkness. Wishing had never worked for him.

He was about to turn and leave when a sound made him stop. A shuffling, rustling sound. He wasn't alone. Suzu scanned the darkness. Although he couldn't see them, he was suddenly acutely aware of multiple presences. He had been careless. The sounds came again, and now he knew what they were: the soft rustle of clothes, slow deliberate steps. They were closing in on him.

Suzu was keenly aware that he had no weapon and was grossly outnumbered. Shadowy figures moved into his line of sight. He counted four – four that he could see, who knew how many there were on his blind side, he couldn't move his head and risk giving away his weakness. But he didn't need to see them to know he was surrounded. They had to have been waiting for him, hiding in the dark, motionless. Suzu tensed, balled his hands into fists and waited. Should he try to make a run for it? He had the feeling he wouldn't get far. Waiting for them to strike first wasn't exactly the better option, but he wouldn't go down without a fight either. And he wasn't as helpless as they might assume, even without a weapon. He knew how to defend himself, how to cause real hurt, even permanent damage. Haldor had not been teaching him any civilised, respected forms of close combat – he had taught Suzu how to fight dirty.

But they kept their distance.

A light appeared from the far side of the grounds, from beyond the ashen remains of the dojo. It seemed to move through the high wall that hadn't only been the border of the estate but was also the border between Yūgao and Eigetsu. As it approached, Suzu saw who held the lantern aloft: Nobu.

A vertiginous surge of purest hate rushed through Suzu's veins at the sight of the man. It was so strong, it made him dizzy.

"I knew you'd come back here," Nobu said as nonchalantly as if they were meeting for tea. And perhaps it was Nobu's airiness, but Suzu's anger changed its form. Had it been a roaring wildfire before, untamed, burning blindingly bright, its bite now became colder than ice. With it came a sharp edged clarity and focused purpose. Reckless impulsivity became calculation.

"And what? You've been sitting here in the dark waiting for me like a lovesick fool? I know I should feel flattered, but..."

Nobu stepped forward into the circle of his men, an indulgent smile on his lips. "I told you, you'd regret rejecting my offer," he said, ignoring Suzu's mockery.

"Regret?" Suzu spat. "They had nothing to do with whatever this is between you and me."

"Wrong! They had everything to do with it. Don't you see? If you had never crossed paths with them, if they hadn't loved you, they'd still be happily alive."

"Fuck you, Nobu!"

"Tsk. Language, please."

"Yeah, I'll give you language, you lousy excuse of a monk. I know what you're trying to do – it won't work. Their blood is on your hands! And for what? Because you can't bear someone telling you no."

Nobu came to stand in front of him, so close Suzu could feel the monk's body heat, smell the lingering scent of sandalwood on his clothes and his skin. "You don't seem to understand that you are in no position to refuse me. So, last chance: You can join me, or I promise you'll wish I'd just kill you."

Suzu rolled his eyes and sighed. Those threats were getting old – not that he didn't believe Nobu would see them through. "All of this? Why?"

"I'm just taking what should have been mine from the start," Nobu replied matter-of-factly. "My father was a nobleman. My mother, unfortunately, was his servant. Did you know, unlike you Furyusha servants have neither protection nor support, no law that would have forced my father to acknowledge me. That's just wrong, don't you think? But my father would have acknowledged me eventually, if it hadn't been for *her* – that Ethereal witch!" Nobu spat. *Ah*, Suzu thought, *that explains a few things*. "She wasn't of noble birth either, but she used her unnatural charm on my father and made him marry her. And when my mother died, he sent me off to the temple. That wily creature robbed me of my birthright!"

"So," Suzu drawled, "what you're saying is, you're throwing a tantrum like a little child because you didn't get what was never yours in the first place?" Anger flashed across Nobu's face. "You do know that you have no claim to the Moonlight Throne, even if your father had acknowledged you, don't you?"

"Debatable." Nobu sniffed. "You don't seriously believe in a sign from the Goddess, or that anyone can be the next chosen emperor or empress – all that nonsense. It's all about politics. It's a game, you pull the right strings, move the right pieces – and the price will be yours."

"And do your co-conspirators know that you intend to put yourself on the throne?"

"Of course not, I operate on a strictly need to know basis. But I have better things to do than play with you, so… What's it going to be?"

"Hmm, how shall I put this? You are positively begging me to join your gang, and no offence, but I absolutely despise you, and all I want is to kill you – very slowly."

Nobu inhaled sharply, his nostrils flaring. A nasty, malicious smile contorted the man's face. "Yes, I know, but I had thought you were smarter. Making decisions based on emotions – really?" He clicked his tongue, then leaned closer to Suzu and said softly into her ear, "But just in case, I've already made arrangements. Something very special, just for you. One of my… sponsors… has a very particular – shall we say… appetite. One that saw him banned for life from Yūgao – and the rest of Getsuro." Nobu chuckled. "He's looking forward to finally meeting the famous Yūzuki no Suzu. I promise you, he'll take good care of you. Unfortunately, though, he has the bad habit of breaking his toys, so I guess, we'll see how long you last."

Suzu felt sick. People like that were the nightmare of Yūgao's Furyusha, the terror of every prostitute and unfortunate all over the empire. When caught, they faced the harshest forms of punishment, ranging from exile, over forced castration, to execution. But more often than not, they were rich, powerful people, who knew how to keep their atrocities hidden. Not even Yūgao could always protect its people – as the ashes Suzu was standing on proved.

He took a step back from Nobu, and stomped down on his rising panic. There was a satisfied smirk on Nobu's face that Suzu decided needed to be wiped off.

He struck, without warning and fast as lightning, putting his entire weight behind it. The punch sent Nobu sprawling on the charred grass, the lantern falling from his hand, the light sputtering and flickering, but it didn't go out. Suzu was about to pounce on the prone monk, when Nobu's men rushed towards him. He swerved sideways, aimed a kick at one man's leg. A satisfying crunch preceded the yowl of pain as his foot collided hard with the man's knee.

Suzu whirled around, fists flying, and hit another square in the face, before a fist, coming at his blind side, sent him staggering. It was a close thing, but he managed to stay on his feet. He couldn't evade the hands that grasped him, however. Vice like, bruising, one on each arm, cutting his rampage short – too short. He could feel another presence behind him a moment before his head was yanked back by the hair. Nobu had gotten back to his feet with the help of the scarred man, who was now holding Nobu's lantern up high, so Suzu could see his face in the light.

"Still a real spitfire, aren't you?" the man said with some amusement.

"Sorry, am I supposed to know you?" Suzu asked with venom in his voice, glaring. The other man was taller and broader than Nobu. The badly healed scar disfigured half of his face, his nose was crooked as if it had been broken and not set right. In the gloomy light of the lantern his lank hair seemed oddly colourless, but Suzu remembered it was a dirty ashen blond.

"What? You recognised Nobu at once but you don't remember me? I'm offended," the man mocked. Suzu scowled. There was no way he'd forget a mug that ugly. The man did look familiar, had so from the start, and it irked Suzu that he couldn't – wait! He squinted at the man again, the colourless hair, the burly statue – and then it dawned on him.

"Ugh," Suzu sighed. "Of course. Steren."

"Aww, see, I knew you'd remember me."

"What happened? I mean, sure the scar is an improvement to that ugly mug of a face, but…"

"Oh this? Courtesy of that little rat Miki."

"Really? Good for him!" Suzu exclaimed, genuinely delighted.

"Yeah, attacked me with a red hot piece of iron, can you believe it? Just before he and those cowardly uncles of his fled the village."

"Hmm, I see. Pity he didn't manage to take your eye out."

"You little –" Steren lurched forward but, unexpectedly, Nobu held him back.

"Enough!" he snapped. "I've had enough of this nonsense. Just put him to sleep and let's go. I have no time for this."

Steren grunted and nodded at the remaining man, standing in the shadows behind him, who stepped forward at once. Suzu felt a flutter of panic in his chest. If they took him out now, he was done for. There'd be no revenge, wasting away as the toy of some sick pervert.

He struggled against the hold on him, but the men were too strong. A rough, calloused hand grabbed his chin, a small flask held to his lips, and so Suzu did the only thing he could think of: he rammed his knee into the man's groin with a force fuelled by panic and desperation. With a pained grunt, the man toppled over, folding in on himself.

"Oh for fuck's sake!" Steren growled, passed the lantern to Nobu, ripped the flask from the other man's hand and kicked him out of his way. Standing at Suzu's side so Suzu could not repeat his attack, Steren's big hand closed around Suzu's jaw, fingers digging painfully into the joints. Suzu clenched his teeth, but the pain soon became unbearable. Steren immediately took the opportunity to push the flask between Suzu's teeth, tipping the contents into Suzu's mouth. Reflexively Suzu pressed his tongue against the roof of his mouth, knowing he must not swallow whatever it was Steren had given him. He must not. Even when Steren threw the flask aside and pressed Suzu's mouth shut did he refuse to swallow.

"Damn it! Swallow!"

"Just pinch his nose shut!" Nobu snapped impatiently, and Suzu's panic grew. Steren lifted his hand –

"All right, boys, enough playing around for one night!" a familiar voice called out of the darkness. Startled, Steren let go of Suzu, reaching for the sword on his belt. Suzu spat the vile concoction into the grass.

"Who the hell are you?" Steren demanded.

"Ah, that doesn't matter," Risa replied as she sauntered towards them, a hand casually resting on the hilt of her sword.

The painful pull on his hair finally ceased. There came the metallic rasp of a sword leaving its sheath. Numbness spread through Suzu, beginning with his tongue. Had he accidentally swallowed some of the drug?

"How about we take him back now, and you boys run home to mummy?"

"Yeah, I really don't think so," Steren sneered.

"Of course you don't." With a sigh Risa drew her sword.

They shuttered their lamps at the mouth of the alley to not announce their presence and, sticking close to the walls of the estates, crept through the darkness towards the end of the alley where the once proud Singing Dragon had been. Its stone walls still stood, blackened and grim. The beautiful gate, however, was nothing but burnt crumbling wood. At a sign from Risa they all stopped, only Durin, quick-footed and silent like a shadow, continued through the ruined gate.

As they waited, Jin became aware of his pulse pounding loudly in his ears. Taking deep breaths, he tried to calm down, but he was a bundle of nerves, worry and excitement warring inside him. It were probably no more than a few minutes until Durin returned, but they felt like hours.

Durin squeezed between Risa and Jin and said in his quiet voice that didn't carry, "Good news first: we have more men. There are seven of them. One is on the ground, clutching his leg and whimpering. Three are keeping a tight hold of our boy."

"Wait! Three?" Jin blurted in surprise, then clamped a hand over his mouth, afraid he'd been too loud.

"Well, seems like they have their hands full with him, one of them has a bleeding nose." A feeling of pride swelled in Jin's chest. Of course Suzu wouldn't go down without a fight, but who would have thought he'd put up such resistance. Jin certainly would have never expected anything like this from the boy he had grown up with – but then, Suzu had told him he wasn't that boy, hadn't he? "Nevertheless, we should hurry now," Durin admonished, so Risa waved them all closer to give her orders.

"All right, listen up. I will go alone first. The rest of you – spread out. Make sure to stay low and quiet, close off any escape routes. And be ready! You two," Risa turned to Jin and Niall. "You stay back – and don't try anything stupid! As soon as possible you grab Suzu and get the hell out of here. You hear me?"

"Yes, sir," they whispered in unison. Satisfied, Risa nodded, stood up, and nonchalantly strode through the gate. The rest followed, quietly, clinging to the darker patches of night, and dispersed to get into position. Jin and Niall followed more slowly, careful not to trip over any obstacles. A single point of light told them where Suzu and their opponents were. Apart from that there were only shadows.

Niall stopped Jin with a hand on his arm from creeping any closer. But they were close enough to make out Suzu, being held by two men one each side of him, a third pulling his head back by the hair. Jin's worry was replaced by anger at the sight. He gritted his teeth, took a deep breath, and forced himself to watch as yet another of Nobu's henchman came forward and pressed something to Suzu's lips. Suzu sent the man to his knees with a vicious kick between the legs. Next to Jin, Niall snorted quietly, and Jin swatted her shoulder in rebuke, although a grin tugged at the corners of his mouth.

"Oh for fuck's sake!" the man with the lantern snapped. He passed the lantern to the slighter figure beside him. Nobu – Jin recognised the monk's face when the light spilled over his features. The taller one kicked the man on the ground aside and reached for Suzu. They couldn't see what he was doing, but they could hear him growl, irritated, and Nobu snarling impatiently to just pinch Suzu's nose shut.

Risa chose that precise moment to saunter into view, one hand casually resting on the hilt of her sword. "All right, boys, enough playing around for the night," she called cheerfully. The tall man whipped around, his hand going for this sword.

"Who the hell are you?"

"Ah, that doesn't matter." Risa slowly moved forward. The metallic rasp of a sword leaving its sheath rang through the air. A moment later the man who had been pulling Suzu's head back took a step towards Risa. The naked blade of his sword caught what little light there was. "How about," Risa continued as if she hadn't noticed, "we take him back now, and you boys run home to mummy?"

"Yeah, I don't think so," the big man sneered.

Risa sighed. "Of course not." She drew her sword.

Both men advanced on Risa, yet the sudden rustle of clothes and the sound of steps on the charred earth made them stop. Shadows emerged from the deeper darkness. One by one light blinked into being as the shutters of the lanterns were opened.

Nobu spun around, realising quickly that he and his men were outnumbered. The light of his own lantern, though swinging wildly, gave glimpses of his anger-distorted face. Was there, perhaps, even a shred of fear?

Time seemed to have stopped. The scene stood frozen, as if they were waiting for some kind of signal. Yet when it came, it wasn't what Jin – or any of them – had expected.

All of a sudden the big man grabbed Suzu and pulled him along as he started running towards the back of the estate. Nobu followed closely, his lantern swinging so much, burning oil spilt in his wake. It was so unexpected they easily pushed their way through Risa's men. And right when Risa started to follow in pursuit, the rest of Nobu's men attacked. It didn't matter. They were met by the ready swords of Risa's crew. The sound of metal meeting metal rang loudly through the night.

Jin, who was in a better position to quickly follow Suzu and his captors, sprang to his feet, Risa's orders forgotten, and sprinted after them. He ignored Niall calling him back and just ran. He couldn't help but wonder why Suzu wasn't putting up more of a fight, the way he had before, instead of letting himself be dragged off like this. But when he caught up to them, Suzu was indeed digging his feet in, throwing wild, uncoordinated punches, struggling against being pulled through what seemed like a hole in the wall.

"Suzu!" Jin yelled and put on a last burst of speed, threw his arms around Suzu, locking them around Suzu's chest, and heaved the slighter man backwards. With the sound of ripping fabric, Jin pulled him from the grasp of Nobu's lackey.

"Damn it, leave him!" Nobu hissed from the other side of the broken wall – and then Jin and Suzu were suddenly alone. Jin sighed and stumbled backwards as Suzu slumped against him.

"Are you all right?" he asked.

"Fine," Suzu drawled, his voice slurred as if he had just woken from slumber. "Just a bit... numb... or dizzy... not sure."

Jin frowned, worried. He had to find Niall. "Can you walk?" Suzu nodded and took an unconvincing, stumbling step forward – in the wrong direction. Jin put one of Suzu's arms across his shoulders, and his own around the younger man's waist, and steered them both in the direction of the others. Only now did he realise the sounds of fighting had stopped, instead there was only the murmur of voices. Picking their way through the dark, across rubble and burnt earth was slow-going, but at last they reached a ring of lanterns in which Risa and Niall stood. Neither looked happy.

"You!" Risa spat, angrily pointing a finger at Jin the moment she noticed their approach. "What did I say before?"

"I'm sorry, but –"

Risa waved him off. "Whatever. You two all right?"

"Splendid," Suzu slurred, earning himself dubious looks from the two women. Niall picked up one of the lanterns and held it up to peer into Suzu's face. "Suzu, did you hit your head? That's going to be a nasty bruise right there." She carefully prodded at Suzu's cheekbone to make sure it wasn't broken. "Does this hurt a lot?"

"Nope," Suzu replied cheerfully, and Niall raised her eyebrows.

"All right, so if you didn't hit your head... they tried to make you swallow something, didn't they?"

"Nasty stuff... tongue's all numb." Suzu stuck his tongue out as if to show just how numb it was. "Spat it out though... tasted yuck."

"Has he been poisoned?" Jin asked anxiously. "Can you somehow find out with what? Do you have an antidote?"

Niall shushed him impatiently. "Suzu, did they say what it was? What it was supposed to do?"

"Sleep."

"Sleep? ... Oh... oh, that's all right then, it's just a sleeping draught. Still, to be on the safe side – because I wouldn't even trust them with my tea – I'll prepare a purge, and Jin and I will stay with you and keep you awake till we're sure the effects have worn off."

Suzu groped clumsily at Jin's shirt until he had a hold of it, then he glared up at him – although it took him some effort to focus on Jin's face.

"I'm not... to Naloc..."

"We won't go to Naloc, we're going home," Niall responded, and Suzu grunted assent and let go of Jin's shirt front.

Out of the corner of his eyes Jin noticed Risa grinning broadly. He scowled at her, but she only wriggled her eyebrows at him suggestively and laughed. He chose to ignore her. It would have been a lie to say he wasn't at least a little nervous about spending the night alone with Suzu, but it was neither the time nor the situation to entertain any fantasies. Besides, Suzu was not Kari, Jin had to accept that.

"Um..." Jin cleared his throat. "What about Nobu's men?"

"Escaped – mostly. We caught one who wasn't quick enough, thanks to Suzu." Risa chuckled and winked at Suzu. "He's being taken to the guard. We'll see if we can get anything useful out of him. Get yourselves home now, the rest can wait till tomorrow."

With Jin supporting Suzu and Niall lighting their way, the three were on their slow, laborious way home.

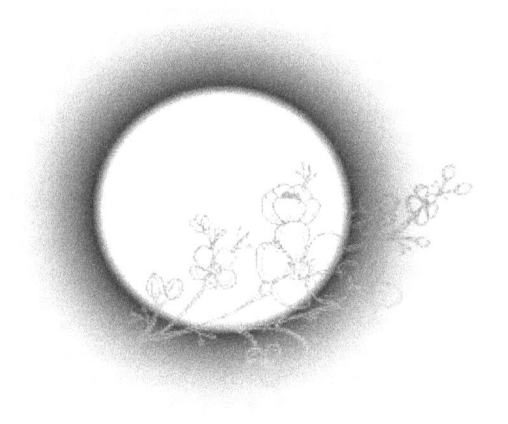

Chapter 30

The long way to Jin's house was exhausting, but Niall had decided there was no better way to get the drug out of Suzu's system then by walking it off. And so they walked. Through the unusually quiet and dark streets of a grieving Yūgao and deep into Kigetsu. Their progress was slow. It was laborious. But eventually Suzu's head became clearer, the numbness receded from his limbs. By the time they arrived at Jin and Niall's home, he was exhausted and footsore, but sober.

Niall pushed the simple wooden gate open. By now the sky had brightened to a deep indigo, the twilight revealing two identical small houses, standing side by side beyond a wide, square lawn. Just to the right of the gate stood an impressive old tree, a table and a couple of chairs beneath its canopy. They followed the pebbled path towards the houses, and Suzu was surprised to see there was a brook running between them with a tiny bridge, no more than a plank, across. It was too dim yet to make out where the brook came from or where it went.

"This one's Jin's," Niall said, pointing at the house they stood in front of. "And that one's mine," she added, hopping across the little brook instead of taking the bridge. "Go and get some sleep now, both of you. That's an order. And if anyone dares to come knocking on my door before I emerge of my own volition, I will rip their head off and turn it into a planter. Good night!" Her door slammed shut with finality, leaving the two young men alone.

Suzu glanced uncertainly at Jin. Their last encounter hadn't exactly been friendly – and yet Jin had come for him. Perhaps, Suzu reckoned, it was time for him to forgive Jin, now that he knew the truth about what had happened five years ago.

Jin shuffled his feet nervously. "So... um... let's go inside?" Suzu nodded and motioned for Jin to go ahead. The house was a single spacious room with a high ceiling and narrow windows. Thanks to the thatched roof, whose eaves hung low, the interior was still draped in deepest night. Suzu had to wait for Jin to light a lantern, then followed close behind him, afraid he would run into or stumble over various objects. They passed a sunken hearth, unlit and cold, the hook, hanging on a chain from a beam above it, was missing a kettle. A wooden screen partitioned the room into living and sleeping area. Jin opened a wall cabinet and pulled out a futon and a thin blanket.

"Sorry, it's not aired out, but at least it's washed," he said, laying the futon next to what was clearly his own.

Suzu nearly collapsed onto the futon, grateful to finally be off his feet. "Thank you," he said softly. And when Jin shook his head, Suzu looked up straight at him and said in a louder voice, ringing with deep sincerity, "I mean it: thank you. For coming for me."

Jin rubbed a hand through his messy hair, the blush creeping up his cheeks visible even in the sparse light of the lantern. He flopped down on his futon, grunted something utterly unintelligible, and quickly dowsed the lantern. In the dark Suzu didn't even try to hide his smile – this was the Jin he knew.

"I would have been screwed if you hadn't shown up when you did."

"I really didn't do anything. It was Risa and the rest, you ought to thank them."

"You know that's not true. If you hadn't followed when they dragged me off, I would have probably already been shipped off to serve some sick bastard as his new sex toy."

Jin sat up abruptly. "Is that what Nobu wanted to do with you?" he cried, as shocked as he was disgusted. "By the gods! How could I've ever been so wrong about someone? I thought he was kind and gentle – I thought he was my friend."

"Don't worry, you weren't the only one he fooled – and certainly not the last."

"But you never were. Why?"

Suzu sighed and put an arm behind his head, staring up at the ceiling he couldn't see. "Takes one to know one, I guess," he said at last. Jin didn't comment. Suzu could hear him lie down again, the rustle of fabric as Jin tried to find a comfortable position – and then quietness. It lasted long enough for Suzu's eyes to droop.

"Hey," Jin said suddenly, "that big fellow... was that...?"

Suzu chuckled sleepily. "Ah yes, I didn't recognise him at first either, he's even uglier than before. But it's Steren."

"Steren?"

"The village bully himself."

"Goddess! I mean... I didn't get a good look at him, but I thought there was something familiar about him. But... Steren? ... Wait. There's something wrong with his face, though, isn't it?"

Glee, like a second blanket settled over Suzu. Perhaps it was wrong and mean and petty of him to be gleeful about another person's disfigurement, but he couldn't help it. Steren was the kind of person who revelled in others' misery, who loved to torment those weaker than him. And Suzu's resentment against the man for the part he played in his downfall – then and now – was like a living thing, a wild beast that tore apart all sympathy, all decency, with a swipe of its claws.

"Apparently," he gloated, "Miki rearranged it for him with a hot iron bar."

Jin barked a laugh at this. "Miki? But he's always been so... gentle and sweet. Timid."

"Yes, until he wasn't. You know, he was the only one who stood up for me at that farce of a trial. The only one to defend me. He and his uncles – they alone did not turn their backs on me." Suzu could feel Jin's eyes on him, wondered if he'd ask him about the trial. But he didn't. So instead Suzu quietly added, "I wonder where Miki is now."

"Perhaps we could try and find him... when this is all over, I mean."

"Perhaps," Suzu agreed half-heartedly, for he couldn't imagine a time after.

For now, sleep claimed them both.

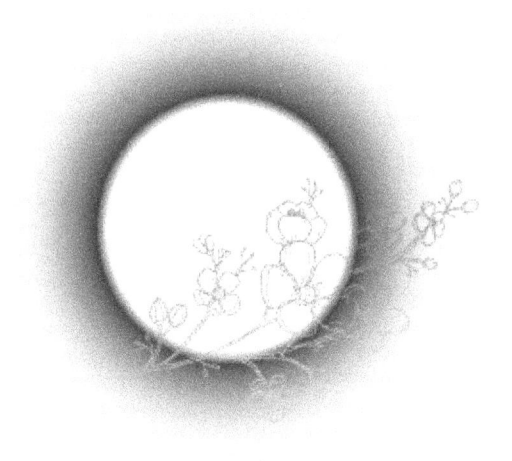

Chapter 31

When Suzu woke again the room was mottled with golden sunlight. He sat up slowly and took a look around, his brain sluggishly putting together the events of the night before. When his gaze fell on Jin's sleeping figure next to him, Suzu was transported miles and years away for the short span of time of a single breath. For a moment he let his eyes linger on the young man. How strange it was, all the contrasting intense feelings Suzu had had for this man in his life. Once he had thought his love for Jin so great he had thought of him is sole reason for living. Once he had felt a hate for Jin which could have devoured worlds. Now – he couldn't say. There were so many emotions roiling inside Suzu it was difficult to pick a single one to examine – and Suzu didn't want any of them. But as he sat in this little house, looking at his childhood friend, the absence of resentment towards him stood out. As if the truth, like a deluge of cold water, had doused the conflagration of hate.

Suzu rubbed his face vigorously. Gods, he'd been so stupid last night. Just what had he been thinking? His revenge would have been snuffed out like a candle in a tempest if Jin and the others hadn't come. Why had Jin come anyway? One ought to think after the way Suzu had treated him, Jin would avoid him at all cost. So why had he come? Suddenly Suzu felt the estrangement between them, a yawning chasm that had never been there, as if they were strangers. And perhaps they were.

The rather persistent pressure on his bladder finally forced Suzu to get up. He left the house as quietly as possible and rounded the house in search of the outhouse.

Done with his urgent business, Suzu determined to take a closer look around. First, he had to find out where that brook came from and where it went. Seeing as the grounds weren't big – there was enough room for the two houses to sit comfortably next to each other, and a small patch of green – all it took for Suzu to find where it came from, was to follow it with his eyes. There, a small arch low in the northern wall. The little stream entered, running straight from the neighbouring property through the arch in the wall, and continued between the two houses. Frowning, Suzu followed its course, eyes on the sparkling water – and thus didn't notice he wasn't alone. Sudden movement at the edge of his vision startled him. He whirled towards it, body tensed, ready for a fight.

Naloc sat beneath the old ginkgo tree. "Please, join me," he said, pointing at the chair opposite him. Suzu went warily, sat down and crossed his arms in front of his chest, glaring. Naloc smiled indulgently. "I know you want to blame me for what happened, and it's fine. I blame myself. I underestimated the danger, but do you really think I would have put my own wife in danger for my own gain?"

"Perhaps not your wife. But the rest of us...?" Suzu shrugged, making it clear he didn't think Naloc would have any scruple sacrificing a few unimportant Furyusha and servants.

"Never," Naloc snapped furiously, giving Suzu pause. "Look, I knew without a doubt – as did Kazue – that the Earl would never harm you. He's head over heels for you. Besides, occasionally selling some information is part of the business, everyone knows that."

"Our customers tell us things because they trust us to keep their secrets," Suzu hissed, irritated. "Perhaps other houses do this kind of *business*, but not the Singing Dragon."

"Your honesty and loyalty honour you. Kazue didn't want to ruin it, so we decided never to ask you to betray your customers confidence. But it is also the reason why she didn't want you to stay in that line of business indefinitely. You are neither naïve nor stupid, you must know that's how Yūgao – how the world works. So don't pretend otherwise, don't be judgemental about it."

Of course, he knew, it didn't mean he had to like it, or be part of it. Had Kazue sold information on the General? Toshi? Any of his other customers? After all he had never kept any secrets from her. The boys had always spoken freely amongst themselves, had discussed their customers. Perhaps he had just turned a blind eye and a deaf ear to it, perhaps for some childish reason he had just assumed the Singing Dragon to be above such things. It was ridiculous. They sold lies and dreams, wearing masks and personas like fine clothes. And Suzu had made it an art. So who was he to judge, to feel righteous.

"Fine," he relented, "it's always been that way, it always will be. And yet! You had no right to put your nose into things that you neither fully understand nor got a full picture of. Who do you think you are? If you think there is a plot against the emperor, than take the issue to the Silver Guard and let them deal with it. You think you and your motley band are some kind of heroes, meant to save emperor and empire? That's ridiculous. It's hubris. And all this just to satisfy your own greed for power."

Naloc sighed. It was a resigned, not an exasperated sigh. "You do know that I am on the Crescent Council, don't you?" Suzu nodded an affirmative. "And do you also know that I hold the First Seat?" Suzu hadn't known that. His surprise must have shown on his face, for Naloc continued, "Yes. I already have all the power I could ever wish for. But the position comes with a heavy burden: I'm responsible for the people of Kigetsu. It is my duty to care for their well-being, to protect them. Without the Crescent those stuck-up snobs in Mangetsu would just gladly forget we even existed. Oh, certainly, things have improved greatly since Mitsuhige's reign, but let's be honest, we are far from equality. And Kjell is a fool who cares more about women and parties than about his people. But someone who'd go so far as to take the throne by force, against the will of the gods – that spells disaster for all of us. So you see, I don't get blindly involved in things I might not understand because of a hunger for power, but because it is my duty. And I cannot take this to the Silver Guard without irrefutable evidence."

Suzu mulled this over. As much as he hated to admit it, Naloc had a point in as such that there was more at stake than personal revenge. Still, one didn't exclude the other. And so Suzu leaned back in his chair and looked Naloc straight in the eye. "All right, I can accept that. However, I will not stay put and let you do whatever it is you are going to do about it. I made a promise to my dead family – and I intend to keep it. If that means having to work with you, then so be it. But you will not tell me to stay out of it for my own good."

Naloc rubbed a hand across his face, looking tired and drawn. Yet he did not argue. Instead he reached down beside him, then put a cloth parcel on the table between them. Stuck through the knot of the parcel was Suzu's short sword.

"I feared you would say that. There are new clothes in there and some of the money that is rightfully yours. And your sword, as you can see. I'll agree to your demands, if you promise not to do anything reckless anymore."

"Deal," Suzu cringed, refraining from arguing that he had not intended to be reckless last night, he had only wanted to go home.

With nothing more to say to each other they sat in awkward silence until Niall, emerging from her house, saved them. She stretched, saw them, and ambled over to the table. Her eyes were still a little puffy from sleep and her auburn hair was tangled and knotted. She stopped beside Suzu, looked down at him and smiled, a little sleepily. There was a smattering of tiny freckles running across the bridge of her nose, and the faintest of lines around her dark blue eyes. Her sharp features and the slightly crooked grin lent her a somewhat foxy appearance. Suzu thought she was gorgeous. Niall wasn't pretty in the conventional sense, perhaps, but her natural charm, her authenticity – there was no artifice about her, neither in her attitude nor her appearance – made her beautiful.

It wasn't until Niall raised an eyebrow that Suzu noticed he had been staring. He looked away, mumbling a short greeting.

Niall laughed and ruffled his hair, then laughed some more when he pushed her hand away, blushing.

"Niall," Naloc interrupted, and for a moment Suzu was glad about the man being here. "Could you please wake up Jin or the boy won't get up before week's end. I've brought you all breakfast." He once more reached down beside his chair and lifted a basket onto the table. Curious as to what else the man may have hidden in this auspicious spot next to himself, Suzu leaned over and peeked beneath the table – but there was nothing but grass. As he straightened, Suzu studiously ignored the amused expression on Naloc's face. From behind him, Suzu could hear a door slam. Niall's wake up call routine seemed to include being as noisy and intrusive as possible.

"Still a late riser, is he?" Suzu asked.

A confused expression, there and gone again in a single heartbeat. "Ah! Yes, I forgot that you grew up together. It's a mystery to me how he coped with temple life."

"Exceedingly badly – that's how. He was never truly able to conform to the strict rules, the rigidity, the narrow-mindedness."

"But you were?"

Suzu shrugged. He didn't want to talk about his past, especially not with Naloc. But the question wasn't unjustified. Had he adapted to the rules, the way of life the Brotherhood dictated? Had there ever been a time, perhaps before he realised his feelings for Jin were more than brotherly affection, in which he had considered taking the vows, dedicating his life to the Path? All he remembered of that time now was dyed in rage and hurt and betrayal. The days, the years before the destruction of his life then were hazy, even the memories of Jin. Only that fateful day remained sharp, clear, as if it had only happened yesterday. The moment of betrayal, the feeling like having a dagger made of ice plunged deep into his heart. The anguish of his soul echoing in every fibre of his body. The pain he had screamed out into the night until his voice broke. Would it be like this this time? Would he, years from now, still feel the pain, the hate, the rage, the hollowness, while the good and happy memories sank in a flood of loss and grief, buried, out of his reach?

"Suzu?" A voice, at once so familiar, warm and golden like sunshine, and yet so strange, giving sound to his name. Suzu turned his head, found dark brown, almost black eyes looking unflinchingly back at him. Jin was crouching beside him, a hand hovering above Suzu's shoulder, uncertain if the touch would be welcome. Slowly, Suzu became aware of his white-knuckled grip on his short sword, the frown between Naloc's brows, Niall hovering on his other side. He forced his hands to unclench, and took a deep breath. *Not now, not yet.* There would come a time for him to let go, to break and shatter, to never be whole again – but not until he had fulfilled his promise.

Suzu stomped down on the rising panic, forced it down beneath righteous anger and purpose, and blinked away treacherous tears.

"Suzu? Are you all right?" Jin asked again.

"I'm fine." Lie. He'd never be fine again. Jin looked unconvinced as well, but he dropped the issue.

They had just finished their meal when Aika came bursting through the gate, sweaty and gasping for air.

"Niall, quick," she panted, panic ringing in her voice. "You have to come. Hurry!"

Niall, neither hesitating nor asking any questions, got up and hurried into her house. Jin and Naloc, too, got to their feet. "What is it? You father? Risa?" Jin asked anxiously.

"No, it's... Niall, come on, hurry!" Aika fidgeted, ready to bolt. Naloc put a hand on her shoulder, squeezing reassuringly.

"Take a breath, girl. Tell me what happened."

"I don't know! They were attacked. Enzo... my father – he's all right, well not really, but... Enzo is... and oh gods... Feli. Naloc, Feli is..." Her voice broke, tears welling up in her eyes. Aika swallowed hard and shook her head. Jin felt as if the ground beneath his feet had broken open. It had only been last evening that they had all sat together, laughing and joking. Feli had always been the soothing gentle counterpart to Enzo's bluntness. How could he be gone just like that?

Before another word was spoken, Niall was back, her doctor's bag slung over her shoulder. She was still wearing the clothes she had slept in, her hair even messier than before but bound back. Without so much as a word she hurried past them, Aika following.

"I should go, too," Naloc stated. Jin, shocked and uncertain, turned to look at Suzu. The other boy was deathly pale, Jin felt torn between rushing off to the side of his friends and staying behind with Suzu. He had no idea how much his struggle must have shown on his face, until Suzu suddenly took a deep breath and squared his shoulders, and said, determined, "What are we waiting for? Let's go!"

Jin threw him a grateful look, and then they were running after the others.

It felt like it took them an unreasonably long time to reach Naloc's house. The courtyard was full of people, an anxious, sad, angry buzz lay in the air. They pushed through the crowd and went straight for the guest wing. The sounds of crying and pain filled groans rang through the hallway. Suzu fell behind as the others entered one of the rooms, suddenly becoming aware of being nothing but a stranger. What right did he have to be here? He had just blindly followed Jin; he shouldn't be here.

The room seemed crowded. The body of a young man lay by the wall, a white cloth covering his face. Two women were sitting beside him, crying and clutching each other. Kuroto, Aika's father, was sitting in a corner, hollow eyed and white as a sheet. There was blood on his clothes and he was cradling his left arm. Niall was bent over another person, working furiously. Risa, grim-faced, held the man's hand, talking quietly to him. Whatever she was saying, her words were drowned out by the man's moans and the women's weeping.

As Niall sat up to rummage through her bag, Suzu could see the man's face. It was Enzo. The man who had challenged him to some sparring, who had laughed at himself after Suzu had knocked him on his arse. Suzu didn't know the man, but he had liked his cheerful nature, his boisterousness. Seeing all of Enzo's light extinguished, seeing him writhe in pain and fight for his life – it wasn't right. This wasn't right.

Suzu suddenly felt dizzy, he felt helpless, useless. Naloc was now sitting with the two women, holding a hand of each in one of his, head bowed. Jin was assisting Niall; it seemed practised, as if he had done so a thousand times before. Aika was with her father, her arms around his neck. There was no room for Suzu, nothing for him to do. He was an intruder.

Slowly, he backed away and stumbled down the dark, empty hallway. At its end Suzu found an open door. It was a sparsely furnished room with nothing more than a low table and a flower arrangement by the wall, beneath a calligraphy. The door to the garden stood open. Suzu went out on the verandah and sat down. It was deceptively quiet here, serene.

Suzu took a shuddering breath, drew his knees up to his chest, and pressed the heels of his hands into his eyes. His breath hitched. Images flashed through his mind. Flames, smoke, people running to and fro. The tiny remains of his family, huddled together, weeping, hurt. He imagined he could still hear Enzo's cries and moans. Then they turned into the harsh rattle of Ryū's seared, smoke filled lungs.

Suzu fought against the rising tide of grief that threatened to drown him, fought to force air into his lungs. Three days. Had it already been three days? Had it only been three days? Another image: Nobu's hateful, handsome, smiling face. The very object of Suzu's rage. He held on to it, let it stoke the flames, until the fury burnt away the grief, the loss, the loneliness. Let it burn, he thought, bright and destructive like a supernova. Let it lay waste to the entire world if it must. Let it consume.

A mournful cry made Suzu jump. He looked up and found himself almost face to face with a magnificent peacock, the wheel of its tail in full, glorious display. Confused by the sudden appearance of the bird, it took Suzu a moment to realise that this was *the* peacock: the General's beloved pet bird, stolen by Naloc, the knave. Suzu huffed a little laugh. Was he supposed to steal the bird back, now that he had found it?

The peacock folded its tail, hopped up onto the verandah, where it unceremoniously, but gracefully, plopped down next to Suzu, and laid its head into his lap. Surprised and uncertain of what the bird wanted, Suzu froze. Tentatively he ran his fingers gently over the soft feathers of the animal's neck and was rewarded with a soft coo.

As he continued to stroke the bird's silky neck, Suzu's mind wandered. The thought of the General made him think of Toshi. They hadn't parted in the best way. Suzu wanted to be angry with the man, and found he could not. Toshi had done what he had thought was right, he was hardly the first to miscalculate Nobu's actions. If he hadn't gotten Suzu out of there, Suzu wasn't certain he would still be alive to even consider being angry at him. Nor was a he certain it was a good thing. And admittedly, even Suzu wouldn't have been able to predict this kind of reaction. The monk had gotten worse, more erratic, more... insane? Until now Suzu had not truly considered Nobu mad, there was too much method, too much deliberation in what he did, but now... Perhaps killing Nobu wouldn't only be the fulfilment of his revenge, or doing the world a favour, perhaps it also meant putting the monk out of his misery.

The sun was already setting, shadows stretching and lengthening into grotesque figures, when Jin found him. With a soul weary sigh the boy sat down beside Suzu, looking drawn and pale.

"Are you all right?" Suzu asked.

After a moment's hesitation Jin nodded. "You?"

"Fine. How... how is Enzo?"

"Alive – for now. Niall did what she could, it's up to him now. Enzo is tough, he'll pull through." It sounded like Jin was trying to convince himself more than Suzu, though.

"What happened? Do you know?"

Jin ran a hand through his hair, messing it up even more. "Kuroto, Enzo, and Feli were out for some lunch. Can you believe it? Feli was eating takoyaki just a few hours ago." Jin looked at Suzu, a wobbly smile on his lips and tears in his eyes.

Suzu's heart broke a little for Jin, for the two weeping women, for the young man he hadn't known who now lay cold, his face hidden beneath a white cloth. In the rough cracks of his heart, rage burnt a little brighter yet.

"They were just eating and laughing," Jin continued, his voice rough. "Then... there was a man who came to stand behind Feli, you know, just stood there, and... and before they could ask him what he wanted, he – the man, he ran Feli through with his sword. Just like that. Put his sword straight through Feli's heart. Feli – he was –" Jin's voice broke. He stopped. Suzu could see the other boy's Adam's apple bob as he swallowed his tears. "Kuroto... said it was chaos after that. Can't recall what exactly happened. There were more of them, he and Enzo were fighting – and losing. Suddenly the guard was there... but by then Kuroto's arm was broken and... Enzo... the guard brought them back, sent men after the attackers... I don't think they'll ever find those bastards." With a sudden burst of ferocity Jin slammed his fist into the hardwood floor of the verandah. Suzu didn't blame him.

"You do know that this was Nobu's doing, don't you?" Suzu said. Teeth clenched, Jin nodded. "He needs to be put down, Jin. He won't ever stop hurting others." Slowly, Jin nodded again. Perhaps when he had calmed down, he would change his mind, but for now it seemed he finally understood. But Suzu had no intention of letting anyone else have his prey.

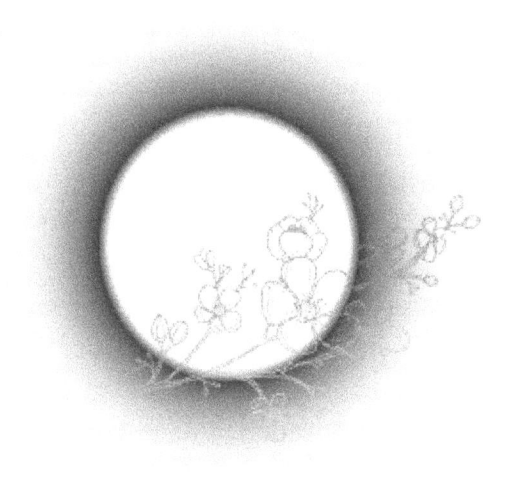

Chapter 32

Another long night. The captain of the town guard had come by to talk to Naloc about what had happened, and left believing the attackers had been some random hoodlums. Niall didn't move from Enzo's side, vigilant of any sign his condition might take a turn for the worse. Risa, Aika, and Kuroto, however, joined the small procession bringing Feli home. As was the custom in the north, it fell upon his mother and sister to prepare his body for the wake.

Jin and Suzu remained in the tea room all night. They didn't talk, hardly acknowledged each other's presence, lost in their own thoughts.

Eventually, Suzu must have fallen asleep, for he suddenly opened his eyes to dazzling sunshine flooding the room. He sat up and stretched. Jin was sitting, slumped against the wall, his chin on his chest, breathing slow and even. A servant passed by the room. Seeing that Suzu was awake, she hurried back in the direction from where she'd come, only to return a short time later with a tray full of little bowls and a small tea pot. Suzu thanked her for bringing him breakfast. Yet lifting the lid from a bowl of miso soup, Suzu felt his appetite missing. In the end, when Jin woke at last, there was still food aplenty left for him.

Only a little time later Naloc and Niall joined them. Both had dark circles under their eyes, Niall looked even more dishevelled than she had the day before. Whereas Naloc seemed to lack appetite as much as Suzu had, Niall devoured her breakfast in such a short amount of time, Suzu doubted she had even tasted what she ate. The moment she had washed down the last bite with the rest of her tea, Niall heaved herself to her feet, stretched, and left without a word.

"She gets like that when she is caring for a patient," Jin explained, before lapsing into silence again.

Until Suzu couldn't stand it anymore. Turning to Naloc, he repeated what he had said to Jin the night before, "You know who's doing this is."

"Yes."

"So, what are you going to do about it?"

"If I knew that, I'd already be doing it. No!" Naloc held up a hand to forestall Suzu's argument. "I won't alert the guard without any real evidence. They might not take it seriously enough or even believe it otherwise."

"I'm not talking about the guard, though. Why not go to the Earl directly? And do not tell me because you think he's a traitor, I've had enough of that nonsense."

"No."

"Fine, then go to the General!"

Naloc sighed tiredly. Frustrated, Suzu turned away before he ended up strangling the man. Naloc's refusal to seek help from members of the Moon Council was ridiculous. The solstice was drawing nearer by the day and they had nothing, except dead and injured people. Even more frustrating was that they were turning in circles. No evidence also meant no proof of Toshi's innocence. Sitting around and doing nothing was starting to take a toll on Suzu, he needed to take action. To hell with the emperor and all the rest, he didn't give a damn about them. He had made a promise – and he intended to keep it, no matter the cost. But he had no chance to get to Nobu on his own now.

The arrival of a lanky youth pulled Suzu back to the present. "Boss," the boy said, his voice had a strange but familiar softness.

"Daikichi," Nobu acknowledged him. "What is it?"

"We've found the maid and the gardener."

Jin and Naloc abruptly sat up straighter, eyes suddenly keen, new life in both of them. "Then we shouldn't lose any time. Take us to them."

They took Naloc's carriage – he hated the vehicle, but not only was time of the essence, it would also hide them from spying eyes as hardly anyone knew it belonged to him. Just to make sure, though, they took a way that made it look as if they were on their way to the warehouse.

"The warehouse?" Suzu asked. While Niall had remained behind to tend to her patient, Suzu had insisted on coming, and to Jin's amazement Naloc had agreed without much of a fuss.

"Yes, warehouse. I am, after all, a merchant," Naloc replied waspishly. As that seemed to be all he had to say about it, Jin quietly explained to Suzu that Naloc used to be a travelling merchant before setting up shop in town. By then he had made connections and gained loyal customers all over the empire. Thanks to those he had quickly grown into one of the most successful merchants in town.

"And what are you trading in?"

"Cloth. The finest there is." Naloc huffed, obviously offended Suzu hadn't already known that. "All those pretty kimono of yours – almost all of them were made of my cloth." Although Suzu raised an eyebrow at the pride in Naloc's voice he didn't comment.

The warehouse was situated in the far west of Kigetsu like most warehouses and workshops. It was also where Durin's boys had at last found their missing young couple.

They drove the carriage straight to Naloc's warehouse, entered – and left through a side entrance to follow Daikichi's directions on foot.

"This is it." Jin pointed at a small old storehouse. It looked abandoned and in need of repairs, but the roof seemed sturdy enough – as did the door. The windows were boarded up, the grass around it had grown wild. Larger, more modern warehouses surrounded it, the town wall was looming behind it, you could see the western gate from here. They carefully picked their way across the overgrown grass, vigilant, hands on their swords.

The moment they had reached the door, however, it swung open – silently, hinges well-oiled. A tall figure stood in the shadows within, barring their way. Jin's sword had half left its sheath before Suzu's hand on his stopped him.

"Kagetora?" Suzu asked, surprised.

The dark figure nodded and stepped aside. "Please come in. Quickly now." And Suzu did, without hesitation. Jin glanced at Naloc uncertainly, but his boss only shrugged and followed Suzu. Another quick look around, but the streets were empty but for a pair of crows fighting over a morsel of food – and then he ducked inside. The door closed behind him at once, plunging them all into darkness.

After a moment Jin's eyes adjusted, allowing him to make out the forms of shelves and crates along the walls in what little light came through the boarded up windows. Kagetora brushed past them, sure-footed and purposeful as if he could see perfectly fine – or as if he knew the lay of the room by heart. To Jin's eyes the man was just a patch of darker blackness that joined another shadowy figure in the depth of the room. There came the sound of a flint being struck, sparks in the dark. A light bloomed into life and the patches of darkness were revealed as Kagetora and –

"Toshi?" Suzu gasped. He took a stumbling step towards the man, almost involuntarily, before he stopped himself. Jin couldn't read the boy's expression, but the familiarity, the emotion with which Suzu said the Earl's name made his heart twinge.

"Suzu," the Earl began, but Naloc cut him off.

"You are not who we expected to find here."

The Earl's face darkened. It was as if walls had suddenly come up, hiding away the unexpected gentleness with which he had looked at Suzu. Now he was all sharp edges and thorns, warmth replaced with icy coldness. Jin had never really met the Earl of Tsukikage before, but this was exactly the version of the man he had always pictured: intimidating, harsh, aloof.

"I am well aware of who you were expecting, Murasaki no Naloc," the Earl snapped. "But I am quite curious as to why you were looking so desperately for my employees." Jin took note of the Earl calling Numie and Genta employees not servants. It annoyed him that perhaps Suzu was right about the man.

"Oh, I think you know exactly why. What have you done with them?"

"I got them out of town – them, and their families. Thanks to your blundering men looking for them left and right, hiding them here became too great a risk."

"And I'm to believe you didn't kill them?"

"I don't care what you believe, Murasaki-tan." From the Earl's mouth the name sounded like an insult. Naloc bristled. The atmosphere in the small stifling room felt charged, a single spark enough to ignite it. Jin shuffled his feet, uncomfortable, and realised too late that Suzu might be that spark. The boy pushed Naloc aside and stepped between him and the Earl. Anger radiated off of him. Jin couldn't honestly say who was more intimidating: the Earl or Suzu.

"And I don't care about any of your posturing. What I care about is avenging my family – and trust me, I will. Even if I have to tear down this whole damn town! So you two can either play nice, or get out of my way."

Jin had been subjected to Suzu's intense anger once already. The sheer devastating potential of it. Therefore he didn't blame Naloc for being momentarily speechless or that his hand unconsciously went to the hilt of his sword. What did confound him, however, was the smile that ghosted over the Earl's face.

"Suzu's right," the man relented. "This is not the time for us to squabble. Let's talk this out like civilised people." He sat down, gesturing for the rest of them to join him. Reluctantly Naloc did as asked, giving Suzu the side-eye. Only Kagetora remained standing. The Earl addressed him, "Please make sure they weren't followed and that we remain undisturbed." Again, Jin noticed the man did not treat his... attendant – butler? Bodyguard? – like a servant but almost like... a friend.

"My lord," Kagetora began, looking warily at Naloc and Jin, but Suzu interjected, "Don't worry, I won't let anything happen to him."

Jin felt a stab of jealousy at the words, which only grew worse when Kagetora, without hesitation, accepted Suzu's claim with a curt nod, a quick clasp of the younger man's shoulder, and left. Jin, in all honesty, couldn't tell if he was jealous of Suzu being willing to defend the Earl, come what may, or of a man like Kagetora acknowledging Suzu's ability to do so. Probably both, for Jin could not deny the unreasonable antipathy he felt for the Earl, nor the fact that he would stand no chance against any of the men in this room should it come to that.

"We weren't followed," Naloc sniffed, offended. "We're not idiots, you know."

"Really? I couldn't tell from the way your men were stumbling all over Kigetsu and Eigetsu looking for my employees – and Nobu."

"In all fairness, until only days ago my men were under the impression they were looking for either a young couple that had eloped – or two bodies."

The Earl smirked. "You are lucky it were some of my people, who recognised them. And even luckier that they didn't draw too much of Nobu's attention or I might have had to eliminate the risk of them leading Nobu straight here." Naloc stiffened, but he had no riposte. "But it seems Nobu has finally – and most unfortunately – taken note of you. I'm sorry for what happened to your men. When I heard what happened, I knew it was time to get Genta and Numie out of here – and time that we met."

Naloc frowned. "You made sure the boys would spot them."

The Earl nodded in affirmation. Jin glanced at Suzu, who seemed unsurprised, his expression unreadable. Naloc, on the other hand, looked ready to explode, fists clenched, jaw tight, taking deep, deliberate breaths. His view of the nobility was greatly tinged with the idea that they were all greedy, self-centred idiots who knew nothing of cunning or subtlety if it didn't involve petty court intrigue. That the Earl proved him wrong in so many ways had to grate on him.

"Why? What for?"

"Because it is high time for us to have this conversation. I'm glad you didn't try to keep Suzu out of it – you and Jarick are really quite similar, did you know? Always trying to decide who has to know what and ignoring the fact that sometimes involving the right people is better for all concerned. I've told him repeatedly it was time to bring you in on this, but he wouldn't have any of it. You can take a wild guess as to why he is not fond of the idea of working with you – a little hint: It has feathers." Suzu snorted; Jin quickly hid his smirk when Naloc glared at him and coughed deliberately. At least he had the decency to look embarrassed.

"Toshi," Suzu said, "just tell me what this is. I know you are no traitor." He cast a quick glowering glance at Naloc. "You would never join hands with a man like Nobu. But... the things that happened..." It was then that Jin realised how desperately Suzu needed for the Earl to be the man he believed him to be. Taking this away from the boy would be akin to dealing him a death blow. Despite feeling bad about it, Jin couldn't shake off the jealousy that simmered inside his heart.

For a moment, looking at Suzu, the Earl's face softened. "Don't worry, Suzu, I'm not." Then he turned back to Naloc and his expression hardened again. "So for your information: No, I do not plan to overthrow the emperor, nor am I in league with a madman. On the contrary, I am trying to prevent any of this from happening – as is my job. You didn't really think he just spontaneously came up with this, did you? We've had our eyes on Nobu for years. It took me two damn years to gain that blasted monk's trust enough for him to share his plans with me – or parts of it. That is one sly bastard, I can tell you that. After all those years, we still don't have a full list of his co-conspirators – hell, not even they know who they are, he makes sure of it. It's also why he keeps hiring groups of thugs from outside the town and discards them after one job. The less they know... That also goes for his plans: Everyone only knows as much as they need to know. It's frustrating and irritating, and we are running out of time."

They had to let that sink in for a moment.

"Who precisely is 'we'?" Naloc asked all of a sudden.

"The Hidden Moon."

Jin gasped. Beside him Suzu and Naloc sat up straighter. The Hidden Moon was a whispered rumour, a myth; the possibility of it was a thrilling thought and cold shiver running down one's spine. They worked in the dark, protecting the empire from threats from within and without. Who they were? Anyone and no-one. Apparently not even the emperor knew.

"You're joking," Jin blurted. He could feel Suzu's eyes boring into him. Sure enough, the Hidden Moon was exactly the kind of grand and impossible dream Jin had dreamt of as a child. They should not be real, that name should not have been thrown around so casually.

"Afraid not," the Earl sighed. "And I do not have to tell you that nothing about this leaves this room. I hope you appreciate the risk I am taking, telling you this. Not even family members are supposed to know, we're making a huge exception, which ought to tell you how dire the situation is."

Naloc, looking simultaneously miffed and as if he had just received the best present in his life, leaned forward. "You won't, by any chance, be able to give us some names – for credibility's sake."

The Earl raised an eyebrow. "I'd say knowing two is more than enough."

"Two? Oh!" Realisation dawned on Naloc's face, mirrored on Suzu's who then grinned to himself. Only Jin felt like he had missed something, but then Naloc growled, "Damn that old wolf." Of course. General Jarick ax Varg.

"So, but if no-one except Nobu knows his plan, how do you intend to prevent it from happening?" Suzu asked, returning to their topic.

The Earl smiled. It was a terrible smile, full of dark promise and righteous wickedness. "Nobu might be clever, I grant him that. But the Hidden Moon has played this game for far longer than he. How do you think we even learned of this conspiracy in the first place? We have eyes and ears everywhere. You plant the right people in his way, ask the right people very nicely." The way he said it made it clear what kind of nice asking they had done. Jin couldn't find it in him to be shocked. "And in the end we put all the pieces together. We know exactly what is going to happen, the problem is that we still don't know exactly who is involved."

"You think he has people inside the palace," Naloc interjected, but when the Earl only kept his steady gaze on him, neither confirming nor denying, he added in a slightly more scandalous tone, "Members of the Moon Council?" Now that was a shock. It was unheard of. Insiders of the palace were one thing, there always were disgruntled, unhappy servants and guards, but council members? They were the most loyal to the empire and closest confidants of the emperor, for any of them to commit treason... And yet, hadn't Naloc accused the Earl of the very same crime? No wonder the Hidden Moon had not yet interfered. To get rid of a nasty weed you had to pull it out by the roots. They could not risk missing any traitors.

"But to what end?" Jin queried, confused.

"To gain the throne, of course."

"But... that's not how this works."

"Jin," Suzu said, "according to law, who can be chosen as emperor?"

"Anyone."

"But who gets chosen?"

Even more confused than before, Jin shook his head. Naloc answered in his stead. "One of the Seven. It is always a member of the Seven, the oldest, most powerful clans in the empire. The Mori clan is one of them, isn't it? And if I'm not completely wrong there have been three Mori emperors so far."

The Earl gave an affirmative nod. "It's nothing but a lovely fairy tale, spun for the common people, that the emperor is chosen by the gods from amongst the people," he said. "The high priests of the Five Temples may seem to convey the will of the gods, but in truth it's a very earthly will they bow to. It's all politics and money, the gods have no say in it. And more often than not, it's the Moon Council who holds all the power, with the emperor its puppet.

"Nobu, having them all in his pockets, through blackmail and threats, is reaching for the Moonlight Throne itself.

Imagine him ruling the empire together with a council as ruthless and power-hungry as he is. He has been planning this for a very long time, and he knows what he's doing. No-one becomes high priest at that young an age without the right backing – and from what we gathered, Nobu disposed of the original candidate through rather underhanded means. Drove the poor old man into seclusion through heartbreak and shame. He died two years ago..." The Earl trailed off; he must have noticed the equally dark expressions on Jin's and Suzu's faces.

Jin's heart was pounding furiously, his blood roaring in his ears. Slowly he looked around at Suzu, found the other boy staring back at him, fury burning in his eyes. There it was, the why they hadn't had an answer to. They had been used, their lives as they had been destroyed – all to break a gentle old man's heart, his spirit, his soul. For greed, for power.

"Brother Askr didn't deserve this," Jin murmured, his voice wavering. "He didn't deserve this, he was a good man, he was..." *Our father.* Jin's voice failed him. Brother Askr had accepted Jin when his own father hadn't wanted him. Gods, he had tried the old man's patience so many times, exasperated him, angered him. Brother Askr had never given up on him even when everyone else had. Jin remembered how the big monk had lifted him and Kari, spun them both around, laughing and screeching. How strong and invincible he had seemed. Jin remembered the man chasing after him, strong muscular arms wrapping around Jin's small frame, soothing and comforting him when his parents had abandoned him.

Suddenly the small room felt stifling. Jin felt caged in; no, he felt like he was falling; no, he was suffocating. When had he stood up, begun to pace. It was just one thing after another. The pain Nobu had caused Suzu, everything he had taken away from him. The way in which he had used Jin, like a tool, a weapon – used and then thrown away. And Brother Askr... It was too much.

Hands on his shoulders stopped him in his frantic pacing. Jin raised his head and found himself looking into Suzu's mismatched eyes. "Calm down, Jin. He'll pay for all he's done, I'll make sure of it." There was a conviction and a determination in those words that were beyond dispute. It would happen, Nobu would pay for his crimes, for every life he had taken or destroyed, every pain he had caused, every drop of blood, every single tear – this was fact, any alternative was unimaginable.

"What are we missing here?" the Earl asked quietly. Both he and Naloc were looking at Jin and Suzu with almost identical frowns between their brows.

"He used us," Jin mumbled. It was all he felt capable of saying at that moment, not trusting his voice or his words for the turmoil of his emotions. Rage and shock. Sadness and guilt. He listened in silence while Suzu told their story. Only occasionally he looked at the other boy, whenever Suzu added a part of his and Nobu's ill-fated story to the parts Jin had lived, events he had never known about. Other than that Jin kept his eyes downcast, too afraid of the judging looks of the Earl and Naloc.

Silence answered Suzu's recount, the expressions on Naloc's and the Earl's faces spoke louder and clearer than any words could have. Abhorrence. Rage.

"There's one more thing," Suzu added. "I think I know why he is doing this – well, not all of this, but the trying to gain the throne part. Nobu is the illegitimate son of a minor nobleman. His mother was a servant in the man's household – he cast her out when she got pregnant. And when she died, the man gave Nobu to the temple instead of raising him himself. Nobu always felt he had been robbed of his birthright, he... well... he feels he's justified in what he is doing because he's only claiming what should rightfully be his."

"But his father wasn't one of the Seven," Naloc argued.

"At this point I don't think he cares about the details anymore," the Earl answered. "We could speculate all we want, who can tell what is really going on in another's head – especially that of a madman's. Right now, all we have to focus on is to stop him from succeeding, and trust me when I say I have been having sleepless nights and a lot of headaches over this. Knowing his plans unfortunately doesn't do us much good without knowing who's backing him. We need to cut off all the beast's heads at once or we will only end up delaying the inevitable. And we are running out of time. So... any ideas?"

Jin could relate to how frustrated the Earl must have been feeling, he, too, was getting a headache from it, and he hadn't been working against Nobu for months already. There had to be a way, something no-one had though of yet.

"So let them get poisoned. Those still standing are your conspirators." Jin wasn't the only one to gasp and gape at Suzu, nonchalantly suggesting they'd just let at least half of the Moon Council and possibly the emperor die. "Oh stop it," Suzu snapped. "I'm not talking about killing them all. Switch the poison, make it look like they succeeded when in reality the emperor and councillors are only... I don't know... unconscious, dreaming sweet dreams until this is all over. And in the meantime, you know who the traitors are and can do... whatever it is you do." The ruthlessness was shocking, but Jin could see the logic of it – and Naloc and the Earl seemed to earnestly consider it.

"So, if we find out who's supposed to poison the wine, we could switch either the poison or the poisoner," the Earl mused. "But the real problem is Nobu's choice of poison. Deva's Breath – they commonly call it Dreamless Sleep. A pretty name that implies a painless death, but in truth it's a most excruciating one. I have – luckily – never seen anyone die of it, but they say it feels like your skeleton is trying to claw its way out of your skin. I doubt the poisoned one just topples over and that's the end of it."

Jin swallowed hard. Now that was a mental image he could have done without – and definitely didn't ever want to witness first hand.

Naloc rubbed his chin and mused, "So, he wants to create a spectacle. Which means the moment people just keel over and lie still, he'll know something's up. What we need then is a poison that mimics the death throes typical to Dreamless Sleep, without actually killing anyone. Yes, that shouldn't be difficult at all."

Just then, a thought crossed Jin's mind. "Wait," he said, "that apothecary who sold the ingredients needed for the poison – he's probably the best in town, I'm certain he could come up with something."

"I'm going to ignore the fact that you knew there was someone in town who not only sells something as dangerous as Deva's Breath, but is also able to distil it – and did not think of mentioning it," the Earl growled.

Naloc nonchalantly waved the remark away and turned to Jin. "Pay another visit to our potions master and convince him to make us what we need."

"Tell me the name, for gods' sake," the Earl demanded. It seemed to Jin that this meeting ought to draw to an end before the man once and for all lost his patience with them. So he readily provided the name. It drew a bitter laugh from the Earl. "Azhar – of course, I should have known. Just stroke his ego, that should do the trick. And in case it doesn't, tell him General Jarick ax Varg sends his regards and urges him to remember the vow he has taken."

"Do I want to know?"

"No."

It wasn't much of a plan, but at least they had something. The Earl, too, had people to report to, to consult with. With a promise to contact them again as soon as possible and to include them on everything that was going to happen from here on out, their business was done for the day. Before Naloc opened the door, however, the Earl asked, genuine curiosity in his voice, "Why were you so eager to find my employees?"

"Because I was certain they had run afoul of their employer." Naloc stressed the word employer as if he still doubted the Earl's sincerity. "And because they are people of Kigetsu, it is my duty to take care of them."

The Earl regarded Naloc for a long moment, appraising. "Well, you weren't completely wrong, they unfortunately did hear something they shouldn't have. Nobu wanted them dead – I told him I would take care of it. Because like you, I have a duty to take care of my people." The tension between them felt as oppressive as the air moments before a storm breaks. There were things that had been left unspoken, too much to read between the lines. For the first time Jin questioned his boss. Had the man really acted out of a sense of duty and worry, or because of personal grievances?

Without another word Naloc tentatively opened the door, scanned the area before he went outside. Jin and Suzu made to follow him.

"Suzu," the Earl said, his voice so much softer than before. "A word, please? Alone." Throwing a glance at Jin, Suzu nodded and turned back.

"I'll wait outside," Jin mumbled, more to himself. There was a feeling in his chest, one he had had occasionally for weeks now, something he shouldn't be feeling: jealousy – ugly and unasked for. Suzu was not Kari, he thought he had understood that, so why couldn't Jin get rid of this disgraceful feeling.

"I'm so sorry, Suzu," Toshi said the moment they were alone. "I'm sorry I dragged you into this. I'm sorry I didn't think... I couldn't...I couldn't save them."

Even before Toshi stopped talking Suzu was already shaking his head. "It's not your fault," he cut him off before Toshi could continue to apologise. "Look, I'm done blaming the wrong people, I've learned my lesson. There is only one person who's at fault here and that person is Nobu, and Nobu alone. I will even admit that Naloc isn't really to blame for any of it – but don't you dare tell him."

"But –"

"Toshi, stop. Perhaps it's fate – the way Nobu, Jin, and I ran into each other again at the same time. What's certain is that it was inevitable that something really bad happened. Not when it comes to that sorry excuse of a monk. You didn't drag me into anything. Nobu – and Steren, that ugly thug – they recognised me. It was no mistake or recklessness that he gave you that message in front of me, they wanted me to know. I mean... did you know he came to the Dragon, told me in very clear terms to either join hands with him or – well, or..." Suzu fell silent, swallowing the sudden thickness in his throat. Toshi was looking at him with a mixture of bewilderment and a sadness as deep as the ocean.

"I still don't understand why he hates you so."

"Because we have always recognised each other as what we really are, seen the real person behind the mask, I guess. Love or hate – it was either or, but never anything in between."

There was a tension between them, anticipation – a moment of truth. It had nothing to do with Nobu and his plans, and yet, in a strange, twisted way, it had everything to do with the monk. Once upon a time Suzu had thought that to be loved he had to be the person his beloved wanted him to be. He had been prepared to spend the rest of his life in a prison of his own making, to be someone he wasn't. The older he got the harder it became, and the more he realised that you didn't miraculously become another person just because you pretended long enough. In the end, a part of him had secretly been grateful to Nobu for tearing down the walls of his false paradise.

Suzu hadn't been supposed to fall in love again – and yet it had happened. And once again, it wasn't his true self that had found love.

"Toshi, I'm the one who ought to apologise." So that was it. The moment of truth – and the end. The moment, in which he was going to lose all that was left to him. But Suzu was exhausted, he couldn't pretend any longer nor did he want to. He hadn't thought he could feel any more pain – he had been wrong. "I'm so sorry, but I am not the person you think I am, and I'm afraid I'll never be. The person you love... Toshi, I... I'm sorry, that... that person is an illusion." How was Toshi going to react – nothing had ever terrified Suzu as much as this. Closing his eyes, he steeled himself against an outburst, against a blow, against the inevitable rejection.

The brush of fingers against his cheek, light as feathers, made Suzu flinch. "Do you know when I first saw you?"

Suzu opened his eyes, warily looked up into Toshi's face. "When the General dragged you to the Dragon two years ago."

Toshi smiled ruefully. "No. It was years before that." That couldn't be right, Suzu would have remembered that. The first time they had met, he had been nothing but a fledgling and so nervous. The Earl of Tsukikage had been this intimidating, aloof, fiendishly handsome and powerful man – and Suzu had felt drawn to him like a moth to the flame.

Toshi gently ran a finger along the thin scar cutting through Suzu's brow and all the way to his cheekbone. "Business had taken me to the Dragon – I needed information and Kazue was the one who could give it to me. But she was busy, so I waited and wandered the garden. Light came from the dojo, sounds. I was wondering who was still training at such a late hour, so I went to take a look. And there was a boy – skinny, badly beaten up, his hair crudely shorn, a bandage covering half his face – and he was attacking a training dummy with a wooden sword like a wild beast. Vicious. Relentless. The rage he put into each stroke was a well-nigh tangible thing.

"I stood there and stared. At this feral creature, who could hardly keep himself on his feet, and yet… All that rage… the pain. Just watching you hurt so much. And yet I just stood there and couldn't take my eyes of you nor did I dare approach you. I have no idea for how long, but Kazue was suddenly standing next to me. She watched you quietly for a while, then looked at me – and told me to come back for you in a few years." Toshi smiled ruefully, shaking his head. "I didn't intend to. But I couldn't get that feral boy out of my head. Every once in a while I would find myself wondering how he was doing, if he was still in so much pain, if his wounds had healed… When Jarick told me the Dragon had a new Furyusha that might interest me, I knew it was you. He didn't even have to try to persuade me or drag me there. Told myself it was nothing but curiosity and this was a one time only thing. But then – you entered that room – and you were breathtaking. Oh, you acted all meek and mild-mannered, but I could see the fire in you, and instead of having sated my curiosity I suddenly made it my personal challenge to make you show me your true self. It was almost like a game, trying to catch glimpses of the real you, finding out what was mask and what not. And before I knew it, I had hopelessly fallen in love with you, Suzu."

A tear rolled down Suzu's cheek; he had no idea where it had come from, but he didn't wipe it away. Looking into Toshi's storm-grey eyes, he saw truth. Why had he never noticed before? He had always prided himself with being able to read people so well.

"Suzu," Toshi continued in a quiet, gentle tone. "You gave me something precious – I can be myself when I'm with you. Not the Earl of Tsukikage, not the little brother who accepts his burdens uncomplainingly, gladly. Nor any other version the world makes of me. Just... Toshi. You allow me to set aside all masks, all pretence. I've only ever hoped to do the same for you. You have no idea how happy it makes me every time your mask slips just a little, without you even noticing."

"I always thought you wouldn't like the real me," Suzu confessed.

Toshi took a step towards him, raising his hand as if he wanted to touch Suzu, but uncertain, he stopped himself. "There is only you, Suzu. For me, there is no-one else, never has been, never will be. I love your gentle side, and – perhaps even more – I love your ferocity. All that you are, everything that makes you you."

Warmth unlike any suffused Suzu. His cracked, broken heart felt soothed, reinforced, mended with purest gold – so much stronger, so much more precious than before. He grabbed Toshi by the front of his shirt and pulled the man into a kiss. Not a tender one, not gentle or chaste, but almost desperate, trying to convey all the love and gratitude he felt and could not put into words. Toshi's arms encircled him, pulling him closer still. They kissed as if it were the first time, as if it would be the last time. They clung to each other, breathless, unable, unwilling to let go.

"I doubt you'll allow me to take you away from all this here," Toshi said eventually. It wasn't a question.

Suzu shook his head. "You know me." It felt strange and wonderful and so true, saying it out loud made Suzu smile.

"I do. The Singing Dragon's Little Moon."

"They told you that, didn't they? I don't deserve to be held in such high regard when I couldn't even keep them safe."

"It was never about you keeping them safe."

His throat constricted, but not even here, in Toshi's arms, could he allow himself to give in to grief. Perhaps especially not now, not when the temptation to let himself fall into the warmth and comfort of a love he had never thought could be his was so close. He'd never have the strength to pull himself out of it and do what he had to do. No, it wasn't strength he needed but harshness, ruthlessness. He needed his wrath.

"Toshi, this… I need to do this. I need to. But… but afterwards – I mean, when this over and you still… perhaps…" Why was this so difficult? Was it because he had fought so long and hard against his own feelings, or did he still fear being rejected?

"Of course, my love," Toshi whispered into his ear. "I've waited so long for you, I can wait a little longer."

For the first time since the Singing Dragon had burnt down Suzu could almost believe that in the end all would be well.

Smiling, he laid his head against Toshi's shoulder and allowed himself a moment of peace with the man he loved.

Jin was leaning against the wall of the warehouse, his heart pounding uncomfortably in his chest. Brother Askr had always chided him for being too nosy. *Eavesdroppers only end up hearing things they don't want to hear*, the old monk had repeatedly told him. How right he had been. And how stupid of Jin to do it anyway. What had he been hoping for? Jin had thought he had understood that Suzu was not the same boy he had grown up loving – so why had he still been hoping?

It seemed like the Earl had a better understanding of people than Jin would ever have, for he had never noticed Kari putting on an act. For him.

Jin exhaled deeply. A moment ago he had thought that jealousy would eat him alive. Strangely, though it hurt, it hurt a lot, he found that he could finally let go and move on. Perhaps sometimes eavesdropping wasn't so bad.

Suzu emerged from the warehouse, squinting against the bright sunlight. It took him a moment to notice Jin. Squinting turned into scowling. "Have you been standing there the entire time?"

"Yes." Jin saw no point in trying to lie. Suzu regraded him for a long moment, then he shrugged and punched Jin in the arm.

"Well, let's get out of here."

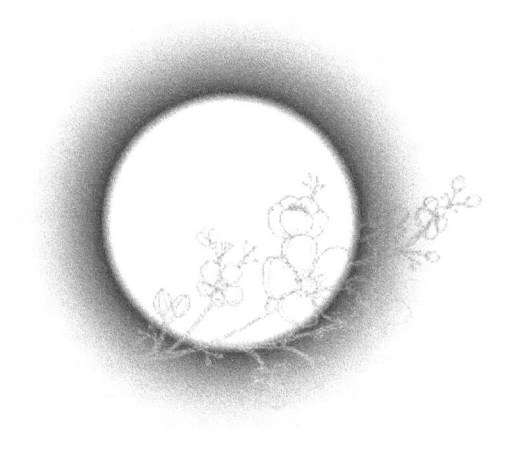

Chapter 33

"Hold still," Yuuko snapped, giving Jin's hair a rather vicious tug. Niall had introduced the woman as the unbeaten mistress of disguise – and Suzu was beginning to believe it as he watched in fascination how she transformed first Niall and now Jin into completely different people.

"Is this really necessary?" Jin whined.

"Yes, we've been over this," Niall snapped back. "We don't know who works for Nobu, and we can't be seen going to that apothecary. Hence – disguises!"

When they had come back from their meeting with Toshi, they had been relieved to learn that Enzo had pulled through and Niall was sleeping the sleep of the just. While devouring the most enormous breakfast Suzu had ever seen, she had informed them that it would take more than a month for Enzo to recover, but at least he was out of the woods. And after they had filled her in on what had transpired the day before, she had immediately sent for her friend Yuuko at the Golden Crane Theatre. Not an hour later the woman had arrived, laden with bags.

"But why can't I come with you?" Suzu groused – and not for the first time. Naloc had promised they wouldn't try to keep him out of this any more. Apparently, however, this particular task was better left to Niall and Jin as they 'had experience in these things'. Whatever that meant.

"Because, my beauty," Yuuko replied, putting the finishing touches to Jin's transformation, "I'd need half a day to make you unrecognisable." With a clever artistic use of paint she had added edges and shadows to Jin's face that hadn't been there before. The optical illusion withstood all but the closest inspection. Even at only a small distance Jin's cheekbones seemed higher and more prominent, his chin weaker, his eyes set deeper. Heavier brows and crow's feet added years to his appearance, his messy hair was hidden beneath a wig of shoulder-length wavy dark brown hair.

"What? Why?" Suzu asked, taken aback. For the millionth time his eyes strayed to Niall in utter fascination of her transformation. The northern style summer dress she wore was padded in just the right places, lending generous curves to her boyish figure. Her hair was bound back into a severe knot, her cheeks rosy and plump, her nose seemed smaller and her lips fuller.

"It's your eyes – you can't hide those unless you wear tinted glasses, and how many people wearing tinted glasses have you ever seen on these streets? They'd invite people to take a closer look at you, which would be a problem. These disguises," Yuuko gestured at Jin and Niall, "they are quick jobs. They won't hold up to scrutiny, so they have to be unassuming, something people don't necessarily look at twice." Although Suzu wasn't fully convinced, he dropped the issue.

"Hello, now those are some delicious curves!"

"Shut it, she-ogre!" Niall snapped, whipping around and aiming a kick at Risa's shin, who had just stepped into the room. Risa nimbly danced out of the way, roaring with laughter.

"Oh, how deceiving looks can be! And here I thought it was a pretty, demure governess – but no, it's Niall, prickly as ever!" Risa laughed, harder than before when Niall flipped her a rude gesture. Naloc, coming in behind her, pushed her aside.

"Excellent work as always, Yuuko-tan."

"Thank you, Murasaki-tana." Yuuko beamed, putting her tools away.

"Well then," Naloc said, turning to Niall and Jin, "you know what to do and how important this is. Oh," he held a letter out for Niall to take, "this just came. Seems the Earl feels the need to insure our success with the apothecary."

"Why? What is it?"

"The old wolf's seal," Naloc grumbled.

"Ah, right. Jin, didn't you say the Earl mentioned invoking the General's name in case Azhar wasn't keen on helping," Niall remarked. "And that makes you so grumpy because...?"

Naloc sniffed, affronted. "The General added a note – about the peacock."

Whereas Risa and Yuuko weren't very successful at hiding their snicker, Jin did a better job, albeit only just. Niall shook her head – it wasn't clear if at Naloc or the others. Suzu rolled his eyes in exasperation. How was it two powerful men like the General and Naloc kept fighting over that poor bird like little children fighting over their favourite toy even with the safety of the realm at stake?

After pocketing the seal, Jin and Niall left; Yuuko, having packed up all her pots of paint and brushes, accepted Naloc's invitation to a cup of tea, and both vanished down the hall. Suzu was left standing in the middle of the room with no idea what to do with himself and full of restless energy.

A nudge to his shoulder made him look around. He hadn't noticed Risa still being here, or perhaps she had come back, he couldn't tell. At this very moment, however, Suzu couldn't have been more happy about seeing the woman, a hand on her hip, the other on the hilt of her sword, head cocked, a crooked grin on her lips. "Well, come on then, I need someone to spar with me who actually knows what he's doing."

They took a rickshaw all the way to Azhar's apothecary. It was the middle of the day – a hot and sunny day – and they had hoped to find the shop empty of customers. They had no such luck. There were several servants, their liveries marking them as such, sent to pick up whatever potions and medications their masters had ordered. And there was a gaggle of young women, browsing the shelves, pointing out certain jars and flasks to each other, giggling and whispering behind their fans. Their impractical and too hot attire betrayed them as daughters of the aristocracy, or at least of the rich and fashionable.

Niall rolled her eyes at Jin. On the way here she had continuously groused about her dress and how it was too warm for the muggy hotness of the day. It wasn't the first time she had ranted about the idiocy of the nobility insisting on northern fashion with its many layers and heavy cloths, so unsuited to the southern climate. No wonder, she sneered, that those high-born ladies were so prone to fainting.

"Ugh, look," she whispered. "I bet they are looking for love potions or salves to increase a man's manhood or some such nonsense."

"Or they are a bunch of young sheltered ladies, here on an errand for one of their grandmas..." Jin trailed off at the look Niall gave him that made it unmistakably clear how unlikely she thought that was, and how much of a buffoon he was for even suggesting it.

Unable to discuss their business with any customers in the shop, they settled into a corner by the door, pretending to be busy inspecting various blends of herbs – and dissuading any new arrivals from entering. Niall jabbed her elbow into Jin's ribs, giving him a meaningful look, when it turned out that the young ladies were indeed shopping for a hopefully unforgettable wedding night. Jin nearly choked on his suppressed laughter.

When at last the last of the giggling blushing girls had left, Jin closed the door after them and threw the lock. Behind his counter, Azhar watched with a frown between his elegant eyebrows, yet he showed no sign of distress, nor did he so much as flinch as they purposefully strode up to the counter.

"How may I help you?" he asked politely.

"You might not recognise us," Niall said, leaning onto the counter. "We've had an interesting chat about the production and selling of a poison commonly known as Dreamless Sleep."

It was impressive, the man's ability of hiding his reaction behind a mask of unconcerned pleasantness, and yet Jin noticed a dark flicker in those golden eyes, the tightening of Azhar's jaw muscles. "I remember. And I remember telling you that I do not sell that particular poison." His voice was cool, professional, almost detached if not for the almost unnoticeable waver.

"Well, that's not quite as I recall it. I seem to remember that not only did you boast about being the only person in this town able to brew it, you also sold a huge quantity of its key ingredient."

"I did not boast, nor did I –"

"Save it," Niall cut him off harshly. "We know you did. You might not be brewing the stuff yourself, but someone is. And you were aware of that the moment you sold them the Deva's Breath, seeing as there is little other use to that blasted weed."

Slowly, fear bled into Azhar's eyes. He drew himself to his full considerable height – ready for flight or fight, it was hard to tell which.

"Lucky for you," Jin drawled, "we're here to present you with an opportunity to redeem yourself."

"And to be clear," Niall added, "no for answer is unacceptable."

Azhar snorted derisively. "Do I look like someone who is easily threatened by the likes of you? I have connections –"

With whom, they never found out. For Azhar abruptly broke off when Niall delicately put something on the polished counter, pushed it gently towards Azhar and lifted her hand to reveal the General's seal. At last the pleasant mask cracked, yielding to an almost panicked expression.

"Funny," Jin said, "so do we. And ours aren't traitors."

"Trai-- what? No, I didn't... I mean... I didn't know," Azhar stammered, flustered.

"Not knowing isn't a very good excuse when you sell rare ingredients that can only be used for deadly poisons, is it?"

Azhar hung his head, shifting uncomfortably from one foot to the other, hugging himself. Jin felt a stab of pity for the man.

How hard it must have been, being one of the very few to find his way into the empire, having to learn a completely new language, a strange new culture, to adjust and integrate into this society, knowing no matter what, you're always going to be an outsider. And how horrible must his life before have been for him to brave the perilous way hardly anyone ever survived, to choose a life away from everyone and everything that was familiar, that was part of who you were. But how could he not have known?

"All right," Azhar relented. "I'll do whatever I must to prove that I'm no traitor. What do you need?"

"A sedative," Niall replied. "Strong enough to knock out even the strongest man within seconds." Relief flickered across the apothecary's face, only to be met with a rather malicious grin on Niall's fox like face. "Imitating – and this is very important, mind you – imitating the typical symptoms shown by those poisoned by Dreamless Sleep – sans the fatality, naturally."

Azhar's mouth hung open in shock and he was slowly shaking his head. "Impossible!" he cried. "Dreamless Sleep causes excruciating pain. It is said to feel as if your skeleton tries to claw its way out of your body."

"So we've heard."

"Then you should know it's the pain that kills you. Can you imagine it? Pain so strong it kills you? Convulsions, rigidity – that is what I'd have to induce. Do you have any idea how risky that is? There is no guarantee there won't be any nasty side effects."

"I'm a doctor," Niall snapped, "of course I know that. But we don't have a choice. It doesn't need to be an exact imitation, hardly anyone has ever seen the effects of Dreamless Sleep first hand anyway. Make it a quick kill – a short convulsion, a momentary rigidity, and then – blessed unconsciousness." But Azhar was still shaking his head. "Look, we'll have people stand by to take care of them as soon as possible and take them to the medical college. We're taking a risk, that's true, but it's still better than having a whole bunch of definitely dead people."

"Making something like that – it needs experimentation, research, a trial run... it would take months just to –"

"You have one and a half weeks."

"O-one an-an-and a –" Azhar sputtered. By now there was none of his former composure left. His mouth opened and closed like a fish's on land, but except for a soft whimper not a single sound escaped him.

"Come now, if anyone can do it, it's you!" Niall declared with an encouraging smile. It didn't do much good, the apothecary looked from her to Jin as if they had lost their minds, and Jin couldn't blame him. "May I remind you," Niall sighed, "that you don't have a choice?" She tapped the General's seal, still lying on the counter top. "This is your chance for redemption. So I suggest, you close your shop for the next ten days and get to work." Defeated, Azhar leaned against the counter, his hands flat on the polished top. He looked close to tears but he nodded his agreement. "Don't worry," Niall added more gently, "the General has arranged for some very competent and trustworthy assistants to help you. They will be here first thing tomorrow morning."

Azhar didn't seem cheered by the promise of competent help, he merely nodded, his eyes downcast. Niall grunted, satisfied, picked up the General's seal and headed for the door without looking back. Jin felt bad for the man.

"Hey," he said softly, waiting till Azhar had lifted his head to look at him with glittering golden eyes. "It'll be fine. After all – you are the best apothecary in town, if not in the entire empire, right? And in a few days, all will be back to normal." Jin wasn't sure if he was trying to convince Azhar or himself, his burst of optimism sounded forced even to his own ears. But it did earn him a small, wobbly smile from Azhar.

"Right," the man agreed and took a deep, steadying breath.

Outside, Niall had already flagged down a rickshaw and was unrestrainedly flirting with the strapping young man pulling it. His eyes were drinking in Niall's voluptuous – and very fake – curves. When Jin joined them, the boy's face dropped in disappointment. As they pulled out into the street, Jin nodded his head questioningly at the back of the rickshaw driver. Niall just shrugged.

"I didn't know there were going to be people standing by, ready to take the poisoned ones to the medical college, or that there were any assistants for Azhar," Jin whispered.

"Well, there better be, no matter how good Azhar might be, we can't just give people some untested drug and leave them to fend for themselves. As for the assistants – the General said so in the note he sent Naloc – I think they are supposed to keep an eye on the apothecary as much as help him."

"Naloc didn't mention that."

"Probably because as soon as he had read it, he burnt it and started grumbling something like, 'That blasted old bastard, thinking he can order me around,'" Niall replied in a terribly bad imitation of Naloc that made Jin laugh.

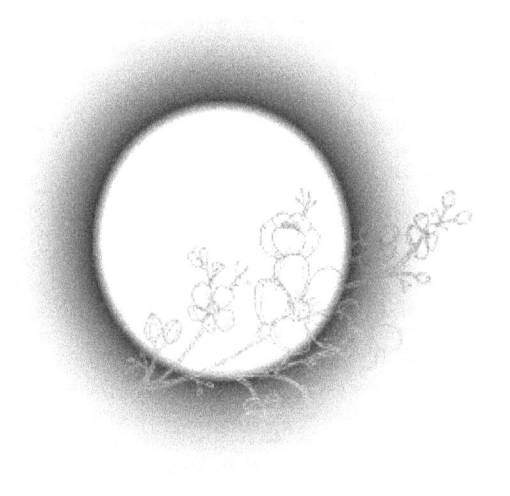

Chapter 34

It was sweltering. After an intensive sparring session during which Risa had taught Suzu almost all of her dirty tricks, they were lounging on the verandah, eating shaved ice. Suzu had peeled off the sweat-soaked top of his jinbei, as Risa had the top half of her yukata, only to keep scratching irritatedly at the bindings around her chest.

"Ugh, it's sticky, and it's tight, and it itches," she complained.

"You know, you don't have to torture yourself for my sake. If you want to take it off, go ahead."

Risa burst out laughing. "What? And get told off for gross indecency again? No thanks."

"Oh? You have experience with that?"

Risa flicked a piece of ice at Suzu. "You know your biggest advantage?" she said, suddenly changing the topic. Suzu had noticed she had a habit of jumping from one topic to the next. "People underestimate you. They look at you, and see all this grace and impossible beauty, and just assume you are as fragile as a flower. It's beyond their imagination that you're a demon with a sword."

Suzu snorted. "Demon? That's a bit of an exaggeration, don't you think?"

"Nope."

They fell into a companionable silence, and for the first time in days Suzu's mind was pleasantly blank, anchored in the moment. For the first time in days, he felt relaxed. Risa, however, wasn't one to enjoy silence for long. With a startling suddenness, she turned her whole body towards Suzu. "I mean, even I can appreciate it – in a purely aesthetic sense, you know? I absolutely do get why people like to ogle you – or want to jump your bones. What I'm saying is – I don't usually care... or even notice a man's looks, right? But I can appreciate your... beauty, I guess."

"In an aesthetic way."

"Exactly." Risa grinned broadly.

"All right, I get it, it's the same for me with women."

"Jin isn't like that," Risa commented, matter-of-factly.

"Oh, I know."

"Do tell."

Suzu rolled onto his side, propping his head in his hand. Risa's warm dark brown eyes glittered with mischief as she waited for him to provide her with stories of Jin's escapades she had not known before. And so he told her about Saya, the girl from the village who they had grown up with, the girl, who had spitefully condemned him. He told Risa how he had thought Saya to be his friend when they were little, only to soon realise it was only Jin she liked. How childish affection had grown into something a little more serious by the time they were youths. And how Jin, once so oblivious to Saya's fondness, had basked in her attention, had flirted outrageously with her.

"Wait! He did what?" Risa interrupted. "That doesn't sound like Jin at all. He flirted with that girl, *although* he had you?" Suzu confirmed with a nod. "What the hell? The way he kept talking about you – annoying us all to death, more like– you would've believed his entire world had consisted only of you! And now you tell me he was making eyes at some hussy from the village?"

Laughing at Risa's outrage, Suzu sat up, and shook his head. "Strange, how the Jin I grew up with and the Jin you know seem like two different people sometimes, isn't it? The Jin I knew was proud, headstrong, he didn't like to be told what to do, he never doubted, never hesitated. And he very much enjoyed being the centre of attention."

"I'm not saying he isn't a flirt – because he is. But everyone always knew that he was just... you know... trying to find some distraction.... I got to say, he does have a type," Risa said with a pointed look at Suzu, which he chose to ignore. "So, what happened with the home wrecker?"

There it was again. How often had he recounted the events of five years ago in the last couple of weeks? Risa didn't seem to have heard the story yet, though. He assumed he could as well tell it once more.

So Suzu told her everything. The accusations, Saya's horrible lies. The verdict. The banishment. Being beaten and shunned. About wandering aimlessly, delirious, only propelled onwards by force of will and anger.

"That bitch!" Risa exclaimed. "All right, I get it, Nobu is just plain evil, I don't think anyone will argue that at this point. But that girl! Being jealous is one thing. Being mean to the competition, perhaps even a little intrigue – but that! That is a level of cruelty that makes me speechless. Which doesn't happen often. There's just such a thing as taking it too far." Suzu shrugged. He had learned that people like Nobu and Saya knew no 'too far' when it came to achieving their goals. "Hey, you didn't believe any of what she said, did you?"

"Sometimes," Suzu admitted with a sigh. And before Risa could protest, he added, "Look, the tale Nobu spun – it was very convincing. He even presented a letter in Jin's handwriting that corroborated everything that was being said. And as much as I didn't want to believe any of it, the fact remained that he had drugged me, left me helpless, and abandoned me. I know the truth now, but for the last five years..." he trailed off. Risa looked thoughtful, scowling at a spot on the hardwood floor they sat on. She also looked ready to stab someone. Suzu knew the feeling, he had had it for the last five years, every single time something had reminded him of Jin or the past. For a short glorious moment he had thought the matter resolved, the anger abated – and then Nobu had set Suzu's world ablaze anew. Now, his fury was a barely controlled inferno, a leashed wild beast, that would consume him, too, if he wasn't careful.

"Well," Risa said eventually. "I just want you to know, that Jin – and everyone here will tell you the same – is head over heels for you and only you. He may have found consolation in other beds, but trust me, not one of 'em ever stood a chance against you."

"Only I am not who Jin loves, who he has missed and searched for for five years. I do feel sorry for him, but I can't go back to being someone who never existed in the first place."

"I see. And the Earl?"

Toshi. Their last meeting had been a revelation, a shock, relief – and a permission. Suzu smiled tentatively. Admitting it to himself, in the quietness of his mind, was one thing, to give voice to his feelings, however, sent an anxious prickle down his spine. Nevertheless. "Toshi sees me as I am and loves who I am. And... and I love him."

Risa nodded as if she had already expected this answer. "The damn Earl of fucking Tsukikage, though," she exclaimed, and Suzu burst out laughing. He hadn't laughed like this, carefree, in too long a time. It wouldn't last, but for just a little while at least, Suzu allowed himself to forget the pain, the anger, the grief.

Jin could hardly wait to wash off the itching make-up; looking at Niall, he was also worried his friend might end up with a heatstroke in all that padding. They entered as they had left – through a concealed door at the back of the estate – and found Suzu and Risa lying spread-eagled on the verandah. A pitcher of water, cups, and empty glassware, with the remains of colourful syrup still clinging to the bottom, littering the space around them. The view of Suzu's naked torso made Jin miss a step. Snickering, Niall slapped him on the back hard enough to make him stumble forward.

"How come we have to run through half the town in this heat, while you two are lazy as cats," Niall complained, good-humouredly. She flopped down between Suzu and Risa and hopefully grabbed the nearest piece of glassware – only to put it back down with a disappointed huff.

"We weren't lazy," Risa protested, sitting up. "We were enjoying a well-earned rest. While chatting about you, Jin, my little puppy," she added with grin. Jin hated it when she called him a puppy. When Niall had first brought him here and he had met Risa, she had thought he looked like a kicked puppy. The unfortunate pet name had stuck, but luckily never really caught on with the others.

Although he wasn't in the mood for getting teased by Risa, Jin sat down and poured himself a glass of water.

"I take it, it was a very boring conversation," he grumbled.

"Not at all, not at all. I certainly got a much clearer picture of our friend the shady monk – rotten from the start. Learned a few interesting things about you, puppy, as well. For example that you should be more careful who you flirt with." Jin rolled his eyes. Niall, however, gave him one of her 'I keep telling you so' looks. If Suzu had told Risa about Saya, he couldn't argue. He knew now that he had been stupid, arrogant, and prideful. Not for one second had he thought about Suzu's feelings, or how Saya would react if she found out he had never regarded her as more than a friend. "You know," Risa continued, "I get why Suzu is Nobu's sworn enemy. But I don't get – and I still haven't gotten an answer – why this... whatshisname... you know, the big ugly fellow..." Risa gestured wildly in the air as if that might conjure up an image of the man.

"Steren," Suzu provided helpfully.

"That one! Why's he going after Beautiful like this? Come on, tell me, what did you do to him? Jin, do you know?"

Jin thought about it seriously for a moment, and Risa was right. Steren had been the village bully practically since birth, but now that he thought about it, Jin noticed Steren's behaviour towards them, especially towards Suzu, had always been rather... strange. Always? No, it hadn't been always.

"I have honestly no idea. He was a bully, he was mean to everyone. He was taller and older – all the kids, in the village and in the temple, were scared of him and his cronies. And then, all of a sudden," Jin snapped his fingers for emphasis, "he stopped. I mean, he was still glaring and growling, and occasionally shoving, but by and large he left us alone." Jin's brows furrowed as he remembered something else. "He also started to go out of his way to avoid Suzu and me... saw him glaring daggers at Suzu all the time, though. Why...? Hmm... now that you mention it..."

Slowly, Jin turned to look at Suzu, as did the other two. Suzu, for his part, was oddly quiet and indifferent to their conversation, and much more interested in the wooden beam just off to Jin's side. He didn't react, despite three pairs of eyes boring into him. Not even when Niall asked him if he had anything to add. Not until Risa poked him in the ribs – hard.

"Ouch, all right!" he cried, swatting Risa's hand away. "Perhaps... well... I might, possibly, have... you know... taught him a lesson, so to speak. Made it clear to him that... well, he ought to stop bullying us – or any of the other kids." Suzu fell silent, a faint blush colouring his cheeks at the incredulous looks the others gave him. Neither Risa nor Niall, however, had any idea just how mind-boggling this admission was, they hadn't been there, hadn't known Suzu as Jin had known him, nor... "You were like... ten!" Jin squeaked. But Suzu merely shrugged.

For the length of two heartbeats all was quiet, then Risa burst out laughing so hard, tears welled up in her eyes. Niall, too, was laughing, but it was hard to tell if she was laughing with Risa or at Jin's befuddled expression.

Still laughing and wiping the tears from her eyes, Risa threw an arm around Suzu's shoulders. "Honestly, I love this guy. He's like the little brother I never wanted."

After Jin and Niall had reported back to Naloc, and Niall had checked in on her patient, they began their convoluted track back home. With potential enemies theoretically lurking around every corner, they moved along secret passages, obscure little alleys, through clandestine doorways, and across people's properties who pointedly pretended not to see them. Despite this route taking them twice as long in the stifling heat of the late afternoon Suzu found himself enjoying it.

When they at last stopped in front of a familiar looking wall, Suzu had lost all orientation. There was a small arch low in the wall to allow one of the many rivulets that ran like veins through Kigetsu to pass through. Niall pressed a stone, smaller than the others, right next to the arch. There came a loud click, and a section of the wall swung open at her touch. It opened right unto Jin's and Niall's property.

"This is amazing," Suzu marvelled appreciatively, watching Jin push the hidden door closed. With another loud click the wall was whole once more, seamlessly fitting together.

As intriguing as it was, and as much as Suzu would have liked to take a closer look at the mechanism, a bath and clean clothes held more allure. Looking at Jin, Suzu could tell the young man felt the same. The thick make-up had begun to melt and mingle with his sweat, streaking his face and neck with dirt. His usually messy hair lay flat, finally defeated by the heat and humidity. Suzu didn't even want to know what Niall was going through in all those layers of fabric and padding.

When Suzu came back into the yard, long tresses of wet hair soaking the back of his fresh top, the other two were already sitting beneath the big old tree.

Niall had promised supper and she had more than lived up to it, serving them a dish of grilled vegetables, seasoned with fresh herbs and only a pinch of spices, rice, and cold tea.

But it was still sweltering, the air humid and close, the charged atmosphere made Suzu's nerve endings tingle. A sudden deep rumble they felt vibrating through their bodies, and the first spatter of rain put a quick and early end to their little gathering. They had just enough time to gather all the dishes, when suddenly the wind picked up and the rain started in earnest. Jin slammed the door shut on the howling wind, then flew across the room, with a lot of clattering and swearing, to close the half open shutters on the windows. The sudden darkness was cut through by a flash of lightning that made Suzu jump. He hunkered down, closed his eyes, and covered his ears. The roar of thunder followed moments later – still far away. Taking a deep breath, Suzu opened his eyes. A light bloomed in the darkness; Jin had lit the oil lamp. Warm, golden light shone through the cracks in the wooden screen that divided the room. Suzu pushed himself to his feet and followed the light, drawn to it like a moth.

"Are you all right?" Jin asked as Suzu stepped around the screen. "Are you... I mean, do you still..."

"I'm fine," Suzu claimed – only to have it proven a lie when he flinched hard at another clap of thunder. Closer now. The look Jin gave him, the warmth in his dark eyes, the small indulgent smile, it was so achingly familiar, so strangely calming.

Suzu plopped down on his futon, legs crossed, and looked straight at Jin. He was determined to simply ignore the storm raging outside, and so he racked his brain for a conversational topic. Anything. The storm was laughing at him, wind howling and shaking the small house, rain so heavy it pelted the roof like stones.

"So why –" A deafening roar of thunder interrupted him. Suzu clenched his teeth, clawed his fingers into the thin duvet. Then he continued stubbornly, "Why are you working for Naloc? Or rather – why are you trusting him so much?"

For a long moment Jin just looked at him blankly. He clearly hadn't expected that question. "I guess, because if not for him and Niall I would be dead by now."

Suzu frowned. "Explain."

"Ah, guess with everything that has happened lately and... our past, I haven't told you what happened to me those last five years," Jin said, a little uncomfortable and perhaps a little sheepishly. "So, when I left the temple it was late spring, remember? So while on the road it was no problem making camp outside, and when I first came to town I even found a tiny room to rent with the money Nobu had given me. Gods, I really thought luck would always be on my side, that it would all be so easy." Jin chuckled ruefully and bitter. "Managed to get myself an apprenticeship with a blacksmith, but turned out I don't have what it takes for the job. Took me just one lousy month to get kicked out. But I didn't have enough money to find a new apprenticeship, and I was running late on rent as it was, so I took on whatever jobs I could find each day. The money I made was hardly enough to keep me fed, let alone pay my rent. Eventually I ate only every other day, but because of the hunger I made more and more mistakes, so I earned less and less, and eventually I ended up on the streets. Of course by then, summer was over and the weather had taken a nasty turn. So there I was: no money, no roof to sleep under, no food, not even any warm clothes." Jin fell quiet. His eyes had taken on a faraway look as if he could see into the past. "To be honest, I don't remember much about those days, they are all kind of blurry. I know I was ill and half frozen, starving… delirious. This is the one thing I'll never forget, though: Niall's face, her blue eyes intent on me – I was so damn sure she was a reaper, who had come to collect my soul. I was very confused when I woke up in a bed and there were the same blue eyes staring at me." This time Jin's chuckle was less bitter, yet it still had a self-deprecating edge that was painful to hear. In the last five years Suzu, in his blind misguided rage, had often imagined Jin leading a life of joyful debauchery, not a care in the world, not wasting a single thought on the boy he had thrown away. How wrong he had been, about so many things.

"Then isn't it Niall rather than Naloc you owe your life to?" Suzu asked, prodding Jin to continue.

"True. And I can't tell you just how grateful I am to her. But it was Naloc who gave me a home, a place to belong to, a name – and he's never given up on me. He got me one apprenticeship after the other, even though I failed every single one of them. He even tried apprenticing me himself, but… you know my problems with reading and writing… Well, it's just… I'm simply not good at anything or for anything, eventually I always mess up. But Naloc, he kept on trying and he didn't kick me out. He pays me a wage, gives me all sorts of jobs – he even gave me this house… well, he gave it to Issei and me – ah, Issei is my best friend, he's out of town for a while though."

Suzu listened and watched Jin belittle himself with a rueful smile on his lips, and felt the anger rise with every word the other boy spoke. It was painful to see the once wild and confident boy he had grown up with so small. He was like a proud tiger caged and beaten into compliance. Suzu couldn't take it anymore. Furious, he slammed his fist down on the floor, startling Jin into silence. "Is that really what you think?" Suzu growled. "That you are no good?"

"I –"

"The Jin I knew would have never just rolled over and let himself be disregarded. You've always had problems reading and writing, but that has never stopped you before. There are tons of jobs out there that don't require you to write. And yes, well, we both know you're not always paying attention to what you are doing – but I have seen how you focus on things you are interested in. If anything, the Jin I know is persistent, tenacious. He would never just hang his head in defeat and follow orders like an obedient dog."

Once upon a time, Jin had been like the sun in Suzu's eyes: brightly burning, full of energy, full of life. From the moment he had met him, Suzu had wanted to be engulfed in this light forever, to a point at which he had been willing to live behind a mask for the rest of his life. The young man in front of him now was nothing like that. He was colourless, washed-out, a poor imitation. It made Suzu so angry he wanted to punch Jin in the face, despite the voice in his head telling him that he had no business getting angry, Jin was nothing to him anymore, he had long since banished the boy from his heart, his life. And yet. If he shook him hard enough, would some broken pieces fit back together?

Jin opened his mouth, but before he could speak, Suzu leaned leaned forwards, glowering so ferociously Jin froze like a rabbit before a snake. "You listen to me now, idiot," Suzu hissed. "Just because you haven't found what you're good at yet doesn't mean you are no good for anything."

"Tell that to my former masters," Jin grumbled, and despite how quietly he said it, there was a bite in his voice that made Suzu hope there was still some defiance in him.

"What was that?" Suzu asked deliberately.

Jin's head snapped up. Anger flashed in the depth of his black eyes. *There he is*, Suzu thought, hiding a smile. "It's just that..." Jin broke off, took a deep breath, reigning the anger in. "From day one they would yell at me, scold me for being too slow, grumble about having to show me how to do things again and again. Then I finally make a mistake big enough so they can sack me, and that's it. Every single time."

Suzu frowned. "And how long did your longest apprenticeship last?"

"One month," Jin said, deflating visibly.

For Suzu, however, a final piece fell into line. There had been enough tradesmen and merchants amongst his customers that he knew about their rather elaborate network of relations and about how they treated their apprentices. It seldom happened that apprentices were mistreated, for the most part they were cherished and well taken care of. Apprentices were usually carefully selected, if not for their connections than for their talent, which was why most masters tested them before accepting them. The smith Jin had found apprenticeship with must have been in need of an apprentice without many to choose from, or they had tried to do some good, giving a poor country boy a chance. The other ones, the ones Naloc had found for him – well, those were probably another matter.

"Jin," Suzu said, "it's possible that you simply picked the wrong professions for you. Normally they test you to see if you have what it takes – the masters in this town are very picky, you know. So... How shall I put it... I guess, Naloc's influence got you threw the door. But... the problem is, most of the masters and merchants have long standing arrangements with others, it's why it is so damn difficult to find someone to take you on if you don't have the right connections. Those arrangements – it's not just a question of money and standing, but honour. They probably thought they couldn't say no to Naloc, but they could just make sure to have an excuse to get rid of you as quickly as possible."

Jin mulled this over, not looking convinced. No wonder, Suzu could see now how failure after apparent failure had eroded Jin's confidence. Naloc should have known this would happen. Had he done it on purpose? Was this how the man 'created' people loyal to him? By making sure they had nowhere else to go? Suzu gave himself a mental slap. For all he knew Naloc had been sincere and had not seen his mistake. Just because he couldn't find it in him to like the man, didn't mean Naloc was a villain.

When he saw Jin fighting some inner struggle that would probably only drag him further down the spiral of self-deprecation, Suzu reached out and took Jin's hand. "What I'm saying is they demanded far too much from you, knowing you wouldn't be able to do it. You never got a chance to find out what you are good at."

"It doesn't matter," Jin argued. "I make mistakes all the time. I always mess up."

"Because you're waiting for it to happen, you idiot! You expect to screw up and you fixate on it – until it happens. It's like a self-fulfilling prophecy." He could see it in Jin's eyes, the moment he realised Suzu might be right. It wouldn't miraculously turn Jin back into the self-reliant, confident boy he used to be, but it might be a start. "Don't just give up on yourself, Jin, it doesn't suit you."

And there, at last, was the smile Suzu had missed. It came slowly, transforming Jin's entire being, turning his dark eyes into glittering pools, a smile that made the young man glow from within. "Thank you," Jin whispered.

Suzu replied with a smile of his own and a last squeeze of Jin's hand, before he let go, lay down on his futon, and closed his eyes. He heard a soft rustle, then the lamp went out. The sound of Jin settling down was followed by silence. The storm had blown out without Suzu noticing.

Chapter 35

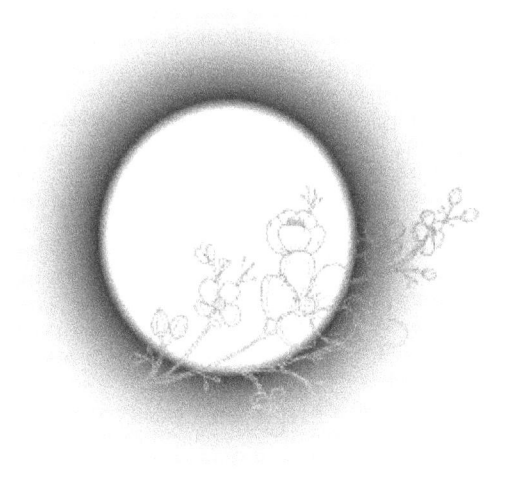

The next morning the only sign there ever had been a storm was a freshness in the air that had been missing the days before. The brook between the houses carried more water, and here and there a flower lay broken, mercilessly ripped out by the wind or trampled by the heavy rain.

When Suzu emerged from the house he found Jin and Niall already in what seemed to be a rather heated debate.

"I just don't think it's a good idea," Jin argued.

Niall's counterargument, however, never came, for at this moment she noticed Suzu and chose to remain silent. Annoyed Suzu demanded, "What's not a good idea?"

"Going out into the streets instead of sneaking through gardens and back alleys," Niall replied too quickly and too readily. "But I have patients to visit, so what am I supposed to do, right?" Suzu wasn't convinced this was the truth – or at least not the sole reason for their debate, but he let it go. Niall, although she hadn't taken over her father's surgery yet, had a flock of patients who wouldn't accept any other physician. She wasn't going to neglect them only because there was a power-hungry psychopath out there who might or might not have his eyes on them. So there must have been a kernel of truth in it at least.

"She's right," Suzu relented. "We can't hide and hope the storm passes. That way we're only doing what Nobu wants us to do. Come on, we are warned and vigilant – and not stupid enough to go out alone." He directed the latter part at Niall, who had the grace to look rueful.

"Fine," Jin snapped.

Hours later Suzu regretted having chosen Niall's side. It was a tense affair, making their way from one patient to the next, always aware of every single person out in the streets, every movement down a dark alley, every rustle behind a bush. Standing watch outside the patients' homes until Niall was done and ready to go to the next one.

After the third one Suzu was disoriented by the nonsensical streets and alleys of Kigetsu, he had no idea if they were closer to the river or closer to home – or perhaps closer to the warehouses and workshops on the other side of the borough. The sun relentlessly burnt down on them, every last puddle, every last drop of water the rain had brought the night before evaporated in a short time. Suzu felt sore-footed and parched.

When they passed a flower shop, the sight of a familiar figure made Suzu stop in his tracks. A lanky boy, tall for his age, dirt on his clothes and holding a small flower arrangement in his hands, stood in front of the shop. For a moment they just stared at each other.

"Miharu," Suzu gasped, breathless. The flower arrangement dropped to the ground, porcelain shattered, flower petals scattered. And then he was there, arms locked tight around Suzu's neck, sobs racking the boy's body, tears soaking Suzu's shirt where he pressed his face into Suzu's shoulder. It was almost impossible for Suzu to draw air into his lungs through the tightness in his chest. With Herculean effort he fought off the tears, and slowly, mechanically lifted his arms and put them around Miharu.

The younger boy had been the only one beside Suzu who had not been at the Singing Dragon the day it burnt. That very morning he had moved out to live and apprentice with Aiyana, the *kadoka* who had made all of the Singing Dragon's flower arrangements. It was a small mercy that this gentle, kind-hearted, sensitive boy had been spared the horror.

Miharu clung to him like a drowning man. "Hush, it's all right. I'm here," Suzu soothed, his voice breaking.

It took a long time for Miharu to calm down and let go of Suzu, sniffling, wiping his reddened eyes. His gaze drifted past Suzu to where Jin and Niall stood sentinel over them, and blushed furiously that they had witnessed his tearful display. Then he suddenly grabbed Suzu's arm and tried to pull him towards the shop. Mistress Aiyana stood in the door, smiling gently, her eyes filled with sadness.

"Suzu, thank the gods," she said. "We didn't know where you were, if you were hurt. The boys were sick with worry."

"The boys?"

Aiyana nodded. "Yes. Come, Akito will be so relieved to see you."

"Akito? You know where he is?"

"He's here. He's staying with Miharu and me."

"How is he?" Suzu demanded, remembering the wounds on the boy's face and hands.

"He was badly burnt and had a high fever for days. Oh, but this lady," Aiyana indicated Niall, who gently smiled back, "she came and treated him, showed us what to do, and he got better." Suzu, taken aback, looked at Niall. He hadn't known. She hadn't said a word. Suzu tried to say something, anything, but there were no words to express how grateful he was. Ryū, Rani, Mother, all the others that couldn't be saved, were lost forever. Fragments were all that was left of his family now, every little piece of it so much more precious for it. Words would never be able to encompass all the emotions inside Suzu's perilously mended heart. Niall seemed to understand, however, smiling, giving his hand a quick gentle squeeze.

But then Miharu started to pull at him again. "Wait. Miharu, where are we going?"

"To see Akito, of course," Aiyana said in Miharu's stead.

Suzu dug his heels in and tried to pull free of the boy's grasp. It was an automatic, unconscious reaction, but when Miharu looked back at him, eyes huge, Suzu found he couldn't breathe. The edges of his vision were beginning to grow fuzzy and dark. He shook his head vehemently. "I can't," Suzu whispered breathlessly.

Miharu's eyes pleaded with him. Seeing the hurt and the confusion on the boy's face felt like a dagger being driven into Suzu's heart, but he couldn't stop himself from taking a step backwards.

"I... I can't." He'd break. He'd shatter once and for all beyond repair. There was no way his resolve, the walls he had built around his heart and soul, holding the grief and pain at bay like a dam, would not crumble, faced with what he had lost. And the knowledge that he was the cause of it. He had brought this on them, he had caused all this pain, this misery, this death. They suffered because of him. He couldn't face them – not yet, not before he had fulfilled his promise and avenged them. Suzu flinched when his back hit something warm and solid. Jin stood behind him, blocking his retreat.

"It's all right," Niall said in this soothing, calm voice she used with her patients. "Calm down, Suzu, everything is all right. Breathe. Now listen, just go with the lad, only for a moment. Those boys, they are scared and so terribly worried about you, just let him see you are all right, hmm?"

Suzu shook his head again. Miharu was still standing in the entrance to the shop with Mistress Aiyana, hugging himself, tears streaming down his cheeks. He was the very picture of misery. It twisted the dagger in Suzu's heart. Drawing one shallow breath after the other Suzu tried to force his lungs to work, but the air seemed to have not enough oxygen.

"They need you," Niall continued mercilessly. Suzu couldn't understand why she was so cruel, why she couldn't see what it cost him. Perhaps she didn't care. "Just for a moment."

"I can't," Suzu repeated more forcefully.

"You can! And I will drag you in there myself if I have to." There was no more patience, no more soothing gentleness in Niall's voice, only cold authority. Suzu could see she would not relent and let him go, and he doubted Jin would either, not if Niall had ordered it. Running away did not seem an option either unless he wanted to sleep in the streets from now on.

Suzu pressed the heels of his hands into his eyes and concentrated on fortifying his walls. He couldn't falter now. Repeating his own mantra of *Not yet, not yet*, Suzu took a deliberate breath. This time, his lungs cooperated, if only from being starved of air. He let Niall's harsh sternness fuel his anger and cloaked himself in it. When he opened his eyes at last, he glared at Niall, perversely satisfied when she involuntarily shied away from him. Then he tore free from Jin's hold and went to Miharu.

"I'm sorry," he whispered, hugging the boy. This time he followed him inside.

A staircase in the back of the shop led to the rooms above. Upstairs, at the end of the hall was the room Miharu now shared with Akito. Miharu hurried ahead.

It was futile, trying to keep control over the trembling in his body, but Suzu nevertheless willed himself to enter the room.

"I told you this was a bad idea," Jin groaned, leaning against the wall of the flower shop, a hand over his eyes. There was the dull pressure between his brows that so often preceded a headache.

"It's not," Niall countered. "He's too focussed on revenge. I thought the Earl would do something against it, but…"

Jin shook his head. "Let me tell you this: I might not know him as I once thought I did, but I do know one thing – there's not a single person in this world more stubborn than Suzu. You won't stop him. And don't try telling him how he's supposed to grieve."

Niall sighed and leaned back against the wall beside him. "Fine. But what about those boys? Hmm? They kept asking me about him. They need to see him. All of those who are left, but especially Akito and Miharu. They are still children. You have no idea what Suzu means to all of them – I think not even Suzu knows."

Jin hung his head and exhaled. Niall was right – as usual. It didn't mean this would go according to her plan, Suzu was unpredictable. Who could tell how he was going to react to seeing the boys now, their need for him to be there, Akito's injuries, a constant reminder of all that was lost. Did Niall think Suzu was on some kind of suicide mission and meeting Akito and Miharu would remind him why he had to live? But that wasn't the Suzu he had gotten to know in the last couple of weeks. He wouldn't just throw his life away. And he did know there was still enough reason for him to live.

The image of Suzu and the Earl came unbidden and with too much bitterness. He had no right to feel jealous and yet there was a tiny voice inside his head that said, *It should be me*. The self-disgust that flooded him at that unworthy thought left a foul taste in Jin's mouth.

Suddenly, Niall's face was right in front of him, so close, they were almost rubbing noses. She was squinting at him as if she would like to dissect him, peel away skin and bone to see what lay beneath.

"What?" Jin snapped defensively.

"You're still in love with him, aren't you?"

"I don't even know him."

"Pish-posh!" Niall dismissed. "Name one person who's exactly the same as they were as a child. It's called development."

"You don't get it, the Suzu I knew – or rather Kari – he was this sweet, gentle thing, he hardly ever got angry, and certainly not as devastatingly as he does now."

"And who says he isn't sweet and gentle now?" Niall countered. "All right, perhaps not with you, but what about those boys up there?" She gestured at the rooms above them. "Let me tell you this, as someone, who is old enough to look back on her younger years and realise how stupid she was then: When teenagers stop being all over the place and know themselves – the who and what they are – the apocalypse is nigh!"

Jin snorted and rolled his eyes at his friend. It didn't change the fact that Suzu had not felt that he could be himself with Jin, that he had thought he had to hide a part himself, regulate himself, make himself smaller. Nor did it change the fact that Jin knew it was the fault of his own neediness, his shortcomings – and his selfishness. And regardless of it all, it didn't change the simple fact that sometimes people grew apart.

"You haven't answered my question yet. Are you still in love with him?" Niall pestered him.

"What does it matter? He and the gods damned Earl are head over heels for each other. As soon as this is all over, Suzu will be gone anyway."

"By Mei Mei's tits, stop being so dramatic and self-pitying. no-one says the two of you can't be friends. Isn't that better than losing him again?"

"Friends," Jin repeated the word as if it felt strange on his tongue. He thought about last night, how angry Suzu had gotten on Jin's behalf. About how easily they had fallen back into an age old routine of Jin keeping Suzu's mind off the storm, raging outside. Last night, for the first time since they had run into one another again, they had felt comfortable with each other. Perhaps there really was a chance for the fragile, wary equilibrium between them to blossom into friendship.

Satisfied with having driven her point home, Niall reclaimed her spot next to Jin, leaning back against the cool wall, a complacent smile on her lips.

"Suzu," Akito said, his voice breathless and raspy, completely void of its usual exuberance. Suzu stood frozen in the door and fought to gain control over the barrage of emotions. He shouldn't be here, not now, but the last thing he wanted was to hurt the boys any more than they already had been. The sight of Akito, however, nearly undid him. He wanted to scream, to cry, to rage, to tear apart the whole damned town until he found Nobu, until he could tear out the monk's throat with his bare hands. Instead, he took a deep breath and went to kneel beside the boy.

Akito immediately reached for Suzu's hand and squeezed it tightly as if reassuring himself Suzu was really there. The boy's left side was almost entirely covered in bandages, from his head, down the side of his face, his arm, his hand. He caught Suzu staring and tried to smile, but it turned into a pained grimace. "It's not as bad as it looks," he said. "That nice doctor says it's healing really well... only... the scars." Akito's voice broke on the word.

"That's of no matter," Suzu hurried to reassure the boy. "What's important is that you heal – and that you're alive!"

"Suzu, where were you?" the boy asked. "We couldn't find you. The doctor, she said... she promised you were all right, but –"

"I'm fine, everything is all right. I'm staying with an old friend."

"Can't you stay with us?"

Confronted with the boys' pleading, Suzu wavered, if only for a moment. They were all that was left of his family, and they needed him. But he had a promise to keep. He had to make this right, or nothing would ever be right again. If he stayed with them, he didn't think he could do it. And it would be too dangerous for them to be around him. So Suzu shook his head.

Before they could argue he added, "Not yet. There's something I have to do. It's not safe for you to be near me at the moment."

"Why? We are always safe with you," Akito objected vehemently, and Miharu nodded his head along in agreement with his friend.

A bitter laugh tore itself from Suzu's throat. *We are always safe with you* – he had told Nobu, that he wouldn't fall for it, that he wouldn't end up blaming himself for what Nobu did, but wasn't it true? If not for him, Nobu would have never had a reason to hurt any of them. Suzu pressed the heels of his hands into his eyes.

"Suzu?"

Gods, if it hadn't been for him... No! Nobu had done this – and Nobu would pay for it! Ah, there it was, roaring awake, glorious in its all-consuming intensity: the monster that kept him awake at night more than the pain and the grief, the monster that kept him going, that would never stop until it had what it wanted. And Nobu had to die, he had a debt to pay that could only be paid in blood. Suzu would be the one to collect the payment, he had to, it was the only way to atone for his failure, for bringing death and misery to the people who loved him.

"I'm sorry." Suzu stood up abruptly. For a moment the room spun. He couldn't stay here; he should never have come. "I have to go. I'm sorry."

"When will you come back?"" Akito enquired anxiously.

"I... I don't know." Soon. Never. He couldn't tell them. Didn't want to make them worry, didn't want to make promises he might not be able to keep. "There's something I have to do, something important and... I won't be able to see you until it is done. Sorry. I..."

He turned and fled the room. Neither Akito calling after him nor Aiyana's questioning look could stop him. He broke out into the street as if he broke the surface of water, gasping for breath and grasping for a lifeline. He didn't stop. Someone was calling his name. He didn't stop. Not until there was enough distance between him and the remnants of his family.

In a small side alley Suzu finally stopped, hands on his knees, taking deep gulps of air. There was no way to tell which one was worse at the moment: the rage or the pain. It felt like being agonizingly slowly torn apart, layer after layer after layer being peeled away.

A familiar presence stood behind him, blocking the entrance of the alley. Jin.

"Niall?" Suzu asked; he didn't think he could face her right now and not lash out.

"Seeing to her patient. Are you... all right?"

"Yes, just give me a moment."

And so Jin, like a silent sentinel, kept watch over him, shielding Suzu from curious glances. He didn't say a word, didn't pry, didn't try to lighten the mood, didn't try to apologise. And Suzu was grateful for that.

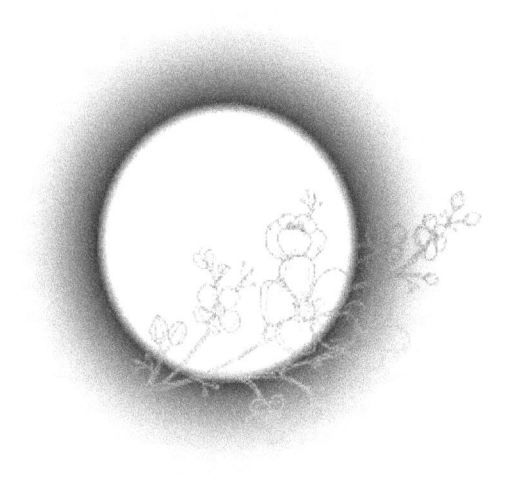

Chapter 36

The wait was the worst of it. Idly spending their days as if they had not a worry in the world. But there wasn't anything else for them to do other than wait for a word from the General or the Earl.

Suzu hadn't spoken a single word to anyone since he had fled from Akito and Miharu. He was sitting on Naloc's verandah, lost in thought, and stared out at the garden without seeing it. For the first two hours Jin had told himself that the boy had a lot to consider, too many emotions to deal with. Now, however, he was starting to get worried. He thought about asking Niall for help, but when she came back from her rounds at last, she gave Suzu a look so filled with sadness and pity, he dismissed the idea at once. Instead, he went to sit beside Suzu and endured the silence.

It was getting dark and Jin, Suzu, and Niall were about to go home for the night, when the summons came: the Hidden Moon had finally found a lead.

In the moonless dark the academy had a strange, foreboding atmosphere. The enormous northern style building complex with its spires and turrets looked otherworldly and hostile, the emptiness of the usually busy, bustling place gave it a haunted impression. They nervously huddled together as they followed the instructions to an annex behind the main building.

A shadow peeled away from the deeper darkness of the small building as they approached. A dim light bloomed between them, a shutter lamp providing just enough light to make out the woman who held it.

"Your entourage will have to wait for you here," she said in a voice that hardly carried.

"What?" Jin and the others exclaimed in unison.

"Don't be difficult, we don't have time for this," Naloc snapped. "Stay here, or better yet, wait at that stone pavilion we just passed by."

"No, we had a deal, remember?" Suzu retorted angrily.

The woman held her lamp aloft, looked from Naloc to Suzu and back. "Actually, he's invited. Explicitly."

"Why?"

"Hey, I'm just the guide, don't ask me."

Suzu smiled smugly. He was sure Toshi had made sure that he would be included.

There followed a short whispered discussion. Risa argued, she was Naloc's bodyguard and therefore should be allowed to go with him, but the guide seemed rather amused by that. She patiently assured Risa and Naloc that no-one intended to cause him any harm.

Jin and Niall didn't say much. They knew they didn't have a good reason to be here, but they were clearly unhappy about being excluded. It wasn't as if they had a choice, though. And so, dragging a reluctant Risa along, they vanished back into the darkness, to wait until Naloc and Suzu returned.

Satisfied, their guide bade them to follow and lead them around the corner of the building to an iron studded door.

"How archaic," Suzu commented in a low whisper at the sight of the dungeon like door. The woman chuckled and pushed the door open. Despite its looks, its well-oiled hinges made barely a sound.

"What is this place?" Naloc asked as the door fell shut behind them with an ominous finality, plunging them into total darkness. Then the little plum of light from the woman's lamp grew stronger as she fully unshuttered it. She led them down a narrow hall.

"It is whatever it needs to be at any given time," she said. "To the general populace, however, it's a storehouse – which is precisely what you will tell anyone who asks." She suddenly stopped and looked back over her shoulder at them. It was too dark to see her face, but Suzu had the impression, she was grinning at them.

It was hard to tell how far they walked, until there was finally a dim light ahead of them. At the end of the hall a – thankfully lit – staircase led downwards, where another door barred their way. The woman knocked, then opened it without waiting for an answer.

"There you go," she announced, waving them through the doorway. As Suzu passed her, she winked at him and whispered, "Have fun."

Suzu stepped into sudden brightness. When his eyes had adjusted he saw they were in a room big enough to fit Jin's entire house inside. In its centre stood the biggest table he had ever seen. The people seated around it turned towards the newcomers. General Jarick ax Varg sat at the table's head, his silver hair swept back, wearing a rather casual black suit. There was always something rakish and mischievous about the man, but now his eyes, large and strangely coloured, almost yellow like those of the wolves of the north, were hard, stern, and calculating.

To the General's right sat Toshi, Kagetora standing behind his chair. Suzu didn't know any of the others.

"I see you've found your way here," the General remarked sardonically, eyes fixed on Naloc.

"Yes, I bet you were hoping I'd get lost in the dark" Naloc retorted, crossing his arms in front of his chest and glaring at his favourite enemy.

The General snorted and looked at Suzu instead. "Glad you made, Suzu. I hope you'll forgive me if I'm taking you by surprise, but we seem to be in need of your special abilities."

"Special abilities?" a tiny woman asked. Her brown eyes, far too big for her delicate face, bored into Suzu as if she might be able to see his every secret if only she looked hard enough.

"He's a Furyusha," the man next to her replied as if she should have known that.

"More importantly," another said, "he's Ethereal." Suzu turned to look at the person who had spoken. They met Suzu's eyes straight on, appraising him perhaps, Suzu had a hard time trying to read them. He never had difficulties reading a person – well, that wasn't true, was it? He had read Toshi wrong.

"What exactly is this about?" Naloc demanded.

"I'll explain in a minute, but first, please sit down." Suzu and Naloc complied, taking the offered seats next to the General. The stranger across from Suzu still hadn't taken their eyes off of him. It was as if they were waiting for something.

"The reason I called you here is because we have... apprehended a man this evening, who we believe to have vital information for us," the General stated. "Perhaps to be more precise, he seems to be just the person we've been looking for."

"And what makes you presume so?" Naloc inquired.

A man of such unremarkable, common features it was difficult to describe him, replied. "He is a member of the Silver Guard, which gives him access and opportunity. And unlike his colleagues he is drowning in debts. It seems to be well-known that he loves to squander his money gambling or in the pleasure houses, several have already barred him from entering. However, just last night, he was flush with money, throwing it around as if there was no morrow. Seemed he was also rather deep in his cups, as he kept boasting about this important secret job he had been entrusted with, and that he soon would be having even more money."

"Suspicious as this may be, it's no proof he's involved," Naloc argued, but the General was already waving away his objection.

"We don't just apprehend people on a hunch, we've done our investigation, and there's no doubt that he is involved. But, the man isn't talking. We can, of course, force him to spill everything he knows, but it won't be pretty, and we won't be able to let him go afterwards, which in itself could pose a problem later. In any case we have no time to lose."

"So, is he why you need my help?" Suzu asked.

"Yes."

"All right... You say he likes to spend his money in Yūgao – did he ever visit the Singing Dragon?"

Uncomfortable looks were exchanged around the table. It was clear that what had happened to the Singing Dragon and its inhabitants was weighing on everyone's conscience.

Kagetora replied at last, "He tried, but he didn't even get past the gate."

Suzu nodded at the man and got to his feet. "All right, then what are we waiting for?"

In his mind he could heard Ryū's voice: *Suzu, your biggest strength is neither your beauty nor your skills with the sword, it is your charisma, your aura, people gravitate towards you, and do whatever you want them to do.* Suzu had scoffed at him and asked if he was talking about Suzu's bad temper. Ryū had just laughed. Then, a few days later, a fight between two groups of customers had broken out in the Singing Dragon. Luck had it that that very day Haldor had been out on another engagement. Mother and Ryū had been unable to talk them down. Suzu, for his part, had been especially angry all day and this had been the last straw. He had stomped right into the middle of the melee, wooden training sword in hand, and slammed the tip of it down so hard the sword splintered and the floor board ever since had sported an impressive dent. The fighting had ceased immediately, and after suffering a verbal flogging by Suzu, they had left peacefully, chastised, with many an apology and a generous compensation. Bad temper or something else – whichever it was, it did seem to work.

What Suzu had never told Ryū was that what he had called charisma was one of his Ethereal gifts. Oh, it was by far not as powerful as people liked to claim, Ethereals could not bewitch other people. At least not enough to subdue them. But since the accusations at the temple – false and malicious as they had been – Suzu was hesitant to use the full force of his allure. But there were exceptions, of course. And everything that brought him closer to his revenge counted as an exception.

There was a cacophony of voices, disharmonious in their disagreement. Varying versions of "sure that he can do it?", "you can't be serious" and "absolutely not" like the chorus of a badly composed song. It grated on Suzu's nerves. They had no time for this nonsense.

There was only one person who wasn't arguing: the stranger sitting across from Suzu, regarding him curiously, appraising, measuring. Suzu stared straight back at them, unflinchingly, until the stranger's lips twitched – not quite a smile.

Ah, he had enough of this. Suzu slammed his hands down on the table. The debate ran dry, quelled by the impressive glower Suzu subjected each and every one of them with, one by one.

"Good. Can someone lend me a knife?" A few raised eyebrows answered him. "Just in case."

The stranger across from Suzu flicked their wrist and a small leaf shaped blade appeared in their hand, which they held out to Suzu. Startled, he hesitantly accepted the *kunai*. He was amazed by how perfectly balanced the weight was, how beautiful the characteristic leaf shaped blade. The stranger gave him a knowing wink.

"Suzu," said Toshi, a hand on Suzu's arm.

"I'll be fine."

"Actually... I am more worried about that man."

Although no-one did laugh out loud, no-one did a good job at hiding their amusement either. Suzu grinned. "I promise, I will only scare him a little. Don't worry."

Suzu followed the General out of the room and further down another dimly lit hallway to a heavy door flanked by two guards. "He's going in," the General told them. "You will not open the door unless you hear him telling you so. When he's done, bring him back to the war room."

"The war room?" Suzu raised an eyebrow at the General. "Really?"

The old man shrugged. "Not my idea, my predecessors gave it that name. Well then, see you in a bit. Don't get too wild."

The room was windowless and confined, with a pallet in one corner, a low table beside it, carrying a pitcher and a single cup: a prison cell. Gas lamps like those in the hallway illuminated the dreary chamber. A man sat on the pallet. Glum, scruffy, his uniform untidy and wrinkled. There was the shadow of a beard along his jaw, his eyes were sunken and bloodshot. Suzu thought he did look slightly familiar, but you could find his type by the dozen all over Getsuro. He almost sprang to his feet, eyes round with a mixture of wonder and suspicion.

"You're Yūzuki no Suzu," he said in this strange tone that suggested this was a fact as surprising to Suzu as it was to him.

"I am. What is your name?"

"Goro. Onishi Goro... Why are you here?"

Suzu took a step forward, eyes coyly downcast. Only the faintest hint of a smile, like a secret, on his lips. The room was so small this single step brought him so close to the other man that he could smell his sweat and stale breath. Suzu reached out to toy with one of the brass buttons on Goro's uniform. "I'm here to help."

"Help?" Goro's body swayed involuntarily towards Suzu, like a flower towards the sun. Suspicion, visible in his eyes, the furrowed brows, however, held him back. "Oh, I see. Hadn't taken the Earl for the kind of man who'd whore out his own lover to get what he wants." Suzu refrained from punching the sneer on the man's face, but only just. "Tell him it's not gonna work, I'm not a snitch."

Suzu slipped his hand inside Goro's open jacket and laid it flat against the man's chest, feeling the heat of his skin seep through the thin shirt of the uniform, the rapid rhythm of his heart. And then he turned the full force of his Ethereal appeal on the man. It felt like finally relaxing a muscle one wasn't even aware of having tensed all the time.

"You know they won't kill you that easily," Suzu said quietly, still averting his eyes. "Not until they get all the information they want from you. And they will be ruthless, and cruel... I just... I thought, perhaps it doesn't need to come to that... perhaps... well... perhaps I could persuade you in another way."

"Oh, and how would you persuade me?" The man's desire was so strong it was almost tangible. It resembled the air pressure just moments before the thunder. Suzu's nerve endings prickled. He felt sick.

"What is it you'd want me to do?" he whispered.

Goro's arm came around Suzu's waist, one big rough hand groping his buttocks. Suzu knew how to put on a face and play along, hiding his thoughts, his feelings, but he could hardly suppress the urge to tear the man's hand off. Instead, he affected a demure gasp that had Goro chuckling as he drew him closer. Suzu gritted his teeth.

"You now exactly what I want you to do, don't you? That's what you're here for, aren't you?" Goro whispered into Suzu's ear. Suzu didn't even try to suppress the shudder that ran through him, he knew the man would misinterpret it. The leer he received was confirmation enough.

"Well..." Suzu drawled. He'd had enough of this game now.

Slowly he lifted his head, let Goro see the hate and fury in his eyes, and watched with gratification as the leer slipped off the man's face. Before he could react, however, Suzu pushed him back against the cold wall and jammed the *kunai* he'd had hidden in his sleeve between the man's legs – not enough to cause injury, but enough to let Goro feel its bite. Goro's entire body went rigid, his hands came off of Suzu, held up in surrender, as he let his eyes wander down to the knife threatening his manhood.

"The way I see it, you can either make this easy and tell me all I want to know, or you don't. But you should know that those guards outside the door? They have orders to remain outside no matter what they hear, unless *I* tell them otherwise."

Goro gulped. "B-but I don't know anything. I d-don't –"

"If that were true, you would have said so hours ago already, instead of refusing to speak, pretending to be some kind of martyr."

"You don't understand," Goro cried, trying to wriggle away. Suzu pushed the *kunai* deeper into the man's groin, eliciting a yelp from Goro. "Please... you don't understand what they'll do if they find out I –"

"Oh I understand perfectly. I know better than anyone what that lousy rotten monk is capable of." There was no way Goro didn't know what had happened to the Singing Dragon. Even if he hadn't known that Nobu and his minions were behind it, he had no problems making the connection, Suzu could see it in his eyes. "And let me tell you this: I will go to any length to make him pay for what he did, and you'd better not be standing in my way. I can promise you that I will make you spill everything – and when I'm done, you will beg me to kill you." The dread on Goro's face sent a thrill through Suzu. He had no intention of torturing the man, but having him believe he did, gave him an odd sense of satisfaction. Here was one of Nobu's lackeys. It didn't matter that he had had nothing to do with the attack on the Singing Dragon, it didn't matter why he was doing it – Goro was helping Nobu get what he wanted, he might as well have been Nobu's little finger. And Suzu did mean to break it.

"So," he breathed, "are you going to sing? Or do you want to play?" As he spoke those words a demonic grin spread across his lovely face.

"Well, you better brace yourselves," Suzu announced as he strode back into the war room, twirling the *kunai* between his deft fingers. More than one pair of eyes were drawn to it, frowns forming between brows, exclamations and questions forming on lips. Before they were given voice, Suzu brushed them off. "Don't worry, he's alive and unmaimed." He held the small knife out for its owner to take back, but they just smiled and shook their head. With a nod of gratitude Suzu slipped it back inside his sleeve. Then he sat down and recounted exactly what Goro had confessed to him: How he had eventually lost more money gambling than he'd ever be able to pay back. And how a woman had approached him with the promise of a way out of his misery. Although he had presumed she worked for a loan shark, having no other choice left, he had followed her. But the assumed loan shark had turned out to be a monk – no, not any monk, a high priest – and all Goro had to do was to deliver a package as little favour. As simple as that: the money to pay off his debts in exchange for accepting a package at a specific time and delivering it to a specific person – become a traitor for gold.

"Come on, lad, tell us who he's supposed to bring it to!" Naloc snapped, rudely cutting through Suzu's dramatic pause. Suzu refrained from rolling his eyes at him, the man had no sense for good story telling and how to create tension. Then again, perhaps now really wasn't the right time for it.

"The emperor's personal bodyguard."

The shock that ran through the room at this disclosure crackled with static like a lightning bolt, eliciting a multitude of emotions from speechless terror to explosive anger.

"Leif ax Ari, that hypocritical, spineless bastard!" the General roared, slamming his fist down on the table and leaving a veritable dent in the wood. His yellow eyes glinted dangerously. For Suzu, who only knew the old man as a kind, funny, warm-hearted father-figure, this was the first time he fully understood why General Jarick ax Varg was feared by many, why they called him the Grey Wolf. "I personally gave him a letter of recommendation when he was nothing but a common little soldier, got him placed with the Dregan Clan.

For fuck's sake, he was Kjell's bodyguard even before Kjell became emperor! This is... it's... unforgivable!"

It was no secret that the General had on more than one occasion made it abundantly clear how little he thought of the man wearing the divinely granted crown. The Moon Throne as an institution, the realm itself and its people – that was where the General's loyalties lay. And he demanded no less from the people subordinate to him. Leif ax Ari's betrayal was a personal affront in his eyes.

"Don't worry, General," Suzu said. "You'll get your chance to teach him a lesson he won't forget." The General huffed and settled down, grumpy and no doubt plotting all sorts of horrible deaths for the emperor's bodyguard, but calmer. "On the positive side, Onishi Goro is willing – no, *enthusiastic* about doing whatever it takes to not be tried as a traitor." This did cheer up not only the General but the others as well.

"How exactly did you make him talk?" Naloc asked curiously.

Suzu smiled. A dazzling smile, hiding secrets, and flavoured with only a hint of smugness. "I'm a Furyusha – people tell me things."

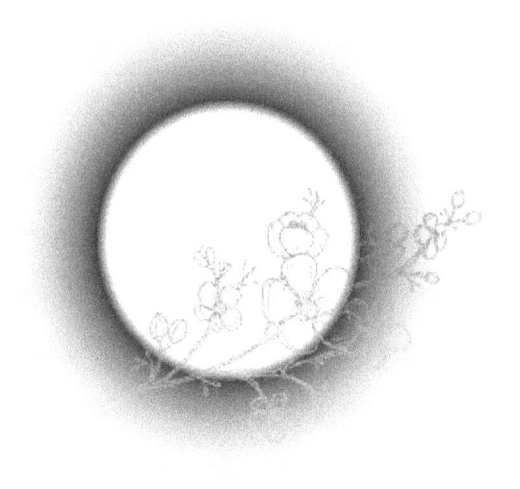

Chapter 37

This was easily the biggest map Jin had ever seen, which they were all crowded around. It showed the lay of Moonlight Palace with its entire grounds, Moonlight Square, and even the Moon Goddess's temple. Jin wondered where Naloc had gotten it from. Then again, perhaps the General had brought it along.

The night before, Suzu and Naloc had only given them a short summary of what had transpired during the meeting with the Hidden Moon. Naloc, in particular, had seemed preoccupied on their way home.

Now, unlike the night before, Jin, Niall, and Risa were included in the meeting – as was the rest of the Crescent, a selection of their people, the General, the Earl, and other members of the Hidden Moon – or so Jin presumed. There was also a tiny elderly woman, who Jin recognised as High Priestess

Tsukiko. She moved with a grace and strength that belied her frail appearance, her eyes were clear and intense, and she radiated authority. Jin felt more intimidated by her than he ever had of any of the monks at the Temple of Hôjô. Two acolytes flanked her, both built and moving like well-trained fighters.

The biggest difference was that they had met in the Crescent's hall, in the middle of the day. Several of their spies had reported that Nobu, only days before Tsuki no Matsuri, seemed to have ceased all activities and was lying low. It was the last chance for them to plan their counterattack.

"Remind me again, what we got to do with this," Fukuda no Fumie grumbled. The old crow looked even less happy to be here than she usually did. Why she was still a member of the Crescent was anyone's guess. Rumour had it that she told her son he'd have to pry her position and her business out of her cold dead hands – and now refused to die.

"You know why," Naloc retorted. "I've explained the situation in detail at least three times already."

"Yes, and? Just because your wife died doesn't mean you have to drag the whole town into this. Let them noble ones deal with their own mess."

Naloc sighed, clearly having reached the limits of his patience. "This is not the time for you to be contrary. Might I remind you that an attack against the throne will have consequences for the entire empire. That includes Kigetsu. That even includes you."

"Then perhaps you should have informed the council earlier, instead of presenting us a fait accompli."

"Well, circumstances didn't allow me to appraise you of the situation earlier. But seeing as I'm First Seat, I can inform you whenever I want anyway. Be glad that we are having this meeting now, instead of me just ordering you and your people to do exactly what I want them to do, when I want them to do it."

The old crone harrumphed, but remained quiet at last. Naloc glared at the other members of the Crescent, daring anyone else to object, but as so often Fukuda no Fumie was the only one who had any complains.

"Good, then let's continue. Jin, you and Niall were checking up on our apothecary friend."

Jin swallowed as all eyes turned on him. Nervously he rubbed his suddenly sweaty hands on his trousers. Why was Naloc putting him on the spot like this? Why not ask Niall? "Y-yes... um... we... he... A-Azhar is working day and night on... the not... not lethal poison..."

"The counterfeit," Niall provided in a whisper.

"The counterfeit. He's been working on the counterfeit, and... well, he's really done wonders. He promises he has enough ready in time, including an antidote, which he says we have to administer, just in case." Jin turned to Niall, in case he had forgotten anything, but his friend smiled at him and nodded her head. He sighed, relieved. From across the table Suzu gave him a surreptitious thumbs-up that made him smile.

"So," a grey-haired lady who looked vaguely familiar to Jin said. "We will really go through with it then. Does that mean I have to let myself get knocked out and just trust you to handle everything?"

"Of course not, Freya, dear," the General chuckled. And Jin remembered now: this was Freya ax Asuka of the Feichun Clan – one of the Seven – Countess of Tel Mân. She was known for her generosity but also for her ruthlessness and the mercilessness with which she took down any who dared challenge her. "Just pretend you're drinking it. Like all the traitors probably will. It'll require a bit of acting on our part, however, we don't want to tip them off too soon after all. But no-one would believe you to be a traitor – unless this was your very own coup d'état." The countess snorted rather unladylike.

"Well then, before we go into any tactical details, allow me to address another concern," General ax Varg continued. "The fact that the emperor's bodyguard is actively involved in the plot makes it clear that there is no doubt there are traitors amongst the Silver Guard. We've all known it's a possibility. But the real danger lies not so much in that we don't know who amongst them is on the monk's side, or even their fighting skills, but that the Silver Guard has access to firearms."

A murmur went through the room. In a country as peaceful as theirs, with no big conflicts, there was no need for firearms. Yes, they existed, and yes people used them – to hunt big game, usually. On occasion smaller varieties could be found in Getsuro; some people in the north apparently preferred them to swords, but by and large they weren't common. It was no wonder then that, until now, not one of them had thought about the use of firearms.

"I guess that's my cue," a man to Jin's left spoke up. He had a bit of a scruffy look, with his beard and wild, shoulder length wavy hair. Fukuda no Fumie wrinkled her nose and turned away from him, clearly not interested in giving the man even a moment of her attention. The General and his entourage weren't quite as disapproving.

"And you are?" the Earl inquired.

"Ah, sorry. I wasn't a member of the Crescent the last time the Moon Council deigned us a meeting." If he had hoped to raise any kind of reaction out of the nobles, he got sorely disappointed. The council members just looked back at him without so much as twitching an eye. The man shrugged and introduced himself. "I'm Higa Osamu, a gunsmith by trade and easily the best shooter you will find in this town – or most of the empire, to be honest. I don't hold with modesty. And chances are the guns the Silver Guard uses are some of mine, after all there aren't that many gunsmiths."

"What he is trying to say," Naloc interrupted impatiently, "is that he can provide firearms and people who know how to use them."

Higa spread his hands and smiled. The General leaned towards the Earl and Lady Freya, having a whispered discussion.

"And what is it you demand in return?" the General asked at last.

Higa opened his mouth to answer, but Naloc was quicker. "The knowledge that he is defending the throne and the people of this town will suffice," he said in a voice that brooked no argument, his slate grey eyes boring into his fellow council member. Higa, his smile never faltering, nodded his assent. Jin couldn't help but wonder if Naloc was overstepping his authority.

"Well, now that that's settled," Naloc continued. "I think it's time we put all the cards on the table and come up with an actual plan."

Once everyone was on the same page – some were quite shocked to learn of certain events or fact they hadn't known yet – High Priestess Tsukiko gave them a rundown of how the Tsuki no Matsuri celebrations would take place:

As was tradition, Tsuki no Matsuri would begin with the emperor and the Moon Council presenting offerings to the Moon Goddess at Her temple and praying for Her blessing, for prosperity and good fortune for the Empire of Tsukiyama. This would be followed by the High Priestess's blessings. The only difference this time would be that her two assistants would be hiding weapons beneath their wide flowing robes.

Afterwards, the emperor and the councillors would go on foot to the stage that was going to be set up on the border between the palace grounds and Moonlight Square. There, they would renew their vows of continued servitude to the Goddess, the realm, and the people, before raising their glasses to toast the heavens.

Normally, this would be followed by celebrations everywhere across town, all night long. This time, however...

For the next two hours they pored over the giant map, dividing people into groups and distributing them at critical points across Moonlight Square, making sure everyone knew exactly what their job was. Avoiding panic amongst the people as much as possible was their first priority, which was why most of them were tasked with evacuating the square before all else.

"Remember this: trust no-one you can't be two hundred percent certain of being on our side," the General admonished. "Some of the traitors will fight, but there will also be those who'll try to vanish back into the shadows when they notice we're onto them. Which is why, pay close attention to who remains conscious on that stage. Anyone other than myself, Toshi, and Freya – apprehend them at once! As for the rest of Nobu's forces... well... I'd say anyone who attacks you or doesn't follow orders – it's safe to assume they are the enemy. Don't let anyone escape!"

Jin's head was spinning. How could they be sure of anyone and anything? This entire plan – if you wanted to call it that – was riddled with uncertainty. They could only hope they could keep collateral damage small.

Jin stared at the map where markers showed each group's position. Three days. Only three more days. In four days they would know if risking that many lives had been worth it. The hardest part now: wait and remain calm.

It was finally over. Suzu hadn't thought it was this difficult to organise that many people. Perhaps he had always assumed that someone like the General would just bark orders and everyone would follow his lead. That was obviously not the case, at least not with this ragtag group, consisting of various factions, each with their own agenda and goals. At last they had all agreed on one plan.

Now the room was slowly clearing, Suzu noticed Toshi hanging back. He looked at Jin, who seemed to have noticed as well. Though it looked a little forced, Jin smiled at him and said, "I wait outside."

When the last person had finally left the room and the door closed behind them, Toshi put a thick bundle on the table. "I got a few things for you. Just a few clothes – I hope they fit."

In lieu of an answer, Suzu threw his arms around the taller man's middle and pressed his face into Toshi's chest. Toshi hugged him back, fiercely, and whispered into Suzu's hair, "Promise me you'll be careful."

"I promise."

"And that you won't take any unnecessary risks."

"I won't."

"And that if someone is in a better position to deal with that blasted monk, you'll just accept it as an unexpected gift."

Suzu lifted his head, mismatched eyes meeting winter sky grey eyes, and huffed. "But I won't like it. I will grouse about it for months, I'll be grumpy and insufferable about it."

"Deal," Toshi laughed.

Suzu smirked. Then he raised himself on tiptoes and pressed his lips to Toshi's. It was a kiss that spoke more than a thousand words ever could. It told of their fears, their hopes, their feelings. It was just one tender, lingering kiss. It was a promise.

Part 4

Revenge

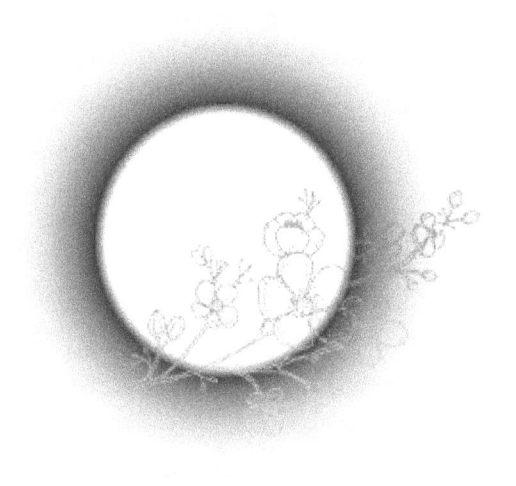

Chapter 38

Three days had never felt so long and simultaneously so short. The mornings and evenings Suzu spent with Risa and her people, training. The rest of the time with Jin, while Niall was doing her rounds, taking care of her patients. Despite the tension, Suzu was surprised to find he enjoyed Jin's company. Perhaps it was the nostalgic feeling he got, sitting with Jin in the garden. For the first time since their reunion they spoke as they once used to: unrestrained, hopping from topic to topic, without any taboos. Thus Suzu soon found out how wrong and frankly ridiculous Jin's idea of Yūgao and especially the pleasure houses was. In that regard, nothing scandalised him more than the fact that the General, who was like a father to Toshi, frequently engaged the services of Toshi's lover.

Suzu couldn't hold back the roaring laughter that burst out of him. He laughed so long and hard his stomach hurt.

"By the gods, Jin," he gasped. "How can you still be so ignorant after all these years? Why in the world do you still stick to those honestly moronic ideas the temple taught you? You? Especially you, who always rebelled against the Path's rigidity and narrow-mindedness." Seeing Jin flush furiously all the way to the tips of his ears, and the confused but pouting expression on the boy's face, made Suzu laugh even harder. Jin said nothing. He plucked some grass, embarrassed, and refused to look at Suzu.

Eventually, Suzu took pity on him. After a few deep breaths and a big gulp of water, he explained, "Look, the first thing you need to know is that Furyusha and prostitutes aren't exactly the same. In fact, prostitution is prohibited within the boundaries of the capital. Though it's true that Furyusha have sex with their customers – occasionally. It is not the primary motivation for engaging a Furyusha's services."

"If that's not what you're after, why visit a pleasure house? I mean, it's in the name, isn't it? 'Pleasure house.'"

"Why? To enjoy and admire beauty, after all we live in a society that appreciates beauty in all its forms. And we give them a respite from their everyday sorrows, their life, from the world outside the window. We are a dream, a way of escapism. We are whatever our customers want us to be – and what they need. Intimacy can be a part of it, which is why the houses usually serve only either male or female customers, rarely both."

Jin furrowed his brows. He didn't look convinced. "But what if – and I mean, I know that you, for example, only like men – so what if you're in a house that serves only women, and your customer wants you to sleep with her? Could you really do it? Would you still be all right with it then?" he demanded to know.

"Actually, I'd have just changed houses then," Suzu retorted, and when he saw that he had lost Jin again, he elaborated, "Here's a very important fact: It's forbidden to force anyone in Yūgao to do anything they don't want to do. You find yourself in a house that only serves male customers but you are uncomfortable with the possibility of sleeping with a man? Tell the house's owner and they arrange for you a place in another house. A certain customer makes you uncomfortable? You are free to refuse them. You find you cannot or do not want to work as a Furyusha? There are other jobs that need to be done in a pleasure house."

Jin was looking at him as if he had sprouted a second head. Well, to be fair, when Mother had picked him up from the streets, he, too, had assumed 'pleasure house' was just a fancy name for brothel. The idea of having been saved by people who sold their bodies after he had been cast out for his "promiscuous and immoral behaviour" – well, the irony of it had been most delightful.

"So... the General?"

"Treats me like his child. He loves to spoil me, we joke, we play games, we talk for hours..."

Jin nodded his head slowly. It was hard to tell if all this new information was disorienting him, overthrowing most of his world view, or if he was struggling to accept how wrong he had been.

"But... but people – children – are sold into the houses," Jin protested.

"True, but it's not so much different to your parents abandoning you at the temple. It's... it's complicated." Suzu rubbed a hand across his eyes. He wasn't sure he could explain it so Jin would understand. The fact that the houses *did* pay money, which in turn bound one to them was indisputable, but also a complicated and delicate matter.

It was the truth that people sold themselves, but also children, into service to the pleasure houses – and they did so out of despair. And while it was fact that they had to stay and work until they had paid back what the house had invested in them, it wasn't a peonage. First – in accordance with the rules that regulated everything in Yūgao – it had to be possible to pay back one's debts within a reasonable amount of time, which required at least a minimum wage to be paid. Furyusha, especially, earned well. The money that wasn't used to pay back their debts was theirs, to spend as they liked or save for their future. But the most important difference was that no-one could be forced into anything they didn't feel comfortable with. The houses provided them with an education and taught them all sorts of useful skills. But in the end it was one's own decision how one earned one's money, be it as Furyusha or as an attendant. Once the house had been repaid, one was free to leave – with the means to lead a good life.

Suzu tried to explain all this; he saw Jin making an effort to understand, but ultimately he wasn't sure the young man really did grasp the difference. In the end, however, Jin mercifully decided he was satisfied with the knowledge that Suzu had neither been forced nor held captive and had been quite happy with his life at the Singing Dragon.

"Hmm." Jin fidgeted with a loose thread on the hem of his shirt, clearly wanting to ask something but not daring to do so. Suzu waited. From the way Jin was not meeting his eyes, searching for the right words, to the blush colouring his cheeks, Suzu had a hunch what this was about. "You… you said some of your customers w-wanted to… hmm… sleep with you.

So, the Earl... um..." Aha! Suzu had been right, Jin was trying to ask about how Suzu and the Earl had become lovers and didn't know how. But how was Suzu to explain how he and Toshi had been drawn to each other as if it had been inevitable. They had collided like two celestial bodies in a cosmic explosion that had been written in the stars aeons ago. How futile it had been for Suzu to deny it for so long, how foolish.

"No. Toshi... it's never been like that," he said after a moment. "Toshi and I – we simply happened."

"Oh." Jin smiled. For a moment there was something bittersweet in his smile, a darker emotion flickering across his dark eyes – there and gone again – then his smile grew warmer, genuine. It was a smile full of comforting familiarity, this smile – like sunshine.

It was at this precise moment that Suzu decided he wanted Jin in his life after all. Once upon a time, in another life, that boy had been his brother, his best friend, his first lover. He had been his home. A lot had happened between them that wasn't their fault. It felt wrong not to bridge that chasm between them.

Suzu looked up at the bright silver orb of the moon. A mere sliver was missing yet. The full moon was upon them – and with it Tsuki no Matsuri. Only one more day.

"Are you all right?" Suzu asked quietly, eyeing Jin worriedly, who seemed more nervous than he had ever seen him.

Jin nodded, but it was hardly convincing. "It's just... don't you think that entire plan is... kind of... half-baked?" Jin confided. He wasn't wrong.

"There is no such thing as a perfect plan," Niall retorted. She looked resigned and unhappy, and Suzu wondered again why she was here. They shouldn't risk a talented doctor like her. Well, anyway, she wasn't wrong either. And taking a look around it became obvious that there was not a single person who was happy about it. What choice did they have, though, they were out of time.

"Too late to back out now," Niall sighed. She petted herself down, checking once more that she hadn't forgotten anything, and that all of her needles and small knives were well hidden and secure. Like Jin, Niall wasn't handy with a sword, but the things she could do with her long acupuncture needles were enough to make even Risa respectfully avoid any confrontations with her. "Well then," she said and stepped up to Suzu. For a long moment she stared straight into his eyes, before – unexpectedly – throwing her arms around him and squeezing him tight.

"You take care. Don't take any stupid risks, you hear? I expect the three of us to share a drink in our garden tomorrow evening." Taken aback, Suzu slowly hugged her back and murmured a promise and a "You better be careful, too." Niall smiled brightly at him as she let go. With a nod in Jin's direction, she gave Suzu's arm a last squeeze and left the two young men alone.

Without her, there was a sudden awkwardness between them. This was not how Suzu wanted them to part. "Well, you heard her. Drinks tomorrow. I expect there to be something more drinkable then that swill you call sakè." Jin's lips twitched into a semblance of a smile. "Oh come now." Suzu thumped the boy's shoulder. "It'll be fine. Just do your job, be careful, and have a little faith in the rest of us. And by tomorrow this will all be over."

Slowly, as if he had to convince himself, Jin nodded his head. "All right. But... but there's... well... I don't want this to be... over."

"What?"

"Ah no, that's not what I meant," Jin said quickly. "I..." With what seemed to be a world shattering effort Jin met Suzu's eyes. "I don't want to lose you again." Such small and simple words – falling at his feet with such crushing weight. For a moment Suzu forgot to breathe, his heart skipped a beat, then pounded twice as fast. A single tiny word – and yet it was such a profound difference: 'lose' – Jin had *lost* him once, he had never *abandoned* him. His world, once thrown out of joint, was finally right again. Whatever it was Jin expected of him, whatever he hoped for – all of this could wait, for now it was enough to know the rift between them was healing. In the end Nobu had failed to tear them apart.

"You won't, you idiot! We're friends, are we not?" It came slowly and uncertainly, but this time it was Jin's real smile. Suzu had no chance to say more, before Jin had his arms around him and hugged him tightly. Stupidly Suzu wondered when his friend had grown so big and put on so much muscle.

"Be careful," Jin whispered.

"You, too... idiot." The teasing earned Suzu a quiet chuckle.

He watched Jin and Niall leave through the secret door in the garden wall, waving goodbye, then went to find Risa. The swordswoman and her troop were assembled in the front yard, checking and rechecking their equipment, giving their swords a last polish and a critic eye.

"Are they off?" Risa asked as he approached. Suzu gave her an affirmative nod. "Don't worry, they'll be fine. Here." She held out the sword she had just been checking over. "As good as new. It should serve you well." With a small bow Suzu accepted the sword. Risa hadn't promised too much, it lay well in his hand, weight and length just right for him. He drew the katana from its sheath, sunlight glinted off the polished blade. After a quick inspection and a couple of practice swings he sheathed it again, the soft metallic click a familiar sound, reminding him of Haldor.

"Thanks, it's perfect." Risa grinned. She was just about to say something when Naloc's voice came from the main house.

"Suzu, a moment, please." Suzu raised a questioning eyebrow at Risa but she only shrugged. Having no choice, Suzu slowly made his way over to Naloc, grumbling. But the second Naloc saw him coming, he turned around and vanished into the house, gesturing over his shoulder for Suzu to follow. Suspicious, Suzu complied.

"No weapons in the house," Naloc snapped, stopping Suzu from entering the dim hallway with his new sword in hand. Resisting the urge to hurl it at the man, Suzu leaned it against the wall, and pulled his short sword out of his sash, but when Naloc turned away and headed deeper into the house, he quickly stuffed it into his shirt. He checked that his kunai was securely strapped to the inside of his arm before he ran after Naloc.

They ended up in the guest wing, or more precisely in the exact same room Suzu had been taken to after the tragic events at the Singing Dragon only weeks ago. He wondered what they were doing here. This couldn't be about the vase Suzu had accidentally broken the other day, could it? One would have thought Naloc would choose a more appropriate time to complain about his mistreated property. Entering the room, however, Suzu noticed the slim window he had fled through was now boarded up, an oil lamp the only source of light.

"What is this?" he asked suspiciously.

Naloc turned to look at him, his expression unreadable. "Sorry about this, lad, but I will have you stay here until this is over."

"What? We had a deal!"

"I know, but... Kazue loved you like a son. I will not – cannot risk you getting killed, too. I owe her that."

"No!" Suzu growled. "She would have never locked me in, she would have sent me off, wishing me luck. You owe her to keep your promises. You owe *us* our revenge!"

"Su–"

"No! You can't keep me here." Suzu whirled around – and found the door blocked by a man who would have even dwarfed Haldor. He had to tilt his head sideways just to be able to stand beneath a ceiling too low for him; arms thick with muscles were crossed in front of his chest as he glared down at Suzu.

"I had to call in a favour to secure Vidar's service for tonight. He'll make sure you remain put. I'm really sorry, and perhaps I'm being selfish, but I just can't let you rush to your doom." And with those words Naloc slipped out of the room behind the giant and was gone. A moment and a glare later, Vidar stepped out of the room as well and slammed the door shut, leaving Suzu behind, stunned.

His bewilderment was short-lived, however, his rising anger burnt it away like snow in a conflagration. He pulled his tantō out of its sheath and – stopped himself a second before he stabbed his guard through the thin paper door. The man was only doing what he was getting paid for, he had nothing to do with the grudge between Naloc and Suzu and even less with Suzu's raging need for revenge.

Backing away slowly from the door, Suzu took a shuddering breath and reined in his anger. He forced himself to turn around and focus on examining the boarded up window. They had made sure he couldn't repeat his vanishing act a second time, it was nailed shut from the outside

Suzu took a look around the room. It had been stripped of everything Suzu might break or use as a weapon, except for the oil lamp... Bad idea. No, Suzu was certainly not going to start a fire; he needed another plan. What did he have on his person? A short sword, a kunai.

Stabbing the man in the back was out of the question, so he needed another plan. And fast.

Chapter 39

Moonlight Square was bustling. Hundreds of people were standing shoulder to shoulder, chatting and laughing. Little children, hoisted onto their father's shoulders, were craning their necks to be the first to catch a glimpse of the royal procession.

Jin pushed his way through the exited crowd with a mantra like stream of "Excuse me, excuse me", with Niall clinging to the back of his shirt so she would not get lost. When at last they reached their designated position in the front row, Jin was sweaty and exhausted. Niall wordlessly passed him a bamboo flask of water. Now that they were standing still, Jin could hear the beat of drums over the crowd's chatter. They had made it just in time.

The pistol he had hidden beneath his shirt seemed to weigh a ton. Jin wasn't comfortable with having it, and less so with the possibility of using it. But he couldn't deny that going into a fight unarmed was even worse.

Higa Osamu had pulled him aside the moment they had arrived at the meeting place.

"Why in the world are you unarmed?" he demanded.

"Um... I... I'm not any good with a sword," Jin replied sheepishly.

"So? There are other weapons. Your friend here," Higa pointed at Niall, "I know that she always has those devilish needles on her."

"And a dagger."

"And a dagger! And what about you?"

"My... fists?"

Higa closed his eyes for a moment and took a deep breath. "I know Naloc is a bit out of it ever since his wife died, but letting you go in there like this? That's neglect. All right." He pulled the pistol at his hip out of its holster and held it out to Jin. "Take it."

"W-w-what? No way! I don't – I have no idea how to –"

"Relax. Look, it's already loaded, and because we neither have the time for me to explain to you how to load it, or for you to practice it, you'll only have two shots. All you have to do is: cock the hammer, point, squeeze the trigger. Easy! And if you're lucky, you'll actually hit your target," Higa laughed, pushing the pistol into Jin's hands and clapping the young man's shoulder. "Remember, two shots!" And then he had left, leaving Jin with a weapon in his hands he was utterly unfamiliar with.

Jin looked at the people around them, full of joyful excitement, the many children. This would be the first time for many of them to witness the procession and the royal blessing.

"Are we really going through with this?" Jin asked apprehensively.

"What choice do we have now?" Niall sounded as unhappy about the situation as Jin felt.

"Do you think Azhar really succeeded? Do you think they managed the switch without anyone noticing?"

"You better hope they did, I don't want to imagine the alternative."

Jin nodded and sent a silent prayer to the Moon Goddess for Her protection, and after short contemplation he added a prayer to Hôjô. The god of his childhood was not one inclined to help the unfaithful, but he was a righteous god who stood against evil and extended a helping hand to the weakest members of society. The gods were not known to meddle in the affairs of mortals, but even if Hôjô wasn't smiting that blasphemous, murderous high priest of his, perhaps he'd at least bless those who were trying to stop him.

The drums were getting louder, the sound of hundreds of small bells accompanying them was still faint but audible now.

"Can you see anything?" Niall called. Jin craned his neck but – there! Temple maidens of the Goddess in black and white robes, wearing silver masks, preceded the procession. With each step they rammed their long staffs on the ground, causing the myriad of silver bells hanging on filigree chains from the silver sickle moon on their tops to ring out. Behind them, set on wheeled platforms and pulled by a dozen strong men, came the two great drums.

They moved in a slow, studied rhythm, steadily nearing the elevated platform facing the crowd. Like a wave accompanying the emperor's advance the people bowed low as their regent passed, smiling and waving benevolently from his open sedan chair, resplendent in midnight blue and silver. He was followed by the members of the Moon Council.

At the platform, the drum players stopped and stood to right of it, whereas the temple maidens proceeded to the left side of the stage, where the royal family, the families of the councillors, and honoured guests were seated.

Jin scrutinised the honoured guests. As they had expected, Nobu was amongst them, standing out in his blood red robes, declaring him the High Priest of the Brotherhood of Hôjô. Next to him sat another monk of the Brotherhood. Steren was nowhere to be seen, but Jin doubted he was far.

The emperor and his councillors took their places on the platform behind a long low table. Only the emperor remained standing. Gradually the crowd fell silent. The temple maidens rang their bells once more, followed by a single, final beat of the great drums. Then all was silent.

Emperor Kjell, 26th bearer of the Moonlight Crown, regent of Tsukiyama, bowed deep to his people. The people bowed back. Then he raised his hands in benediction.

"Our Celestial Mother," the emperor's deep, booming voice rang out across the square, and thus he began the traditional prayer.

"Damn it!" Suzu cursed. He took a deep breath, swallowing an outburst of frustration. There was nothing with which he could get rid of those blasted boards, and besides the noise of him hammering against them would no doubt draw the attention of the giant guarding him. Sitting around, contemplating one stupid, impossible idea after the next was getting him nowhere, and time was running out – he needed to get out of here right now. It was time for desperate measures.

The oil lamp was flickering merrily with not a care in the world. Oh, he really didn't want to do this, what if it got out of control. No, if anything happened Naloc had himself to blame for going back on his promise and locking Suzu up. Still, this was the stupidest idea he'd had in a long time, Suzu thought as he carefully picked up the lamp.

"Oi!" he bellowed. "Unless you want me to burn this bloody house down, you should better let me go. Now."

"Nice try," came the rumbling reply. "You're not stupid enough to start a fire with you in the same room and no way out."

"Am I not? How do you know? I might just be desperate enough to do something seriously stupid."

"Nah."

"Fine. Let me just make something clear to you: I have absolutely nothing left to lose." It wasn't quite the truth but it was close enough. "I'm fully prepared to die tonight, are you?" That, on the other hand, was the truth. There was no way he would accomplish what he intended to do if he wasn't.

Vidar, on the other hand, didn't seem inclined to court death just yet, for he finally opened the door. The irritated expression on the man's face changed into shock the second he saw Suzu standing in the middle of the room, the lamp in his hands.

"Put that down," Vidar growled. Suzu took a step back. "I said, put it down. Nice and easy."

"Let me go, and I will."

"No can do."

Suzu sighed. "Looks like I have no choice then." As he had hoped, Vidar slowly crept towards him, hands reaching for the lamp. Suzu took another step, Vidar followed. Another step, this one to the side, Vidar did not notice, too focussed on the lamp.

"Come now, put it down, don't be stupid, hm?" Vidar coaxed as if he were talking to a spooked horse. Suzu sent a mental prayer to whichever god might be listening that he wouldn't end up regretting this till the end of his days – and tossed the lamp at Vidar. Startled, the big man grabbed for it on reflex. At the same time Suzu dodged past him and dashed through the door. A wordless bellow followed him, then a stream of cursing. Suzu didn't stop to see if he had caused a fire or injury but raced down the hall, pushing a frightened housemaid out of his way in the process. The sound of loud, thundering footsteps told him Vidar was after him. At least nothing had caught on fire then.

His moment of relief was short-lived when two figures appeared in front of him. "Catch him!" Vidar's voice rang through the hall. Alarmed, the two turned around, they didn't seem to be fighters. Suzu used their surprise to his advantage. Instead of slowing down or stopping as they might have expected, Suzu put on more speed and charged them head on. His hands on his chest and his elbows turned outwards, he crashed into them. The force was enough to push them aside, gasping, and allowed Suzu to stumble onwards. Vidar's steps grew louder, he was gaining on Suzu. Regaining his balance, Suzu ran flat out down the hallway, out the door and straight across the yard. He yanked the gate open and was through it before Vidar had even reached the porch.

Toshi scanned the crowd surreptitiously, slowly sinking down onto the sitting cushion. He couldn't spot a single familiar one in the sea of faces. Good, that meant Nobu couldn't either. The mere thought of the monk galled Toshi, he wished he could have just ripped the man's throat out and be done with it. He deserved a hundred deaths for what he had done. But taking Nobu out too soon was like cutting the head off a weed, its roots intact, just waiting to grow and blossom once more. The seed of treason had been germinating for a long time already, all it had needed was the right spark, someone with a vision and the drive to see it through.

The emperor was the last one standing. The temple maidens rang their bells: seven times, once for each phase of the moon. Toshi found it hard to focus, his mind drifting as so often to Suzu. The boy was burning for revenge and Toshi couldn't deny it to him, despite his fear that it might consume Suzu. Unlike Naloc, Toshi hadn't even tried to keep Suzu from tonight's events, from the inevitable bloodshed. Yet if possible, he'd kill Nobu before he let Suzu sully himself with the monk's blood.

It wasn't a purely altruistic thought, Toshi *wanted* to kill the man, no, to make him suffer, make him beg for death. The intensity of his wrath still took him by surprise. He had never had friends. His sister, Kagetora, Jarick – they were family and he loved them dearly. But Suzu – Suzu was to him, what he had never even thought he could have; until it had happened he had not believed love like this to be more than a fantasy, something the poets wrote about, something the romantics yearned for. Suzu had become his heart, his very soul. And Suzu's family had become the first real friends he had ever had. Now they were gone, sacrificed for a single man's ego and ambition. One way or another, Nobu was going to pay for what he had done.

The thunderous beat of the great drums jerked him out of his thoughts. Twilight. Torches were being lit in front of the platform. In the firmament the moon was rising in all Her glory, full and huge.

The emperor lifted his hands in benediction towards his people. "Our Celestial Mother," he began the age old prayers. Toshi bowed his head, sending his own prayers to the goddess.

The longer the prayer went on, the more anxious Jin became. The tension made his nerve-endings tingle and caused an uncomfortable fluttering sensation in his stomach. Niall put a hand on his arm to keep him from fidgeting. He took a deep breath, trying to steady his nerves.

"Blessed be Your land and all life that inhabits it," the prayer closed at last. The temple maidens again rang the Seven Bells of the Moon Goddess seven times, each chime was followed by the beat of the great drums. Then there was silence. The emperor took his seat. Servants came forward, filling the waiting ornate glass cups of His Majesty and his council.

Jin grabbed Niall's hand. If Azhar hadn't delivered as promised, or if the exchange had failed, what came next would be a disaster. Jin wondered if the emperor would drink or if he had been cautioned against it.

Emperor Kjell lifted his cup high. The council members and honoured guests followed suit. "To our realm. To the peace and prosperity that has been granted to us. To the people. To the Celestial Mother – to Her eternal glory!"

"To Her eternal glory!" echoed the people.

And thus, the emperor brought his cup to his lips, as did the members of his council, as did his honoured guests.

Jin held his breath. Niall was squeezing his hand so tightly it hurt. The length of a single heartbeat – that was all it took. At first, there was a gasp, loud enough for Jin and Niall to hear where they stood. A cup slipped out of someone's grasp and shattered on the low table, shards of glass catching the torchlight. Two, three of the council members simply keeled over and lay motionless. Others clawed at their throats, their chests. Eyes protruding in panic, streaming tears, beseechingly searching the crowd in front of them for help that wasn't there. Rasping, choking, feeble wails – voices robbed, unable to scream out their fear, their anguish. The betrayal.

It happened so fast. The crowd stared in horror. Until the first terror filled scream rang through the night and Jin was jolted out of his petrification. At last he took a real look at the stage, took note of who was writhing in apparent agony, who lay quietly, and who – more importantly – was fine. He saw that not only the General, but also the emperor lay quiet, both pretending. He saw the Earl sitting tensely by, waiting for the right time, his jaw clenched. Jin looked towards the guest table, to Nobu, and found the monk observing the scene with a triumphant smile on his face. The yellow clad monk beside him was clawing futilely at his own throat.

For a moment, looking at Nobu, hatred filled Jin unlike anything he had ever known or thought himself capable of. Then Niall gripped his arm tightly and the moment was gone. Another scream followed the first. Sudden movement went through the crowd like a wave. Panic was setting in. This was why they had been sent here, he, Niall, and all the others: to take control of the crowd, to minimise the harm. Out of the corner of his eyes Jin saw dark figures darting towards the stage from all directions, saw the Earl and the General rising to their feet, swords being drawn.

"Jin!" Niall yelled.

He gave her a terse nod and grabbed the person next to him. "Quick! Take your family and get out of here. Don't push back. Head straight for the bridge, but don't run. Try to remain calm until you are across the bridge, do you understand?" The man stared at him with wide eyes, looking spooked, but he nodded, clutched his little daughter tighter to his chest with one arm and grabbed his wife's hand. Determined, they followed Jin's instructions.

They had to get those closest to them as quickly as possible across the bridge before the crowd started pushing towards them in blind panic. And so Jin and Niall moved from one to the next, directing them, trying to calm them down, moving them along. Although fear hung in the air like fog, it seemed the strategy they had developed was working out. For now.

With their people in position, they were like wave breakers: diffusing, steering. Slowly the crowd began to disperse, fleeing across the bridges into Kigetsu or deeper into the streets of Mangetsu.

The effect was as spectacular as it was horrifying. It also became abundantly clear very quickly why the apothecary had additionally provided them with an antidote in the end. Whatever did cause those symptoms could not be healthy, the last they needed was for anyone to die of the apparently harmless surrogate.

Toshi tore his eyes away from his convulsing neighbour and instead took stock of who was still completely safe and sound. Jarick and Freya ax Asuka were both pretending to be unconscious, as did the countess's niece. At the other end of the table Lord Otani gaped at the scene, sickly pale, his eyes filled with horror. Too late for any qualms now, Toshi thought. The man had chosen his side, now he had to live with the consequences.

To the emperor's right side, Count Helva and his friends observed their doing with an air of victory, sneering and contemptuous. Toshi mentally rolled his eyes. No surprise. That pompous bastard had cultivated his disdain for the emperor ever since Kjell was crowned. Everyone knew Helva thought he should have been sitting on the Moonlight Throne. His friends, though, they were nothing but mindless followers and lackeys. One of the greatest mysteries had always been how they had even gained a seat on the council in the first place.

And there, just a step below the platform stood Nobu in his brilliant red robes, face alight with triumph. The monk was revelling in his apparent victory, so much so he hadn't noticed yet the people converging on the stage or anything else amiss. Members of the Silver Guard, hand-picked by Jarick, were trying to round up the royal family to herd them to safety. The emperor's wife struggled in the grip of a burly guard, screaming and crying for her husband. Toshi hadn't thought she cared so much about him – or perhaps she was only afraid of all that she would lose if he died.

The crowd, at first frozen in shock, was now in motion. There was screaming, yelling, children crying, calls for order, directions, commands. But no panicked stampede, no mindless terror driving the masses – at least not yet. Slowly, the crowd dispersed. Toshi released a breath of relief.

Well then, he guessed, this was it. Time to give Nobu and his cronies a good taste of bitter disappointment.

He stood up. At his side, Jarick rose to his feet, as did both the Countess and her niece. Even from the distance Toshi could see the frown of confusion forming between Nobu's brows. Then the monk snarled and drew the sword of the man sitting slumped and unconscious beside him.

"What is this?" Count Helvar demanded. "Oi, Tsukikage, what the hell do you think you are doing? Why is the General –" As Nobu stepped up onto the platform he fell silent.

"Somehow I doubt this is just about your little whore, is it?"

"Well, yes and no," Toshi drawled. "You are all under arrest for high treason and conspiring to murder the emperor of Tsukiyama and members of the Moon Council. Resist and you will die right here and now – by which, of course, I mean, please do resist. I'll make sure you die as painfully as possible."

"Ah, I take it that last part is about him," Nobu remarked casually, but his nonchalance was crumbling as he realised his plan had failed.

Lord Otani squeaked in fright and tried to run, but the Countess and her niece easily caught him before he even got off the platform. He fell to his knees in front of them, whimpering and pleading. Freya ax Asuka looked at him as if he were something disgusting she had found beneath a rock.

The Count and his friends, on the other hand, recovered quickly and drew their swords. And then, all of a sudden, they were all plunged into chaos. Ignoring the unconscious men and women at their feet, fighters from both sides drove each other across and off the platform. More armed people were converging on them from all sides, some of them allies, others enemies. The sound of steel clashing with steel rang through the night, loud enough to drown out the screaming and the cries from the scattering crowd.

It was then that the first gunshot rang through the night. It had been foolish to hope the traitors wouldn't go that far. The sound of it was so loud and shocking, even the fighting on the stage drew to a halt. Only a second later panic erupted in the square, those who had not yet been evacuated fled in blind terror, running for their lives, screaming and yelling for their friends and family to hurry.

A nasty smile spread across Nobu's face. "Well, I bet you thought you had already won just because you foiled my little plan with the poison. I did try to avoid a bloodshed, but if that's what you want..."

Toshi rolled his shoulders and adjusted his stance, ready to attack. "You don't seriously consider yourself merciful," he asked disdainfully. Another gunshot rang out, followed by another, and another in more rapid succession. "I wouldn't be so sure about your victory just yet," Toshi added, mimicking Nobu's smile.

The torches set around the platform made it difficult to discern anything that happened beyond it, but Toshi knew those gunshots did not come from one group alone. Nobu did not. Still sure about having the upper hand, the monk ignored Toshi's comment and instead attacked.

Toshi blocked the strike easily, but as they dealt blows back and forth, cutting, stabbing, slashing, and parrying, he had to admit that the man, unfortunately, wasn't half-bad. To the sound of clashing steel, screaming, and the roar of firearms they fiercely crossed swords, neither giving way, neither gaining the upper hand.

Suddenly someone crashed into Toshi's side, sending them both sprawling. He pushed the person off, they were like a rag doll, limp and lifeless, crimson spreading across the front of their white and silver uniform from the bullet hole in their chest. As he scrambled out from beneath the dead guard, Toshi saw Nobu's henchman pulling at the monk's arm urgently, saying something Toshi couldn't hear. He didn't need to, the snarl Nobu gave him before he let his minion drag him away was enough for Toshi to know Nobu had finally been informed that his side wasn't he only one with guns. At last the man's confidence waned. He had to know that he had no chance of winning anymore.

Toshi pushed himself to his feet, yet before he could follow Nobu, a nameless attacker cut his way off. It didn't take him long to divest himself of the man, but by then Nobu was gone. He whirled around, searching frantically for any sign of him, but the monk had vanished.

All around him was chaos. With only the moonlight and a few sparse torches, it was hard to tell who was on whose side. Guards were fighting guards, people who had been friends for years were now crossing swords and throwing punches. Impromptu barricades had sprung up, from behind which two groups were exchanging fire; by this point it seemed the crucial question was, which side would run out of ammunition first.

The General was engaged in fierce battle with Leif ax Ari, the – now former – bodyguard of the emperor. The Countess and her niece were taking care of Count Helvar and his friends with ruthless efficiency.

"Toshi!" He turned into the direction of where the call had come from. Kagetora was standing on the edge of the platform, beckoning. So Toshi struggled back the way he had come.

"Hurry," Kagetora urged as he jumped down from the platform and grabbed Toshi's arm to pull him around the corner of the stage. "Nobu and his thug are fleeing towards Emperor's Bridge!"

The knot of people unravelled. The people of Getsuro showed immense self-discipline, following orders and directions, and taking care of those who might have otherwise have been left behind. Until the deafening roar of a gunshot broke down the final barrier and panic swept through the people.

The steely ring of swords clashing mingled with the sound of crying children and the screams of fear. Jin, ushering an elderly woman towards the bridge, looked back over his shoulder, just as another gunshot rang out. He pulled the old woman against himself, trying not to be swept away by the wave of people, fleeing the fighting.

The enormous silver orb of the moon washed the scene in cold silver light. It looked like utter chaos with no way to tell who was who, who was on which side. A young guard was locked in a heated battle with a guard captain. A young lady, wearing a beautifully patterned kimono, drove a burly man away from the group of temple maidens. The drummers used their big drum sticks like clubs, swinging them wildly at a couple of guards, while the drum bearers were brawling with another group.

And then there was a group of Silver Guards carrying firearms. As they took aim, another shot roared through the night and one of the guards fell. Higa and his people had arrived on the battle field.

Jin fought his way onwards, the old woman trembling like leaves in the wind, clutching at him with surprising strength. Again and again someone, running in blind panic, bumped into them, more than once nearly causing them to fall. But Jin pushed on. Until at last a middle-aged man, wide-eyed and dishevelled, came running towards him, yelling for his mother. The old woman in Jin's arms finally looked up and cried out.

Depositing her safely into the arms of her son, Jin turned back. He had to find Niall. And fast. His friend and he had been charged with delivering the antidote after all.

Pushing his way back towards the platform, Jin shouted his friend's name, but it was difficult to hear anything over the noise of the fighting and the screams.

A figure suddenly rushed at him. If not for the moonlight glinting off the blade of their sword, Jin wouldn't have noticed them until it was too late. As it was, he stumbled sideways, only just avoiding the sharp edged blade. Shocked, he turned towards his attacker, hoping the cold light to reveal an ally who had mistaken him for an enemy. But his hope died quickly. His opponent raised their sword again.

Jin backed away as fast as he could without taking his eyes off of them, fumbling to draw his pistol. All that saved him was the fact that the attacker was either not very skilled or not quite clear in the head, if the blood running down the left side of their face was any indicator.

Pistol finally free, Jin aimed it at the strange swordsman with shaking hands and cocked the hammer... He couldn't do. He couldn't pull the trigger.

The swordsman decided for him, raising his sword above his head and coming at Jin screaming. Startled, Jin pulled the trigger. The report was deafening, the recoil nearly put him on his arse.

He stood trembling, staring at the man who had just a moment ago tried to kill him, lying face-down on the cobblestones at Jin's feet now. The pistol was still smoking.

"Jin!" Someone grabbed his arm, making Jin jump. A frightened yelp escaped him, before he realised it was Niall, who had found him.

"N-N-Niall, I..."

"It's all right. Come – we... we need to get to the platform... stage... whatever."

He let Niall pull him along, but he couldn't take his eyes off of the dead man. It wasn't that Jin had been naïve enough to believe no-one would die this night, or that he wouldn't have to kill anyone. But knowing the possibility wasn't the same as actually doing it. He wanted to fling the pistol far away from himself, and yet he found he couldn't let go of it. That man had intended to kill Jin, it hadn't been much of a choice. What if the next one came after Niall?

At last, Jin pulled his gaze away and instead looked at the scene before him. Squinting, he tried to make out any familiar faces. There – the General was crossing swords with a tall man, who Jin thought was the emperor's bodyguard. A few paces away from the platform, he found Risa disposing one opponent after the other with obvious relish. Her devilish grin was visible even from a distance. Not far from her Naloc and Aika were fighting back to back.

One group, armed with firearms, was barricaded behind what looked like overturned tables, no doubt the same ones the guests of honour had sat at only a short time ago. The other group of shooters was using one of the giant drums as a shield, popping out to quickly fire a shot at the other group, than ducking back behind it.

"Jin!" Niall cried, pulling at Jin's arm. "Come on, we need to get up onto that platform." Jin glanced towards the stage. The fighting by now had moved away from there. A few of the poisoned had already overcome most of it on their own, it seemed, sitting dazed and confused on the platform. Two or three shadowy figures were moving between them, tending to them. So far so good, but to get to them, Jin and Niall still had to cross a small battle field. Jin took a deep breath and lifted his pistol. He had only one shot left.

"All right." He held his hand out to Niall. "Don't let go! And assume to be attacked from everyone you don't recognise at once."

Niall checked the bamboo flask with the antidote was securely tied to her belt, drew her own knife, and grasped Jin's hand tightly. A nod, and then they were running, dodging fighting pairs, a sword swung in their direction. Jin reeled back. Not wanting to waste his shot, he instead brought the butt of the pistol down on the woman's wrist hard. With a yelp she dropped her sword, and Jin and Niall took the opportunity to hurry on.

Niall punched her small wickedly pointed dagger into a particularly painful body part of another attacker – the man went down, howling. But at last they were through the worst of it. Before they could enter the platform, however, a young woman barred their way, levelling her sword at them.

Niall held up the bamboo flask. "We have the antidote!"

The woman looked at her, suspicious. "How do I know you're not lying?"

"Why should I lie now?"

At that moment another woman appeared out of the shadows. It took Jin a second to recognise her as the one who had met them at the General's secret lair at the Academy.

"Let them through, they're Murasaki's." Her colleague huffed but did as told. Only seconds later Niall had fully turned into her physician self, calling orders, administering the antidote, checking vital signs. Jin just followed along and did as she told him.

Suzu cursed loudly when he saw people running across the bridges spanning the River Opal. From across the river came shouts and the metallic clang of clashing swords. Escaping his guard had taken Suzu far too long. Now he was standing on top of a low wall, watching the deluge of people fleeing Moonlight Square in dismay. He had to get across the river. Worrying his lower lip with his teeth, Suzu thought about his options. Taking a bridge further south would mean he would have to backtrack through the streets of Mangetsu, which no doubt would be full of scared people. That left him with only one option: Emperor's Bridge. It would be heavily guarded for it led directly onto palace grounds, but it was the only way. With any luck, the guards would be occupied otherwise.

Grinding his teeth with impatience, Suzu jumped down from his perch and fought his way through the crowd, then sprinted all the way to Emperor's Bridge.

He ground to a halt. The bridge, instead of being heavily guarded, was deserted. The lanterns and the stone lions on either side of it were the only sentinels left. Suzu wondered if the guards really had left their post because they were needed elsewhere.

Wary, Suzu slowly moved forward and drew his short sword. Something felt off. This wasn't right.

The bridges across the river weren't flat but gentle arches. No sooner than Suzu stepped onto the peek of the bridge did it become clear why it had seemed deserted. He quickly crouched down in the deeper shadows along the balustrade.

There were four of them. Two lay on the ground, not moving. A third one was kneeling in front of a person raising their sword. From what Suzu could make out in the cold moonlight, all four of them were Silver Guards.

"Why are you doing this?" the one, kneeling, asked. Her voice sounded distorted with pain. She didn't receive an answer. Instead, the person she had once trusted with her life cut her down. Moonlight reflected off the blade as the guard, with a flick of her wrist, shook the blood off it.

Before Suzu could decide how to get past them, movement caught his attention. Nobu stepped out of the shadows beyond the bridge. He looked down at the fallen guards, his whole posture spoke of his disdain.

"Let's go," Nobu said.

Suzu stepped out into the middle of the bridge. The moment they saw him, the guard raised her sword again, but Nobu, with a hand on her arm, held her back.

"I was wondering when you'd show up."

"Yes, sorry, I was held up. But you know... promises to keep."

Nobu laughed. "Oh, I see. Hope you don't expect me to hold still and just let you kill me."

Suzu shrugged. "You could."

"And where would be the fun in that? Give me your sword," Nobu demanded, holding his hand out. The woman looked at him in confusion for a moment, obviously torn between her innate sense of guarding her master and not defying his orders. At last she shrugged and handed it over.

"Oi, a High Priest of Hôjô has no business even touching a sword," Suzu mocked.

"Ah, you know me. Always prepared for any kind of situation," Nobu quipped and lifted the sword. It was a slender blade and easily twice as long as Suzu's tantō. He cursed mentally. Just his luck to show up to a sword fight with a knife. He could only hope Nobu's skills with a sword weren't particularly good.

That hope didn't live long; Nobu unceremoniously rushed him. Suzu blocked the thrust only just in time, then sprang back. Nobu, however, didn't give him any time to recover, pressing him with movements as vicious and fast as a viper. And, of course, he kept trying to get at Suzu's blind side. But Suzu had learned from the best. Haldor had taught him two things before anything else: how to make up for his limited vision, and how to guard his right side.

However, Nobu's reach was bigger than Suzu's, putting him on the defence. It was all he could do: defend and wait for an opening, or for the monk to tire himself out.

It was so frustrating that Suzu, annoyed, made a mistake. Trying to push back, he left his right side open. Even realising his mistake at once, he wasn't quick enough to completely evade Nobu's attack. Cold steel drew a line of fire across his arm. Suzu cursed, sprang back – and stumbled. He managed to regain his footing, but he knew this time he would not be able to block the glinting blade cutting through the air towards him.

The sound of steel hitting steel was deafening. Sparks flew as the two blades grated against each other. Nobu nearly lost hold of his sword and hastily retreated.

"Are you all right?"

Suzu looked up at the man, who had just saved him. "Toshi? How did you--?"

"I followed that scum. Got delayed by his thug, though. Kagetora is taking care of him now."

"Oh look, if it isn't the prince come save his little princess," Nobu sneered.

"If you had even a shred of honour in your bones, you would have given Suzu a sword to fight with. And then I could just have stood back and watched him cutting you into pieces. But alas..." Toshi retorted.

"Pah! Honour – that's just what the losing side likes to tell themselves: that at least they fought with honour. I don't give a damn about honour!"

"Clearly," Suzu murmured. And then, as much as he hated it, he stepped back to give Toshi room. It was his own fault, what had he been thinking? That he wouldn't have to fight anyone except Nobu? That the damn monk wouldn't even know how to hold a sword? Stupid. He should have had gotten a sword from somewhere, anywhere. Now all he could do was concede and let Toshi handle this. After all, Suzu had promised not to be stubborn about getting his revenge.

Not a heartbeat later the man he loved and the man he despised with every fibre of his being clashed with the ferocity of demons. Suzu ground his teeth, his rage demanded an outlet, not to be assuaged.

Irritatingly, both men seemed to be evenly matched, driving each other across the bridge, a steady back and forth.

Neither of them was giving, neither relenting, neither gaining the upper hand.

"Well, well, what does a monk know about honour anyway." Suzu whirled around. He had completely forgotten about the guard. Now she was stalking towards him, drawing her tantō. "Don't worry, I will give you an honourable death."

Suzu had no more time to worry about Toshi, as she attacked him with a manic relish.

Many of the high-born insurgents, surprised at having their perfect plan foiled, were quickly subdued. The bigger problem were the turncoats amongst the guard. They knew there was only one way this would end for them, and most of them chose to die here and now, fighting. Perhaps it was also that they intended to take as many people with them as they could. In any way, they fought far fiercer than before. Reckless. Brutal. Former friends, subordinates, brothers- and sisters-in-arms.

Behind the platform were now almost two dozen prisoners, bound and kneeling. They were nobles, guards, and commoners alike. A score of loyal Silver Guards was standing guard over them, regarding their former comrades and friends with disgust.

Niall didn't fault them, the betrayal cut deep and was much more personal than the treason for which they would be going to the gallows.

By now the emperor's own physicians had arrived and taken over command, having seen their most important patient safely installed in his own chambers under heavy guard. With the knowledge that she had done all she could by administering the antidote, Niall gladly relinquished command. She made a mental note to congratulate Azhar, he had accomplished the impossible.

"What now?" asked Jin.

Niall chewed her lip, unsure. Their orders hadn't gone beyond making certain the antidote was administered to everyone and ensuring there were no ugly side effects. Neither Jin nor she were fighters, it would probably be best to stay as far away from any battle as possible. She should see to the injured, though...

"Niall, have you seen Suzu anywhere?" Jin's voice had a worried edge. "Or the Earl?"

Now that Jin mentioned it, the last time Niall had seen the Earl had been on the platform when the fighting had started. Afterwards she had been too busy with the evacuation of the square. She couldn't even recall if the man had still been on the stage by the time she and Jin had reached it. And Suzu? The boy was supposed to be with Naloc and Risa.

"The Earl and his bodyguard went after that lousy high priest," said a voice from behind them. It was a swordswoman neither of them knew, although she looked familiar.

"Do you know in which direction –" Jin began. A cry of agony, coming from the directions of the palace grounds, cut him off.

"That one," the woman answered with a grimace.

They needed no words to know what the other was thinking. With a curt nod to the nameless swordswoman they took off at a run in the direction the scream had come from.

There was no other light save for the moon illuminating the palace grounds. Clouds had formed in the formerly clear sky, occasionally drifting lazily across the moon's face, plunging them into temporary darkness. Because of this they didn't notice the two blood drenched guards standing in the deeper shadows of a tree, until they were almost upon them.

There was no doubt which side they were on. Without preamble they drew their swords. Niall grabbed Jin's arm, tried to steer him into backing away. But instead, Jin lifted his pistol.

His hand was neither steady, nor did he look like he really knew what he was doing. And the guards could tell. With matching ugly grins, they stalked towards Niall and Jin.

"There is no need for this. Just stay back and let us pass," Jin said.

The guards laughed. "Or what?" the one on Niall's right retorted. "Do you even know how to shoot this thing? I tell you what. You just get down on your knees – both of you. And who knows, if your pretty friend here begs nicely enough..." His lewd grin and the way his friend was laughing told Niall exactly what kind of begging they wanted her to do. She gritted her teeth. Let them try. Surreptitiously she pulled one of her long needles out of the band she wore on her arm.

She didn't have to bother. With a low growl, Jin fired a shot at the guard. These kinds of threats – no matter if they were against himself or anyone else – Jin had no tolerance for them.

The retort shattered the relative silence of the palace grounds. Niall's ears were ringing. Shocked, she looked at her friend, standing tense, with gritted teeth and fury in his eyes, the smoking pistol still aimed at the offensive guard. The shot had missed. It had only grazed the man's face. Tentatively he touched his fingers to his bloody cheek.

"You –!" he snarled. But before he had recovered enough to lift his sword again, Jin surprised all of them even more by rushing at the man and, using the spent pistol like a club, bashed it against the guard's head. The man went down like a wet sack.

That was when the fight seemed to go out of Jin. He stumbled back and dropped the pistol.

"Jin," Niall began – but whatever she had intended to say it turned into a scream. The other guard had recovered from his shock. Niall saw him lift his sword, saw him moving to cut down Jin, who just stood there with his head hanging and his shoulders slumped. What little she could do, she wouldn't make it in time. A horrible vision of her best friend, the brother of her heart, cut open and bleeding, flashed before her inner eye. She reached for Jin, cried his name –

The guard stiffened, dropped his sword, and then he fell. Behind him stood a person, dressed all in black, leaning heavily on what appeared to be a katana, a bloody dagger in their other hand.

Jin snapped out of his stupor. "K-Kagetora?"

The Umbrage gave a grunt in response and sat down heavily. Niall ran to him. Kagetora was panting, beads of sweat glistened on his brow. His leg looked wrong.

"What happened?"

"That bastard broke my leg," he gasped.

"Who?"

"The monk's lackey."

"Where is he now? Where's Nobu? Where's your master? Suzu? Have you –"

"Jin," Niall cut her friend off. "I know you're worried, but calm down, please." Jin, clearly unhappy, did as he was told, biting his tongue and clenching his hands into fists. "All right, let me see your leg."

While Niall, as gently as possible, examined the leg, Kagetora kept his eyes fixed on the moon.

"I need to set the bone and fixate it. Jin, make yourself useful and hold him down."

Kagetora was about to protest, but Jin, used to helping Niall with her patients, was quick and efficient as he pushed the man down and pinned him to the ground.

"What exactly happened?" Jin asked, and Niall knew he didn't just ask to distract Kagetora.

Kagetora took a shuddering breath. "I don't really know. We – Toshi and I – we followed Nobu. But we were waylaid by his thug. I told Toshi to go on, that I would take care of him. But gods damn it! That bastard doesn't fight fair. He's got not a shred of honour in his bones. I swear, when I'll – Aaaargh!" he screamed when Niall set the bone in his leg, feeling the broken pieces slide together. Niall was pretty satisfied with her work, but when she looked up at the two men, neither of them seemed very appreciative. Jin was staring into the darkness, Kagetora looked close to fainting, which wasn't really a surprise.

"Now... I need something..." She spotted Kagetora's sword lying in the grass beside them and picked it up, appraising. Then she grabbed a bandage from her satchel and, using the sword, sheath and all, as a makeshift splint, dressed the leg.

"What are you –" Kagetora gasped in shock.

"What? I don't have anything else, do I?" By all rights she should be praised for her ability to improvise, but although Kagetora did not protest further, he seemed neither impressed nor very happy about her quick thinking.

Jin was fidgeting again. His gaze searched the surrounding area. But a shudder ran through him when his eyes fell on the two dead guards. It would take some time for the young man to come to terms with having taken lives this night. Niall could only hope that he could overcome it and would not drown in guilt and nightmares. But she would be there, however long it took, and no matter how often she would have to put him back together when he broke apart, she'd do it.

Right now, however, the nervous energy that came from him almost made Niall snap. She knew he was worried, but what could he do?

"Which direction did they go? Was Suzu with the Earl?" he asked.

"Suzu? No, I don't know where he is. Nobu fled towards Emperor's Bridge. He'll try to vanish back into Eigetsu."

Niall, anticipating what was going to happen, grabbed at Jin before he could spring to his feet and dash off.

"Niall!"

"No! You have... what? A knife? You are no match for that Steren bloke – look what he did to Kagetora!" she snapped when Jin opened his mouth to protest. It was enough to shut him up. Kagetora was an Umbrage, and yet Steren had somehow managed to incapacitate the man. "Go and find Naloc and Risa. Bring them and whoever else is available."

"But –"

"Do as I say!" Niall seldom used her authority on Jin, but when she did Jin knew better than to argue. And so he nodded, turned and took off, back towards the square.

"He's worried about Suzu," Kagetora stated. Niall made an affirmative sound. "To be honest, so am I. I haven't seen him anywhere."

"He'll be fine. He's stronger than any of us." She pulled the bandage tighter, eliciting a grunt of pain from Kagetora. Dissatisfied, Niall clicked her tongue. "This is far from ideal. I can't promise it won't need setting again later. For now, try to keep it as still as possible."

"It doesn't matter, I have to go after Toshi."

"Don't be a fool! You can't stand, much less walk. What use are you in a fight like this?"

"You don't understand. He's not just my master, he's my friend, my... my brother. He's the only family I've ever known!"

Niall looked into the man's eyes, filled with pain, desperate. She felt an unexpected kinship towards him. Kagetora and the Earl – their relationship wasn't so different from what Naloc and Jin were to Niall. Or from Suzu and the family he so desperately wanted to avenge. All of them had found a family in strangers, all of them would fight heaven and hell for them. And so Niall did what she would normally never do: she told her inner doctor to shut the hell up.

"All right. I don't know if I can get you that far, but I'll give it my best." The gratefulness in Kagetora's eyes warmed her heart.

"Perhaps I might be of help."

Startled, Niall looked up and found the General looming over them. She hadn't even noticed his approach. Kagetora had to be in a lot of pain and probably not a little feverish to not have noticed either. Niall ignored the sensible doctor's voice in her head that told her the man needed rest and decent treatment.

"I just ran into your young friend," the General explained. "He told me what happened. He's gone to fetch the old goat." He winked at Niall, who couldn't help but smile. Whatever grudge Naloc held against the man, Niall found she actually liked him.

The General took Kagetora beneath the arms and together they managed to get him on his feet without jostling the broken leg too much. Supporting Kagetora, the three began their laborious way across the vast lawn towards the river and the bridge.

But they hadn't gotten far when they heard a scream that send a shiver through all of them. The despair, the agony, the sheer strength and weight of the emotion it carried almost brought them to their knees. For a short moment, Niall felt disorientated and dizzy, her heart constricted painfully. She gasped, tears blurred her vision. The men, both, drew sharp breaths.

"Suzu," all three whispered in unison. They exchanged shocked looks and continued as quickly as they could.

Suzu allowed the guard to drive him back across the bridge, staying on the defence. She didn't realise he was testing her skills, patiently waiting for an opening. And while she was as fierce a fighter as Risa, she wasn't half as good. Her almost mindless, reckless attacks, however, came in such rapid succession and with such brutish force, it made them almost unpredictable.

"You're good," she said with a wicked grin, as they ground to a halt, swords locked.

Suzu's face lit with an angelic smile. "Thank you. I would love to return the compliment – but I've seen better."

The snub had the desired effect. With an angry roar, the guard pushed – but Suzu, who had been waiting for it, swiftly sidestepped her. She stumbled forward and fell against the railing. Blind with rage, she swung around – leaving herself wide open. Suzu was already there, and drove his sword beneath her rips and up. She gasped. Her sword clattered onto the cobblestones. Her expression was frozen in shock as the light in her eyes already dimmed. The guard was dead before she even hit the ground.

Suzu flicked the blood off his sword and looked up from the dead guard. It was at this moment that the moon appeared from behind a passing cloud and her silver orb bathed the scene on the other side of the bridge in cold light. Toshi and Nobu – much like Suzu and the female guard just moments ago – had come to a standstill, although it seemed Toshi's greater physical strength had the monk in a precarious situation, when suddenly, out of the shadows, a third figure appeared behind Toshi. Light glinted off a blade.

Suzu's eyes widened in shock, his heart began to hammer frantically against his ribs. His ears filled with the sound of rushing blood. Too late, he'd never make it in time. He forced his body to move, but it felt as if he was moving through molasses. It was like being trapped inside a nightmare. His voice wouldn't come; he tried again and again to call out. Perhaps he had no more air in his lungs. Dread filled him. He was halfway across the bridge. Just a little more. He had to move faster.

The blade cut into Toshi as if he was nothing but a doll made of rags. Suzu heard a sharp intake of breath, saw Toshi's back arch as the blade went right through him. A scream finally tore from Suzu's throat, full of anguish and rage.

He reached Toshi just as Steren yanked his sword out. As Toshi fell heavily to his knees. As Nobu took a hasty step back, away from Toshi, away from Suzu. But Suzu paid the monk no heed. He fell to his knees beside his love, pressed his hands against the gaping wound.

"No no no!" Panic rushed through him. Hot blood spilled over his fingers. He had no way to stop it.

"What about him?"

"Just leave him. Let him break from yet another loss. We need to hurry."

Footsteps, receding quickly. Then they were alone.

"Su... -zu."

"Hush, don't speak. I... we need to..." Suzu had no idea what they needed, what he ought to do, to say. His head was filled with a screaming voice. *No, no, no, no, no!* This couldn't be happening. It mustn't. There had to be something he could do.

Blood ran in a hot stream over his fingers. Too much, too fast. The iron stench of it filled his nose.

"...sorry." Toshi's voice was quiet and broken. He slowly lifted his head to look at Suzu. A trickle of blood ran out of the corner of his mouth. There was a horrible gurgling sound as he tried to draw breath. He coughed. Fresh blood bubbled out of his mouth.

"It's all right, Toshi. It's going to be all right. Remember? We promised. I'll come live with you from now on. We're going to be together. Just you and me. We... we can go somewhere quiet for a while... your... your country home. And..." Suzu was babbling. Saying stupid things – to calm himself as much as Toshi. It was all he could do. He sent a desperate prayer to the gods to save Toshi. Beseeching. Promising a thousand different things. Whatever it took. Pleading. Threatening.

"Su..." Toshi dragged his hand across his lap. He was still holding his sword. "Take... it... you... go..."

"No. Toshi, no. I don't care anymore. I'm not leaving you. Please, just... just... please!"

"He's... n... ga..." Toshi's voice was fading.

"No! No, no, no!" Suzu pressed his hands harder against the wound, but the flow of blood would not be staunched. Toshi slumped against him. "No, please!" Carefully, Suzu laid Toshi down. "Don't leave me. I love you, Toshi. You hear? You can't leave me!"

Toshi gave him a weak, weary smile. "So... sorry." The light was leaving his eyes. Those grey eyes that only ever warmed when he looked at Suzu. "Su...zu... I lo--"

Toshi's face lost all expression, his eyes stared unseeingly at the moon above, their light forever extinguished.

"No," Suzu gasped. He couldn't breathe, his lungs refused to take in any air. He grasped at Toshi's lifeless body. A sob racked Suzu's body.

And then something inside him broke. Shattered into a thousand tiny pieces – and the raging infernal storm of rage that had been restrained, contained, for so many years broke free. Like a dragon, awakening, it roared to life. It gripped Suzu's broken heart in its claws, sharpened the pieces to a razor's edge. It fed on all of his grief, his pain.

A sudden deadly calm descended on Suzu.

He took the sword from Toshi's limp hand, brushed the hair from his brow. Suzu used his sleeve to clean his love's face. He gently closed those lovely grey eyes. For one eternal moment, he regarded the still face of the man he loved, washed in silver moonlight. Then he leaned down and pressed his lips against Toshi's for one last kiss. A single tear was all he allowed himself. There would be no tears now, he would not fall apart now. He still had a promise to fulfil – a promise that carried one more name now, a name that weighed heavily.

Suzu gently stroked his beloved's face. Inhale, exhale. Inhale, exhale. The sound of footsteps reached his ears, but he didn't move. A sharp intake of breath. A shocked exclamation.

"Toshi!"

Someone fell to their knees besides Toshi's body. Suzu slowly raised his head. Kagetora, face deathly pale, awkward with a heavily bandaged leg, half knelt, half lay beside his master, his friend. He ran his hands through the air just above the lifeless body, afraid to touch.

The General was there, too, staring in shock and shaking his head as if he refused to believe what he saw was real.

Niall was there, pressing two fingers against Toshi's neck, eyes assessing the damage. There was nothing of her usual cheerfulness.

"Toshi! Oh gods, no, Toshi." Kagetora turned to Niall, pleading. "Please. Can't you do something? You're a doctor! Do something, please! He can't die!" His voice broke. Niall only looked sad and shook her head. The General sat down heavily, face blank.

"Kagetora," Suzu said, startling the others. His voice was eerily calm, empty, hollow. "Tell me where to find Nobu."

"What? I... gods..." Kagetora sobbed.

"Tell me!" Suzu ordered sharply.

"A-at his hideout... I guess. His family's old abandoned manor. I reckon he'll want to leave through the north... through the north gate."

"Where is the manor?"

"Near the gate... it's the old... there's a stone griffin at the front gate, and a small one at the back gate."

"Thank you."

Suzu, sword in hand, stood up and turned to go.

"Wait! Suzu, where are you going?" the General asked, taken aback.

"To fulfil my promise, and end this once and for all." Suzu kept his eyes locked on Kagetora, until he was sure the

Umbrage understood. At last the man lifted his head and looked at Suzu, then gave him a short, grim nod.

"And Kagetora, don't you dare do anything that can't be undone. You know that he wouldn't want you to. So honour his wish!"

Kagetora opened his mouth to speak, but Suzu didn't stay around to listen. Before any of them could stop him, Suzu cast a last glance at his dead love, then turned and went to claim his revenge.

It had taken Jin too long to find Naloc. If he hadn't had a run in with the General, who pointed him in the right direction, he wouldn't have found him at all. Now, Jin, Naloc, and Risa were running towards Emperor's Bridge. They were almost there when they could make out a huddled group of people at the foot of the bridge. Even from afar Jin thought the scene looked wrong.

"Niall?" he called. His friend lifted her head and looked in his direction. She looked more exhausted than he had ever seen her. It wasn't until he heard Naloc and Risa gasping in shock that Jin took notice of the figure on the ground. His heart nearly stopped. For one mad moment, he thought it was Suzu. Then his brain rearranged the image in front of him. It wasn't any less shocking.

Kagetora was awkwardly sprawling on the ground, openly crying. The General was sitting beside him, gently stroking the hair of a bloodied and still body. It was the Earl's.

This isn't right. Of all the things that could go wrong, all the terrible things his brain had invented, for some reason Jin had not once imagined it possible that the Earl could die. The man had always had an aura of power, of strength – now he was but a shattered, empty shell. All of his fire, his intellect, his unexpected gentleness – gone. Snuffed out like a candle in the wind. He had been a force – now he was gone. It was shocking and terrifying, and so wrong.

Another thought hit Jin like a hammer strike: What about Suzu? Die he know? How was he supposed to live with even more loss? No-one deserved so much heartbreak, no-one could cope with so much grief.

"How... what happened?" Naloc inquired in a hushed voice.

Niall stood up and stepped closer to them before replying in a low voice, "I assume Nobu and his goon happened. We don't know for sure. All I can tell you is..." She drew a shuddering breath. "All I can say is that he was run through, there was nothing anyone could have done."

Risa let out a colourful string of curses, kicking the pebbles beneath her feet. Jin pressed the heel of his hand against his brow and took a deep breath. He wanted to scream, he wanted... he wanted that none of this had ever happened. And then Niall made it all worse. "Suzu went after the monk."

Jin's heart stopped for a beat, before it began a frantic tattoo. His head was spinning.

"Wait! Suzu? That can't be," Naloc countered. "I... well... I constrained him at home."

For one dizzy moment Jin felt hopeful. It didn't last long. A low chuckle made them turn. It was the General. Despite a tear running down his face, he had a crooked smile on his lips.

"You didn't really think you could keep that boy from his revenge."

"Where is he? Where has he gone? We can't just let him go alone!" Jin cried with a note of panic in his voice.

It was Kagetora, who answered him, voice broken and tear choked, and not taking his eyes off his dead master. He was still an Umbrage, despite his grief, and gave them as precise a description as he could of the house he believed Nobu was at.

Naloc began issuing orders, to Risa, to Niall – but Jin wasn't listening. He had just noticed the bodies of three guards. It had been a silver glint that had caught his eyes. Without hesitation, Jin went to one of the corpses and grabbed the man's sword.

"Jin?" It was Niall's voice. He didn't look back at her, didn't answer. She would hold him back, tell him to stay, to not be so stupid. And she would be right, of course, but he couldn't just stand back anymore. He felt responsible for bringing Nobu and all the suffering the monk had caused back into Suzu's life. No, that was wrong, it was more than that. This wasn't the first time after all. But this time, he would do something, anything, no matter the cost.

He ran.

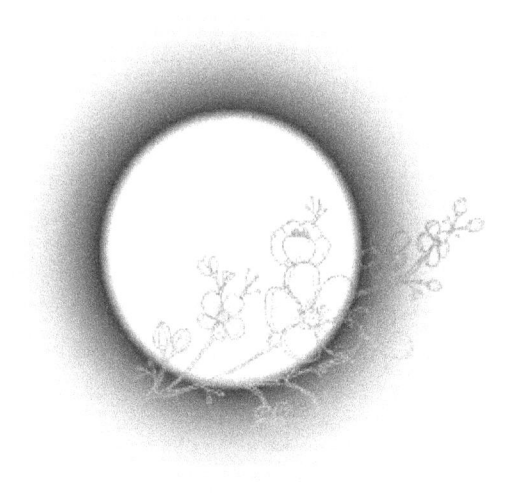

Chapter 40

The streets of Eigetsu were deserted. Even those closest to the river and the palace were dark and silent. The houses were tall and clustered, the moonlight hardly able to reach into the small alleyways.

Impatience and urgency tugged on Suzu's nerves. He needed to get out of this labyrinth. How much further? How much of a headstart did Nobu have? Had he already fled the town?

After what felt like hours, Suzu finally stepped out of a dark alley and onto a moonlight-flooded and wild-grown green belt. Beyond lay the oldest part of the capital, long since abandoned: Ghost Town. Derelict old manor houses, overgrown gardens, wild, green meadows and groves that once were parks. It was an apocalyptic view.

Suzu had never been here, the directions Kagetora had given him didn't mean much to him. Instead he took the shortest route to the wall. From there he would first head to the northern gate and then look for the house Kagetora had described to him: the monk's ancestral family home.

The northern gate rose out of the darkness suddenly and unexpectedly. It was closed, no guards in sight – here, they only cared about who tried to enter the town, not who wanted to leave. But unless Nobu had made it out before they had closed the gate – which was unlikely – he was trapped inside the town until sunrise.

Suzu slowly went down the road, squinting at the ramshackle houses. Kagetora had said Nobu's house was close to the gate, but how far still counted as close? Just when Suzu thought he should try another street, he spotted it: a stone griffin. One wing had broken off, and so had the tip of its tail and a piece of its beak. But this had to be the one.

He went closer cautiously, tightening the grip on his sword. The griffin's pedestal had tilted to one side, it wouldn't take much longer until the stone figure toppled over. One large griffin in front of the house, a smaller one in the back – there was no way to tell which one this one was. The gate the griffin was supposed to guard was half rotted away, the rest of it hanging off its hinges. Readying himself for whatever was to come, Suzu stepped through it into an overgrown garden.

"I was hoping you'd show up!" Sitting on the trunk of a fallen tree, waiting patiently with his sword laid across his legs, was Steren.

The house with the stone griffins. Jin remembered he had seen it before, when he and Issei had been exploring some of the abandoned parts of town. That had been two years ago, roughly. But Jin could still recall the griffins, for it had been the first time he had seen such creatures. Issei had laughed about his childish wonder.

He took the shortest route he knew of, running until, at last, he came to a halt, sweating and panting, in front of a giant roaring stone griffin. The remnants of a gate lay on the overgrown path next to it.

Jin took his time, catching his breath and listening intently for any sounds. There – were those voices? He couldn't quite tell where they came from. Warily, he peered around the statue. The path was empty and dark. There was no light coming from the house. Had Nobu already fled town? Or was he hiding inside?

Jin took a deep breath, gripped his sword tightly, and slowly stepped over the broken gate. A quick glance to the left and to the right to ensure no-one was there, and then he continued slowly down the path.

He was halfway to the house when a shadow peeled off the from the deeper darkness of the porch. Jin stopped and raised his sword. The shadow descended the decrepit stairs.

"Now you're not who I was expecting," Nobu said, stepping into the moonlight. "It's been far too long, don't you think, Jin?"

"Nobu." In the last couple of days Jin had imagined a thousand versions of how this would go. What he would do or say when he finally met Nobu again. What he would feel, knowing what he knew now to be the truth about the monk. The truth was – he didn't know. He had expected to feel furious, betrayed, hurt, but what he felt could not be described in simple words. It was a confusion of warring emotions, a clash of past and present verities. The image of Nobu Jin had had in his mind for all his life lay superimposed over the man in front of him. Part of him didn't want to let go of the Nobu who had been his friend, his confidant. But another part reminded him that that person had never been real in the first place.

"Well," Nobu continued. "I'd love to chit-chat, but I'm a little busy right now, so..."

"The gates are closed, you can't get out of town," Jin blurted.

"So? Do you really think General Jarick ax Varg and that boss of yours are able to rout out every single one of my allies? And even if they do, they got nothing on me, nor will they find anything."

"I think you are wrong about that," Jin argued, but he didn't sound as confident as he had hoped. "Why are you doing this?"

"Why? To take back what is rightfully mine!"

"I don't care... I mean, why are you doing this to Suzu? Back then? Now? Why kill all those innocent people?"

Nobu sighed, exasperated. "Jin, Jin, Jin. You know what I always liked best about you? Not that you were so damn gullible, or so easily manipulated. No. But that you didn't ask so many questions."

Jin gritted his teeth. "What the hell do you think other people's lives are? They are not your tools, or your toys. You can't just ruin them, destroy them, throw them away as if they have no value at all."

"Tsk." Nobu clicked his tongue. "And that's where you're wrong. They don't. They have value as long as they are of use, and when they aren't..." Nobu shrugged.

Jin was speechless. Never in his life had he imagined it possible for someone to have such utter disregard for others' lives. How could he ever have thought Nobu was kind and caring? That he mattered to him?

"Isn't it amazing how little we know the people closest to us?" Nobu chuckled, derisively, as if he had read Jin's thoughts. "Tell me, Jin: How well do you know Suzu? Or rather: How well did you know Kari?"

And there it was, another undeniable truth: He didn't know Suzu at all, he had never known Kari as well as he had thought. It wasn't the other boy's fault. Jin had just never looked beyond what he wanted to see. He had taken everything for granted, had never asked Kari what he wanted, what he needed. And Suzu? Suzu was a stranger with a familiar face and a shared past.

"I did you a favour, back then," Nobu continued. "I freed you of him."

"You freed me? I didn't need any freeing!"

"Did you not? Do you really still think the love between you was real?" Nobu laughed, shaking his head as if the idea alone was ridiculous. "He's an Ethereal, Jin, he bewitched you, it's what they do."

"You're wrong! He didn't. Perhaps he didn't show me who he really is, but he never bewitched me!"

Nobu shrugged exaggeratedly. "How do you know? Oh, of course, if he had, you probably wouldn't have been able to just throw him away like some piece of trash, would you? You're right, my bad."

"That's –" Jin choked on his words. He wanted to deny it, to say he never intended to abandon Kari – but he knew now that it was exactly what he had done, intentionally or not. The knowledge of the harm, the pain he had caused made him to lie awake at night. There was nothing he could do to undo it, but at least he could try.

"You pretend to be such a good person, but aren't you just self-centred and selfish?" Nobu taunted.

The monk's words hit deep, but it wasn't only shame and hurt they incited. At last – at long last, anger stirred within Jin. "You're right, I made mistakes, and my worst mistake was listening to you! It wasn't Suzu who bewitched me, it was you who manipulated me from the start. You were never my friend. I have no idea what Suzu has ever done to you that you hate him so much, and I don't care. He didn't deserve the things you did to him. The people at the Singing Dragon didn't deserve to die like this. The Earl didn't deserve it! You –" The metallic rasp of a sword leaving its sheath cut Jin off.

"I've had enough of you and your whining and your stupid morals." Nobu snapped, irritated. "Let's find out if you know what to do with a sword."

"Steren," Suzu spat the name, disgusted and filled with hatred. But Steren just laughed and slowly stood up, sword ready in his hand.

"I guess loverboy croaked," he said, laughing, as if it were a joke. The pain and rage his words induced made Suzu's knees buckle, his vision went dark for a moment. Clenching his teeth and taking a deep breath, Suzu tried to gain control over his emotions. *Never let your emotions lead your sword.* Haldor had told him again and again, until Suzu had learned to put a leash on his anger. But now his emotions – the pain, the rage –

had become a wild, roaring dragon no leash could ever tame. So perhaps he had to fight fire with fire.

"You know, you really should thank Miki for rearranging your face. I'd call this an improvement. But don't worry, you still have one mean ugly mug."

It had the desired effect. Steren's expression darkened, his nonchalance was cracking. "You've always been an insufferable brat," the man growled. "The only thing you're good for is being fucked."

"And yet, still better than being someone's lapdog, running around and yapping for his master's attention, who couldn't care less if you live or die."

"I'm not... Nobu values me. I'm his right hand after all."

"Tut tut tut," Suzu clucked his tongue, shaking his head, disappointed. "It's nice to have dreams, but you are delusional if you really believe that. Oh yes, I bet he appreciates your opinions and your invaluable input."

Well, Steren might have been delusional, but he didn't miss Suzu's sarcasm. "You!" he snarled and pointed his sword at Suzu. "I should have wrung your skinny little neck a long time ago!"

"Hmm, as I remember, you couldn't even beat me when I was ten."

Now that certainly did the trick. With an angry roar, Steren launched himself at Suzu. In his anger he used his sword more like a club, wildly swinging it at Suzu two-handed as if he wanted to just hack him into pieces. Suzu easily evaded him.

"I will fucking tear you apart, you fucking whore," Steren growled. "I will bash in that pretty face of yours. I'll... I'll..." Steren was tall, lots of muscle, but he lacked brain as well as stamina. The random sword swings became sloppier and less forceful. Suzu blocked another swing, then sprang back out of reach. Steren was already panting heavily.

"You know," the man sneered, "I really enjoyed their screams." For a moment Suzu was confused. But Steren continued. "Did you know, the first ones to stumble out, were that old bitch and a little runt. That runt – actually tried to protect the old hag, can you believe it?" He barked a laugh. "He was so scrawny, I almost cut him in two. Ah, that bitch's screams," Steren drawled. "I bet she loved to be fucked hard, eh? If only there had been the time, I'd have made her beg for death," he laughed.

Suzu felt like he had to vomit. He breathed hard through his nose. His vision was tinged red, his blood was screaming for violence. Too much. The rage was burning him alive. His whole body was trembling from the effort of holding back, of not rushing blindly forward. But why was he holding back? He shouldn't be holding back. *Do it! Do it! Kill him!* a voice screamed inside his head. *KILL HIM!*

Do not let your emotions lead your sword, Suzu! Haldor's voice was like thunder in his mind, silencing the other voice. And suddenly that eery, icy calmness descended on him once more, his mind and his vision became crystal clear.

It was almost as if time had slowed down. Steren was coming at him. Suzu shifted his stance and met Steren's blow. Their swords met with a resounding clang – and then Steren's battered, chipped sword broke. Suzu took advantage of Steren's shock, stepped into the man's space and rammed his kunai into the inside of Steren's thigh. Grunting, Steren stabbed his broken sword at Suzu, who blocked it easily and gave the kunai a vicious twist. Steren cried out in pain.

"That was for all the lies you told five years ago," Suzu snarled. And before Steren could do so much as draw another breath, Suzu, with all the strength he could muster, dragged the small vicious knife through Steren's flesh and across the man's groin, opening a wide gash. Hot, metallic reeking blood gushed over Suzu's hand. Steren, screaming – a blood curdling, almost inhuman scream – fell to his knees.

"That was for Mother and Rani and Ryū and the rest of my family." Suzu took a step back. The moon illuminated the grisly scene he had created. The sultry air was filled with the stench of blood and Steren's whimpers.

Suzu lifted his sword – Toshi's sword. "And this," he said in a voice hard and cold as ice, "is for Toshi." Moonlight glinted off the blade as it descended in a graceful arch – and took Steren's head clean off his neck. There was a dull thump and then – silence.

Suzu stood beneath the light of his goddess, covered in blood and breathing hard. His mind was a blank. Unseeingly, he stared at the mess that used to be the village bully. The man who had taken so much from him, whose hands had spilt the blood of Suzu's loved ones. And he felt nothing. A vast emptiness inside him. A sudden calmness after a raging storm. Treacherous and confounding.

Eventually he heard the sound of clashing swords and jolted out of his stupor. The sound came from close by. And Suzu knew exactly who he would find if he followed it. He wasn't done yet.

"Oh dear, please tell me you've held a sword before," Nobu said with mock concern. "I'm starting to feel bad about this."

"Like you feel bad about stabbing the Earl in the back?" Gods damn it, Jin thought, with a hint of rising panic. He knew he was no swordsman, but one should think a monk had no business knowing how to handle a sword either. At this rate Jin wouldn't be able to keep this up much longer.

"Technically, it wasn't I who did the stabbing, but who cares about details. In any case," Nobu sneered, "I don't think you're really sad about the man being dead."

"What's that supposed to mean?" Jin sputtered.

But Nobu merely laughed, and in the next second, Jin was hard-pressed defending himself against Nobu's renewed attacks. The most frustrating part was, the monk didn't even try, he was only toying with Jin, and Jin knew it. If it weren't for the other man's sadistic streak, Jin would already be dead. Why? Why did it always have to be like this? No matter what he did, Jin always seemed to end up failing. How had he once been so cocky, so self-assured of himself? He had thought, without a doubt, that he could do anything. In his mind he had seen it

clearly. He would come to town, find good work, find a place to make a home of. Then he would fetch Kari, and they would live happily ever after. It had seemed so easy. It had never been true. But he'd be damned if he allowed his own incompetence to get him killed.

Frustrated and angry, Jin threw himself at his opponent, wildly swinging his sword at the man. It was a mistake, of course, but Jin was blind with self-loathing and pent-up frustration. Nobu easily evaded Jin's reckless strike, his blade coming at Jin in one fluid motion.

It was dumb luck that saved Jin from being gutted. His own momentum pulled at him, made him stumble and hastily plant his feet just so to not lose balance. It wasn't elegant, but it was enough for him to avoid a fatal injury.

A line of fire burned across his side, pain shot through his nerves. He fell to one knee, gasping and pressed a hand against his side. It came away bloody.

"Disappointing," Nobu said scornfully. Jin lifted his head, but the monk's face was veiled in shadows. The disdain in his voice, however, was enough. "I wonder, do you think he will be sad about your death, or will he not care?"

Perhaps he deserved this. His own arrogance and his gullibility had only caused pain, his inaptitude brought embarrassment and shame to those he owed gratitude. Perhaps the world was better off without him, he couldn't even save himself.

Moonlight glinted off the sharp edge of the blade. All his life he had thought the man who wielded the sword to be his friend – another mistake, a fatal one, it seemed.

"Why don't you ask him yourself?" a familiar husky voice came out of the darkness, startling Nobu enough to make him whirl around, his prey all but forgotten. Jin strained his eyes see past the monk, the edges of his vision were starting to blur.

Suzu stood in a patch of moonlight. He looked like a god, and he looked like a demon. The goddess caressed his jade white skin, lending it an unnatural glow. Blood dripped from his sword's blade.

Nobu tensed. "You," he spat. "You're really persistent, aren't you?"

"Promises to keep," Suzu replied with a shrug. "Oh... I hope you don't expect your watchdog to show up any time soon. Guess it all became a bit too much for him, he... hmm... lost his head."

It took Jin a moment to figure out the meaning behind Suzu's words, his brain was becoming sluggish. When he finally understood, his initial shock quickly turned into a fierce sense of satisfaction. Steren had had it coming for a long time, Nobu had probably been the reason why the man hadn't gotten himself killed sooner.

"I'm getting rid of you once and for all," Nobu hissed.

"You can try."

They sprang at each other, swords flashing, meeting with a metallic clang. One thrust, one block, one parry, over and over. None gave any quarter, none yielded. The moon seemed to push aside any straggling clouds, burned cold and silver and nearly as bright as day, staring down with intensity at the scene below. And in her light, Jin finally saw a change in Nobu. Saw the man's confidence turn into fear.

Faster and faster they clashed. The only sounds, the ringing of their colliding swords and the harshness of their breathing. It was a thrilling, fascinating, deadly dance. A choreography as eerily beautiful as it was terrifying. Jin found himself unable to look away, although he could hardly comprehend what he was seeing.

Step by step, turn by turn, with each thrust of the sword, each block, each time they sprang apart and circled each other like two tigers, Suzu became a little more otherworldly. Jin couldn't say if it was his imagination, the blood loss, or if Suzu, at last, was revealing his true self.

And eventually, with inhuman ease and grace, Suzu swept aside the blade that was coming for his heart. The sword was torn out of Nobu's hand. Another step, a subtle shift – and Suzu drove his sword straight into the monk's chest.

Nobu drew a sharp breath. Incredulous, he looked down at the blade buried deep between his ribs.

"You –" he breathed. It was the last word he ever spoke. With a spray of blood Suzu yanked the sword free and flicked the blood from its blade. Drops of ruby scattered across the wild-grown grass. And Nobu fell – not slow, not gently. He crumpled to the ground like a puppet cut off its strings.

Caught between awe and relief, Jin stared at Suzu. The young man was trembling and breathing hard. For an eternity, seemingly, the moment was frozen, nothing moved, the only sound, Suzu's ragged breathing.

Pain lanced through Jin's side, shattering the moment. He felt dizzy, his vision growing darker. Blood poured over his hands.

"Suzu," he gasped. It was but a whisper, but Suzu flinched and turned around, eyes wild before they focused on Jin, kneeling on the ground, hands pressed against his wound. Suzu rushed to his side and reached out to peel Jin's fingers away. But the moment he touched Jin's hands, he stopped. The hot sticky blood coating Jin's hands told Suzu all he needed to know.

"What happened? Did that bastard stab you?"

"Just a cut," Jin wheezed.

"It... it's obviously not just a cut," Suzu snapped. "How are you even here? Why?"

"Couldn't just let you do this on your own."

Suzu clicked his tongue and mumbled an almost inaudible "Idiot". One of his sleeves was torn. He grabbed it and tore it off, balling the fabric to press it against Jin's wound. Only now did Jin see the long gash on the other boy's arm. Bloody rivulets ran down to his wrist.

"You're injured," Jin observed unnecessarily.

Sparing but a quick glance at his arm, Suzu retorted, "It's just a cut," glaring at Jin, daring him to object. Jin's lips twitched in an approximation of a smile, it was all he could muster. Why was he so tired? He wanted to lie down and close his eyes, but Suzu suddenly shook him and snarled at him to stay awake. Right. Somewhere in his mind Jin knew that falling asleep now would be a bad idea. He had to stay awake, he had to... he had... he had so much to tell Suzu. So much he wanted to say. Who knew if he got another chance to do so.

"Suzu," he forced himself to speak. "Suzu, the Earl... I'm... I'm so s-sorry."

"I... I need to get you home – no, I need to get you to Niall. Yes. Can you... can you get up?"

"Suzu –"

"Where do you think she is? At the palace? No, guess they have their own physicians there, but perhaps at the square? Do you think you can make it that far?"

"Suzu –"

"No!" Suzu cried, making Jin flinch. "No. Don't. I can't do that now. I just... we need to get to Niall."

Ah. Staring at Suzu, with his vision growing dimmer and dimmer, Jin could finally see them, all the cracks, how close the young man was to falling apart, how much effort it cost him not to shatter.

"I... I think she's coming for us... with Naloc and Risa..." Jin said at last. Speaking hurt. Breathing hurt.

"All right. That's good. We... um... we should try and... meet them?"

With Suzu's help Jin heaved himself to his feet. The pain wasn't so bad compared to the wave of dizziness that washed over him and nearly made him keel over. Thanks to Suzu taking the brunt of Jin's weight, he didn't fall flat on his face.

They made slow progress. Jin had no more strength left to lift his feet, so Suzu had no choice but to half carry, half drag him.

"Damn it!" Suzu growled. "Come on, Jin. And don't you dare fall asleep, you hear?" Jin gave a non-committal noise. "I mean it. You will be in so much trouble. Remember when Brother Hanjo caught you in his kitchen, snitching some of his beloved sugar cookies? That will be nothing compared to the trouble you'll be in if you die on me!" Jin chuckled softly. He had no doubt that Suzu would carry out his threats, whatever it took. But his eyelids were so heavy. His body felt as if it were made of lead, he tasted iron on his tongue.

And then, suddenly, there was a noise: several pairs of feet running – running towards them. Voices. Hands grabbing him.

"All right! Let me take a look." Niall's voice. Jin had never been so glad to hear the voice of his friend. "Gods damn it!" Niall cursed. Jin wanted to tell her it wasn't as bad as it looked, but he couldn't make his mouth work. There was a buzzing in his ear, he couldn't understand what was said, but it sounded like several people arguing. He was suddenly lifted up, only to be laid down on something hard a moment later.

"Now move, move, move! Hurry up! I don't care if this piece of garbage breaks down as long as it does after we've arrived home! Now get going!" Jin smiled – or he thought he did. Niall was always so bossy, especially when she was being a doctor.

The ground beneath him began to rattle, jostling him, but he didn't feel any pain anymore. Only cold and exhaustion.

"Jin... Jin?" Suzu's voice was so close to his ear, he could feel the boy's breath hot against his skin.

"Hm?" Jin hummed – and knew no more.

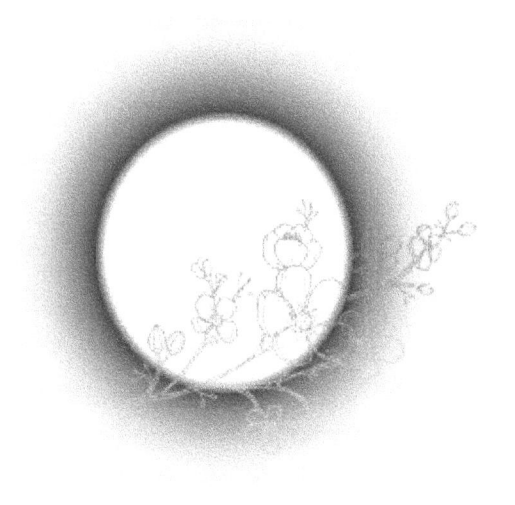

Chapter 41

Suzu watched Niall berating Jin. After she had stitched him up and given him some kind of concoction, Jin had eventually regained consciousness. He was exhausted and in pain, but he was alive. Although he probably wished to be unconscious again, given the dressing down Niall was giving him for running off on his own and getting injured. Despite it, Niall had worry and relief written all over her face.

For his part, Suzu felt... numb. The confrontation with Steren had left him full of adrenaline and a sense of satisfaction, yet the relief, the feeling of justice having been delivered had been missing, nor had it come with Nobu's death. Instead, he was left with an ominous calm. As if he was standing in the eye of a storm. The calm serenity that prefaced pandemonium. He felt detached, watching from outside his own body, waiting with bated breath for the inevitable to come. There was a brittleness about his very being, as if the mere brush of butterfly wings would make him crumble.

Others had followed them to Jin and Niall's home, worried. Suzu could feel their looks on him, heard their whispers. They had found the bodies, they had seen the punishment he had brought down on Steren. They were afraid, perhaps, repulsed. No-one tried to approach him, not even Naloc.

And so he stood in the open door, holding onto Toshi's sword as if it were a rock to hold onto amidst the wild surf, waves breaking around him, the tide pulling at him. He could feel them still. Pity. Fear. Anticipation – of what, he didn't know. Perhaps they were waiting for him to break. He would not give them the satisfaction.

In the sky more and more clouds were gathering, hiding the moon as if she didn't want to watch anymore. Suzu didn't blame her. The wind picked up, carrying the smell of rain. The night grew sultry, oppressive.

Eventually, someone did approach Suzu. It was the stranger who had gifted him the kunai. They regarded Suzu solemnly, without pity or fear, and spoke not a single word. After a little while, Suzu presented Toshi's sword to them, holding it gently, balanced on both hands.

"Will you bring it back to him," he asked softly.

"I will."

"Tell Kagetora... tell his family that... tell them he... his soul can rest easy now."

The stranger bowed deeply to Suzu and accepted the sword deferentially. "I will," they promised again. Then they were gone. And Suzu still stood there, alone and empty-handed, beneath the hidden moon.

How much longer? Perhaps he would stay like this forever, caught in a kind of stasis like a bug caught in amber. He had kept his promise, what was left now for him in this world? His family was gone. Toshi was gone – and he had taken what was left of Suzu's heart with him. Perhaps it wouldn't be so bad to never feel again. No pain. No loss.

Niall got to her feet, at last, brushing her clothes down, and stretched.

"All right, enough for one day. I will go to bed now and sleep like a log, and I suggest you do the same. See you in the mor– no probably in the afternoon. Come fetch me if there's anything you need, though."

She patted Suzu's shoulder as she brushed past him through the door. As he closed it after her, Suzu heard Niall shooing the others away, telling them all would be fine and they ought to go home and sleep now. It didn't sound like anyone was arguing.

He slowly, uncertainly, crossed the room. Wind rattled the shutters and made the lamp flicker. Suzu felt Jin's eyes on him. He looked up and saw an expression on Jin's face he had never seen there before: a deep, profound sadness.

Suzu swallowed hard, his breath hitched. He – Jin wordlessly opened his arms.

The brush of butterfly wings. Suzu crumbled. His heart broke into million tiny pieces. His soul shattered. The walls went down and all the pain, all the grief, all the terrible, unspeakable feelings washed over him like a tidal wave. He was drowning. He was burning. He was being ripped apart and scattered in the wind.

He stumbled forward and, with a cry of anguish, fell into Jin's arms, clinging to him, all that was left, all that was real. He cried. He wailed. He screamed. And Jin held him tight, uttering not a single useless word of consolation, offered not another gesture of futile comfort. He only held him – held Suzu tight, held him together.

And in the sky above, the moon veiled her face in dark, dark clouds, and the rain began to sing a dirge. A beautiful, sorrowful lament that lasted throughout the night.

Chapter 42

For two days Suzu lay in the dark. He didn't speak. He didn't move. He refused to eat, and Niall had to force what little he drank on him. Jin never left his side, telling Suzu about his life those last five years, enriched with little anecdotes that normally would have earned him a smile at least.

At night, despite his exhaustion, Suzu found he couldn't sleep, too afraid of dreams. Exhaustion won in the end. But when the dreams came, they were not the nightmares, filled with the lifeless faces of his dead loved ones, as he had feared.

So at last, on the third morning, Suzu, much to Jin's and Niall's relief, got up and joined them for breakfast. Then he washed, dressed, and sent a message to the few remaining members of his family.

They were already waiting for him in the small room above Aiyana's flower shop. Every single one of them seemed anxious. For a moment, Suzu silently studied each of them. Miharu's wide hopeful eyes. Akito's scarred face. Sabia's bandaged arms and legs, and the heavy wrappings around Tomiko's clever hands. Aurin's reddened eyes and haggard face. Hayato leaning against him, ashen-faced.

And at last, Suzu took a deep, shuddering breath and told them he had fulfilled his promise.

Suzu wandered the streets of Yūgao. It was mid-day and Yūgao an islet of serenity in the hectic hubbub of the town. These days, wherever one went, people were discussing the events of Tsuki no Matsuri, speculating, reliving their own experiences. Jin and Niall couldn't leave the house without drawing the attention of a curious crowd, badgering them with questions. And to Suzu's exasperation, the people of Kigetsu didn't seem to tire of singing Naloc's praise for his and his people's involvement in the events. For his part, Suzu had not yet spoken more then two words with the man. Naloc had tried to apologise for trying to keep Suzu locked away, but Suzu had only glowered at the man and left him standing.

Yūgao seemed like an entirely different world. In a sense it always had, but all of a sudden it had lost its feeling of being home. It was as if a part of its soul had died with the Singing Dragon.

Suzu left the main road and rounded the corner into the street that had welcomed him home for five years. It had taken him some time to gather the courage to come, but in the end he had to admit it wouldn't become easier the longer he dragged it out. The meeting with his brothers had been painful but cathartic. As they had shared tears and comfort in each other, not only the unreasonable fear that they would blame him for all their loss, but with it the feeling of immense guilt were lifted off of him. They were still his family and always would be.

He kept his eyes, burning with tears, on the ground as he made his way towards his home. Only when he had finally reached the end of the street and stood before the charred remains of the once glorious gate did he raise his head and perceive the terrible wound in Yūgao's heart.

Suzu gasped. The last time it had been dark. Here, in the dazzling sunlight the true devastation was visible. The rubble had been cleared away, as had all other remains, but nothing could hide the blackened earth, the emptiness, the unnatural stillness that lay over this plot of land. Gone was the lush green of the grass and the trees. Gone the splashes of colour from the flowers. Gone the beautiful mansion. Gone. It was truly all gone.

"I..." Suzu began and had to stop, sobbing. He took several shaking breaths before he tried again. "I... I kept my p-promise. They are d-dead. You... you can rest now." Unable to hold back the tears any longer, Suzu sank to his knees and buried his face in his hands. The tears were hot against his palms.

Only when the tears finally stilled and the sobs abided, did Suzu become aware he wasn't alone anymore. He slowly looked over his shoulder. Astrid smiled sadly at him. She stood amidst Chihiro, Enya, Masami, and Hiroki – the owners of Yūgao's most renowned houses and the members of Yūgao's council.

Suzu quickly wiped his eyes and stood up. He was taken aback when all six of them bowed deeply to him.

"I... what...?" Astrid laid a hand on his arm and stilled his stammering. She still had this sad gentle smile on her face.

"Oh sweetling," she sighed. "Come. Come with us."

She took his hand and led him away from the ruins of his home and to her own house, the Golden Lotus. The girls, already busy preparing for the evening, nodded gravely at Suzu and made way to let them pass.

Astrid's parlour was a beautiful, sun-flooded room filled with flowers. A calligraphy, embellished with gold paint, adorned one wall – it was a poem, about love found and lost. Astrid's late wife had written it.

"Suzu," Chihiro said in her raspy voice when the young girls serving them tea had departed. She was the oldest member of the council, and therefore her word carried the most weight. "I hope you know that all of Yūgao shares your loss." Suzu nodded, although it was hard to imagine anyone else understanding his pain.

"The light of Yūgao has been diminished by this tragedy," Masami continued. "Yūgao will never forget."

"Suzu, my sweet boy." Astrid reached across the table and took Suzu's hand. "I know this is very hard, but there is something we need to know. What do you wish us to do about the Singing Dragon?"

Suzu frowned. "I don't understand."

"Do you want to rebuild it?"

"Rebuild the Dragon? I... sorry, why are you asking me this? It's not my decision to make."

"But it is. The Dragon, the entire estate – it's yours."

"What? Mine?" Suzu shook his head, confused. "No. No, you got this wrong. Ryū... Ryū is... was Mother's heir."

"And that is true," Chihiro agreed. "However, a while ago Kazue and Ryū came to us with a rather unique request: to bequeath the Singing Dragon to you. Not as Kazue's heir, but as the owner."

Suzu looked from Chihiro to Astrid, to the others. How could this be? He had never heard any of this before.

Seeing his confusion, Astrid said quietly, "They wanted to ensure you knew you always had a home to return to, whatever the future would hold. It's yours now, Suzu, yours alone. You alone decide what happens to it now."

Suzu closed his eyes against the renewed burn of tears. Love – he felt enveloped by it. Why had he never realised how loved he had been. Gratitude and the warmth of love mellowed the grief that held him in a tight grasp. It felt like the first rays of sunshine, breaking through the clouds after months of rain.

"No," he said at last, opening his eyes. "I won't rebuild it. It would never be the same as it was before, so let it rest. Let the Dragon rest with its people."

"Are you sure?"

"Yes." He looked each of them in the eyes and knew exactly what to do. "You said Yūgao will always remember. So make it a place to remember them."

It were the hardest days of Suzu's life.

All of Yūgao was shrouded in mourning colours, all came to pay their respect and share the grief. Jin had not left Suzu's side even for a moment during the preparations for nor during the day of the funeral. It was the first time Suzu thanked the gods that their paths had crossed again. He would not have been able to go through this, had he not known there was someone to catch him should he fall.

One thing, however, he felt he had to do alone. And so, on the day of Toshi's public funeral – only a day after he had laid his family to rest – Suzu quietly left the house without telling Jin.

The streets were wet from a recent shower, raindrops glistening like little jewels on flower petals. The overcast sky promised more rain, so Suzu decided to buy an umbrella and get breakfast on the way. It felt strange walking the streets of the town and feeling people's gazes following him. It wasn't that he wasn't used to this, but where those gazes had been appraising, admiring, or even jealous before, now they were... not pity, although it was there, under the surface. No, there was still admiration, but of a different kind: respect, acknowledgment. No-one approached him directly, but he heard whispers of "That poor boy" and "It's the Earl's funeral today, isn't it?"And he had noticed how the umbrella maker had given him his most exquisite umbrella without charging a higher price, or the street vendor, who had given him the freshest bun.

He didn't know what to make of it. He felt detached and yet touched by the display of compassion and sympathy from all those strangers. A gentle rain began to fall. The air filled with the comforting fragrance of wet earth and hydrangeas. Suzu opened the umbrella. It was midnight blue with golden peonies. Suzu smiled, it was something Toshi would have picked for him.

Mangetsu's cemetery was situated behind the Academic Quarter. When Suzu arrived at last, he had no problem finding the funeral party. Hundreds of people filled the cemetery grounds, converging on a single spot. Suzu was taken aback by the crowd. For common people it was usual that friends, acquaintances, business partners attended the wake, yet it was alone the family's prerogative to carry the ashes to their final resting place. He understood now why they called it a 'public' funeral. Noble families did not have the right to mourn alone.

Suzu made out the members of the Moon Council – those who had not turned out to be traitors – still a little pale, and their families. He saw Toshi's employees huddled together, crying openly. He couldn't find the General or Toshi's family, however, the crowd, like a wall, surrounding them.

Suzu kept his distance, skirting the edges of the funeral party until he found a big maple tree from where he could follow the funeral, but stay relatively hidden. His new vantage point also allowed him a glimpse of Toshi's family at last. Toshi's nephew, Takara, clung to his mother like a small child, the General, standing right behind him, had a steadying hand on the boy's shoulder. He would be the Earl of Tsukikage now. Suzu felt pity for the boy, having to shoulder such a burden at such a young age.

Kagetora, head bowed and leaning heavily on his crutches, stood next to the General. And on the man's other side, Suzu was surprised to see Emperor Kjell. No wonder there were Silver Guards all over the cemetery, some giving him curious looks.

The rain shower ceased, the blanket of clouds broke apart and sun reached through, tingeing the raindrops golden. Suzu leaned against the tree and waited. He didn't listen or care about the words of the priestess or the emperor's. He was tired of funerals, of saying goodbye, but one more time – there were still so many things he needed to say, so many things he had no words for. And he needed to be alone for this. So he waited.

Slowly, unbearably slowly, the funeral party broke up, the emperor – naturally – the first to leave, trailing guards. He was watching impatiently as the crowd dispersed, when he noticed Kagetora hobbling towards him. For a long moment, they simply stared at each other.

"I'm glad you are still around," Suzu said at last.

Kagetora smiled briefly. "Well, you were right, you know. He wouldn't have wanted me to follow, always thought it a stupid custom that made no sense. He would be giving me a good thrashing in the beyond if I had... you know." This time they shared a smile. "Toshi, he... he told me once – actually, he made me swear – to take care of Takara, should anything ever happen to him. It's just... I never actually thought he would go before me."

"Isn't that what we like to believe? That not just we, ourselves, but our beloved ones are immortal? Only to find out just how fragile and fleeting life is."

Tears glistened in Kagetora's eyes. He bowed his head in acknowledgment. Then he took a deep breath and looked Suzu in the eyes. "Thank you, Suzu," he said huskily. "Thank you for making him happy, for loving him... for... for giving him peace."

Suzu's throat felt tight. He didn't trust himself to speak, so he merely nodded and blinked the tears away. Unsuccessfully. Like raindrops, they slowly ran down his cheeks. Trying to make them stop, Suzu looked up, and noticed a group of people approaching them slowly.

The General, his wife at his arm, was the first to reach them. Toshi's employees stopped at a respectful distance. Among them was a young woman, leaning against a burly young man, who had his arm around her waist. Of all of them, they seemed to be taking their employer's death the hardest. They bowed to Suzu when they noticed him looking at them.

"Suzu, lad, how are you holding up?" The General's gentle tone made Suzu cry. Nevertheless, he nodded his head, implying he would be all right, though he didn't know if it was true. Mori no Akari reached out and brushed the tears away. She didn't say a word. There was no need. What was there to say, anyway? They all shared the same pain.

"Y-Yu-Yūzuki-tana," a timid voice said from Suzu's right – his blind side. He turned his head – and bowed when he saw who stood before him.

"Takara-tana – I mean… my lord." Takara stood between his parents. He looked even younger than his sixteen years. Suzu felt a painful stab in his heart. Toshi, who had to take over the title of earl at the age of fourteen, had never wanted his nephew to be burdened with it so early.

"Oh, p-please, don't… don't be so formal," the boy stammered. "J-just Takara. Please."

Suzu smiled. "Only if you call me Suzu."

The boy blushed furiously and seemed momentarily too flustered to speak, so instead his mother spoke up. "Yūzuki no Suzu, we have to thank you for everything you did for my brother."

"I didn't –"

"Oh, sweet boy, you have no idea how much you did for him. My greatest fear had always been that he would be lonely and never know love. And then he met you. You gave him so much. I only wished you didn't have to part so soon. Thank you – for loving him."

The sob that racked his body seemed to come from his very soul. Suzu had to turn away from the others, closing his eyes and taking deep breaths until he finally had himself under control again. His were not the only tears being shed.

"If..." Suzu took a deep shuddering breath and tried again. "If there is anything I can do, please let me know. Please?"

"There is!" Takara blurted, surprising Suzu as much as himself. "Um... what I mean is – well, technically you'd be my uncle – that is, I don't mean to presume or anything, but... I know Uncle would have... and we... I... You are family! So... don't be a stranger?"

Suzu was speechless. He had expected anything, that Toshi's family would blame him, that they regretted the two had ever met, that they never wanted to see him again. Or, if he was generous to himself, that they would simply depart, all of them going their separate ways, living their separate lives. Never would he have dared to even hope for this. There was a sudden warmth suffusing his body. It felt as if Toshi was hugging him, whispering into his ear that everything would be all right. He had lost most of his family, his love, but perhaps he had gained a new one as well.

"I promise," he said, breathless.

Takara smiled, then grabbed the sword hanging at his waist. It was his uncle's sword. He held it out to Suzu. "It is yours. My uncle would have wanted you to have it."

"What? No, I can't! That's –"

"Yes, you can. It's already yours."

With shaking hands, Suzu accepted the sword and held it close. "Thank you."

Takara nodded, and once more smiled shyly at Suzu before he and his parents and his little sister took their leave. They had gone but a couple of steps, when Takara looked back over his shoulder and said, "Oh, by the way, its name is Zangetsu!"

Suzu gaped at his new sword in wonder. Had Toshi given it the name? Or had the sword been in the family long before Toshi became earl? *Zangetsu* – the morning moon.

A broad hand landed on his shoulder. Suzu looked up into the General's gentle eyes. "Whatever you need, whenever – you're always welcome in our house, Suzu, never forget that." Smiling, he gave Suzu's shoulder a little squeeze. Akari actually gave Suzu a soft kiss on his cheek, before she accepted her husband's arm and they, too, left. Kagetora went with them. And at last, Suzu was alone, with no-one but the dead for company.

The grave stone glittered in the sun with a hint of quartz. 'Mori' was engraved in its surface, above the family crest of the double moon. Suzu took an incense stick out of the box and lit it. The incense holder was already full, a cloud of fragrant smoke rising into the sky.

"I'm sorry, I didn't come to the wake, Toshi. We were laying our family to rest – I'm sure you understand. And I guess, you knew that already. I wonder, did you all meet in the beyond? Did they tell you I'm the owner of the Singing Dragon? Though I wouldn't be surprised if Mother and Ryū had told you already. I've decided to turn the estate into a little park. A place of serenity. A place to remember." He fell silent and let the tears fall. "Gods, Toshi, it hurts so much. Waking hurts. Sleeping hurts. I can't breathe. Toshi, I don't know how to live like this. I know I am not alone. There's your family and the General. And what is left of my family. And... Jin. But I've never felt so lonely. I don't know if I can do this, if I can go on like this. I feel nothing but pain anymore, it'll drive me mad. And I haven't even told you once, because I was too stubborn and too stupid, and I should have just... I should have just told you how much I love you."

He hugged his legs and pressed his forehead against his knees. And then he cried. He cried so bitterly, for a long, long time, until he felt exhausted, until he felt he had no more tears to left to cry.

The sun was once more hidden behind a thick layer of clouds. The slow patter of the first raindrops broke Suzu out of his petrification. Slowly, he wiped his face on his sleeve and stood up. With a last, whispered goodbye, Suzu took his sword, opened his umbrella, and turned to leave.

A lone figure was waiting for him beside a tall, ancient hydrangea with vivid red flowers. Even though his face was hidden beneath his umbrella, Suzu knew him at once. Strange, but he would always know him, Suzu realised. No matter where, no matter how long they were apart. The thought brought a small smile to Suzu's lips.

"How long have you been waiting?"

Jin looked up. "Oh. I don't know. A while, I guess."

Suzu stopped in front of his childhood friend and looked up into his face. Jin was still paler than usual, his wound had not had time to heal yet, but – as Niall pointed out, fed up – his pigheadedness was incurable. Eyes so dark they seemed black found Suzu's. Jin was taller than he had been five years ago, his face more angular, the shadow of a beard gracing his jaw. He seemed calmer, more settled, perhaps. He wasn't the Jin Suzu had once known any more than he was Kari. And yet, there was a familiarity, a warmth, a comfort in the young man's presence that was like balm for Suzu's wounded soul, his broken heart.

"Niall will skin us both if those stitches open," Suzu remarked.

"They won't," Jin replied with a crooked smile. It was short-lived, however. Serious, Jin took a deep breath before he said, "Suzu... I've been thinking – or... wondering. What will you do now? Where will you go?"

"I don't know. I guess I need time to figure that out."

"Of course. Which is... what I mean is..." Jin drew himself to his full height, as if he was readying himself for a fight. "Don't leave. Please. You can stay at my place – at least for now, until you've figured out what you want to do."

"Jin –"

"No! It's not like that, I swear. Look, I understand that you're not Kari, that whoever Kari was, he wasn't real – well, not all of it, anyway. And honestly, it just shows how little I actually knew. I guess I really only saw what I wanted to see. No wonder it was so easy for Nobu to manipulate me."

"Jin –"

"Let – let me finish, please. It's... Kari or Suzu – I just don't want to lose you again. I want to get to know you, the real you. Do it right this time. Please, just let me stay by your side. Let me be your friend."

See, my love? You are not alone. Suzu blinked, his heart beating so fast he felt dizzy. Toshi – had he sent Jin after him? Suzu tilted his head back and let the rain fall on his face. This pain would probably never go away, his soul and his heart would for ever carry scars, deeper than any sword could leave. But right here, in this very moment, he felt he could breathe a little easier.

Suzu smiled, looking at Jin. Before he had been Suzu's enemy, before he had ever been his lover, Jin had been a brother and a friend. Perhaps they were bound by fate. And perhaps, amidst all that he had lost, fate had given Suzu what he needed – a friend.

"I'd love that."

Appendix

Calthean: 'the mountainous area'; northern region before it merged with the southern Tsukishima to form the Empire of Tsukiyama.

Crescent, The: The Crescent was formed in Kigetsu about a hundred and fifty years ago in answer to a corrupt Moon Council and a puppet emperor, to fight against the neglect of the nobility and put an end to the suffering of the lower classes. The first and foremost duty of the Crescent is to care for the people of Kigetsu and their concerns.

To become a member requires an invitation from the council and sponsorship from at least one member. The First Seat – leader of the council – is elected and appointed for life, unless they resign or lose the trust of the council.

Deva's Breath: a poisonous plant. The toxin of the same name is very difficult to extract and needs to be done by a highly skilled professional. Despite what its common, Dreamless Sleep, implies, Deva's Breath one of the strongest, most fatal, and also most cruel poisons in the world.

Eigetsu: waxing moon. Oldest part of Getsuro, used to be where the nobility and upper classes lived before they left it for the other side of the river. Now Eigetsu is the home of the poorest of Getsuro's inhabitants, parts of it are even completely abandoned. Those parts are commonly known as Ghost Town.

Ethereal: descendants of the so-called 'god-blessed'. When the gods still interfered with the mortal world, millennia ago, they often found individuals who they favoured above all else. Those individuals were gifted a spark of divinity, which granted them beauty, strength, longevity, and more individual talents.

Over the centuries that spark diminished, but the descendants inherited those gifts, even though they, too, are not as strong as they once were.

What distinguishes Ethereals the most, is the colour of their eyes, which – depending on the god that once blessed their ancestors – are very intense or even unnatural shades. Just like the eye colour, there are certain talents that reveal their patron deity. The stronger the talents and the more intense the eye colour, the purer the blood line – but hardly any full-blooded Ethereals remain now.

Suspicion and jealousy has led to almost superstitious prejudice against Ethereals, e.g. they are often believed to be shape-shifters and tricksters, who bewitch the unwary.

Furisode: a formal type of kimono with long sleeves, usually worn by unmarried young women.

Furyusha: the 'Graceful Ones'. In a society that values and admires beauty their first and foremost job is to be admired. They sell illusions and dreams to their customers, providing them with entertainment, comfort, and companionship, fulfilling their customers needs.

Getsuro: 'dew in which the moon reflects'. Capital of the empire of Tsukiyama, seat of the Moonlight Throne.

Hidden Moon: a kind of secret agency, charged with monitoring and protecting the empire and its people against all threats. They remain hidden in the shadows and become something like a myth in the collective mind – this, of course, is their strongest weapons and allows them to have eyes and ears everywhere.

The members of the Hidden Moon come from all walks of life.

Jinbei: a casual set of clothing, consisting of loose trousers and a side-tied kimono style top.

Kanzashi: hair ornament

Kigetsu: waning moon. The most populated and busiest part of Getsuro; some claim Kigetsu is the real Getsuro.

Kunai: knife with a characteristic leave-shaped blade; usually used as tools, they are also excellent throwing and stabbing knives.

Mangetsu: full moon. District east of the Opal River; home of the Moonlight Palace and its grounds, the Moon Goddess's temple, the nobility and the wealthy upper classes, and the Academic Quarter.

Moon Fair: Getsuro's night market, held during the full moon each month.

Moon Council: officially the emperor's advisers. In reality, the council holds as much power as the emperor, if not even more. It consists of members of the nobility – a position that is inherited, but not necessarily by the legal heir of a council member, therefore the name of the successor is taken down in a special ledger at the council and can't be disputed.

Nagajuban: a thin robe worn beneath a kimono.

Nemaki: a nightwear type of kimono.

Seven, The: the founding clans of the empire. Those are the clans Mori, Furyutsuki, Hinode, Mizutama, Drekan, Aesoc, and Feichun

Silver Guard: elite guard serving also as palace guard.

Tantō: a short sword, usually accompanying a katana

Tsukishima: 'moon island'; southern region before it merged with Calthean to form the Empire of Tsukiyama.

Tsuki no Matsuri: the highest holiday of Tsukiyama, celebrating the Moon Goddess, patron goddess of the empire, showing gratitude and asking for the goddess's continued protection. It is held during the night of the full moon around the summer solstice.

Umbrage: fighters, who are highly skilled in unarmed combat, various weapons, and espionage. Many of the old clans have tight relations with Umbrage clans. It is not rare for children of the two clans to grow up together and be bound to each other for life.

Old customs had it that should the Umbrage fail to protect their master, they follow them into death. This has long been abolished but some still hang on to it.

Yūgao: 'moonflower' or 'Evening Glory'; Getsuro's entertainment district, nestled between Kigetsu and Eigetsu. It is the home of the Furyusha houses (commonly known as pleasure houses), as well as gambling houses, theatres, bars, tea houses etc.

Yūgao has its own rules and laws, which are accepted and respected even by the Moonlight Crown.

Yukata: a cotton summer kimono, more casual and less expensive than a kimono.

Yūzuki: 'evening moon'; the moon that can be seen in the evening sky. Name of one of the Moon Goddess's Seven Sacred Bells, which is said to produce the most beautiful sound in the world. Suzu has been named after it.

Zangetsu: 'morning moon'; the moon that can be seen in the morning sky. Name of Toshi's sword.

Honorifics:

Honorifics are used to express respect towards another person.

While people in Tsukiyama may address others by certain titles, such as Master, Teacher, Doctor, or titles of nobility, they also use honorifics.

-**tan**: used for people one is not very close to or familiar with or who are older, but of equal status (compare Japanese -san)
-**tana**: used for people of higher status (compare Japanese -sama)
(Yes, they sound very much like the Japanese honorifics, but trying to come up with original ones resulted in them either sounding so very very wrong, or, alternatively, always just came back to the Korean -shi.)

Names in Tsukiyama::

There are two naming systems in Tsukiyama, one who originated in the southern part, formerly known as Tsukishima; the second, which originated in what used to be Calthean.

Northern style: The northern style is a matronymics/patronymics system, the 'ax' in the name means as much 'child of'. Usually female children are named after their mother, male children after their father. This is not the rule, however, but every individual's choice.
Niall, e.g., used her father's name because she never knew her mother, which is why she is called Niall ax Corbin (Niall, child of Corbin).

<u>Southern style</u>: The southern style uses clan and family names. The use of 'no', meaning 'of', signifies if a person is part of a clan or not.

Jin, as a de facto orphan, didn't have a clan nor a family name. After Naloc took him in, he adopted Naloc's name Murasaki, but because he is not part of the clan, he is simply called Murasaki Jin, whereas Naloc is Murasaki no Naloc (Naloc of the Murasaki Clan). Many family names came into being this way.

Furyusha names, however, are special. They also use the 'no', but not to signify affiliation to any clan.

Acknowledgements

Fifteen years – and then I stopped counting.

Fifteen years, in which Suzu, Jin and their story has been part of my life.

To say they mean a lot to me is almost an understatement. But our time together isn't over yet, we still have a long way ahead of us. So this is not a goodbye, this is a "Finally!" Finally, this story is out there in this world, finally we can share it with others. And if you are one of those – welcome, and thank you.

Stories need to be shared, they need to be told and they need to be heard/ read. The author creates, but it's through the reader that a story can truly live. Therefore, thank you. Thank you for letting this story live.

And, of course, I need to thank my best friend, my sister of my heart, Ellen. Not only did you read every little snippet I've ever thrown at you, no, you even read the entire first manuscript. The manuscript – not a draft, a finished manuscript – I completely scrapped in the end. I really felt bad about that, which was the reason why I insisted, the next time you read any of it, it's the ultimate final version. Tada! Hope you liked it.

Lots of thanks to my Beta reader, ASC, for cheering me on and helping me to turn this book into its best possible version.

Last but not least, I need to thank my eARC readers, for being interested and enthusiastic about this book without even knowing what to expect. You had to stoically ignore typos and weird phrases (not to mention the converter messed up the early epub version) – I'm really sorry about that, and thank you for not grousing about it.

Special thank you also to those who joined the Cover Reveal. Your posts were absolutely gorgeous, I loved every single one of them so much. Thank you, thank you, thank you!

About the Author

Iris Retzlaff has a MA in British and American Studies, but likes to say it's in Escapism with a minor in Procrastination. They live in a tiny forgotten corner of the world with a head full of imaginary people and their stories.

Milton Keynes UK
Ingram Content Group UK Ltd.
UKHW021203271124
3180UKWH00044B/542